KU-762-507

An Armada Three-in-One

Three Great Secret Stories

The Secret Island

The Secret of Killimooin

The Secret of Moon Castle

by Enid Blyton

Armada
An Imprint of HarperCollins*Publishers*

This Armada Three-in-One
first published in the UK in 1993

Armada is an imprint of HarperCollins Children's Books, a division of
HarperCollins Publishers Ltd, 77-85 Fulham Palace Road, Hammersmith,
London W6 8JB

All rights reserved

The Enid Blyton signature is the trademark of
Darrell Waters Ltd

Printed and bound in Great Britain
by HarperCollins Book Manufacturing Ltd, Glasgow

Conditions of Sale
This book is sold subject to the condition that it shall not, by way of trade
or otherwise, be lent, re-sold, hired out or otherwise circulated without the
publisher's prior consent in any form of binding or cover other than that in
which it is published and without a similar condition including this
condition being imposed on the subsequent purchaser.

Contents

The Secret Island

The Secret Island was first published in the UK
by Basil Blackwell Ltd in 1938

First published as a single volume by Armada in 1964

Copyright reserved Enid Blyton 1938

The Beginning Of The Adventures

Mike, Peggy and Nora were sitting in the fields, talking together. They were very unhappy. Nora was crying, and would not stop. As they sat there, they heard a low call. "Coo-ee!"

"There's Jack," said Mike. "Dry your eyes, Nora. Jack will cheer you up!"

A boy came running by the hedge and sat down by them. He had a face as brown as a berry and bright blue eyes that shone with mischief.

"Hallo!" he said. "What's up, Nora? Crying again?"

"Yes," said Nora, wiping her eyes. "Aunt Harriet slapped me six times this morning because I didn't wash the curtains well enough. Look!"

She showed him her arm, red with slaps.

"It's a shame!" said Jack.

"If only our father and mother were here they wouldn't let us live like this," said Mike. "But somehow I don't believe they'll ever come back now."

"How long is it since they've been gone?" asked Jack.

"It's over two years now," said Mike. "Dad built a fine new aeroplane, you know, and he set off to fly to Australia. Mother went with him, because she loves flying, too. They got nearly there—and then nothing more was heard of them!"

"And I know Aunt Harriet and Uncle Henry think they will never come back again," said Nora, beginning to cry once more, "or they would never treat us as they do."

"Don't cry any more, Nora," said Peggy. "Your eyes

will get so red and horrid. I'll do the washing instead of you next time."

Jack put his arm round Nora. He liked her best of them all. She was the smallest, although she was Mike's twin. She had a little face, and a head of black curls. Mike was exactly like her, but bigger. Peggy had yellow hair and was a year older. Nobody knew how old Jack was. He didn't know himself. He lived with his grandfather on a tumble-down farm, and worked as hard as a man, although he wasn't much bigger than Mike.

He had made friends with the children as they wandered through the fields. He knew how to catch rabbits. He knew how to catch fish in the river. He knew where the best nuts and blackberries were to be found. In fact, he knew everything, the children thought, even the names of all the birds that flew about the hedges, and the difference between a grass snake and an adder, and things like that.

Jack was always dressed in raggedy things, but the children didn't mind. His feet were bare, and his legs were scratched with brambles. He never grumbled; he never whined. He made a joke of everything, and he had been a good friend to the three miserable children.

"Ever since Aunt Harriet made up her mind that Mummy and Daddy wouldn't come back, she has been perfectly horrid," said Nora.

"And so has Uncle Henry," said Mike. "We none of us go to school now, and I have to help Uncle in the fields from morning to night. I don't mind that, but I do wish Aunt Harriet wouldn't treat the two girls so badly. They are not very old, and she makes them do all the work of the house for her."

"I do every bit of the washing now," said Nora. "I wouldn't mind the little things, but the sheets are so big and heavy."

"And I do all the cooking," said Peggy. "Yesterday I burnt a cake because the oven got too hot, and Aunt Harriet sent me to bed for the rest of the day without anything to eat at all."

"I climbed through the window and gave her some bread and cheese," said Mike. "And Uncle caught me and shook me so hard that I couldn't stand up afterwards. I had to go without my supper, and my breakfast this morning was only a small piece of bread."

"We haven't had any new clothes for months," said Peggy. "My shoes are dreadful. And I don't know what we shall do when the winter comes, because none of our coats will fit us."

"You are much worse off than I am," said Jack. "I have never had anything nice, so I don't miss it. But you have had everything you wanted, and now it is all taken away from you—you haven't even a father and mother you can go to for help."

"Do you remember *your* father and mother, Jack?" asked Mike. "Did you always live with your old grandfather?"

"I never remember anyone except him," said Jack. "He's talking of going to live with an aunt of mine. If he does I shall be left all alone, for she won't have me, too."

"Oh, Jack! Whatever will you do?" asked Nora.

"I shall be all right!" said Jack. "The thing is what are *you* three going to do? I hate to see you all unhappy. If only we could all run away together!"

"We should be found at once and brought back," said Mike gloomily. "I know that. I've read in the papers about boys and girls running away, and they are always found by the police and brought back. If I knew some place where we would never be found, I *would* run away—and take the two girls with me too. I hate to see them slappd and worked hard by Aunt Harriet."

"Now listen to me," said Jack suddenly, in such an earnest voice that all three children turned to him at once. "If I tell you a very great secret will you promise never to say a word about it to anyone?"

"Oh, yes, Jack, we promise," said all three.

"You can trust us, Jack," said Mike.

"I know I can," he said. "Well, listen. I know a place where nobody could find us—if we ran away!"

"Where is it, Jack?" they all cried in great excitement.

"I'll show you this evening," said Jack, getting up. "Be by the lakeside at eight o'clock, when all your work is done, and I'll meet you there. I must go now, or Grandpa will be angry with me, and perhaps lock me into my room so that I can't get out again to-day."

"Good-bye, Jack," said Nora, who was feeling much better now. "We'll see you this evening."

Jack ran off, and the three children made their way slowly back to Uncle Henry's farm. They had taken their dinner out into the fields to eat—now they had to go back to work. Nora had a great deal of ironing to do, and Peggy had to clean the kitchen. It was a big stone kitchen, and Peggy knew it would take her until supper-time—and, oh dear, how tired she would be then! Aunt Harriet would scold her all the time, she knew.

"I've got to go and clean out the barn," said Mike to the girls, "but I'll be in at supper-time, and afterwards we'll see about this great secret of Jack's."

They each began their work, but all the time they were thinking excitedly of the evening. What was Jack's secret? Where was the place he knew of? Could they really and truly run away?

They all got into trouble because they were thinking so hard of the evening that they did not do their work to Aunt Harriet's liking nor to Uncle Henry's either. Nora got a few more slaps, and Peggy was scolded so hard that

12

she cried bitterly into her overall. She was made to scrub the kitchen floor all over again, and this made her late for supper.

Mike was shouted at by Uncle Henry for spilling some corn in the barn. The little boy said nothing, but he made up his mind that if it was possible to run away in safety he would do so, and take the girls with him, too.

"Nora and Peggy ought to be going to school and wearing nice clothes that fit them, and having friends to tea," said Mike to himself. "This is no life for them. They are just very hard-worked servants for Aunt Harriet, and she pays them nothing."

The children ate their supper of bread and cheese in silence. They were afraid of speaking in case their aunt and uncle shouted at them. When they had finished Mike spoke to his aunt.

"Please may we go for a walk in the fields before we go to bed?" he asked.

"No, you can't," said Aunt Harriet in her sharp voice. "You'll just go to bed, all of you. There's a lot of work to do tomorrow, and I want you up early."

The children looked at one another in dismay. But they had to do as they were told. They went upstairs to the big bedroom they all shared. Mike had a small bed in the corner behind a screen, and the two girls had a bigger bed between them.

"I believe Aunt Harriet and Uncle Henry are going out tonight, and that's why they want us to go to bed early," said Mike. "Well, if they do go out, we'll slip down and meet Jack by the river."

"We won't get undressed then," said Nora. 'We'll just slip under the sheets, dressed—and then it won't take us long to run down to the lake."

The three children listened hard. They heard the front door close. Mike popped out of bed and ran to the front

13

room. From there he could see the path to the gate. He saw his uncle and aunt walk down it, dressed to go out.

He ran back to the others. "We'll wait for five minutes," he said, "then we'll go."

They waited quietly. Then they all slipped downstairs and out of the back door. They ran down to the lake as fast as they could. Jack was there waiting for them.

"Hallo, Jack," said Mike. "Here we are at last. They sent us to bed, but when they went out we slipped down here to meet you."

"What's your great secret, Jack?" asked Nora; "we are longing to know."

"Well, listen," said Jack. "You know what a big lake this is, don't you, perfectly wild all round, except at the two ends where there are a few farmhouses and cottages. Now I know a little island, a good way up the south side of the lake, that I'm sure nobody knows at all. I don't think anyone but me has ever been there. It's a fine island, and would make the best hiding-place in the world!"

The three children listened, their eyes wide with astonishment. An island on the big lake! Oh, if only they could really go there and hide—and live by themselves— with no unkind aunt and uncle to slap them and scold them and make them work hard all day long!

"Are you too tired to walk down the lakeside to a place where you can see the island?" asked Jack. "I only found it quite by chance one day. The woods come right down to the lakeside opposite the island, and they are so thick that I don't think anyone has ever been through them, and so no one can have seen my island!"

"Jack! Jack! Take us to see your secret island!" begged Nora. "Oh, we must go. We're all tired—but we must, *must* see the secret island."

"Come on, then," said Jack, pleased to see how excited the others were. "Follow me. It's a good way."

The bare-footed boy took the three children across the fields to a wood. He threaded his way through the trees as if he were a rabbit. The wood thinned out and changed to a common, which, in turn, gave way to another wood, but this time the trees were so thick that it seemed as if there was no way through them at all.

But Jack kept on. He knew the way. He led the children without stopping, and at last they caught sight of the gleam of water. They had come back to the lakeside again. The evening was dim. The sun had sunk long since, and the children could hardly see.

Jack pushed his way through the trees that grew down to the waterside. He stood there and pointed silently to something. The children crowded round him.

"My secret island!" said Jack.

And so it was. The little island seemed to float on the dark lake-waters. Trees grew on it, and a little hill rose in the middle of it. It was a mysterious island, lonely and beautiful. All the children stood and gazed at it, loving it and longing to go to it. It looked so secret—almost magic.

"Well," said Jack at last. "What do you think? Shall we run away, and live on the secret island?"

"Yes!" whispered all the children. "Let's!"

An Exciting Day

The three children thought of nothing else but Jack's secret island all the next day. Could they possibly run away and hide there? Could they live there? How could they get food? What would happen if people came to look for them? Would they be found? How busy their minds were, thinking, thinking, planning, planning! Oh, the excitement of that secret island! It seemed so mysterious and lovely. If only, only they were all there, safe from slappings and scoldings!

The first time the children had a little time together to talk, they spoke about the island.

"Mike, we *must* go!" said Nora.

"Mike, let's tell Jack we'll go," said Peggy.

Mike scratched his curly black head. He felt old and worried. He wanted to go very badly—but would the three of them really be able to stand a wild life like that? No proper beds to sleep in—perhaps no proper food to eat—and suppose one of them was ill? Well, they would have to chance all that. They could always come back if things went too wrong.

"We'll go," said Mike. "We'll plan it all with Jack. He knows better than we do."

So that night, when they met Jack, the four of them laid their plans. Their faces were red with excitement, their eyes were shining. An adventure! A real proper adventure, almost like Robinson Crusoe—for they were going to live all by themselves on a lonely island.

"We must be careful in our plans," said Jack. "We

mustn't forget a single thing, for we ought not to go back to get anything, you know, or we might be caught."

"Could we go over to the island and just see what it's like before we go to live there?" asked Nora. "I would so love to see it."

"Yes," said Jack. "We'll go on Sunday."

"How can we go?" asked Mike. "Do we have to swim?"

"No," said Jack. "I have an old boat. It was one that had been left to fall to pieces, and I found it and patched it up. It still gets water in, but we can bale that out. I'll take you over in that."

The children could hardly wait for Sunday to come. They had to do a certain amount of work on Sundays, but usually they were allowed to take their dinner out and have a picnic afterwards.

It was June. The days were long and sunny. The farm garden was full of peas, broad beans, gooseberries, and ripening cherries. The children stole into it and picked as many pea-pods as they could find, and pulled up two big lettuces. Aunt Harriet gave them so little to eat that they always had to take something else as well. Mike said it wasn't stealing, because if Aunt Harriet had given them the food they earned by the hard work they did, they would have twice as much. They were only taking what they had earned. They had a loaf of bread between them, some butter, and some slices of ham, as well as the peas and lettuces. Mike pulled up some carrots, too. He said they would taste most delicious with the ham.

They hurried off to meet Jack. He was by the lakeside, carrying a bag on his back. He had his dinner in it. He showed them some fine red cherries, and a round cake.

"Mrs. Lane gave me those for hoeing her garden yesterday," he said. "We'll have a fine dinner between us."

"Where's the boat, Jack?" said Nora.

"You wait and see!" said Jack. "I don't leave my secret things out for everyone to see! No one else but you three knows about my boat!"

He set off in the hot June sunshine, and the three children followed him. He kept close to the lakeside and although the children kept a sharp look-out for the boat they did not see it until Jack stopped and showed it to them.

"See that great alder bush hanging over the lake just there?" he said. "Well, my boat's underneath it! It's well hidden, isn't it?"

Mike's eyes shone. He loved boats. He did hope Jack would let him help to row. The children pulled out the boat from under the thick tree. It was quite a big one, but very, very old. It had a good deal of water in, and Jack set everyone to work baling it out. There was an old pair of oars in the boat, and Jack put them in place.

"Now get in," he said. "I've a good way to row. Would you like to take an oar, Mike?"

Of course Mike would! The two boys rowed over the water. The sun shone down hotly, but there was a little breeze that blew every now and again. Soon the children saw the secret island in the distance. They knew it because of the little hill it had in the middle.

The secret island had looked mysterious enough on the night they had seen it before—but now, swimming in the hot June haze, it seemed more enchanting than ever. As they drew near to it, and saw the willow trees that bent over the water-edge and heard the sharp call of moorhens that scuttled off, the children gazed in delight. Nothing but trees and birds and little wild animals. Oh, what a secret island, all for their very own, to live on and play on.

"Here's the landing-place," said Jack, and he guided the boat to a sloping sandy beach. He pulled it up on the sand, and the children jumped out and looked round. The

18

They rowed across to the secret island

landing-place was a natural little cove—a lovely spot for a picnic—but picnickers never came here! Only a lonely otter lay on the sand now and again, and moorhens scuttled across it. No fire had ever been made on this little beach to boil a kettle. No bits of old orange peel lay about, or rusty tins. It was quite unspoilt.

"Let's leave our things here and explore a bit," said Mike, who was simply longing to see what the island was like. It seemed very big now they were on it.

"All right," said Jack, and he put his bag down.

"Come on," said Mike to the girls. "This is the beginning of a big adventure."

They left the little cove and went up through the thick trees. There were willows, alders, hazels, and elderberries at first, and then as they went up the hill that lay behind the cove there were silver birches and oaks. The hill was quite steep, and from the top the children could see a very long way—up the lake and down the lake.

"I say! If we come here to live, this hill will make an awfully good place to watch for enemies from!" said Mike excitedly. "We can see everything from here, all around!"

"Yes," said Jack. "Nobody would be able to take us by surprise."

"We *must* come here, we must, we must!" said Nora. "Oh, look at those rabbits, Peggy—they are as tame as can be, and that chaffinch nearly came on to my hand! Why are they so tame, Mike?"

"I suppose because they are not used to people," said Mike. "What's the other side of the hill, Jack? Shall we go down it?"

"There are caves on the other side of the hill," said Jack. "I haven't explored those. They would make good hiding-places if anyone ever came to look for us here."

They went down the hill on the other side. Gorse grew there and heather and bracken. Jack pointed out a big cave in the hillside. It looked dark and gloomy in the hot sunshine.

"We haven't time to go there now," said Jack. "But a cave would be an awfully good place to store anything in, wouldn't it? It would keep things nice and dry."

A little way down the hill the children heard a bubbling noise.

"What's that?" asked Peggy, stopping.

"Look! It's a little spring!" cried Mike. "Oh, Jack! This shall be our water-supply! It's as cold as can be, and as clear as crystal!"

"It tastes fine, too," said Jack. "I had a drink last time I was here. Lower down, another spring joins this one, and there is a tiny brook."

At the bottom of the hill was a thick wood. In clear patches great bushes of brambles grew. Jack pointed them out.

"There will be thousands of blackberries in the autumn," he said. "And as for hazel nuts, you should see them! And in another place I know here, on a warm slope, you can find wild raspberries by the score!"

"Oh, do show us!" begged Mike. But Jack said there was not time. Besides, the raspberries wouldn't be ripe yet.

"The island is too big to explore all over to-day," said Jack. "You've seen most of it—this big hill with its caves, the springs, the thick wood, and beyond the wood is a grassy field and then the water again. Oh, it is a glorious place!"

"Jack, where shall we live on this island?" said Peggy, who always liked to have everything well settled in her mind.

"We shall build a house of wood," said Jack. "I know how to. That will do finely for the summer, and for the winter we will have to find a cave, I think."

The children gazed at one another in glee. A house of wood, built by themselves—and a cave! How lucky they were to have a friend like Jack, who had a boat and a secret island!

They went back to the little landing-place, hungry and happy. They sat down and ate their bread and ham, carrots and peas, cherries and lettuces, and cake. It was the loveliest meal they had ever had in their lives, they thought. A little moorhen walked up to them and seemed surprised to see so many people in its home. But it did not run away. It ran round, pecking at the lettuce leaves, saying, "Fulluck, fulluck!" in its loud voice.

"If I could live here on this secret island always and always and always, and never grow up at all, I would be quite happy," said Nora.

"Well, we'll have a shot at living here for a good while at least!" said Jack. "Now, when shall we come?"

"And what shall we bring?" said Mike.

"Well, we don't really need a great deal at present," said Jack. "We can make soft beds of heather and bracken to lie on at night. What would be useful would be things like enamel mugs and plates and knives. I'll bring an axe and a very sharp woodman's knife. We'll need those when we build our house. Oh—and matches would be *most* useful for lighting fires. We shall have to cook our meals. I'll bring my fishing-line along, too."

The more the children talked about their plan, the more excited they got. At last they had arranged what to bring. They were gradually to hide things in a hollow tree by the lakeside, and then, when the time came, they could carry them to the boat and row off to the secret island, ready to set up house there.

"A frying-pan would be useful," said Nora.

"And a saucepan or two," said Peggy, "and a kettle. Oh! What fun it will be. I don't care how much we are

22

slapped or scolded now—I shall think of this exciting plan all day long!"

"We had better fix a day for starting off," said Jack. "What about a week from now? Sunday would be a good day for running away, because no one will come to look for us until night-time, when we don't go home!"

"Yes! A week to-day!" cried everyone. "Oooh! How happy we shall be!"

"Now we must go home," said Jack, setting off to the boat. "You can row if you like, Mike, and I'll bale out the water as we go. Get in, you girls."

"Ay, ay, Captain!" they sang out, full of joy to think they had such a fine leader as Jack! Off they all went, floating across the water in the evening light. What would they be doing next Sunday?

The Escape

All that week the three children carried out their plans. Aunt Harriet and Uncle Henry could not understand what was different about the children—they did not seem to mind being scolded at all. Even Nora took a slapping without tears. She was so happy when she thought of the secret island that she couldn't shed a tear!

The children took all the clothes they possessed down to the hollow tree by the lakeside. Mike took four enamel cups, some enamel plates, and two enamel dishes. Nora smuggled down an old kettle that Aunt Harriet had put away in a cupboard. She did not dare to take one of those on the stove. Peggy took a frying-pan and a saucepan to the hollow tree, and had to put up with a dreadful scolding when her aunt could not find them.

Jack took a saucepan too, and an axe and a fine sharp knife. He also took some small knives and forks and spoons, for the other children did not dare to take these. There were only just enough put out for them and their aunt and uncle to use. So they were glad when Jack found some and brought them along.

"Can you get some empty tins to store things in?" asked Jack. "I am trying to get sugar and things like that, because we must have those, you know. Grandad gave me some money the other day, and I'm buying a few things to store."

"Yes, I'll get some empty tins," said Mike. "Uncle has plenty in the shed. I can wash them out and dry them. And could you get matches, Jack? Aunt only leaves one box out, and that won't go far."

"Well, I've got a small magnifying glass," said Jack, and he showed it to the others. "Look, if I focus the rays of the sun on to that bit of paper over there, see what happens. It burns it, and, hey presto, there's a fire ready-made!"

"Oh, good!" said Mike. "We'll use that on a sunny day, Jack, and save our matches!"

"I'm bringing my work-basket in case we need to sew anything," said Peggy.

"And I've got a box of mixed nails and an old hammer," said Mike. "I found them in the shed."

"We're getting on!" said Jack, grinning, "I say—what a time we're going to have!"

"I wish Sunday would come!" sighed Nora.

"I shall bring our snap cards and our game of ludo and our dominoes," said Peggy. "We shall want to play games sometimes. And what about some books?"

"Good for you!" cried Mike. "Yes—books and papers we'll have, too—we shall love to read quietly sometimes."

The old hollow tree by the lakeside was soon full of the queerest collection of things. Not a day went by without something being added to it. One day it was a plank of wood. Another day it was half a sack of potatoes. Another day it was an old and ragged rug. Really, it was a marvel that the tree held everything!

At last Sunday came. The children were up long before their uncle and aunt. They crept into the kitchen garden and picked a basket of peas, pulled up six lettuces, added as many ripe broad beans as they could find, a bunch of young carrots, some radishes, and, putting their hands into the nest-boxes of the hens, they found six new-laid eggs!

Nora crept indoors and went to the larder. What could she take that Aunt Harriet would not notice that morning? Some tea? Yes! A tin of cocoa from the top shelf. A packet of currants and a tin of rice from the store

25

shelf, too. A big loaf, a few cakes from the cake-tin! The little girl stuffed them all into her basket and raced out to join the others. Long before Aunt Harriet was up all these things were safely in the hollow tree.

Peggy didn't quite like taking anything from the larder, but Mike said that as Aunt and Uncle wouldn't have to keep them after that day, they could quite well spare a few odds and ends for them.

"Anyway, if they paid us properly for our work, we would have enough to buy all these things and more," he said, as he stuffed them into the tree.

They went back to the farm for the last time, to breakfast. Peggy cooked the breakfast, and hoped Aunt would not notice that her long iron cooking spoon was gone. She also hoped that Aunt would not want to get another candle from the packet in the larder, for Peggy knew Mike had taken the rest of them, and had taken an old lantern of Uncle's, too!

The children ate their breakfast in silence.

Aunt Harriet looked at them. "I suppose you think you are going off for a picnic today!" she said. "Well, you are not! You can stay and weed the kitchen garden, Peggy and Nora. And I've no doubt Uncle Henry can set Mike something to do. *Someone* has been taking cakes out of my tin, and so you'll all stay in today!"

The hearts of the three children sank. Today of all days! As soon as the girls were washing up alone in the scullery, Mike looked in at the window.

"You girls slip off down to the lake as soon as you get a chance," he said. "Wait there for me. I won't be long!"

Peggy and Nora felt happier. They were to escape after all, then! They washed up a few more things and then saw their aunt going upstairs.

"She has gone to look out Uncle's Sunday suit and shirt," whispered Nora. "Quick! Now's our chance. We can slip out of the back door."

26

Peggy ran to the cupboard under the dresser and took out a long bar of soap. "We forgot all about soap!" she said. "We shall want some! I just remembered in time!"

Nora looked round for something to take, too. She saw a great slab of margarine on the dresser, and she caught it up.

"This will help us in our frying!" she said. "Come on, Peggy—we've no time to lose."

They raced out of the back door, down the path, and out into the fields. In five minutes' time they were by the hollow tree, well out of sight. Jack was not yet there. They did not know how long Mike would be. He would not find it so easy to get away!

But Mike had laid his plans. He waited for the moment when his aunt discovered that the girls had gone, and then walked into the kitchen.

"What's the matter, Aunt Harriet?" he asked, pretending to be very much surprised at her angry face and voice.

"Where have those two girls gone?" cried his aunt.

"I expect they have only gone to get in the clothes or something," said Mike. "Shall I go and find them for you?"

"Yes, and tell them they'll get well slapped for running off like this without finishing their work," said his aunt in a rage.

Mike ran off, calling to his uncle that he was on an errand for his aunt. So Uncle Henry said nothing, but let him go. Mike tore across the fields to the lakeside and met the two girls there. They hugged one another in joy.

"Now, where's Jack?" said Mike. "He said he would meet us as soon as he could."

"There he is!" said Nora; and sure enough, there was Jack coming across the field, waving to them. He carried a heavy bag into which he had crammed all sorts of things at

27

the very last moment—rope, an old mackintosh, two books, some newspapers, and other things. His face was shining with excitement.

"Good! You're here!" he said.

"Yes, but we nearly couldn't come," said Nora, and she told Jack what had happened.

"I say! I hope this won't mean that your uncle and aunt will start to look for you too soon," said Jack.

"Oh, no!" said Mike. "It only means that they will make up their minds to whip us well when we get back this evening, but we shan't go back! They'll think we've gone off on our usual Sunday picnic."

"Now we've got a lot to do," said Jack seriously. "This is all fun and excitement to us—but it's work, too—and we've got to get on with it. First, all these things must be carried from the hollow tree to the boat. Mike, you get out some of them and give them to the girls. Then we'll take the heavier things. I expect we shall have to come back to the tree three or four times before it's emptied."

The four of them set off happily, carrying as much as they could. The sun was hot, and they puffed and panted, but who cared? They were off to the secret island at last!

It was a good walk to the boat, and they had to make four journeys altogether, carrying things carefully. At last there was nothing left in the hollow tree. They need not come back again.

"I'm jolly glad," said Mike. "Every time I get back to that hollow tree I expect to find Aunt or Uncle hidden inside it, ready to pop out at us!"

"Don't say such horrid things," said Nora. "We're leaving Aunt and Uncle behind for ever!"

They were at the boat, and were stowing things there as well as they could. It was a good thing the boat was fairly big or it would never have taken everything. The children had had to bale out a good deal of water before they could put anything in the bottom. It leaked badly, but as long as someone could bale out with a tin it was all right.

"Now then," said Jack, looking round at the shore to see that nothing was left behind, "are we ready?"

"Ay, ay, Captain!" roared the other three. "Push off!"

The boat was pushed off. Mike and Jack took an oar each, for the boat was heavy and needed two people to pull it. It floated easily out on to the deeper water.

"We're off at last!" said Nora, in a little happy voice that sounded almost as if she were going to cry.

Nobody said anything more. The boat floated on and on, as Mike and Jack rowed strongly. Peggy baled out the water that came in through the leaks. She wondered what it would be like not to sleep in a proper bed. She wondered what it would be like to wake up under the blue sky—to have no one to make her do this, that and the other. How happy she felt!

It was a long way to the island. The sun rose higher and higher. The adventurers felt hotter and hotter. At last Nora pointed excitedly in front.

"The secret island!" she cried. "The secret island."

Mike and Jack stopped rowing for a moment and the boat floated on slowly by itself whilst the four gazed at the lonely little island, hidden so well on the heart of the lake. Their own island! It had no name. It was just the Secret Island!

Mike and Jack rowed on again. They came to the little sandy cove beneath the willow trees. Jack jumped out and pulled the boat in. The others jumped out too and gazed round.

"We're really here, we're really here, we're really here!" squealed Nora, jumping up and down and round and round in delight. "We've escaped. We've come to live on this dear little hidden island."

"Come on, Nora, give a hand," ordered Jack. "We've a lot to do before night, you know!"

Nora ran to help. The boat had to be unloaded, and that

was quite a job. All the things were put on the beach under the willow trees for the time being. By the time that was finished the children were hotter than ever and very hungry and thirsty.

"Oh, for a drink!" groaned Mike.

"Peggy, do you remember the way to the spring?" asked Jack. "You do? Well, just go and fill this kettle with water, will you? We'll all have a drink and something to eat!"

Peggy ran off up the hill and down the other side to the spring. She filled the kettle and went back. The others had put out enamel mugs ready to drink from. Mike was busy looking out something to eat, too. He had put out a loaf of bread, some young carrots, which they all loved to nibble, a piece of cheese each, and a cake.

What a meal that was! How they laughed and giggled and chattered! Then they lay back in the sun and shut their eyes. They were tired with all their hard work. One by one they fell asleep.

Jack awoke first. He sat up. "Hey!" he said. "This won't do! We've got to get our beds for the night and arrange a good sleeping-place! We've dozens of things to do! Come on, everyone, to work, to work!"

But who minded work when it was in such a pleasant place? Peggy and Nora washed up the mugs and dishes in the lake water and set them in the sun to dry. The boys put all the stores in a good place and covered them with the old mackintosh in case it should rain. To-morrow they would start to build their house.

"Now to get a sleeping-place and bedding," said Jack. "Won't it be fun to sleep for the first time on the Secret Island!"

The First Night On The Island

"Where do you think would be the best place to sleep?" said Peggy, looking round the little cove.

"Well," said Jack, "I think it would be best to sleep under some thick trees somewhere, then, if it rains tonight, we shall not get too wet. But I don't think it will rain; the weather is quite settled."

"There are two nice, big, thick oak trees just beyond the cove," said Mike, pointing. "Shall we find a place there?"

"Yes," said Jack. "Find a bramble bush or gorse bush near them to keep any wind off. Let's go and see what we think."

They all went to the two big oak trees. Their branches swung almost down to the ground in places. Below grew clumps of soft heather, springy as a mattress. To the north was a great growth of gorse, thick and prickly.

"This looks a fine place to sleep," said Jack. "Look. Do you see this little place here, almost surrounded by gorse, and carpeted with heather? The girls could sleep here, and we could sleep just outside their cosy spot, to protect them. The oak trees would shelter us nicely overhead."

"Oh, I do think this is fine; I do, I do!" cried Nora, thinking that their green, heathery bedroom was the nicest in the world. She lay down on the heather. "It is as soft as can be!" she said; "and oh! there is something making a most delicious smell. What is it?"

"It is a patch of wild thyme," said Jack. "Look, there

31

is a bit in the middle of the heather. You will smell it when you go to sleep, Nora!"

"All the same, Jack, the heather won't feel quite so soft when we have lain on it a few hours," said Mike. "We'd better get some armfuls of bracken too, hadn't we?"

"Yes," said Jack. "Come on up the hill. There is plenty of bracken there, and heaps of heather too. We will pick the bracken there, and put it in the sun to dry. The heather doesn't need drying. Pick plenty, for the softer we lie the better we'll sleep! Heyho for a starry night and a heathery bed!"

The four children gathered armfuls of bracken and put it out in the sun to wither and dry. The heather they carried back to their green bedroom under the oak tree. They spread it thickly there. It looked most deliciously soft! The thick gorse bushes kept off the breeze, and the oaks above waved their branches and whispered. What fun it all was!

"Well, there are our bedrooms ready," said Jack. "Now, we'd better find a place to put our stores in. We won't be too far from the water, because it's so useful for washing ourselves and our dishes in."

The children were hungry again. They got out the rest of the cakes, and finished up the bread, eating some peas with it, which they shelled as they ate.

"Are we going to have any supper?" asked Mike.

"We might have a cup of cocoa each and a piece of my cake," said Jack. "We must be careful not to eat everything at once that we've brought, or we'll go short! I'll do some fishing to-morrow."

"Shall we begin to build the house to-morrow?" asked Mike, who was longing to see how Jack meant to make their house.

"Yes," said Jack. "Now you two girls wash up the

mugs again, and Mike and I will find a good place for the stores."

The girls went to the water and washed the things. The boys wandered up the beach—and, at the back of the sandy cove, they found just the very place they wanted!

There was a sandy bank there, with a few old willows growing on top of it, their branches drooping down. Rain had worn away the sandy soil from their roots, and underneath there was a sort of shallow cave, with roots running across it here and there.

"Look at that!" said Jack in delight. "Just the place we want for our stores! Nora, Peggy, come and look here!"

The girls came running. "Oh," said Peggy, pleased, "we can use those big roots as shelves, and stand our tins and cups and dishes on them! Oh, it's a proper little larder!"

"Well, if you girls get the stores from the cove and arrange them neatly here," said Jack. "Mike and I will go and fill the kettle from the spring, and we'll see if there isn't a nearer spring, because it's a long way up the hill and down the other side."

"Can't we come with you?" asked Peggy.

"No, you arrange everything," said Jack. "It had better all be done as quickly as possible, because you never know when it's going to turn wet. We don't want our stores spoilt."

Leaving Peggy and Nora to arrange the tins, baskets, and odds and ends neatly in the root-larder, the two boys went up the hill behind the cove. They separated to look for a spring, and Mike found one! It was a very tiny one, gushing out from under a small rock, and it ran down the hill like a little waterfall, getting lost in the heather and grass here and there. Its way could be seen by the rushes that sprang up beside its course.

"I expect it runs down into the lake," said Mike. "It's a very small spring, but we can use it to fill our kettle, and it won't take us quite so long as going to the other spring. If we have to live in the caves during the winter, the other spring will be more useful then, for it will be quite near the cave."

They filled the kettle. It was lovely up there on the hillside in the June sun. Bees hummed and butterflies flew all round. Birds sang, and two or three moorhens cried "Fulluck, fulluck!" from the water below.

"Let's go to the top of the hill and see if we can spy anyone coming up or down the lake," said Jack. So they went right up to the top, but not a sign of anyone could they see. The waters of the lake were calm and clear and blue. Not a boat was on it. The children might have been quite alone in the world.

They went down to the girls with the full kettle. Nora and Peggy proudly showed the boys how they had arranged the stores. They had used the big roots for shelves, and the bottom of the little cave they had used for odds and ends, such as Jack's axe and knife, the hammer and nails, and so on.

"It's a nice dry place," said Peggy. "It's just right for a larder, and it's so nice and near the cove. Jack, where are we going to build our house?"

Jack took the girls and Mike to the west end of the cove, where there was a thicket of willows. He forced his way through them and showed the others a fine clear place right in the very middle of the trees.

"Here's the very place," he said. "No one would ever guess there was a house just here, if we built one! The willows grow so thickly that I don't suppose anyone but ourselves would ever know they could be got through."

They talked about their house until they were tired out. They made their way back to the little beach and Jack said they would each have a cup of cocoa, a piece of cake, and go to bed!

He and Mike soon made a fire. There were plenty of dry twigs about, and bigger bits of wood. It did look cheerful to see the flames dancing. Jack could not use his little magnifying glass to set light to the paper or twigs because the sun was not bright enough then. It was sinking down in the west. He used a match. He set the kettle on the fire to boil.

"It would be better tomorrow to swing the kettle over the flames on a tripod of sticks," he said. "It will boil more quickly then."

But nobody minded how slowly the kettle boiled. They lay on their backs in the sand, looking up at the evening sky, listening to the crackle of the wood, and smelling a mixture of wood-smoke and honeysuckle. At last the kettle sent out a spurt of steam, and began to hiss. It was boiling.

Nora made the cocoa, and handed it round in mugs. "There's no milk," she said. "But there is some sugar."

They munched their cake and drank their cocoa. Though it had no milk in it, it was the nicest they had ever tasted.

"I do like seeing the fire," said Nora. "Oh, Jack, why are you stamping it out?"

"Well," said Jack, "people may be looking for us to-night, you know, and a spire of smoke from this island would give our hiding-place away nicely! Come on, now, everyone to bed! We've hard work to do tomorrow!"

Peggy hurriedly rinsed out the mugs. Then all of them went to their green, heathery bedroom. The sun was gone. Twilight was stealing over the secret island.

"Our first night here!" said Mike, standing up and looking down on the quiet waters of the lake. "We are all alone, the four of us, without a roof over our heads even, but I'm so happy!"

"So am I!" said everyone. The girls went to their hidden

green room in the gorse and lay down in their clothes. It seemed silly to undress when they were sleeping out of doors. Mike threw them the old ragged rug.

"Throw that over yourselves," he said. "It may be cold tonight, sleeping out for the first time. You won't be frightened, will you?"

"No," said Peggy. "You two boys will be near, and, anyway, what is there to be frightened of?"

They lay down on the soft heather, and pulled the old rug over them. The springy heather was softer than the old hard bed the two girls had been used to at home. The little girls put their arms round one another and shut their eyes. They were fast asleep almost at once.

But the boys did not sleep so quickly. They lay on their heathery beds and listened to all the sounds of the night. They heard the little grunt of a hedgehog going by. They saw the flicker of bats overhead. They smelt the drifting scent of honeysuckle, and the delicious smell of wild thyme crushed under their bodies. A reed-warbler sang a beautiful little song in the reeds below, and then another answered.

"Is that a blackbird?" asked Mike.

"No, a reed-warbler," said Jack. "They sing as beautifully as any bird that sings in the daytime! Listen, do you hear that owl?"

"Oooo-ooo-ooo-oooo!" came a long, quivering sound; "ooo-ooo-ooo-ooo!"

"He's hunting for rats and voles," said Jack. "I say, look at the stars, Mike?"

"Don't they seem far away?" said Mike, looking up into the purple night sky, which was set with thousands of bright stars. "I say, Jack, it's awfully nice of you to come away with us like this and share your secret island."

"It isn't nice of me at all," said Jack. "I wanted to. I'm doing just exactly what I most want to do. I only hope we shan't be found and taken back, but I'll take jolly good care no one finds us! I'm laying my plans already!"

But Mike was not listening. His eyes shut, he forgot the owls and the stars; he fell asleep and dreamt of building a house with Jack, a lovely house.

Jack fell asleep, too. And soon the rabbits that lived under their gorse-bush came slyly out and peeped at the sleeping children in surprise. Who were they?

But, as the children did not move, the rabbits grew bold and went out to play just as usual. Even when one ran over Mike by mistake, the little boy did not know it. He was *much* too fast asleep!

The Building Of The House

What fun it was to wake up that first morning on the island! Jack awoke first. He heard a thrush singing so loudly on a tree near by that he woke up with a jump.

"Mind how you do it," said the thrush, "mind how you do it!"

Jack grinned. "I'll mind how I do it all right!" he said to the singing thrush. "Hi, Mike! Wake up! The sun is quite high!"

Mike woke and sat up. At first he didn't remember where he was. Then a broad smile came over his face. Of course—they were all on the secret island! How perfectly glorious!

"Peggy, Nora! Get up!" he cried. The girls awoke and sat up in a hurry. Wherever were they? What was this green bedroom—oh, of course, it was their heathery bedroom on the secret island!

Soon all four children were up and about. Jack made them take off their things and have a dip in the lake. It was simply lovely, but the water felt cold at first. When they had dried themselves on an old sack—for they had no towels—the children felt terribly hungry. But Jack had been busy. He had set his fishing-line, and, even as they bathed, he had seen the float jerk up and down. It was not long before Jack proudly laid four fine trout on the sand of the cove, and set about to make a fire to cook them.

Mike went to fill the kettle to make some tea. Peggy got some big potatoes out of the sack and put them almost in the fire to cook in their skins. Jack found the frying-pan in their storeroom and put a piece of margarine in to fry the fish, which he knew exactly how to clean.

"I don't know what we should do without you," said Mike, as he watched Jack. "Goodness! How I shall enjoy my breakfast!"

They all did. The tea did not taste very nice without milk. "It's a pity we can't get milk," said Jack. "We shall miss that, I'm afraid. Now let's all wash up, and put everything away—and then we'll start on our house!"

In great excitement everything was washed up and put away. Then Jack led the way through the thick willow trees, and they came to the little clear place in the centre of them.

"Now, this is how I mean to build the house," he said. "Do you see these little willow trees here—one there —one there—two there—and two there. Well, I think you will find that if we climb up and bend down the top branches, they will meet each other nicely in the centre, and we can weave them into one another. That will make the beginning of a roof. With my axe I shall chop down some other young willow trees, and use the trunk and thicker branches for walls. We can drive the trunks and branches into the ground between the six willow trees we are using, and fill up any cracks with smaller branches woven across. Then if we stuff every corner and crevice with bracken and heather, we shall have a fine big house, with a splendid roof, wind-proof and rain-proof. What do you think of that?"

The other children listened in the greatest excitement. It sounded too good to be true. Could it be as easy as all that?

"Jack, can we really do it?" said Mike. "It sounds all right—and those willow trees are just the right distance from one another to make a good big house—and their top branches will certainly overlap well."

"Oh, let's begin, let's begin!" cried Nora, impatient as usual, dancing up and down.

"I'll climb up this first willow tree and swing the branches over with my weight," said Jack. "All you others must catch hold of them and hold them till I slip down. Then I'll climb another tree and bend those branches over too. We'll tie them together, and then I'll climb up the other trees. Once we've got all the top branches bending down touching one another, and overlapping nicely, we can cut long willow-sticks and lace our roof together. I'll show you how to."

Jack swung himself up into one of the little willow trees. It was only a young one, with a small trunk—but it had a head of long, fine branches, easy to bend. Jack swung them down, and the girls and Mike caught them easily. They held on to them whilst Jack slid down the tree and climbed another. He did the same thing there, bending down the supple branches until they reached and rested on top of those bent down from the other tree.

"Tie them together, Mike!" shouted Jack. "Peggy, go and find the rope I brought."

Peggy darted off. She soon came back with the rope. Mike twisted it round the branches of the two trees, and tied them firmly together.

"It's beginning to look like a roof already!" shouted Nora, in excitement. "Oh, I want to sit underneath it!"

She sat down under the roof of willow boughs, but Jack called to her.

"Get up, Nora! You've got to help! I'm up the third tree now—look, here come the top branches bending over with my weight—catch them and hold them!"

Nora and Peggy caught them and held on tightly. The branches reached the others and overlapped them. Mike was soon busy tying them down, too.

The whole morning was spent in this way. By

dinnertime all the six trees had been carefully bent over. Jack showed Mike and the girls how to weave the branches together, so that they held one another and made a fine close roof. "You see, if we use the trees like this, their leaves will still grow and will make a fine thick roof," said Jack. "Now, although our house has no walls as yet, we at least have a fine roof to shelter under if it rains!"

"I want something to eat," said Nora. "I'm so hungry that I feel I could eat snails!"

"Well, get out four eggs, and we'll have some with potatoes," said Jack. "We'll boil the eggs in our saucepan. There's plenty of potatoes, too. After the eggs are boiled we'll boil some potatoes and mash them up. That will be nice for a change. We'll nibble a few carrots, too, and have some of those cherries."

"We do have funny meals," said Peggy, going to get the saucepan and the eggs, "but I do like them! Come on, Nora, help me get the potatoes and peel them whilst the eggs are boiling. And Mike, get some water, will you? We haven't enough."

Soon the fire was burning merrily and the eggs were boiling in the saucepan. The girls peeled the potatoes, and Jack washed the carrots. He went to get some water to drink, too, for everyone was very thirsty.

"You'd better catch some more fish for tonight, Jack," said Peggy. "I hope our stores are going to last out a bit! We do seem to eat a lot!"

"I've been thinking about that," said Jack, watching the potatoes boiling. "I think I'll have to row to land occasionally and get more food. I can get it from Granddad's farm. There are plenty of potatoes there, and I can always get the eggs from the hen-house. Some of the hens are mine—and there's a cow that's really mine too, for Granddad gave her to me when she was a calf!"

"I wish we had hens and a cow here!" said Peggy. "We should have lots of milk then and plenty of eggs!"

"How would we get hens and a cow here?" said Mike, laughing. "I think Jack's idea of rowing across to land sometimes is a good one. He can go at night. He knows the way, and could get back before day breaks."

"It's dangerous, though," said Peggy. "Suppose he were caught? We couldn't do without Jack!"

The children ate their dinner hungrily. They thought that eggs and potatoes had never tasted so nice before. The sun shone down hotly. It was simply perfect weather. Nora lay down when she had finished her meal and closed her eyes. She felt lazy and sleepy.

Jack poked her with his foot. "You're not to go to sleep, Nora," he said. "We must get on with our house, now we've started. We've got to clear up as usual, and then we must get back to the house. We'll start on the walls this afternoon."

"But I'm sleepy," said Nora. She was rather a lazy little girl, and she thought it would be lovely to have a nap whilst the others got on with the work. But Jack was not the one to let anyone slack. He jerked Nora to her feet and gave her a push.

"Go on, lazy-bones," he said. "I'm captain here. Do as you're told."

"I didn't know you were captain," said Nora, rather sulkily.

"Well, you know now," said Jack. "What do the others say about it?"

"Yes, you're captain, Jack," said Mike and Peggy together. "Ay, ay, sir!"

Nobody said any more. They washed up in the lake and cleared the things away neatly. They put some more wood on the fire to keep it burning, because Jack said it was silly to keep on lighting it. Then they all ran off to the willow thicket.

Jack made himself busy. He chopped down some willow

saplings—young willow trees—with his axe, and cut off the longer branches.

"We'll use these to drive into the ground for walls," said Jack. "Where's that old spade, Mike? Did you bring it as I said?"

"Yes, here it is," said Mike. "Shall I dig holes to drive the sapling trunks into?"

"Yes," said Jack. "Dig them fairly deep."

So Mike dug hard in the hot sun, making holes for Jack to ram the willow wood into. The girls stripped the leaves off the chopped-down trees, and with Jack's knife cut off the smaller twigs. They trimmed up the bigger branches nicely.

Everyone worked hard until the sun began to go down. The house was not yet built—it would take some days to do that—but at any rate there was a fine roof, and part of the wall was up. The children could quite well see how the house would look when it was done—and certainly it would be big, and very strong. They felt proud of themselves.

"We'll do no more today," said Jack. "We are all tired. I'll go and see if there are any fish on my line."

But, alas! there were no fish that night!

"There's some bread left and a packet of currants," said Peggy. "And some lettuces and margarine. Shall we have those?"

"This food question is going to be a difficult one," said Jack thoughtfully. "We've plenty of water—we shall soon have a house—but we must have food or we shall starve. I shall catch rabbits, I think."

"Oh, no, Jack, don't do that," said Nora. "I do like rabbits so much."

"So do I, Nora," said Jack. "But if rabbits were not caught, the land would soon be overrun with them, you know. You have often had rabbit-pie, haven't you? And I guess you liked it, too!"

"Yes, I did," said Nora. "Well, if you are sure you can

catch them so that they are not hurt or in pain, Jack, I suppose you'll have to."

"You leave it to me," said Jack. "I don't like hurting things any more than you do. But I know quite well how to skin rabbits. If it makes you feel squeamish, you two girls can leave it to Mike and me. So long as you can cook the rabbits for dinner, that's all you need worry about. And ever since Peggy said she wished we had a cow and some hens, I've been thinking about it. I believe we could manage to get them over here on to the island—then we *would* be all right!"

Mike, Peggy, and Nora stared at Jack in amazement. What a surprising boy he was! However could they get a cow and hens?

"Let's hurry up and get the supper," said Jack, smiling at their surprised faces. "I'm hungry. We'll think about things tomorrow. We'll have our meal now and a quiet read afterwards, then to bed early. Tomorrow we'll go on with the house."

Soon they were munching bread and margarine, and eating lettuce. They saved the currants for another time. Then they got out books and papers and sprawled on the soft heather, reading whilst the daylight lasted. Then they had a dip in the lake, threw on their clothes again, and settled down for the night in their heathery beds.

"Good-night, everyone," said Mike. But nobody answered—they were all asleep!

Willow House Is Finished

The next day, after a meal of fish and lettuce, the children were ready to go on with the building of their house in the willow thicket. It was lucky that Jack had caught more fish on his line that morning, for stores were getting low. There were still plenty of potatoes, but not much else. Jack made up his mind that he would have to take the boat and see what he could bring back in it that night. There was no doubt but that food was going to be their great difficulty.

All morning the four children worked hard at the house. Jack cut down enough young willows to make the walls. Mike dug the holes to drive in the willow stakes. He and Jack drove them deeply in, and the girls jumped for joy to see what fine straight walls of willow the boys were making.

The willow stakes were set a little way apart, and Jack showed the girls how to take thin, supple willow branches and weave them in and out of the stakes to hold the walls in place, and to fill up the gaps. It was quite easy to do this when they knew how, but they got very hot.

Mike went up and down to the spring a dozen times that morning to fetch water! They all drank pints of it, and were glad of its coldness. The sun was really very hot, though it was nice and shady in the green willow thicket.

"It begins to look like a house now," said Jack, pleased. "Look, this front gap here is where we shall have the door. We can make that later of long stakes interwoven with willow strips, and swing it on some sort of a hinge so that it opens and shuts. But we don't need a door at present."

That day all the walls were finished, and the girls had gone a good way towards weaving the stakes together so that the walls stood firmly and looked nice and thick.

"In the olden days people used to fill up the gaps with clay and let it dry hard," said Jack. "But I don't think there's any clay on this island, so we must stuff up the cracks with dried bracken and heather. That will do nicely. And the willow stakes we have rammed into the ground will grow, and throw out leaves later on, making the wall thicker still."

"How do you mean—the stakes we have cut will grow?" asked Mike in surprise. "Sticks don't grow, surely!"

Jack grinned. "Willow sticks do!" he said. "You can cut a willow branch off the tree—strip it of all buds and leaves, and stick it in the ground, and you'll find that, although it has no roots, and no shoots—it will put out both and grow into a willow tree by itself! Willows are full of life, and you can't stamp it out of them!"

"Well—our house will be growing all the year round, then!" cried Nora. "How funny!"

"I think it's lovely!" said Peggy. "I like things to be as alive as that. I shall love to live in a house that's growing over me—putting out roots and shoots and buds and leaves! What shall we call our house, Jack?"

"Willow House!" said Jack. "That's the best name for it!"

"It's a good name," said Peggy. "I like it. I like everything here. It's glorious. Just us four—and our secret island. It's the loveliest adventure that ever was!"

"If only we had more to eat!" said Mike, who seemed to feel hungry every hour of the day. "That's the only thing I don't like about this adventure!"

46

"Yes," said Jack. "We'll have to put that right! Don't worry. We shall get over it somehow!"

That night there was nothing much to eat but potatoes. Jack said he would go off in the boat as soon as it was dark, to see what he could find at his old farm.

So he set off. He took with him a candle, set in the lantern, but he did not light it in case he should be seen.

"Wait up for me," he said to the others, "and keep a small fire going—not big, in case the glow could be seen."

The other three waited patiently for Jack to come back. He seemed a long, long time. Nora stretched herself out on the old rug and fell asleep. But Mike and Peggy kept awake. They saw the moon come up and light everything. The secret island seemed mysterious again in the moonlight. Dark shadows stretched beneath the trees. The water lapped against the sand, black as night, close by them, but silvered where the moon caught it beyond. It was a warm night, and the children were hot, even though they had no covering.

It seemed hours before they heard the splash of oars. Mike ran down to the edge of the water and waited. He saw the boat coming softly over the water in the moonlight. He called Jack.

"Hallo, there, Jack! Are you all right?"

"Yes," said Jack's voice. "I've got plenty of news too!"

The boat scraped on the sand and stones. Mike pulled it up the beach, and Jack jumped out.

"I've got something here for us!" said Jack, and they saw his white teeth in the moonlight as he grinned at them. "Put your hands down there in the boat, Nora."

Nora did—and squealed!

"There's something soft and warm and feathery there!" she said. "What is it?"

"Six of my hens!" said Jack. "I found them roosting in the hedges! I caught them and trussed them up so that

47

they couldn't move! My word, they were heavy to carry! But we shall have plenty of eggs now! They can't escape from the island!"

"Hurrah!" cried Peggy. "We can have eggs for breakfast, dinner, and tea!"

"What else have you brought?" asked Mike.

"Corn for the hens," said Jack. "And packets of seeds of all kinds from the shed. And some tins of milk. And a loaf of bread, rather stale. And lots more vegetables!"

"And here are some cherries," said Nora, pulling out handfuls of red cherries from the boat. "Did you pick these, Jack?"

"Yes," said Jack. "They are from the tree in our garden. It's full of them now."

"Did you see your grandfather?" asked Mike.

"Yes," grinned Jack, "but he didn't see me! He's going away—to live with my aunt. The farm is to be shut up, and someone is to feed the animals until it's sold. So I think I shall try and get my own cow somehow, and make her swim across the lake to the island!"

"Don't be silly, Jack," said Peggy. "You could never do that!"

"You don't know what I can do!" said Jack. "Well, listen—I heard my Granddad talking to two friends of his, and everyone is wondering where we've all gone! They've searched everywhere for us—in all the nearby towns and villages, and in all the country round about!"

"Oooh!" said the three children, feeling rather frightened. "Do you suppose they'll come here?"

"Well, they may," said Jack. "You never know. I've always been a bit afraid that the smoke from our fire will give the game away to someone. But don't let's worry about that till it happens."

"Are the police looking for us, too?" asked Peggy.

"Oh yes," said Jack. "Everyone is, as far as I can make

48

Mike shone the lantern onto the hens

out. I heard Granddad tell how they've searched barns and stacks and ditches, and gone to every town for twenty miles round, thinking we might have run away on a lorry. They don't guess how near we are!"

"Is Aunt Harriet very upset?" asked Peggy.

"Very!" grinned Jack. "She's got no one to wash and scrub and cook for her now! But that's all she cares, I expect! Well, it's good news about my Granddad going to live with my aunt. I can slip to and fro and not be seen by him now. My word, I wished you were with me when I got these hens. They did peck and scratch and flap about. I was afraid someone would hear them."

"Where shall we put them?" said Mike, helping Jack to carry them up the beach.

"I vote we put them into Willow House till the morning," said Jack. "We can stop up the doorway with something."

So they bundled the squawking hens into Willow House, and stopped up the doorway with sticks and bracken. The hens fled to a corner and squatted there, terrified. They made no more noise.

"I'm jolly tired," said Jack. "Let's have a few cherries and go to bed."

They munched the ripe cherries, and then went to their green bedroom. The bracken which they had picked and put on the hillside to dry had been quite brown and withered by that afternoon, so the girls had added it to their bed and the boys', and tonight their beds seemed even softer and sweeter-smelling than usual. They were all tired. Mike and Jack talked for a little while, but the girls went to sleep quickly.

They slept late the next morning. Peggy woke first, and sat up, wondering what the unusual noise was that she heard. It was a loud cackling.

"Of course! The hens!" she thought. She slipped off her

50

bracken-and-heather bed, jumped lightly over the two sleeping boys and ran to Willow House. She pulled aside the doorway and squeezed inside. The hens fled to a corner when they saw her, but Peggy saw a welcome sight!

Four of the hens had laid eggs! Goody! Now they could have a fine breakfast! The little girl gathered them up quickly, then, stopping up the doorway again, she ran out. She soon had a fire going, and, when the others sat up, rubbing their eyes, Peggy called them.

"Come on! Breakfast! The hens have laid us an egg each!"

They ran to breakfast. "We'll have a dip afterwards," said Mike. "I feel so hungry."

"We must finish Willow House properly today," said Jack. "And we must decide what to do with the hens, too. They can't run loose till they know us and their new home. We must put up some sort of enclosure for them."

After breakfast the four of them set to work to make a tiny yard for the hens. They used willow stakes again and quickly built a fine little fence, too high for the hens to jump over. Jack made them nesting-places of bracken, and hoped they would lay their eggs there. He scattered some seed for them, and they pecked at it eagerly. Peggy gave them a dish of water.

"They will soon know this is their home and lay their eggs here," said Jack. "Now, come on, let's get on with Willow House! You two girls stuff up the cracks with heather and bracken, and Mike and I will make the door."

Everyone worked hard. The girls found it rather a nice job to stuff the soft heather and bracken into the cracks and make the house rain- and wind-proof. They were so happy in their job that they did not notice what a fine door Jack and Mike had made of woven willow twigs. The boys called the girls, and proudly showed them what they had done.

51

The door had even been fixed on some sort of a hinge, so that it swung open and shut! It looked fine! It did not quite fit at the top, but nobody minded that. It was a door—and could be shut or opened, just as they pleased. Willow House was very dark inside when the door was shut—but that made it all the more exciting!

"I'm so hungry and thirsty now that I believe I could eat all the food we've got!" said Mike at last.

"Yes, we really must have something to eat," said Jack. "We've got plenty of bread and potatoes and vegetables. Let's cook some broad beans. They are jolly good. Go and look at my fishing-line, Mike, and see if there are any fish on it."

There was a fine trout, and Mike brought it back to cook. Soon the smell of frying rose on the air, and the children sniffed hungrily. Fish, potatoes, bread, beans, cherries, and cocoa with milk from one of Jack's tins. What a meal!

"I'll think about getting Daisy the cow across next," said Jack, drinking his cocoa. "We simply must have milk."

"And, Jack, we could store some of our things in Willow House now, couldn't we?" said Peggy. "The ants get into some of the things in the cave-larder. It's a good place for things like hammers and nails, but it would be better to keep our food in Willow House. Are we going to live in Willow House, Jack?"

"Well, we'll live in the open air mostly, I expect," said Jack; "but it will be a good place to sleep in when the nights are cold and rainy, and a fine shelter on bad days. It's our sort of home."

"It's a lovely home," said Nora; "the nicest there ever was! What fun it is to live like this!"

The Cow Comes To The Island

A day or two went by. The children were busy, for there seemed lots of things to do. The door of Willow House came off and had to be put on again more carefully. One of the hens escaped, and the four children spent nearly the whole morning looking for it. Jack found it at last under a gorse bush, where it had laid a big brown egg.

They made the fence of the hen-yard a bit higher, thinking that the hen had been able to jump over. But Mike found a hole in the fence through which he was sure the hen had squeezed, and very soon it was blocked up with fronds of bracken. The hens squawked and clucked, but they seemed to be settling down, and always ran eagerly to Nora when she fed them twice a day.

Mike thought it would be a good idea to make two rooms inside Willow House, instead of one big room. The front part could be a sort of living-room, with the larder in a corner, and the back part could be a bedroom, piled with heather and bracken to make soft lying. So they worked at a partition made of willow, and put it up to make two rooms. They left a doorway between, but did not make a door. It was nice to have a two-roomed house!

One evening Jack brought something unusual to the camp-fire on the little beach. Mike stared at what he was carrying.

"You've caught some rabbits!" he said, "and you've skinned them, too, and got them ready for cooking!"

"Oh, Jack!" said Nora. "Must you catch those dear

little rabbits? I do love them so much, and it is such fun to watch them playing about round us in the evenings."

"I know," said Jack, "but we must have meat to eat sometimes. Now, don't worry, Nora—they did not suffer any pain and you know you have often eaten rabbit-pie at home."

All the same, none of the children enjoyed cooking the rabbits, though they couldn't help being glad of a change of food. They were getting a little tired of fish. Nora said she felt as if she couldn't look a rabbit in the face that evening!

"In Australia, rabbits are as much of a pest as rats are here," said Jack, who seemed to know all sorts of things. "If we were in Australia we would think we had done a good deed to get rid of a few pests."

"But we're not in Australia," said Peggy. Nobody said any more, and the meal was finished in silence. The girls washed up as usual, and the boys went to get some water from the spring ready to boil in the morning. Then they all had a dip in the lake.

"I think I'll have a shot at getting my cow along tonight," said Jack, as they dressed themselves again.

"You can't, Jack!" cried Nora. "You'd never get a cow here!"

"I'll come with you, Jack," said Mike. "You'll want someone to help you."

"Right!" said Jack. "We'll start off as soon as it's dark."

"Oh, Jack!" said the girls, excited to think of a cow coming. "Where shall we keep it?"

"It had better live on the other side of the island," said Jack. "There is some nice grass there. It won't like to eat heather."

"How will you bring it, Jack?" asked Mike. "It will be difficult to get it into the boat, won't it?"

54

"We shan't get it into the boat, silly!" said Jack, laughing. "We shall make it swim *behind* the boat!"

The other three stared at Jack in surprise. Then they began to laugh. It was funny to think of a cow swimming behind the boat to their secret island!

When it was dark, the two boys set off. The girls called good-bye, and then went to Willow House, for the evening was not quite so warm as usual. They lighted a candle and talked. It was fun to be on the secret island alone.

The boys rowed down the lake and came to the place where Jack usually landed—a well-hidden spot by the lake-side, where trees came right down to the water. They dragged the boat in and then made their way through the wood. After some time they came to the fields that lay round the house of Jack's grandfather. Jack looked at the old cottage. There was no light in it. No one was there. His grandfather had gone away. In the field nearby some cows and horses stood, and the boys could hear one of the horses saying, "Hrrrumph! Hrrrrumph!"

"Do you see that shed over there, Mike?" said Jack, in a low voice. "Well, there are some lengths of rope there. Go and get them whilst I try to find which is my own cow. The rope is in the corner, just by the door."

Mike stumbled off over the dark field to the tumble-down shed in the corner. Jack went among the cows, making a curious chirrupy noise. A big brown and white cow left the others and went lumbering towards Jack.

Jack cautiously struck a match and looked at it. It was Daisy, the cow he had brought up from a calf. He rubbed its soft nose, and called to Mike:

"Hurry up with that rope! I've got the cow."

Mike had been feeling about in the shed for rope and had found a great coil of it. He stumbled over the field to Jack.

"Good," said Jack, making a halter for the patient

animal. "Now, before we go, I'd like to pop into the old cottage and see if I can find anything we'd be glad of."

"Could you find some towels, do you think?" asked Mike. "I do hate having to dry myself with old sacks."

"Yes, I'll see if there are any left," said Jack, and he set off quietly towards the old cottage. He found the door locked, but easily got in at a window. He struck a match and looked round. There were only two rooms in the cottage, a living-room and a bedroom. All the furniture had gone. Jack looked behind the kitchen door, and found what he had hoped to see—a big roller-towel still hanging there. It was very dirty, but could easily be washed. He looked behind the bedroom door—yes, there was a roller-towel there, too! Good! His grandfather hadn't thought of looking behind the doors and taking those when he went. Jack wondered if the old carpet left on the floor was worth taking, too, but he thought not. Good clean heather made a better carpet!

Jack wandered out to the little shed at the back of the cottage—and there he did indeed make a find! There was an old wooden box there, and in it had been put all the clothes he possessed! His grandfather had not thought it worth while to take those with him. There they were, rather ragged, it is true, but still, they were clothes! There were three shirts, a few vests, an odd pair of trousers, an overcoat, a pair of old shoes, and a ragged blanket!

Jack grinned. He would take all these back with him. They might be useful when the cold weather came. He thought the best way to take them back would be to wear them all—so the boy put on all the vests, the shirts, the trousers, the shoes, and the overcoat over his own clothes, and wrapped the blanket round him, too! What a queer sight he looked!

Then he went out to the garden and filled his many pockets with beans and peas and new potatoes. After that

56

he thought it was time to go back to Mike and the cow. Mike would be tired of holding the animal by now!

So, carrying the two dirty towels, Jack made his way slowly over the field to Mike.

"I thought you were never coming!" said Mike, half-cross. "Whatever happened to you? This cow is getting tired of standing here with me."

"I found a lot of my clothes," said Jack, "and an old blanket and two towels. The cow will soon get some exercise! Come on! You carry the towels and this blanket, and I'll take Daisy."

They went back over the fields and through the thick wood to the boat. The cow did not like it when they came to the wood. She could not see where they were going and she disliked being pulled through the close-set trees. She began to moo.

"Oh, don't do that!" said Jack, scared. "You will give us away, Daisy."

"Moo-oo-oo!" said Daisy sorrowfully, trying her hardest to stand still. But Jack and Mike pulled her on.

It was hard work getting her down to the boat. It took the boys at least two hours before they were by the lake, panting and hot. Daisy had mooed dozens of times, each time more loudly than before, and Jack was beginning to think that his idea of taking her across to the island was not such a good one after all. Suppose her mooing gave them away, and people came after them? Suppose she mooed a great deal on the island? Whatever would they do?

Still, they had at last got her to the boat. Jack persuaded the poor, frightened cow to step into the water. She gave such a moo that she startled even the two boys. But at last she was in the water. The boys got into the boat, and pushed off. Jack had tied the cow's rope to the stern of the boat. The boys bent to their oars, and poor Daisy found that she was being pulled off her feet into deeper water!

It was a dreadful adventure for a cow who had never been out of her field before, except to be milked in a nearby shed! She waggled her long legs about, and began to swim in a queer sort of way, holding her big head high out of the water. She was too frightened to moo.

Jack lighted the lantern and fixed it to the front of the boat. It was very dark and he wanted to see where he was going. Then off they rowed up the lake towards the secret island, and Daisy the cow came after them, not able to help herself.

"Well, my idea is working," said Jack after a bit.

"Yes," said Mike, "but I'm jolly glad it's only *one* cow we're taking, not a whole herd!"

They said no more till they came in sight of the island, which loomed up near by, black and solid. The girls had heard the splashing of the oars, and had come down to the beach with the candle.

"Have you got the cow, Jack?" they called.

"Yes," shouted back the boys. "She's come along behind beautifully. But she doesn't like it, poor creature!"

They pulled the boat up the beach and then dragged out the shivering, frightened cow. Jack spoke to her kindly and she pressed against him in wonder and fear. He was the one thing she knew, and she wanted to be close to him. Jack told Mike to get a sack and help him to rub the cow down, for she was cold and wet.

"Where shall we put her for tonight?" asked Mike.

"In the hen-yard," said Jack. "She's used to hens and hens are used to her. There is a lot of bracken and heather there and we can put some more armfuls in for her to lie on. She will soon be warm and comfortable. She will like to hear the clucking of the hens, too."

So Daisy was pushed into the hen-yard, and there she

lay down on the warm heather, comforted by the sound of the disturbed hens.

The girls were so excited at seeing the cow. They asked the boys over and over again all about their adventure till Mike and Jack were tired of telling it.

"Jack! You do look awfully fat tonight!" said Nora suddenly, swinging the lantern so that its light fell on Jack. The others looked at him in surprise. Yes, he did look enormous!

"Have you swollen up, or something?" asked Peggy anxiously. Jack laughed loudly.

"No!" he said, "I found some clothes of mine in a box and brought them along. As the easiest way to carry them was to wear them, I put them on. That's why I look so fat!"

It took him a long time to take all the clothes off, because they were all laughing so much. Peggy looked at the holes in them and was glad she had brought her work-basket along. She could mend them nicely! The blanket, too, would be useful on a cold night.

"What's that funny light in the sky over there?" said Nora, suddenly, pointing towards the east. "Look!"

"You silly! It's the dawn coming" said Jack. "It must be nearly daylight! Come on, we really must go to sleep. What a night we've had!"

"Moo-oo-oo!" said Daisy, from the hen-yard, and the children laughed.

"Daisy thinks so, too!" cried Peggy.

A Lazy Day—With A Horrid Ending

The next morning the children slept very late indeed. The sun was high in the sky before anyone stirred, and even then they might not have awakened if Daisy the cow hadn't decided that it was more than time for her to be milked. She stood in the hen-yard and bellowed for all she was worth.

Jack sat up, his heart thumping loudly. Whatever was that awful noise? Of course—it was Daisy! She wanted to be milked!

"Hi, you others!" he shouted. "Wake up! It must be about nine o'clock! Look at the sun, it's very high! And Daisy wants to be milked!"

Mike grunted and opened his eyes. He felt very sleepy after his late night. The girls sat up and rubbed their eyes. Daisy bellowed again, and the hens clucked in fright.

"Our farmyard wants its breakfast," grinned Jack. "Come on, lazy-bones, come and help. We'll have to see to them before we get our own meal."

They scrambled up. They were so very sleepy that they simply had to run down to the lake and dip their heads into the water before they could do anything!

Then they all went to gloat over their cow. How pretty she was in her brown and white coat! How soft and brown her eyes were! A cow of their own! How lovely!

"And what a voice she has!" said Jack, as the cow mooed again. "I must milk her."

"But I say—we haven't a pail!" said Mike.

The children stared at one another in dismay. It was true—they had no pail.

60

"Well, we must use the saucepans," said Jack firmly. "And we can all do with a cup or two of milk to start the day. I'll use the biggest saucepan, and when it's full I'll have to pour it into the bowls and jugs we've got—and the kettle, too. We must certainly get a pail. What a pity I didn't think of it last night!"

There was more than enough milk to fill every bowl and jug and saucepan. The children drank cupful after cupful. It was lovely to have milk after drinking nothing but tea and cocoa made with water. They could not have enough of it!

"I say! Daisy has trodden on a hen's egg and smashed it," said Nora, looking into the hen-yard. "What a pity!"

"Never mind," said Jack. "We won't keep her here after to-day. She shall go and live on that nice grassy piece, the other side of the island. Nora, feed the hens. They are clucking as if they'd never stop. They are hungry."

Nora fed them. Then they all sat down to their breakfast of boiled eggs and creamy milk. Daisy the cow looked at them as they ate, and mooed softly. She was hungry, too.

Jack and Mike took her to the other side of the island after they had finished their meal. She was delighted to see the juicy green grass there and set to work at once, pulling mouthfuls of it as she wandered over the field.

"She can't get off the island, so we don't need to fence her in," said Jack. "We must milk her twice a day, Mike. We must certainly get a pail from somewhere."

"There's an old milking-pail in the barn at Aunt Harriet's farm," said Peggy. "I've seen it hanging there often."

"Has it got a hole in it?" asked Jack. "If it has it's no use to us. We'll have to stand our milk in it all day and we don't want it to leak away."

"No, it doesn't leak," said Peggy. "I filled it with water one day to take to the hens. It's only just a very old one and not used now."

"I'll go and get it tonight," said Mike.

"No, I'll go," said Jack. "You might be caught."

"Well, so might you," said Mike. "We'll go together."

"Can't we come, too?" asked the girls.

"Certainly not," said Jack, at once. "There's no use the whole lot of us running into danger."

"How shall we keep the milk cool?" wondered Peggy. "It's jolly hot on this island."

"I'll make a little round place to fit the milk-pail into, just by one of the springs," said Jack, at once. "Then, with the cool spring water running round the milk-pail all day, the milk will keep beautifully fresh and cool."

"How clever you are, Jack!" said Nora.

"No, I'm not," said Jack. "It's just common sense, that's all. Anyone can think of things like that."

"I do feel tired and stiff today," said Mike, stretching out his arms. "It was pretty hard work pulling old Daisy along last night!"

"We'd better have a restful day," said Jack, who was also feeling tired. "For once in a while we won't do anything. We'll just lie about and read and talk."

The children had a lovely day. They bathed three times, for it was very hot. Nora washed the two big roller towels in the lake, and made them clean. They soon dried in the hot sun, and then the two boys took one for themselves and the two girls had the other. How nice it was to dry themselves on towels instead of on rough sacks!

"Fish for dinner," said Jack, going down to look at his lines.

"And custard!" said Nora, who had been doing some cooking with eggs and milk.

"Well, I feel just as hungry as if I'd been hard at work building all morning!" said Mike.

The afternoon passed by lazily. The boys slept. Nora read a book. Peggy got out her work-basket and began on the long, long task of mending up the old clothes Jack had brought back the night before. She thought they would be very useful indeed when the cold weather came. She wished she and Nora and Mike could get some of their clothes, too.

The hens clucked in the hen-yard. Daisy the cow mooed once or twice, feeling rather strange and lonely—but she seemed to be settling down very well.

"I hope she won't moo too much," thought Peggy, her needle flying in and out busily. "She might give us away with her mooing if anyone came up the lake in a boat. But thank goodness no one ever does!"

Everyone felt very fresh after their rest. They decided to have a walk round the island. Nora fed the hens and then they set off.

It was a fine little island. Trees grew thickly down to the water-side all round. The steep hill that rose in the middle was a warm, sunny place, covered with rabbit runs and burrows. The grassy piece beyond the hill was full of little wild flowers, and birds sang in the bushes around. The children peeped into the dark caves that ran into the hillside, but did not feel like exploring them just then, for they had no candles with them.

"I'll take you to the place where wild raspberries grow," said Jack. He led them round the hill to the west side, and there, in the blazing sun, the children saw scores of raspberry canes, tangled and thick.

"Jack! There are some getting ripe already!" cried Nora, in delight. She pointed to where spots of bright red dotted the canes. The children squeezed their way through and began to pick the raspberries. How sweet and juicy they were!

"We'll have some of these with cream each day," said

63

"Look," cried Jack alarmingly, *"some people in a boat."*

Peggy. "I can skim the cream off the cow's milk, and we will have raspberries and cream for supper. Oooh!"

"Oooh!" said everyone, eating as fast as they could.

"Are there any wild strawberries on the island, too?" asked Nora.

"Yes," said Jack, "but they don't come till later. "We'll look for those in August and September."

"I do think this is a lovely island," said Peggy happily. "We've a spendid house of our own—hens—a cow, wild fruit growing—fresh water each day!"

"It's all right now it's warm weather," said Jack. "It won't be quite so glorious when the cold winds begin to blow! But winter is a long way off yet."

They climbed up the west side of the hill, which was very rocky. They came to a big rock right on the very top, and sat there. The rock was so warm that it almost burnt them. From far down below the blue spire of smoke rose up from the fire.

"Let's play a game," said Jack. "Let's play . . ."

But what game Jack wanted the others never knew—for Jack suddenly stopped, sat up very straight, and stared fixedly down the blue, sparkling lake. The others sat up and stared, too. And what they saw gave them a dreadful shock!

"Some people in a boat!" said Jack. "Do you see them? Away down there!"

"Yes," said Mike, going pale. "Are they after us, do you think?"

"No," said Jack, after a while. "I think I can hear a radio playing—and if it was anyone after us they surely wouldn't bring that! They are probably just trippers, from the village at the other end of the lake."

"Do you think they'll come to the island?" asked Peggy.

"I don't know," said Jack. "They may—but anyway it would only be for a little while. If we can hide all traces of our being here they won't know a thing about us."

"Come on, then," said Mike, slipping off the rock. "We'd better hurry. It won't be long before they're here."

The children hurried down to the beach. Jack and Mike stamped out the fire, and carried the charred wood to the bushes. They scattered clean sand over the place where they had the fire. They picked up all their belongings and hid them.

"I don't think anyone would find Willow House," said Jack. "The trees really are too thick all round it for any tripper to bother to squeeze through."

"What about the hens?" said Peggy.

"We'll catch them and pop them into a sack just for now," said Jack. "The hen-yard will have to stay. I don't think anyone will find it—it's well hidden. But we certainly couldn't have the hens clucking away there!"

"And Daisy the cow?" said Peggy, looking worried.

"We'll watch and see which side of the island the trippers come," said Jack. "As far as I know, there is only one landing-place, and that is our beach. As Daisy is right on the other side of the island, they are not likely to see her unless they go exploring. And let's hope they don't do that!"

"Where shall *we* hide?" said Nora.

"We'll keep a look-out from the hill, hidden in the bracken," said Jack. "If the trippers begin to wander about, we must just creep about in the bracken and trust to luck they won't see us. There's one thing—they won't be *looking* for us, if they are trippers. They won't guess there is anyone else here at all!"

"Will they find the things in the cave-larder?" asked Nora, helping to catch the squawking hens.

"Peggy, get some heather and bracken and stuff up the opening to the cave-larder," said Jack. Peggy ran off at once. Jack put the hens gently into the sack one by one and ran up the hill with them. He went to the other side of

66

the hill and came to one of the caves he knew. He called to Nora, who was just behind him.

"Nora! Sit at the little opening here and see that the hens don't get out! I'm going to empty them out of the sack into the cave!"

With much squawking and scuffling and clucking the scared hens hopped out of the sack and ran into the little cave. Nora sat down at the entrance, hidden by the bracken that grew there. No hen could get out whilst she was there.

"The boat is going round the island," whispered Jack as he parted the bracken at the top of the hill and looked down to the lake below. "They can't find a place to land. They're going round to our little beach! Well—Daisy the cow is safe, if they don't go exploring! Hope she doesn't moo!"

The Trippers Come To The Island

Nora sat crouched against the entrance of the little cave. She could hear the six hens inside, clucking softly as they scratched about. Jack knelt near her, peering through the bracken, trying to see what the boat was doing.

"Mike has rowed our own boat to where the brambles fall over the water, and has pushed it under them," said Jack, in a low voice. "I don't know where he is now. I can't see him."

"Where's Peggy?" whispered Nora.

"Here I am," said a low voice, and Peggy's head popped up above the bracken a little way down the hill. "I say — isn't this horrid? I do wish those people would go away."

The sound of voices came up the hillside from the lake below.

"Here's a fine landing-place!" said one voice.

"They've found our beach," whispered Jack.

"Pull the boat in," said a woman's voice. "We'll have our supper here. It's lovely!"

There was the sound of a boat being pulled a little way up the beach. Then the trippers got out.

"I'll bring the radio," said someone. "You bring the supper things, Eddie."

"Do you suppose anyone has ever been on this little island before?" said a man's voice.

"No!" said someone else. "The countryside round about is quite deserted—no one ever comes here, I should think."

The three children crouched down in the bracken and

listened. The trippers were setting out their supper. One of the hens in the cave began to cluck loudly. Nora thought it must have laid an egg.

"Do you hear that noise?" said one of the trippers. "Sounds like a hen to me!"

"Don't be silly, Eddie," said a woman's voice scornfully. "How could a hen be on an island like this! That must have been a blackbird or something."

Jack giggled. It seemed very funny to him that a hen's cluck should be thought like a blackbird's clear song.

"Pass the salt," said someone. "Thanks. I say! Isn't this a fine little island! Sort of secret and mysterious. What about exploring it after supper?"

"That's a good idea," said Eddie's voice. "We will!"

The children looked at one another in dismay. Just the one thing they had hoped the trippers wouldn't do!

"Where's Mike, do you suppose?" said Peggy, in a low voice. "Do you think he's hiding in our boat?"

"I expect so," whispered Jack. "Don't worry about him. He can look after himself all right."

"Oh, my goodness! There's Daisy beginning to moo!" groaned Peggy, as a dismal moo reached her ears. "She knows it is time she was milked."

"And just wouldn't I like a cup of milk!" said Jack, who was feeling very thirsty.

"Can you hear that cow mooing somewhere?" said one of the trippers, in surprise.

"I expect it's a cow in a field on the mainland," said another lazily. "You don't suppose there is a cow wandering loose on this tiny island, do you, Eddie?"

"Well, I don't know," said Eddie, in a puzzled voice. "Look over there. Doesn't that look like a footprint in the sand to you?"

The children held their breath. Could it be true that they had left a footprint on the sand?

"And see here," went on the tripper, holding up something. "Here's a piece of string I found on the beach. String doesn't grow, you know."

"You are making a great mystery about nothing," said one of the women crossly. "Other trippers have been here, that's all."

"Perhaps you are right," said Eddie. "But all the same, I'm going to explore the island after supper!"

"Oh, put on the radio, Eddie," said someone. "I'm tired of hearing you talk so much."

Soon loud music blared through the air, and the children were glad, for they knew it would drown any sound of Daisy's mooing or the hens' clucking. They sat in the bracken, looking scared and miserable. They did not like anyone else sharing their secret island. And what would happen if the trippers did explore the island and found the children?

Nora began to cry softly. Tears ran down her cheeks and fell on her hands. Jack looked at her and then crept silently up. He slipped his arm round her.

"Don't cry, Nora," he said. "Perhaps they won't have time to explore. It is getting a bit dark now. Do you see that big black cloud coming up? It will make the night come quickly, and perhaps the trippers will think there's a storm coming and row off."

Nora dried her eyes and looked up. There certainly was a big black cloud.

"It looks like a thunderstorm," said Peggy, creeping up to join them.

"Oooh!" said Nora suddenly, almost squealing out loud. "Look! Someone's coming up the hill! I can see the bracken moving! It must be one of the trippers creeping up to find us!"

The children went pale. They looked to where Nora pointed—and sure enough they could see first one frond

70

of bracken moving, and then another and another. Someone was certainly creeping up the hill hidden under the fronds.

Nora clutched hold of Jack. "Don't make a sound," he whispered. "No one can possibly know we're here. Keep quiet, Nora. We'll slip inside the cave if he comes much nearer."

They sat silently watching the swaying of the tall bracken as the newcomer crept through it. It was a horrid moment. Was someone going to spring out on them?

"Get inside the cave, you two girls," whispered Jack. "I think you'll be safe there. I'm going to slip round the hill and come up behind this person, whoever he is."

The girls crept just inside the cave and parted the bracken that grew around it to see what Jack was going to do. He was just slipping away when the person creeping up the hillside stopped his crawling. The bracken kept still. This was worse than seeing it move! Oh dear!

Then a head popped out of the bracken, and Nora gave a loud squeal.

"Mike!" she said. "Mike!"

"Sh, you silly chump!" hissed Peggy, shaking her. "You'll be heard by the trippers!"

Fortunately the radio was going loudly, so Nora's squeal was not heard. The three children stared in delight at Mike. It was he who had been creeping up through the bracken after all! What a relief! He grinned at them and put his head down again. Once more the bracken fronds began to move slightly as Mike made his way through them up to the cave.

"Oh, Mike," said Nora, when he came up to them. "You did give us such a fright. We thought you were a tripper coming after us!"

"I got a good view of them," said Mike, sitting down beside the others. "There are three men and two women. They are tucking into an enormous supper."

"Do you think they'll explore the island as they said?" asked Peggy anxiously.

"Perhaps this thunderstorm will put them off," said Mike, looking up at the black sky. "My word, it's brought the bats out early! Look at them!"

Certainly the little black bats were out in their hundreds. The hot, thundery evening had brought out thousands of insects, and the bats were having a great feast, catching the flies and beetles that flew through the air.

It was the bats that sent the trippers away. One of the women caught sight of two or three bats darting round under the trees, and she gave a shriek.

"Ooh! Bats! Ooh! I can't bear bats! I'm frightened of them. Let's pack up and go quickly!"

"I can't bear bats either!" squealed the other woman. "Horrid little creatures!"

"They won't hurt you," said a man's voice. "Don't be silly."

"I can't help it; I'm frightened of them," said a woman. "I'm going!"

"But I wanted to explore the island," said Eddie.

"Well, you'll have to explore it another day," said the woman. "Just look at the sky, too—there's going to be a dreadful storm."

"All right, all right," said Eddie, in a sulky voice. "We'll go. Fancy being frightened of a few bats!"

The children on the hillside stared at one another in delight. The trippers were really going. And no one had discovered them. Goody, goody!

"Good old bats!" whispered Jack. "Would you think anyone would be scared of those little flitter-mice, Nora?"

"Aunt Harriet was," said Nora. "I don't know why. I think they are dear little creatures, with their funny black wings. Anyway, I shall always feel friendly towards them now. They have saved us from being found!"

Daisy the cow mooed loudly. Jack frowned. "If only we had milked Daisy before the trippers came!" he said.

"Did you hear that?" said one of the trippers. "That was thunder in the distance!"

The four children giggled. Nora rolled over and stuffed her hands into her mouth to stop laughing loudly.

"Good old Daisy!" whispered Mike. "She's pretending to be a thunderstorm now, to frighten them away!"

Nora gave a squeal of laughter, and Jack punched her. "Be quiet," he said. "Do you want us to be discovered just when everything is going so nicely?"

The trippers were getting into their boat. They pushed off. The children heard the sound of oars, and peeped out. They could see the boat, far down below, being rowed out on to the lake. A big wind sprang up and ruffled the water. The boat rocked to and fro.

"Hurry!" cried a woman's voice. "We shall get caught in the storm. Oh! Oh! There's one of those horrid bats again! I'll never come to this nasty island any more!"

"I jolly well hope you won't!" said Jack, pretending to wave good-bye.

The children watched the boat being rowed down the lake. The voices of the people came more and more faintly on the breeze. The last they heard was the radio being played once again. Then they saw and heard no more. The trippers were gone.

"Come on," said Jack, standing up and stretching himself. "We've had a very narrow escape—but thank goodness, no one saw us or our belongings."

"Except that footprint and a bit of string," said Mike.

"Yes," said Jack, thoughtfully. "I hope that man called

73

Eddie doesn't read anywhere about four runaway children and think we might be here because of what he heard and found. We must be prepared for that, you know. We must make some plans to prevent being found if anyone comes again to look for us."

A distant rumble of thunder was heard. Jack turned to the others. "Not Daisy mooing this time!" he grinned. "Come on, there's a storm coming. We've plenty to do. I'll go and get Daisy, to milk her. Nora and Mike, you catch the hens and take them back to the hen-yard—and Mike, make some sort of shelter for them with a couple of sacks over sticks, or something, so that they can hide there if they are frightened. Peggy, see if you can light the fire before the rain comes."

"Ay, ay, Captain!" shouted the children joyfully, full of delight to think they had their island to themselves once more!

A Stormy Night In Willow House

There was certainly a thunderstorm coming. The sky was very black indeed, and it was getting dark. Nora and Mike caught the six hens in the little cave, bundled them gently into the sack, and raced off to the hen-yard with them. Mike stuck two or three willow sticks into the ground at one end of the hen-yard and draped the sack over them.

"There you are, henny-pennies!" said Nora. "There is a nice little shelter for you!"

Plop! Plop! Plop! enormous drops of rain fell down and the hens gave a frightened squawk. They did not like the rain. They scuttled under the sack at once and lay there quietly, giving each other little pecks now and again.

"Well, that settles the hens," said Mike. "I wonder how Peggy is getting on with the fire."

Peggy was not getting on at all well. The rain was now coming down fast, and she could not get the fire going. Jack arrived with Daisy the cow and shouted to Peggy:

"Never mind about the fire! Now that the rain's coming down so fast you won't be able to light it. Get into Willow House, all of you, before you get too wet."

"The girls can go," said Mike, running to help Jack. "I'll get the things to help you milk. My goodness—we haven't drunk all the milk yet that Daisy gave us this morning!"

"Put it into a dish and pop it in the hen-yard," said Jack. "Maybe the hens will like it!"

In the pouring rain Jack milked Daisy the cow. Soon all the saucepans and the kettle and bowls were full! Really, thought Jack, he simply *must* get that old milking-pail that

75

the girls had told him of at their Aunt's farm. It was such a tiring business milking a cow like this.

When the milking was finished, Jack took Daisy back to her grassy field on the other side of the island. Mike went to Willow House where the two girls were. It was dark there, and the sound of rain drip-drip-dripping from the trees all around sounded rather miserable.

Mike and the two girls sat in the front part of Willow House and waited for Jack. Mike was very wet, and he shivered.

"Poor old Jack will be wet through, too," he said. "Feel this milk, girls. It's as warm as can be. Let's drink some and it will warm us up. We can't boil any, for we haven't a fire."

Jack came to Willow House dripping wet. But he was grinning away as usual. Nothing ever seemed to upset Jack.

"Hallo, hallo!" he said. "I'm as wet as a fish! Peggy, where did we put those clothes of mine that I brought to the island last night?"

"Oh yes!" cried Peggy, in delight. "Of course! You and Mike can change into those."

"Well, I don't know about that," said Mike. "Jack only brought three old vests, a shirt or two, and an overcoat."

"Well, we can wear a vest each, and a shirt, and I'll wear the overcoat, and you can wrap the old blanket I brought all round you!" said Jack.

The boys took off their wet clothes and changed into the dry ones. "I'll hang your wet ones out to dry as soon as the rain stops," said Peggy, squeezing the rain out of them.

"I can't see a thing here," said Mike, buttoning up his shirt all wrong.

"Well, light the lantern, silly," said Jack. "What do you suppose the candles are for? Nora, find the lantern and light it. It may want a new candle inside. You know where

76

you put the candles, don't you? Over in that corner somewhere."

Nora found the lantern. It did want a new candle inside. She found a box of matches and lighted the candle. Mike hung the lantern up on a nail he had put in the roof. It swung there, giving a dim but cheerful light to the little party huddled inside Willow House.

"This really feels like a house now," said Nora, pleased. "I do like it. It's very cosy. Not a drop of rain is coming through our roof or the walls."

"And not a scrap of wind!" said Jack. "That shows how well we packed the walls with heather and bracken. Listen to the wind howling outside! We shouldn't like to be out in that! What a good thing we've got Willow House to live in! Our outdoor bedroom wouldn't be at all comfortable tonight!"

The thunderstorm broke overhead. The thunder crashed around as if someone were moving heavy furniture up in the sky.

"Hallo! Someone's dropped a wardrobe, I should think!" said Jack, when an extra heavy crash came!

"And there goes a grand piano tumbling down the stairs!" said Mike, at another heavy rumble. Everyone laughed. Really, the thunderstorm *did* sound exactly like furniture being thrown about.

The lightning flashed brightly, lighting up the inside of Willow House. Nora was not sure that she liked it. She cuddled up to Mike. "I feel a bit frightened," she said.

"Don't be silly!" said Mike. "You're as bad as those women trippers over the bats! There's nothing to be frightened of. A storm is a grand thing. We're perfectly safe here."

"A storm is just a bit of weather being noisy!" laughed Jack. "Cheer up, Nora. We're all right. You can think you're lucky you're not Daisy the cow. After all, we do know that a storm is only a storm, but she doesn't."

Crash! Rumble! Crash! The thunder roared away, and the children made a joke of it, inventing all kinds of furniture rumbling about the sky, as each crash came. The lightning flashed, and each time Jack said. "Thanks very much! The sky keeps striking matches, and the wind keeps blowing them out!"

Even Nora laughed, and soon she forgot to be frightened. The rain pelted down hard, and the only thing that worried Jack was whether or not a rivulet of rain might find its way into Willow House and run along the floor on which they were sitting. But all was well. No rain came in at all.

Gradually the storm died away, and only the pitter-patter of raindrops falling from the trees could be heard, a singing, liquid sound. The thunder went farther and farther away. The lightning flashed for the last time. The storm was over.

"Now we'll have something to eat and a cup of milk to drink, and off to bed we'll go," said Jack. "We've had quite enough excitement for today! And Mike and I were so late last night that I'm sure he's dropping with sleep. I know I am."

Peggy got a small meal for them all, and they drank Daisy's creamy milk. Then the girls went into the back room of Willow House and snuggled down on the warm heather there, and the boys lay down in the front room. In half a minute everyone was asleep!

Again Daisy the cow awoke them with her mooing. It was strange to wake up in Willow House instead of in their outdoor sleeping-place among the gorse, with the sky above them. The children blinked up at their green roof, for leaves were growing from the willow branches that were interlaced for a ceiling. It was dim inside Willow House. The door was shut, and there were no windows. Jack had thought it would be too difficult to make windows, and they might let in the wind and the rain too much. So Willow House was rather dark and a bit stuffy when the door was shut—but nobody minded that! It really made it all the more exciting!

The children ran out of Willow House and looked around—all except Nora. She lay lazily on her back, looking up at the green ceiling, thinking how soft the heather was and how nice Willow House smelt. She was always the last out of bed!

"Nora, you won't have time for a dip before breakfast if you don't come now," shouted Peggy. So Nora ran out, too. What a lovely morning it was! The thunderstorm had cleared away and left the world looking clean and newly washed. Even the pure blue sky seemed washed, too.

The lake was as blue as the sky. The trees still dripped a little with the heavy rain of the night before, and the grass and heather were damp to the foot.

"The world looks quite new," said Mike. "Just as if it had been made this very morning! Come on—let's have our dip!"

Splash! Into the lake they went. Mike and Jack could both swim. Jack swam like a fish. Peggy could swim a little way, and Nora hardly at all. Jack was teaching her, but she was a bit of a baby and would not get her feet off the sandy bed of the lake.

Peggy was first out of the water and went to get the breakfast—but when she looked round their little beach, she stood still in disgust!

"Look here, boys!" she cried. "Look, Nora! How those trippers have spoilt our beach!"

They all ran out of the cold water, and, rubbing themselves down with their two towels, they stared round at their little beach, which was always such a beautiful place, clean and shining with its silvery sand.

But now, what a difference! Orange-peel lay everywhere. Banana skins, brown, slippery, and soaked with rain, lay where they had been thrown. A tin that had once had canned pears in, and two cardboard cartons that had been full of cream, rolled about on the sand, empty. A newspaper, pulled into many pieces by the wind, blew here and there. An empty cigarette packet joined the mess.

The children felt really angry. The little beach was theirs and they loved it. They had been careful to keep it clean, tidy, and lovely, and had always put everything away after a meal. Now some horrid trippers had come there just for one meal and had left it looking like a rubbish-heap!

"And they were grown-up people, too!" said Jack, in disgust. "They ought to have known better. Why couldn't they take their rubbish away with them?"

"People that leave rubbish about in beautiful places like this are just rubbishy people themselves!" cried Peggy fiercely, almost in tears. "Nice people never do it. I'd like to put those people into a big dustbin with all their horrid rubbish on top of them—and wouldn't I bang on the lid, too!"

The other laughed. It sounded so funny. But they were all angry about their beach being spoilt.

"I'll clear up the mess and burn it," said Mike.

"Wait a minute!" said Jack. "We might find some of the things useful."

"What! Old banana skins and orange-peel!" cried Mike. "You're not thinking of making a pudding or something of them, Jack!"

"No," said Jack, with a grin, "But if we keep the tin and a carton and the empty cigarette packet in our cave-cupboard, we might put them out on the beach if anyone else ever comes—and then, if they happen to find the remains of our fire, or a bit of string or anything like that—why, they won't think of looking for us—they'll just think trippers have been here!"

"Good idea, Jack!" cried everyone.

"You really are good at thinking out clever things," said Peggy, busy getting the fire going. Its crackling sounded very cheerful, for they were all hungry. Peggy put some milk on to boil. She meant to make cocoa for them all to drink.

Mike picked up the cigarette packet, the tin, and one of the cardboard cartons. He washed the carton and the tin in the lake, and then went to put the three things away in their little cave-cupboard. They might certainly come in useful some day!

Nora brought in five eggs for breakfast. Peggy fried them with two trout that Jack had caught on his useful lines. The smell was delicious!

"I say! Poor old Daisy *must* be milked!" said Jack, gobbling down his breakfast and drinking his hot cocoa.

Suddenly Nora gave a squeal and pointed behind him. Jack turned—and to his great astonishment he saw the cow walking towards him!

"You wouldn't go to milk her in time so she has come to you!" laughed Peggy. "Good old Daisy! Fancy her knowing the way!"

Nora Gets Into Trouble

There seemed quite a lot of jobs always waiting to be done each day on the island. Daisy had to be milked. The hens had to be seen to. The fishing-lines had to be baited and looked at two or three times a day. The fire had to be kept going. Meals had to be prepared and dishes washed up. Willow House had to be tidied up each day, for it was surprising how untidy it got when the four children were in it even for an hour.

"I'll milk Daisy each morning and Mike can milk her in the evenings," said Jack, as they sat eating their breakfast that morning. "Nora, you can look after the hens. It won't only be your job to feed them and give them water and collect the eggs, but you'll have to watch the fence round the hen-yard carefully to see that the hens don't peck out the heather we've stuffed into the fence to stop up the holes. We don't want to lose our hens!"

"What is Peggy going to do?" asked Nora.

"Peggy had better do the odd jobs," said Jack. "She can look after the fire, think of meals and tidy up. I'll see to my fishing-lines. And every now and again one or other of us had better go to the top of the hill to see if any more trippers are coming. Our plans worked quite well last time—but we were lucky enough to spot the boat coming. If we hadn't seen it when we did, we would have been properly caught!"

"I'd better go and get the boat out from where I hid it under the overhanging bushes, hadn't I?" said Mike, finishing his cocoa.

"No," said Jack. "It would be a good thing to keep it always hidden there except when we need it. Now I'm off to milk Daisy!"

He went off, and the children heard the welcome sound of the creamy milk splashing into a saucepan, for they still had no milking-pail. Mike and Jack were determined to get one that night! It was so awkward to keep milking a cow into saucepans and kettles!

Peggy began to clear away and wash up the dishes. Nora wanted to help her, but Peggy said she had better go and feed the hens. So off she went, making the little clucking noise that the hens knew. They came rushing to her as she climbed over the fence of their little yard.

Nora scattered the seed for them, and they gobbled it up, scratching hard with their strong clawed feet to find any they had missed. Nora gave them some water, too. Then she took a look round the fence to see that it was all right.

It seemed all right. The little girl didn't bother to look very hard, because she wanted to go off to the raspberry patch up on the hillside and see if there were any more wild raspberries ripe. If she had looked carefully, as she should have done, she would have noticed quite a big hole in the fence, where one of the hens had been pecking out the bracken and heather. But she didn't notice. She picked up a basket Peggy had made of thin twigs, and set off.

"Are you going to find raspberries, Nora?" called Peggy.

"Yes!" shouted Nora.

"Well, bring back as many as you can, and we'll have them for pudding at dinner-time with cream!" shouted Peggy. "Don't eat them all yourself!"

"Come with me and help me!" cried Nora, not too pleased at the thought of having to pick raspberries for everyone.

"I've got to get some water from the spring," called back Peggy; "and I want to do some mending."

So Nora went alone. She found a patch of raspberries she hadn't seen yesterday, and there were a great many ripe. The little girl ate dozens and then began to fill her basket with the sweet juicy fruit. She heard Jack taking Daisy the cow back to her grassy field on the other side of the island. She heard Mike whistling as he cut some willow stakes down in the thicket, ready for use if they were wanted. Everyone was busy and happy.

Nora sat down in the sun and leaned against a warm rock that jutted out from the hillside. She felt very happy indeed. The lake was as blue as a forget-me-not down below her. Nora lazed there in the sun until she heard Mike calling:

"Nora! Nora! Wherever are you! You've been hours!"

"Coming!" cried Nora, and she made her way through the raspberry canes, round the side of the hill, through the heather and bracken, and down to the beach, where all the others were. Peggy had got the fire going well, and was cooking a rabbit that Jack had produced.

"Where are the raspberries?" asked Jack. "Oh, you've got a basketful! Good! Go and skim the cream off the milk in that bowl over there, Nora. Put it into a jug and bring it back. There will be plenty for all of us."

Soon they were eating their dinner. Peggy was certainly a good little cook. But nicest of all were the sweet juicy raspberries with thick yellow cream poured all over them! How the children did enjoy them!

"The hens are very quiet today," said Jack, finishing up the last of his cream. "I haven't heard a single cluck since we've been having dinner!"

"I suppose they're all right?" said Peggy.

"I'll go and have a look," said Mike. He put down his plate and went to the hen-yard. He looked here—and he looked there—he lifted up the sack that was stretched over one corner of the yard for shelter—but no hens were there!

"Are they all right?" called Jack.

Mike turned in dismay. "No!" he said. "They're not here! They've gone!"

"Gone!" cried Jack, springing up in astonishment. "They can't have gone! They must be there!"

"Well, they're not," said Mike. "They've completely vanished! Not even a cluck left!"

All the children ran to the hen-yard and gazed in amazement and fright at the empty space.

"Do you suppose someone has been here and taken them?" asked Peggy.

"No," said Jack sternly, "look here! This explains their disappearance!"

He pointed to a hole in the fence of the hen-yard. "See that hole! They've all escaped through there—and now goodness knows where they are!"

"Well, I never heard them go," said Peggy. "I was the only one left here. They must have gone when I went to get water from the spring!"

"Then the hole must have been there when Nora fed the hens this morning," said Jack. "Nora, what do you mean by doing your job as badly as that? Didn't I tell you this morning that you were to look carefully round the fence each time the hens were fed to make sure it was safe? And now, the very first time, you let the hens escape! I'm ashamed of you!"

"Our precious hens!" said Peggy, in dismay.

"You might do your bit, Nora," said Mike. "It's too bad of you."

Nora began to cry, but the others had no sympathy for her. It was too big a disappointment to lose their hens. They began to hunt round to see if by chance the hens were hidden anywhere near.

Nora cried more and more loudly, till Jack got really angry with her. "Stop that silly baby noise!" he said. "Can't you help to look for the hens, too?"

"You're not to talk to me like that!" wept Nora.

"I shall talk to you how I like," said Jack. "I'm the captain here, and you've got to do as you're told. If one of us is careless we all suffer, and I won't have that! Stop crying, I tell you, and help to look for the hens."

Nora started to hunt, but she didn't stop crying. She felt so unhappy and ashamed and sad, and it was really dreadful to have all the others angry with her, and not speaking a word to her. Nora could hardly see to hunt for the hens.

"Well, they are nowhere about here!" said Jack, at last. "We'd better spread out and see if we can find them on the island somewhere. They may have wandered right to the other side. We'll all separate and hunt in different places. Peggy, you go that way, and I'll go over to Daisy's part."

The children separated and went different ways, calling to the hens loudly. Nora went where Jack had pointed. She called to the hens, too, but none came in answer. Wherever could they be?

What a hunt there was that afternoon for those vanished hens! It was really astonishing that not one could be found. Jack couldn't understand it! They were nowhere on the hill. They were not even in the little cave where Jack had hidden them the day before, because he looked. They were not among the raspberry canes. They were not in Daisy's field. They were not under the hedges. They were not anywhere at all, it seemed!

Nora grew more and more unhappy as the day passed. She felt that she really couldn't face the others if the hens were not found. She made a hidey-hole in the tall bracken and crouched there, watching the others returning to the camp for supper. They had had no tea and were hungry and thirsty. So was Nora—but nothing would make her go and join the others! No—she would rather stay where she was, all alone, than sit down with Mike, Jack and Peggy while they were still so cross and upset.

"Well, the hens are gone!" said Mike, as he joined Jack going down the hill to the beach.

"It's strange," said Jack. "They can't have flown off the island, surely!"

"It's dreadful, I think," said Peggy; "we did find their eggs so useful to eat."

Nora sat alone in the bracken. She meant to sleep there for the night. She thought she would never, never be happy again.

The others sat down by the fire, whilst Peggy made some cocoa, and doled out a rice pudding she had made. They wondered where Nora was.

"She'll be along soon, I expect," said Peggy.

They ate their meal in silence—and then—then oh, what a lovely sound came to their ears! Yes, it was "cluck, cluck, cluck!" And walking sedately down to the beach came all six hens! The children stared and stared and stared!

"Where *have* you been, you scamps?" cried Jack. "We've looked for you everywhere!"

"Cluckluck, cluckluck!" said the hens.

"You knew it was your meal-time, so you've come for it!" said Jack. "I say, you others! I wonder if we could let the hens go loose each day—oh no—we couldn't—they'd lay their eggs away and we'd never be able to find them!"

"I'll feed them," said Peggy. She threw them some corn and they pecked it up eagerly. Then they let Mike and Jack lift them into their mended yard and they settled down happily, roosting on the perch made for them at one end.

"We'd better tell Nora," said Jack. So they went up the hillside calling Nora. "Nora! Nora! Where are you?"

But Nora didn't answer! She crouched lower in the

bracken and hoped no one would find her. But Jack came upon her suddenly and shouted cheerfully. "Oh, there you are! The hens have all come back, Nora! They knew it was their meal-time, you see! Come and have your supper. We kept some for you."

Nora went with him to the beach. Peggy kissed her and said, "Now don't worry any more. It's all right. We've got all the hens safely again."

"Had I better see to the hens each day, do you think, instead of Nora?" Mike asked Jack. But Jack shook his head.

"No," he said. "That's Nora's job—and you'll see, she'll do it splendidly now, won't you, Nora?"

"Yes, I will, Jack," said Nora, eating her rice pudding, and feeling much happier. "I do promise I will! I'm so sorry I was careless."

"That's all right," said the other three together—and it *was* all right, for they were all kind-hearted and fond of one another.

"But what *I'd* like to know," said Peggy, as she and Nora washed the dirty things, "is *where* did those hens manage to hide themselves so cleverly?"

The children soon knew—for when, in a little while, Mike went to fetch something from Willow House he saw three shining eggs in the heather there! He picked them up and ran back to the others.

"Those cunning hens walked into Willow House and hid there!" he cried, holding up the eggs.

"Well, well, well!" said Jack, in surprise. "And to think how we hunted all over the island—and those rascally hens were near by all the time!"

The Caves In The Hillside

The days slipped past, and the children grew used to their happy, carefree life on the island. Jack and Mike went off in the boat one night and fetched the old milking-pail from Aunt Harriet's farm, and a load of vegetables from the garden. The plums were ripening, too, and the boys brought back as many as would fill the milking-pail! How pleased the girls were to see them!

Now it was easy to milk Daisy, for they had a proper pail. Peggy cleaned it well before they used it, for it was dusty and dirty. When Jack or Mike had milked Daisy they stood the pail of milk in the middle of the little spring that gushed out from the hillside and ran down to the lake below. The icy-cold water kept the milk cool, and it did not turn sour, even on the hottest day.

Jack got out the packets of seeds he had brought from his grandfather's farm, and showed them to the others. "Look," he said, "here are lettuce seeds, and radish seeds, and mustard and cress, and runner beans! It's late to plant the beans, but in the good soil on this island I daresay they will grow quickly and we shall be able to have a crop later in the year."

"The mustard and cress and radish will grow very quickly!" said Peggy. "What fun! The lettuces won't be very long, either, this hot weather, if we keep them well watered."

"Where shall we plant them?" asked Mike.

"Well, we'd better plant them in little patches in different corners of the island," said Jack. "If we dig out a big patch and have a sort of vegetable garden, and anyone comes here to look for us, they will see our garden and know someone is here! But if we just plant out tiny patches, we can easily throw heather over them if we see anyone coming."

"Jack's always full of good ideas," said Nora. "I'll help to dig and plant, Jack."

"We'll all do it," said Jack. So together they hunted for good places, and dug up the ground there, and planted their precious seeds. It was Peggy's job to water them each day and see that no weeds choked the seeds when they grew.

"We're getting on!" said Nora happily. "Milk and cream each day, eggs each day, wild raspberries when we want them, and lettuces, mustard and cress, and radishes soon ready to be pulled!"

Jack planted the beans in the little bare places at the foot of a brambly hedge. He said they would be able to grow up the brambles, and probably wouldn't be noticed if anyone came. The bean seedlings were carefully watched and nursed until they were strong and tall, and had begun to twist themselves round any stem near. Then Peggy left them to themselves, only watering them when they needed it.

It was sometimes difficult to remember which day it was. Jack had kept a count as best he could, and sometimes on Sundays the children could hear a church bell ringing if the wind was in the right direction.

"We ought to try and keep Sunday a day of rest and peace," said Mike. "We can't go to church, but we could make the day a *good* sort of day, if you know what I mean."

So they kept Sunday quietly, and the little island always seemed an extra peaceful day then. They hardly ever knew what the other days were—whether it was Tuesday or Thursday or Wednesday! But Jack always told them when it was Sunday, and it was the one day they really knew. Nora said it had a different feel, and certainly the island seemed to know it was Sunday, and was a dreamier, quieter place then.

One day Jack said they must explore the caves in the hillside.

"If anyone does come here to look for us, and it's quite likely," he said, "we must really have all our plans made as to what to do, and know exactly where to hide. People who are really looking for us won't just sit about on that beach as the trippers did, you know—they will hunt all over the island."

"Well, let's go and explore the cave today," said Mike. "I'll get the lantern."

So, with the lantern swinging in his hand, and a box of matches ready in his pocket to light it, Jack led the way to the caves. The children had found three openings into the hillside—one where the hens had been put, another larger one, and a third very tiny one through which they could hardly crawl.

"We'll go in through the biggest entrance," said Jack. He lighted the lantern, and went into the dark cave. It seemed strange to leave the hot July sunshine. Nora shivered. She thought the caves were rather queer. But she didn't say anything, only kept very close to Mike.

Jack swung the lantern round and lit up all the corners. It was a large cave—but not of much use for hiding in, for every corner could be easily seen. Big cobwebs hung here and there, and there was a musty smell of bats.

Mike went all round the walls, peeping and prying—and right at the very back of the cave he discovered a curious thing. The wall was split from about six feet downwards, and a big crack, about two feet across, yawned there. At first it seemed as if the crack simply showed rock behind

In great excitement they explored the cave

it—but it didn't. There was a narrow, winding passage there, half hidden by a jutting-out piece of rock.

"Look here!" cried Mike, in excitement. "Here's a passage right in the very rock of the hillside itself. Come on, Jack, bring your lantern here. I wonder if it goes very far back."

Jack lifted up his lantern and the others saw the curious half-hidden passage, the entrance to which was by the crack in the wall. Jack went through the crack and walked a little way down the passage.

"Come on!" he cried. "It's all right! The air smells fresh here, and the passage seems to lead to somewhere."

The children crowded after him in excitement. What an adventure this was!

The passage wound here and there, and sometimes the children had to step over rocks and piles of fallen earth. Tree-roots stretched over their heads now and again. The passage was sometimes very narrow, but quite passable. And at last it ended—and Jack found that it led to an even larger cave right in the very middle of the hill itself! He lifted his lantern and looked round. The air smelt fresh and sweet. Why was that?

"Look!" cried Nora, pointing upwards. "I can see daylight!"

Sure enough, a long way up, a spot of bright daylight came through into the dark cave. Jack was puzzled. "I think some rabbits must have burrowed into the hill, and come out unexpectedly into this cave," he said. "And their hole is where we can see that spot of daylight. Well—the fresh air comes in, anyhow!"

From the big cave a low passage led to another cave on the right. This passage was so low that the children had to crawl through it—and to their surprise they found that this second cave led out to the hillside itself, and was no other than the cave into which it was so hard to crawl because of the small entrance.

"Well, we are getting on," said Jack. "We have discovered that the big cave we knew leads by a passage to an even bigger one—and from that big one we can get into this smaller one, which has an opening on to the hillside —and that opening is too small for any grown-up to get into!"

"What about the cave we put the hens into?" asked Nora.

"That must be just a little separate cave by itself," said Jack. "We'll go and see."

So they squeezed themselves out of the tiny entrance of the last cave, and went to the hen-cave. But this was quite ordinary—just a little low, rounded cave smelling strongly of bats.

They came out and sat on the hillside in the bright sunshine. It was lovely to sit there in the warmth after the cold, dark caves.

"Now listen," said Jack thoughtfully. "Those caves are going to be jolly useful to us this summer if anyone comes to get us. We could get Daisy into that big inner cave quite well, for one thing."

"Oh, Jack! She'd never squeeze through that narow, winding passage," said Peggy.

"Oh yes, she would," said Jack. "She'd come with me all right—and what's more, Daisy is going to practise going in and out there, so that if the time comes when she has really got to hide for a few hours, she won't mind. It wouldn't be any good putting her into that cave, and then having her moo fit to lift off the top of the hill!"

Everyone laughed. Mike nodded his head. "Quite right," he said. "Daisy will have to practise! I suppose the hens can go there quite well, too?"

"Easily," said Jack. "And so can we!"

"The only things we can't take into the cave are our boat and our house," said Mike.

"The boat would never be found under those brambles by the water," said Jack. "And I doubt if anyone would ever find Willow House either, for we have built it in the very middle of that thicket, and it is all *we* can do to squeeze through to it! Grown-ups could never get through. Why, we shall soon have to climb a tree and drop down to Willow House if the bushes and trees round it grow any more thickly!"

"I almost wish someone *would* come!" said Peggy. "It would be so exciting to hide away!"

"A bit *too* exciting!" said Jack. "Remember, there's a lot to be done as soon as we see anyone coming!"

"Hadn't we better plan it all out now?" said Mike. "Then we shall each know what to do."

"Yes," said Jack. "Well, I'll manage Daisy the cow, and go straight off to fetch her. Mike, you manage the hens and get them into a sack, and take them straight up to the cave. Peggy, you stamp out the fire and scatter the hot sticks. Also you must put out the empty cigarette packet, the tin, and the cardboard carton that the trippers left, so that it will look as if trippers have been here, and nobody will think it's funny to find the remains of a fire, or any other odd thing."

"And what shall I do?" asked Nora.

"You must go to the spring and take the pail of milk from there to the cave," said Jack. "Before you do that scatter heather over our patches of growing seeds. And Peggy, you might make certain the cave-cupboard is hidden by a curtain of bracken or something."

"Ay, ay, Captain!" said Peggy. "Now we've all got our duties to do—but you've got the hardest, Jack! I wouldn't like to hide Daisy away down that narrow passage! What will you do if she gets stuck?"

"She won't get stuck," said Jack. "She's not as fat as all that! By the way, we'd better put a cup or two in the cave, and some heather, in case we have to hide up for a good many hours. We can drink milk then, and have somewhere soft to lie on."

"We'd better keep a candle or two in the entrance," said Peggy. "I don't feel like sitting in the dark there."

"I'll tell you what we'll do," said Jack thoughtfully. "We won't go in and out of that big inner cave by the narrow passage leading from the outer cave. We'll go in and out by that tiny cave we can hardly squeeze in by. It leads to the inner cave, as we found out. If we keep using the other cave and the passage to go in, we are sure to leave marks, and give ourselves away. I'll have to take Daisy that way, but that can't be helped."

"Those caves will be cosy to live in in the winter-time," said Peggy. "We could live in the outer one, and store our things in the inner one. We should be quite protected from bad weather."

"How lucky we are!" said Nora. "A nice house made of trees for the summer—and a cosy cave-home for the winter!"

"Winter's a long way off yet," said Jack. "I say!—I'm hungry! What about frying some eggs, Peggy, and sending Mike to get some raspberries?"

"Come on!" shouted Peggy, and raced off down the hillside, glad to leave behind the dark, gloomy caves.

The Summer Goes By

No one came to interfere with the children. They lived together on the island, playing, working, eating, drinking, bathing—doing just as they liked, and yet having to do certain duties in order to keep their farmyard going properly.

Sometimes Jack and Mike went off in the boat at night to get something they needed from either Jack's farm or Aunt Harriet's. Mike managed to get into his aunt's house one night and get some of his and the girls' clothes—two or three dresses for the girls, and a coat and shorts for himself. Clothes were rather a difficulty, for they got dirty and ragged on the island, and as the girls had none to change into, it was difficult to keep their dresses clean and mended.

Jack got a good deal of fruit and a regular amount of potatoes and turnips from his grandfather's farm, which still had not been sold. There was always enough to eat, for there were eggs, rabbits, and fish, and Daisy gave them more than enough milk to drink.

Their seeds grew quickly. It was a proud day when Peggy was able to cut the first batch of mustard and cress and the first lettuce and mix it up into a salad to eat with hard-boiled eggs! The radishes, too, tasted very good, and were so hot that even Jack's eyes watered when he ate them! Things grew amazingly well and quickly on the island.

The runner beans were now well up to the top of the bramble bushes, and Jack nipped the tips off, so that they would flower well below.

"We don't want to have to make a ladder to climb up and pick the beans," he said. "My word, there are going to be plenty—look at all the scarlet flowers!"

"They smell nice!" said Nora, sniffing them.

"The beans will taste nicer!" said Jack.

The weather was hot and fine, for it was a wonderful summer. The children all slept out of doors in their "green bedroom," as they called it, tucked in the shelter of the big gorse bushes. They had to renew their beds of heather and bracken every week, for they became flattened with the weight of their bodies and were uncomfortable. But these jobs were very pleasant, and the children loved them.

"How brown we are!" said Mike one day, as they sat round the fire on the beach, eating radishes, and potatoes cooked in their jackets. They all looked at one another.

"We're as brown as berries," said Nora.

"What berries?" said Mike. "I don't know any brown berries. Most of them are red!"

"Well, we're as brown as oak-apples!" said Nora. They certainly were. Legs, arms, faces, necks, knees—just as dark as could be! The children were fat, too, for although their food was a queer mixture, they had a great deal of creamy milk.

Although life was peaceful on the island, it had its excitements. Each week Jack solemnly led poor Daisy to the cave and made her squeeze through the narrow passage into the cave beyond. The first time she made a terrible fuss. She mooed and bellowed, she struggled and even kicked—but Jack was firm and kind and led her inside. There, in the inner cave, he gave her a juicy turnip, fresh-pulled from his grandfather's farm the night before. Daisy was pleased. She chewed it all up, and was quite good when she was led back through the passage once more.

The second time she made a fuss again, but did not kick, nor did she bellow quite so loudly. The third time she seemed quite pleased to go, because she knew by now that a fine turnip awaited her in the cave. The fourth time she even went into the cave by herself and made her way solemnly to the passage at the far end.

"It's an awfully tight squeeze," said Mike, from the back. "If Daisy grows any fatter she won't be able to get through, Jack."

"We won't meet our troubles half-way," said Jack cheerfully. "The main thing is, Daisy likes going into the cave now, and won't make a fuss if ever the time comes when she has to be put there in a hurry."

July passed into August. The weather was thundery and hot. Two or three thunderstorms came along, and the children slept in Willow House for a few nights. Jack suggested sleeping in the cave, but they all voted it would be too hot and stuffy. So they settled down in Willow House, and felt glad of the thick green roof above them, and the stout, heather-stuffed walls.

The wild raspberries ripened by the hundred. Wild strawberries began to appear in the shady parts of the island—not tiny ones, such as the children had often found round the farm, but big, sweet, juicy ones, even nicer than garden ones. They tasted most delicious with cream. The blackberries grew ripe on the bushes that rambled all over the place, and the children's mouths were always stained with them, for they picked them as they went about their various jobs.

Jack picked them on his way to milk Daisy, and so did Mike. Peggy picked them as she went to get water from the spring. Nora picked them as she went to feed the hens.

Nuts were ripening, too, but were not yet ready. Jack looked at the heavy clusters on the hazel-trees and longed for them to be ripe. He went to have a look at the beans.

They were ready to be picked! The runners grew up the brambles, and the long green pods were mixed up with the blackberry flowers and berries.

"Beans for dinner today!" shouted Jack. He went to fetch one of the many baskets that Peggy knew how to weave from willow twigs, and soon had it full of the juicy green beans.

Another time Jack remembered the mushrooms that used to grow in the field at the end of his grandfather's farm. He and Mike set off in the boat one early morning at the end of August to see if they could find some.

It was a heavenly morning. Mike wished they had brought the girls, too, but it would not do to take a crowd. Someone might see them. It was just sunrise. The sun rose up in the east and the whole sky was golden. A little yellow-hammer sang loudly on a nearby hedge, "Little bits of bread and no cheese!" A crowd of young sparrows chirruped madly in the trees. Dew was heavy on the grass, and the boys' bare feet were dripping wet. They were soaked to the knees, but they didn't mind. The early sun was warm, and all the world was blue and gold and green.

"Mushrooms!" said Jack, in delight, pointing to where two or three grew. "Look—fresh new ones, only grown up last night. Come on! Fill the sack!"

There were scores in the field. Jack picked the smaller ones, for he knew the bigger ones did not taste so nice and might have maggots in them. In half an hour their sack was full and they slipped away through the sunny fields to where they had moored their boat.

"What a breakfast we'll have!" grinned Jack. And they did! Fried mushrooms and fried eggs, wild strawberries and cream! The girls had gone out strawberry hunting whilst the boys had gone to look for mushrooms.

Nora learnt to swim well. She and Peggy practised every day in the lake till Jack said they were as good as he and

Mike were. They were soon like fish in the water, and tumbled and splashed about each day with yells and shrieks. Jack was clever at swimming under water and would disappear suddenly and come up just beside one of the others, clutching hard at their legs! What fun they had!

Then there came a spell of bad weather—just a few days. The island seemed very different then, with the sun gone, a soft rain-mist driving over it, soaking everything, and the lake-water as cold as ice.

Nora didn't like it. She didn't like feeding the hens in the rain. She asked Peggy to do it for her. But Jack heard her and was cross.

"You're not to be a fair-weather person," he told her. "It's all very well to go about happily when the sun is shining and do your jobs with a smile—but just you be the same when we get bad weather!"

"Ay, ay, Captain!" said Nora, who was learning not to be such a baby as she had been. And after that she went cheerfully out to feed the hens, even though the rain trickled down her neck and ran in a cold stream down her brown back.

They were rather bored when they had to keep indoors in Willow House when it rained. They had read all their books and papers by that time, and although it was fun to play games for a while, they couldn't do it all day long. Peggy didn't mind—she had always plenty of mending to do.

She showed the boys and Nora how to weave baskets. They needed a great many, for the baskets did not last very long, and there were always raspberries, strawberries, or blackberries to pick. Mike, Jack and Nora thought it was fun to weave all kinds and shapes of baskets, and soon they had a fine selection of them ready for sunny weather.

Then the sun came back again and the children lay

about in it and basked in the hot rays to get themselves warm once more. The hens fluffed out their wet feathers and clucked happily. Daisy came out from under the tree which gave her shelter, and gave soft moos of pleasure. The world was full of colour again and the children shouted for joy.

The beans, radishes, lettuces, and mustard and cress grew enormously in the rain. Jack and Mike picked a good crop, and everyone said that never had anything tasted so delicious before as the rain-swollen lettuces, so crisp, juicy, and sweet.

All sorts of little things happened. The hole in the boat grew so big that one day, when Mike went to fetch the boat from its hiding-place, it had disappeared! It had sunk into the water! Then Jack and Mike had to use all their brains and all their strength to get it up again and to mend it so that it would not leak quite so badly.

The corn for the hens came to an end, and Jack had to go and see if he could find some more. There was none at his grandfather's farm, so he went to Mike's farm—and there he found some in a shed, but was nearly bitten by a new dog that had been bought for the farm. The dog bit a hole in his trousers, and Peggy had to spend a whole morning mending them.

Another time there was a great alarm, because Nora said she had heard the splashing of oars. Jack rushed off to get Daisy, and Mike bundled the hens into a sack—but, as nothing more seemed to happen, Peggy ran to the top of the hill and looked down the lake.

No boat was in sight—only four big white swans, quarrelling among themselves, and slashing the water with their feet and wings!

"It's all right, boys!" she shouted. "It's only the swans! It isn't a boat!"

So Daisy was left in peace and the hens were emptied

out of the sack again. Nora was teased, and made up her mind that she would make quite certain it *was* a boat next time she gave the alarm!

One day Jack slipped down the hillside when he was reaching for raspberries and twisted his ankle. Mike had to help him back to the camp on the beach. Jack was very pale, for it was a bad twist.

Peggy ran to get some clean rags and soaked them in the cold spring water. She bound them tightly round Jack's foot and ankle.

"You mustn't use it for a while," she said. "You must keep quiet. Mike will do your jobs."

So Jack had to lie about quietly for a day or two, and he found this very strange. But he was a sensible boy, and he knew that it was the quickest way to get better. Soon he found that he could hop about quite well with a stout hazel stick Mike cut for him from the hedges—and after a week or so his foot was quite all right.

Another time poor Peggy overbalanced and fell into a gorse bush below her on the hill. She was dreadfully scratched, but she didn't even cry. She went to the lake and washed her scratches and cuts, and then got the supper just as usual. Jack said he was very proud of her. "Anybody else would have yelled the place down!" he said, looking at the scratches all over her arms and legs.

"It's nothing much," said Peggy, boiling some milk. "I'm lucky not to have broken my leg or something!"

So, with these little adventures, joys, and sorrows, the summer passed by. No one came to the island, and gradually the children forgot their fears of being found, and thought no more of it.

Jack Does Some Shopping

The summer passed away. The days grew gradually shorter. The children found that it was not always warm enough to sit by the camp-fire in the evenings, and they went to Willow House, where they could light the lantern and play games. Willow House was always cosy.

They had had to stuff the walls again with heather and bracken, for some of it crumbled away and then the wind blew in. All the willow stakes they had used in the making of the walls had put out roots, and now little tufts of green, pointed leaves jutted out here and there up the sticks! The children were pleased. It was fun to have walls and a roof that grew!

One day Mike got a shock. He went to get another candle for the lantern—and found that there was only one left! There were very few matches left, too, for although the children were careful with these, and only used one when the fire had gone out, they had to use them sometimes.

"I say, Jack, we've only got one candle left," said Mike.

"We'll have to get some more, then," said Jack.

"How?" asked Mike. "They don't grow on trees!"

"Jack means he'll go and get some from somewhere," said Peggy, who was mending a hole in Jack's shirt. She was so glad she had been sensible enough to bring her work-basket with her to the secret island. She could stop their clothes from falling to pieces by keeping an eye on them, and stitching them as soon as they were torn.

"But where could he get candles except in a shop?" said Mike.

"Well, I've been thinking," said Jack seriously. "I've been thinking very hard. The autumn is coming, when we shall need a better light in the evenings. We shall need another blanket, too. And there are all sorts of little things we want."

"I badly want some more mending wool and some black cotton," said Peggy. "I had to mend your grey trousers with blue wool yesterday, Jack."

"And I'll have to have some more corn for the hens soon," said Nora.

"And it *would* be nice if we could get some flour," said Peggy. "Because if I had a bag of flour I could make you little rolls of bread sometimes—I just long for bread, don't you!"

"It would be nice," said Jack. "Well, listen, everyone. Don't you think it would be a good idea if I took the boat and went to the village at the other end of the lake and bought some of the things we badly need?"

The others all cried out in surprise.

"You'd be caught!"

"You haven't any money to buy things with!"

"Oh, don't go, Jack!"

"I shouldn't be caught," said Jack. "I'd be very careful. No one knows me at that village. Anyway, if you're afraid, I'll go on to the next village—only it's five miles away and I'd be jolly tired carrying back all the things we want."

"But what about money, Jack?" said Peggy.

"I'd thought of that," said Jack. "If Mike will help me to pick a sackful of mushrooms early one moning, I could bring them back here, arrange them in the willow baskets we make, and then take them to the village to sell. With the money I get I'll buy the things we want."

"Oh, that *is* a good idea, Jack," said Peggy. "If only you don't get caught!"

105

"Don't worry about that, silly," said Jack. "Now we'd better make out a list of things we want, and I'll try and get them when I go."

"I wish we could have a book or two," said Peggy.

"And a pencil would be nice," said Nora. "I like drawing things."

"And a new kettle," said Peggy. "Ours leaks a bit now."

"And a few more nails," said Mike.

"And the flour and the wool and the black cotton," said Peggy.

So they went on, making up a list of things they would like to have. Jack said them all over, and counted them up so that he wouldn't forget them.

"Mike and I will get the mushrooms from the field over the water tomorrow morning," he said.

"And I say, Jack—do you suppose you could sell some wild strawberries if you took them?" asked Nora eagerly. "I know where there are lots. I found a whole patch yesterday, ever so big, and very sweet!"

"That's a splendid idea," said Jack, pleased. "Look here, we'll make lots of little baskets today, and then we will arrange the mushrooms and strawberries neatly in them and I'll take them in the boat to sell. We should make a lot of money!"

The children were really excited. Mike went off to get a supply of thin willow twigs, and Peggy ran to get some rushes. She had discovered that she could make dainty baskets from the rushes, too, and she thought those would be nice for the strawberries.

Soon all four children were sitting on the sunny hillside among the heather, weaving the baskets. The boys were as good at it as the girls now, and by the time the sun was sinking there was a fine array of baskets. Peggy counted them. There were twenty-seven!

"I say! If we can fill and sell all those, Jack, you will have plenty of money to buy everything," said Mike.

The children went to bed early, for they knew they would have to be up at dawn the next day. They had no watches or clocks, and the only way to wake up early was to go to bed early! They knew that. It was a warm night, so they slept in their outdoor bedroom among the gorse bushes, lying cosily on their heather beds. Nothing ever woke them now, as it had done at first. A hedgehog could crawl over Jack's legs and he wouldn't stir! A bat could flick Mike's face and he didn't even move.

Once a little spider had made a web from Peggy's nose to her shoulder, and when Nora awoke and saw it there she called the boys. How they laughed to see a web stretching from Peggy's nose, and a little spider in the middle of it! They woke Peggy up and told her—but she didn't mind a bit!

"Spiders are lucky!" she said. "I shall have some luck today!" And so she did—for she found her scissors, which she had lost the week before!

The children awoke early, just as the daylight was putting a sheet of silver over the eastern sky. A robin was tick-tick-ticking near by and burst into a little creamy song when the children awoke. He was not a bit afraid of them, for they all loved the birds and fed them with crumbs after every meal. The robin was very tame and would often sit on Peggy's shoulder whilst she prepared the meals. She liked this very much.

They all got up and had their dip in the lake. Peggy thought of one more thing they wanted—a bar of soap! Their one piece was finished—and it was difficult to rub dirt off with sand, which they had to do now they had no soap. Jack added that to the list in his mind—that made twenty-one things wanted! What a lot!

"Mike and I won't be very long picking mushrooms," he

107

said, as he got into the boat and pushed off. "You and Nora go and pick the strawberries, Peggy. Have a kettle boiling on the fire when we come back so that we can have something hot to drink. It's rather chilly this morning."

How busy the four children were as the sun rose! Mike and Jack were away in the mushroom field, picking as many mushrooms as they could, and stuffing them into the big sack they carried. Nora and Peggy were picking the wild strawberries on the island. Certainly the patch Nora had found was a wonderful one. Deep red strawberries glowed everywhere among the pretty leaves, and some of the berries were as big as garden ones.

"Don't they look pretty in our little green baskets?" said Peggy, pleased. The girls had taken some of their baskets with them, and had lined them with strawberry leaves first. Then neatly and gently they were putting the ripe strawberries in.

"I should think Jack could sell these baskets of strawberries for sixpence each," said Peggy. "They are just right for eating."

The girls filled twelve of the rush baskets, and then went back to light the camp-fire. It was soon burning well, and Peggy hung the kettle over the flames to boil. Nora went to feed the hens.

"I'll milk Daisy, I think," said Peggy. "It is getting about milking-time, and the boys won't have time this morning. Watch the fire, Nora, and take the kettle off when it boils."

Soon the boys were back, happy to show the girls such a fine collection of white mushrooms. Peggy had finished milking Daisy and there was soon hot tea for everyone. The tin of cocoa had long been finished, and was added to the list that Jack had in his mind.

Whilst the boys were having breakfast of fried eggs and mushrooms, with a few wild strawberries and cream to

108

follow, the two girls were busy arranging the fine mushrooms in the willow baskets, which were bigger and stronger than the rush strawberry ones. There were more than enough to fill the baskets.

Peggy and Nora carried the full baskets carefully to the boat. They put them safely at the far end and covered them with elder leaves so that the flies would not get at them. The flies did not like the smell of the elder leaves.

The boys set off in the boat. It had been arranged that they should both go to the far end of the lake, but that only Jack should go to sell their goods and to shop. One boy alone would not be so much noticed. Mike was to wait in the boat, hidden somewhere by the lakeside, till Jack returned. Mike had some cold cooked fish and some milk, for it might be some hours before Jack came back.

"Here's a good place to put the boat," said Jack, as he and Mike rowed up the lake, and came in sight of the village at the far end. An alder tree leaned over the water by the lakeside, and Mike guided the boat there. It slid under the drooping tree and Jack jumped out.

"I can easily find my way to the village from here," he said. "I'll be as quick as I can, Mike."

Jack had two long sticks, and on them he threaded the handles of the baskets of mushrooms and strawberries. In this way he could carry them easily, without spilling anything. Off he went with his goods through the wood, and Mike settled down in the boat to wait for his return.

Jack was not long in finding the road that led to the little village—and to his great delight he found that it was market-day there! A small market was held every Wednesday, and it happened to be Wednesday that day!

"Good!" thought Jack. "I shall not be so much noticed if there is a crowd of people—and I should be able to sell my goods easily!"

The boy went to the little market-place, calling "Fine

mushrooms! Ripe wild strawberries!" at the top of his voice.

When people saw the neat and pretty baskets of mushrooms and strawberries they stopped to look at them. Certainly they were excellent goods, and very soon Jack was selling them fast. Shillings and sixpences clinked into his pocket, and Jack felt very happy. What a fine lot of things he would be able to buy!

At last his sticks held no more baskets. The people praised him for his goods and the cleverly woven baskets, and told him to come again. Jack made up his mind that he would. It was a pleasant way of earning money, and he could buy all the things he needed if only he could get the money!

He went shopping. He bought a very large bag of flour. He bought wool and cotton for Peggy. He bought scores of candles and plenty of matches. He bought a new kettle and two enamel plates. Peggy was always wishing she had more dishes. He bought some storybooks, and two pencils and a rubber. A drawing-book was added to his collection, some nails, soap, butter for a treat, some bars of chocolate, some tins of cocoa, tea, rice—oh, Jack had a load to carry before he had done!

When he could carry no more, and his money was all gone, he staggered off to the boat. He kept thinking what fun everyone would have that night when he unpacked the bags and boxes!

Mike was waiting for him impatiently. He was delighted to see Jack, and helped him to dump the things into the boat. Then off they rowed, home to the secret island.

Jack Nearly Gets Caught

What fun it was that evening, unpacking all the things Jack had brought! Mike helped Jack to take everything to the beach, and Nora and Peggy jumped up and down and squealed with excitement.

"Flour! What a lot! I can make you rolls now to eat with your fish and eggs!" cried Peggy in delight. "And here's my wool—and my cotton!"

"And *two* pencils for me—and a rubber—and a drawing-book!" cried Nora.

"And butter—oh, and *chocolate*!" yelled Mike. "I've forgotten what chocolate tastes like!"

"Oh, Jack, you are clever," said Peggy. "Did you sell all the mushrooms and strawberries?"

"Every single basket," said Jack. "And what is more, the people told me to bring more next week—so I shall earn some more money, and lay in a good stock of things for the winter! What do you say to that?"

"Fine, Captain!" shouted everyone joyfully. "We shall be as cosy as can be with candles to see by, nice things to eat, books to read, chocolate to nibble! Hurrah!"

"Have you brought the corn for my hens, Jack?" asked Nora anxiously.

"Yes, there it is!" said Jack. "And what about this new kettle and enamel dishes, Peggy? I thought you'd like those."

"Oh, Jack, isn't it all exciting?" cried Peggy. "Look here—shall we have supper now—and look at all the things again afterwards—and then put them away carefully? You and Mike will have to put up shelves in Willow House for all these new stores!"

Talking all at once and at the tops of their voices the children set to work to get supper. This was a rabbit stew, with runner beans picked by Nora and a baked potato each, with raspberries and cream afterwards. And as a special treat Jack gave everyone half a bar of the precious chocolate! The children were so happy—they really felt that they couldn't be any happier! The girls had been lonely all day without the two boys, and it was lovely to be all together again.

After supper they cleared away and washed the dishes, and then stamped out the fire. They took everything to Willow House, and lighted the lantern that hung from the roof. Jack also lighted another candle to make enough light to see clearly all the treasures he had brought.

"I say! What a nice lot of matches!" said Mike. "We'll have to store those carefully in a dry place."

"And look at the books!" squealed Peggy. "Jack can read them out loud to us in the evening. *Robinson Crusoe*, and *Stories from the Bible* and *Animals of the World* and *The Boy's Book of Aeroplanes*. What a lovely lot! It will be fun to read about Robinson Crusoe, because he was alone on the island, just as we are. I guess we could teach him a few things, though!"

Everyone laughed. "He could teach *us* a few things, too!" said Jack.

Jack had really shopped very well. He had even bought a tin of treacle, so that sometimes, for a treat, Peggy could make toffee! He had got sugar, too, which would be nice in their tea and cocoa. Their own sugar had been finished long ago.

"And we needn't be too careful now of all our things," said Jack, "because I can go each week and sell mushrooms and strawberries and earn money to buy more."

"But what will you do when the mushrooms and strawberries are over?" asked Peggy.

"Then there will be blackberries and nuts," said Jack. "They won't fetch so much money, but at any rate I can get enough to store up plenty of things for the winter. If we can get flour, potatoes, rice, cocoa, and things like that, we shall be quite all right. Daisy can always give us milk and cream, and we get lots of eggs from the hens, fish from the lake, and a rabbit or two. We are really very lucky."

"Jack, read to us tonight," begged Nora. "It's so long since I heard a story."

"We'll begin *Robinson Crusoe* first, then," said Jack. "That seems sort of suitable. By the way, Nora, can you read yourself?"

"Well, I wasn't very good at it," said Nora.

"I think it would be a good idea if we all took a night each to read out loud," said Jack. "It's no good forgetting what we learnt. I'll read tonight—and you shall read tomorrow night, Nora."

So, by the light of the two candles, Jack began reading the tale of Robinson Crusoe to the others. They lay on the heather, listening, happy to be together, enjoying the tale. When Jack shut up the book they sighed.

"That was lovely," said Peggy. "My goodness, Jack, I guess we could write an exciting book if we wrote down all our adventures on the island!"

"Nobody would believe them!" laughed Jack. "Yet it's all true—here we are, living by ourselves, feeding ourselves, having a glorious time on a secret island that nobody knows!"

The next day Jack and Mike rigged up some shelves on which to keep some of their new stores. It was fun

113

arranging everything. The children soon began to make out their next list of things for Jack to buy when he went to market.

"We shall have to keep the days pretty carefully in future," said Jack. "I don't want to miss Wednesdays now because Wednesday is market-day at the village. I shall get better prices then."

So, the next Wednesday, once again there was a great stir just about dawn, and the four children hurried to their tasks of picking mushrooms and strawberries. They had made plenty of baskets again, and Jack and Mike set off two or three hours later with the boat, taking the full baskets with them.

For three or four weeks Jack went to market, sold all his goods, and bought a great many stores for the winter. He and Mike decided to store the bags and sacks of goods in the inner cave of the hillside, as there they would be quite dry—and, as the children would probably have to live in the caves in the winter, the stores would be quite handy there.

As the weeks went by there were not so many wild strawberries to be found. Mushrooms stopped growing in the field, and other market goods had to take their place. The children went nutting in the hazel trees and struck down great clusters of ripe nuts, lovely in their ragged green coats and brown shells. The girls picked baskets of big ripe blackberries, and Jack took these to the market instead of mushrooms and strawberries.

People soon grew to know him at the market. They wondered where he came from, but Jack never told them anything about himself.

"I just live by the lakeside," he said, when people asked him where he lived. They thought he meant somewhere by the lake—they did not know he meant by the lakeside on the secret island—and certainly Jack was not going to tell them!

One day, for the first time, Jack saw a policeman in the village. This struck him as strange, for he had never seen one there before, and he knew that the village was too small to have a policeman of its own. It shared one with the village five miles away. Jack's heart sank—could the policeman have been told that a strange boy was about—and could he be wondering if the boy was one of the lost children! Jack began to edge away, though his baskets of nuts and blackberries were only half sold.

"Hi, you!" called the policeman suddenly. "Where do you come from, boy?"

"From the lakeside, where I've been gathering blackberries and nuts to sell," said Jack, not coming near the policeman.

"Is your name Mike?" said the policeman.

And then Jack knew for certain that the policeman had been told that maybe he, Jack, *was* one of the four runaway children—and he had come to find out.

"No, that's not my name," said Jack, looking very innocent. "Buy some nuts, Mister Policeman?"

"No," said the policeman, getting a strip of paper out of his pocket, and looking at a photograph there. "Come you here, my lad. I think you're one of the runaway children —let's have a look at you."

Jack turned pale. If the policeman had a picture of him, he was caught! Quick as lightning the boy flung down the two sticks on which he had a dozen or so baskets strung, and darted off through the crowd that had gathered. Hands were put out to stop him, but he struggled away, tearing his jacket, but not caring for anything but to escape.

He slipped round a corner and into a garden. He darted round the cottage there and peered into the back garden. There was no one there—but there was a little henhouse at the side. Jack made up his mind quickly. He opened the

115

door of the henhouse, slipped inside, and crouched down in the straw there, hardly daring to breathe. There were no hens there—they were scratching about in the little run outside.

Jack heard the sound of shouting and running feet, and he knew that people were looking for him. He crouched lower, hoping that no one had seen him dart into the cottage garden.

The running feet went by. The shouting died down. No one had seen him! Jack let out a big breath, and his heart thumped loudly. He was really frightened.

He stayed in the henhouse all day long. He did not dare to move out. He was hungry and thirsty and very cramped, but he knew quite well that if he slipped out he might be seen. He must stay there till night. He wondered what Mike would think. The girls would be anxious, too.

A hen came in, sat on a nesting-box and laid an egg. She cackled and went out again. Another came in and laid an egg. Jack hoped that no one would see him if they came looking for eggs that afternoon!

Someone did come for the eggs—but it was after tea and the henhouse was very dark. The door was opened and a head came round. A hand was stretched out and felt in all the boxes. The eggs were lifted out—the door was shut again! Jack hadn't been seen! He was crouching against the other side of the house, well away from the nesting-boxes!

The henhouse did not smell nice. Jack felt miserable as he sat there on the floor. He knew that by running away he had as good as told the policeman that he was one of the runaways. And now the whole countryside would be searched again, and the secret island would probably be explored, too.

"But if I hadn't run away the policeman would have caught me and made me tell where the others were," thought the boy. "If only I can get back to where Mike is waiting with the boat, and get back safely to the island, we can make preparations to hide everything."

When it was dark, and the hens were roosting in the house beside him, Jack opened the door and slipped out. He stood listening. Not a sound was to be heard except the voices of people in the kitchen of the cottage near by.

He ran quietly down the path to the gate. He slipped out into the road—and then ran for his life to the road that led to the wood by the lakeside where Mike was waiting.

But would Mike be waiting there? Suppose people had begun to hunt already for the four children—and had found Mike and the boat! What then? How would he get back to the girls on the island?

Jack forgot his hunger and thirst as he padded along at top speed to where he had left Mike. No one saw him. It was a dark night, for the moon was not yet up. Jack made his way through the trees to the lakeside.

And then his heart leapt for joy! He heard Mike's voice! "Is that you, Jack? What a time you've been! Whatever's happened?"

The Great Hunt Begins

Jack scrambled into the boat, panting. "Push off, quickly, Mike!" he said. "I was nearly caught today, and if anyone sees us we shall all be discovered!"

Mike pushed off, his heart sinking. He could not bear the idea of being caught and sent back to his uncle's farm. He waited till Jack had got back his breath and then asked him a few questions. Jack told him everything. Mike couldn't help smiling when he thought of poor Jack sitting with the hens in the hen-house—but he felt very frightened. Suppose Jack had been caught!

"This is the end of my marketing," said Jack gloomily. "I shan't dare to show my nose again in any village. They will all be on the look-out for me. Why can't people run away if they want to? We are not doing any harm—only living happily together on our secret island!"

After a bit Jack helped Mike to row, and they arrived at the island just as the moon was rising. The girls were on the beach by a big fire, waiting anxiously for them.

"Oh Jack, oh Mike!" cried Nora, hugging them both, and almost crying with delight, at seeing them again. "We thought you were never coming! We imagined all kinds of dreadful things! We felt sure you had been caught!"

"I jolly nearly *was*," said Jack.

"Where is your shopping" asked Peggy.

"Haven't got any," said Jack. "I had only sold a few baskets when a policeman spotted me. I've got the money for the ones I sold—but what's the good of money on this island, where you can't buy anything!"

Mike and Jack pulled hard at the oars

Soon Jack had told the girls his story. He sat by the fire, warming himself, and drinking a cup of hot cocoa. He was dreadfully hungry, too, for he had had nothing to eat all day. He ate a whole rice pudding, two fishes, and a hard-boiled egg whilst he talked.

Everyone was very grave and solemn. They knew things were serious. Nora was really scared. She tried her hardest not to cry, but Jack heard her sniffing and put his arm round her. "Don't be a baby," he said. "Things may not be so bad after all. We have all our plans laid. There is no real reason why anyone should find us if we are careful. We are all upset and tired. Let's go to bed and talk tomorrow."

So to bed in Willow House they went. Jack took off his clothes and wrapped himself in the old rug because he said he smelt like hens. Peggy said she would wash his things the next day. They did not get to sleep for a long time because first one and then another of them would say something, or ask a question—and then the talking would all begin again.

"Now, nobody is to say another word!" said Jack at last, in his firmest voice.

"Ay, ay, Captain!" said everyone sleepily. And not another word was spoken.

In the morning the children awoke early, and remembered what had happened the day before. Nobody felt like singing or shouting or joking as they usually did. Peggy solemnly got the breakfast. Jack went off in his old overcoat to milk the cow, for his things were not yet washed. Mike got some water from the spring, and Nora fed the hens. It was not a very cheerful party that sat down to breakfast.

When the things were cleared away, and Peggy had washed Jack's clothes and set them out to dry, the children held a meeting.

"The first thing to do," said Jack, "is to arrange that someone shall always be on watch during the day, on the top of the hill. You can see all up the lake and down from there, and we should get good warning then if anyone were coming—we should have plenty of time to do everything."

"Shall we have someone on guard during the night?" asked Nora.

"No," said Jack. "People are not likely to come at night. We can sleep in peace. I don't think anyone will come for a few days, anyhow, because I think they will search around the lake-side first, and will only think of the island later."

"I think, as we are not going to the mainland for some time, we had better make a big hole in the boat and let her sink," said Mike. "I've always been afraid she might be found, although she is well hidden under the brambles. After all, Jack, if she is sunk, no one could possibly find her!"

"That's a good idea, Mike," said Jack. "We can't be too careful now. Sink her this morning. We can easily get her up again and mend her if we want her. Peggy, will you see that every single thing is cleared away that might show people we are here? Look, there's some snippings of wool, there—that sort of thing must be cleared up, for it tells a tale!"

"I'll see to it," promised Peggy. Jack knew she would, for she was a most dependable girl.

"Every single thing must be taken to the caves today," said Jack, "except just those few things we need for cooking, like a saucepan and kettle and so on. We can easily slip those away at the last minute. We will leave ourselves a candle or two in Willow House, because we can sleep there till we have to go to the caves."

"Jack, what about the hen-yard?" asked Nora. "It really

121

does look like a yard now, because the hens have scratched about so much."

"That's true," said Jack. "Well, as soon as we know we've got to hide, Mike can pull up the fence round the hen-yard and store it in Willow House. Then he can scatter sand over the yard and cover it with heather. It's a good thing you thought of that, Nora."

"There's one thing, even if we have to hide away for days, we've enough food!" said Peggy.

"What about Daisy, though?" said Mike. "She won't have anything to eat. A cow eats such a lot."

"We should have to take her out to feed at night," said Jack. "And by the way, Peggy, don't light the fire for cooking until the very last minute and stamp it out as soon as you have finished. A spire of smoke gives us away more than anything!"

"What about someone hopping up to the hill-top now?" said Mike. "The sun is getting high. We ought to keep a watch from now on."

"Yes, we ought," said Jack. "You take first watch, Mike. I'll give you a call when it's time to come down. We'll take turns all day long. Keep watch all round. We don't know from which end of the lake a boat might come, though it's more likely to be from the end I was at yesterday."

Mike sped up the hill and sat down there. The lake lay blue below him. Not a swan, not a moorhen disturbed its surface. Certainly no boat was in sight. Mike settled down to watch carefully.

The others were busy. Everything was taken up to the caves in the hillside and stored there. Nora left a sack by the hen-yard ready to bundle the hens into when the time came. She also put a pile of sand by the yard, ready for Mike to scatter after the fences had been pulled up. Nora was no longer the careless little girl she had been. Nor was she lazy any more. She had learned that when she did badly everyone suffered, so now she did her best—and it was a very good best too.

After a while Jack went up to take Mike's place on the hill-top. Mike set to work to sink the boat. She soon sank to the bottom of the water, under the bramble bushes. Mike felt sure that no one would ever know she was there.

Peggy went hunting round looking for anything that might give them away. She did not find very much, for all the children tidied up after any meal or game. Broken egg-shells were always buried, uneaten food was given to the hens, and it was only things like snippings of wool or cotton that the wind had blown away that could be found.

Peggy went on guard next and then Nora. It was dull work, sitting up on the hill-top doing nothing but watch, so Nora took her pencil and drawing-book and drew what she could see. That made the time go quickly. Peggy took her mending. She always had plenty of that to do, for every day somebody tore their clothes on brambles. After every stitch Peggy looked up and down the lake, but nothing could be seen.

That evening Mike was on guard, and he was just about to come down to get his supper when he saw something in the distance. He looked carefully. Could it be a boat? He called Jack.

"Jack! Come quickly! I can see something. Is it a boat, do you think?"

Everyone tore up the hill. Jack looked hard. "Well, if it's a boat, it's very small," he said.

"It's something black," said Nora. "Whatever is it? Oh, I do hope it isn't anyone coming now."

The children watched, straining their eyes. And suddenly the thing they thought might be a small boat flew up into the air!

"It's that black swan we saw the other day!" said Jack,

123

with a squeal of laughter. "What a fright it gave us! Look, there it goes! Isn't it a beauty?"

The children watched the lovely black swan flying slowly towards them, its wings making a curious whining noise as it came. Nora went rather red, for she remembered how frightened she had been the first time she had heard a swan flying over the island—but nobody teased her about it. They were all too thankful it was only a swan, not a boat.

"There's no need to keep watch any more tonight," said Jack, and they all went down the hill. Evening was almost on them. They sat by their fire and ate their supper, feeling happier than the day before. Perhaps after all no one would come to look for them—and anyway, they had done all they could now to get things ready in case anyone *did* come.

The next day the children kept watch in turn again, and the next. The third day, when Nora was on guard, she thought she saw people on the far side of the lake, where a thick wood grew. She whistled softly to Jack, and he came up and watched, too.

"Yes, you're right, Nora," he said at last. "There *are* people there—and they are certainly hunting for something or someone!"

They watched for a while and then they called the others. There was no fire going, for Peggy had stamped it out. They all crowded on to the hill-top, their heads peeping out of the tall bracken that grew there.

"See over there!" said Jack. "The hunt is on! It will only be a day or two before they come over here. We must watch very carefully indeed!"

"Well, everything is ready," said Peggy. "I wish they would come soon, if they are coming—I hate all this waiting about. It gives me a cold feeling in my tummy."

"So it does in mine," said Mike. "I'd like a hot-water bottle to carry about with me!"

That made everyone laugh. They watched for a while longer and then went down, leaving Jack on guard.

For two days nothing happened, though the children thought they could see people on the other side of the lake, beating about in the bushes and hunting. Mike went on guard in the morning and kept a keen watch. Nora fed the hens as usual and Jack milked Daisy.

And then Mike saw something! He stood up and looked—it was something at the far end of the lake, where Jack had gone marketing. It was a boat! No mistaking it this time—a boat it was, and a big one, too!

Mike called the others and they scrambled up. "Yes," said Jack at once. "That's a boat all right—with about four people in, too. Come on, there's no time to be lost. There's only one place a boat can come to here—and that's our island. To your jobs, everyone, and don't be frightened!"

The children hurried off. Jack went to get Daisy. Mike went to see to the hens and the hen-yard. Peggy scattered the dead remains of the fire, and caught up the kettle and the saucepan and any odds and ends of food on the beach to take to the cave. Nora ran to cover up their patches of growing seeds with bits of heather. Would they have time to do everything? Would they be well hidden before the boatload of people came to land on their secret island?

The Island Is Searched

Now that people had really come at last to search the island the children were glad to carry out their plans, for the days of waiting had been very upsetting. They had laid their plans so well that everything went smoothly. Daisy, the cow, did not seem a bit surprised to have Jack leading her to the inner cave again, and went like a lamb, without a single moo!

Jack got her safely through the narrow passage to the inner cave and left her there munching a turnip whilst he went to see if he could help the others. Before he left the outer cave he carefully rubbed away any traces of Daisy's hoofmarks. He arranged the bracken carelessly over the entrance so that it did not seem as if anyone went in and out of it.

Mike arrived with the hens just then, and Jack gave him a hand. Mike squeezed himself into the little tiny cave that led by the low passage to the inner cave, for it had been arranged that only Jack and the cow should use the other entrance for fear that much use of it should show too plainly that people went in and out.

Jack passed him the sack of hens, and Mike crawled on hands and knees through the low passage and into the big inner cave where Daisy was. The hens did not like being pulled through the tiny passage and squawked dismally. But when Mike shook them out of the sack, and scattered grain for them to eat, they were quite happy again. Jack had lighted the lantern in the inner cave, and it cast its dim light down. Mike thought he had better stay in the cave, in case the hens found their way out again.

So he sat down, his heart thumping, and waited for the others. One by one they came, carrying odds and ends. Each child had done his or her job, and with scarlet cheeks and beating hearts they sat down together in the cave and looked at one another.

"They're not at the island yet," said Jack. "I took a look just now. They've got another quarter-mile to go. Now, is there anything we can possibly have forgotten?"

The children thought hard. The boat was sunk. The cow and the hens were in. The fire was out and well scattered. The hen-yard was covered with sand and heather. The yard-fence was taken up and stored in Willow House. The seed-patches were hidden. The milk-pail was taken from the spring.

"We've done *every*thing!" said Peggy.

And then Mike jumped up in a fright. "My hat!" he said. "Where is it? I haven't got it on! I must have left it somewhere!"

The others stared at him in dismay. His hat was certainly not on his head nor was it anywhere in the cave.

"You had it on this morning," said Peggy. "I remember seeing it, and thinking it was getting very dirty and floppy. Oh, Mike dear! Where can you have left it? Think hard, for it is very important."

"It might be the one thing that gives us away," said Jack.

"There's just time to go and look for it," said Mike. "I'll go and see if I can find it."

He crawled through the narrow passage and out into the cave with the low entrance. He squeezed through that and went out into the sunlight. He could see the boat from where he was, being rowed through the water some distance away. He ran down the hill to the beach. He hunted there. He hunted round about the hen-yard. He hunted by the spring. He hunted everywhere! But he could *not* find that hat!

And then he wondered if it was anywhere near Willow House, for he had gone there that morning to store the hen-yard fences. He squeezed through the thickly growing trees and went to Willow House. There, beside the doorway, was his hat! The boy pushed it into his pocket, and made his way back up the hillside. Just as he got to the cave-entrance he heard the boat grinding on the beach below. The searchers had arrived.

He crawled into the big inner cave. The others greeted him excitedly.

"Did you find it, Mike?"

"Yes, thank goodness," said Mike, taking his hat out of his pocket. "It was just by Willow House—but I don't expect it would have been seen there, because Willow House is too well hidden among those thick trees to be found. Still, I'm glad I found it—I'd have been worried all the time if I hadn't. The boat is on the beach now, Jack; I heard it being pulled in. There are four men in it."

"I'm just a bit worried about the passage to this inner cave from the outer cave," said Jack. "If that is found it's all up with us. I was wondering if we could find a few rocks and stones and pile them up half-way through the passage, so that if anyone *does* come through there, he will find his way blocked and won't guess there is another cave behind, where *we* are hiding!"

"That's a fine idea, Jack" said Mike. "It doesn't matter about the other entrance, because no grown-up could possibly squeeze through there. Come on, everyone. Find rocks and stones and hard clods of earth and stop up the passage half-way through!"

The children worked hard, and before half an hour had gone by the passage was completely blocked up. No one could possibly guess there was a way through. It would be quite easy to unblock when the time came to go out.

"I'm going to crawl through to the cave with the small entrance and peep out to see if I can hear anything," said Jack. So he crawled through and sat just inside the tiny, low-down entrance, trying to hear.

The men were certainly searching the island! Jack could hear their shouts easily.

"*Some*one's been here!" shouted one man. "Look where they've made a fire."

"Trippers, probably!" called back another man. "There's an empty tin here, too—and a carton—just the sort of thing trippers leave about."

"Hi! Look at this spring here!" called another voice. "Looks to me as if people have been tramping about here."

Jack groaned. Surely there were not many footmarks there!

"Well, if those children are here we'll find them all right!" said a fourth voice. "It beats me how they could manage to live here, though, all alone, with no food, except what that boy could buy in the village!"

"I'm going over to the other side to look there," yelled the first man. "Come with me, Tom. You go one side of the hill and I'll go the other—and then, if the little beggars are dodging about to keep away from us, one of us will find them!"

Jack felt glad he was safely inside the cave. He stayed where he was till a whisper reached him from behind.

"Jack! We can hear voices. Is everything all right?"

"So far, Mike," said Jack. "They are all hunting hard — but the only thing they seem to have found is a few footmarks round the spring. I'll stay here for a bit and see what I can hear."

The hunt went on. Nothing seemed to be found. The children had cleared everything up very well indeed.

But, as Jack sat just inside the cave, there came a shout from someone near the beach.

"Just look here! What do you make of this?"

Jack wondered whatever the man had found. He soon knew. The man had kicked aside the heather that had hidden the hen-yard—and had found the newly scattered sand!

"This looks as if something had been going on here," said the man. "But goodness knows what! You know, I think those children *are* here somewhere. It's up to us to find them. Clever little things, too, they must be, hiding away all traces of themselves like this!"

"We'd better beat through the bushes and the bracken," said another man. "They may be hiding there. That'd be the likeliest place."

Then Jack heard the men beating through the bracken, poking into every bush, trying their hardest to find a hidden child. But not one could they find.

Jack crawled back to the cave after two or three hours and told the others what had happened. They listened, alarmed to hear that the hen-yard had been discovered even though they had tried so hard to hide it.

"It's time we had something to eat," said Peggy. "We can't light a fire in here, for we would be smoked out, but there are some rolls of bread I made yesterday, some wild strawberries, and a cold pudding. And lots of milk, of course."

They sat and ate, though none of them felt hungry. Daisy lay down behind them, perfectly good. The hens clucked, quietly, puzzled at finding themselves in such a strange dark place, but quite happy with the children there.

When the meal was over Jack went back to his post again. He sat just inside the cave-entrance and listened.

The men were getting puzzled and disheartened. They were sitting at the foot of the hill, eating sandwiches and drinking beer. Jack could hear their voices quite plainly.

"Well, those children *may* have been on this island, and I think they were—but they're not here now," said one man. "I'm certain of that."

"We've hunted every inch," said another man. "I think you're right, Tom; those kids have been here all right — who else could have planted those runner beans we found?—but they've gone. I expect that boy the policeman saw last Wednesday gave the alarm, and they've gone off in the boat."

"Ah yes, the boat!" said a third man. "Now, if the children were here we'd find a boat, wouldn't we? Well, we haven't found one—so they can't be here!"

"Quite right," said the first man. "I didn't think of that. If there's no boat here, there are no children! What about going back now? I'm sure it's no good hunting any more."

"There's just one place we haven't looked," said the quiet voice of the fourth man. "There are some caves in this hillside—it's possible those children may have hidden there."

"Caves!" said another man. "Yes—just the place. We'll certainly look there. Where are they?"

"I'll show you in a minute," said the fourth man. "Got a torch?"

"No, but I've got plenty of matches," said the other man. "But look here—they can't be there if there's no boat anywhere to be seen. If they are here, there must be a boat somewhere!"

"It's possible for a boat to be sunk so that no searcher could find it," said the fourth man.

"Children would never think of that!" said another.

"No, I don't think they would," was the answer.

Jack, who could hear everything, thought gratefully of Mike. It had been Mike's idea to sink the boat. If he hadn't sunk it, it would certainly have been found, for

131

the seach had been much more thorough than Jack had guessed. Fancy the men noticing the runner beans!

"Come on," said a man. "We'll go to those caves now. But it's a waste of time. I don't think the children are within miles! They've gone off up the lakeside somewhere in their boat!"

Jack crawled silently back to the inner cave, his heart thumping loudly.

"They don't think we're on the island," he whispered, "because they haven't found the boat. But they're coming to explore the caves. Put out the lantern, Mike. Now everyone must keep as quiet as a mouse. Is Daisy lying down? Good! The hens are quiet enough, too. They seem to think it's night, and are roosting in a row! Now nobody must sneeze or cough—everything depends on the next hour or two!"

Not a sound was to be heard in the big inner cave. Daisy lay like a log, breathing quietly. The hens roosted peacefully. The children sat like mice.

And then they heard the men coming into the cave outside. Matches were struck—and the passage that led to their cave was found!

"Look here, Tom," said a voice. "Here's what looks like a passage—shall we see where it goes?"

"We'd better, I suppose," said a voice. And then there came the sound of footsteps down the blocked-up passage!

The End Of The Search

The children sat in the inner cave as though they were turned into stone. They did not even blink their eyes. It seemed almost as if they did not even breathe! But how their hearts thumped! Jack thought that everyone must hear his heart beating, even the searchers outside, it bumped against his ribs so hard.

The children could hear the sound of someone fumbling his way along the narrow passage. He found it a tight squeeze, by his groanings and grumblings. He came right up to the place where the children had piled rocks, stones, and earth to block up the passage.

"I say!" the man called back to the others, "the passage ends here in what looks like loose rocks. Shall I try to force my way through—pull the rocks to see if they are just a fall from the roof?"

"No!" cried another man. "If you can't get through, the children couldn't! This is a wild-goose chase—we'll never find the children in these caves. Come back, Tom."

The man turned himself round with difficulty and began to squeeze back—and at the very moment a dreadful thing happened!

Daisy the cow let out a terrific moo!

The children were not expecting it, and they almost jumped out of their skins with fright. Then they clutched at one another, expecting the men to come chasing along at once, having heard Daisy.

There was an astonished silence. Then one of the men said, "Did you hear that?"

133

"Of course!" said another. "What in the wide world was it?"

"Well, it wasn't the children, that's certain!" said the first, with a laugh. "I never in my life heard a child make a noise like *that*!"

"It sounded like a cow," said another voice.

"A cow!" cried the first man, "what next? Do you mean to say you think there's a cow in the middle of this hill, Tom?"

"Of course there can't be," said Tom, laughing. "But it sounded mighty like one! Let's listen and see if we hear anything again."

There was a silence, as if the men were listening—and at that moment Daisy most obligingly gave a dreadfull hollow cough, that echoed mournfully round and round the cave.

"I don't like it," said a man's voice. "It sounds too queer for anything. Let's get out of these dark caves into the sunshine. I'm perfectly certain, since we heard those noises, that no children would be inside those caves! Why, they'd be frightened out of their lives!"

Jack squeezed Nora's hand in delight. So old Daisy had frightened the men! What a glorious joke! The children sat as still as could be, glad now that Daisy had given such a loud moo and such a dreadful cough.

There was the sound of scrambling about in the outer cave and then it seemed as if the men were all outside again. "We'd better just hunt about and see if there are any more caves," said one man. "Look that seems like one!"

"That's the cave where we put the hens when the trippers came!" whispered Jack. "It's got no passage leading to our inner cave here. They can explore that all they like."

The men did explore it, but as it was just a cave and

nothing else, and had no passage leading out of it, they soon left it. Then they found the cave with the low-down, tiny entrance—the one the childen used to squeeze into when they wanted to go to their inner cave—but, as Jack had said, the entrance was too small for any grown up to use, and, after trying once or twice, the men gave it up.

"No one could get in there except a rabbit," said a man's voice.

"Children could," said another.

"Now look here, Tom, if we find children on this island now, I'll eat my hat!" said the first man. "There's no boat, to begin with—and we really haven't found anything except runner beans, which might have been dropped by birds, and a funny sort of sandy yard—and you can't tell me children are clever enough to live here day after day, and yet vanish completely, leaving no trace behind, as soon as we come! No, no—no children are as clever as that!"

"I think you're right," said Tom. "Come on, let's go. I'm tired of this island with its strange noises. The sooner we get back home, the better I'll be pleased. Where those children have gone just beats me. I wish we could find them. There's such a surprise waiting for them!"

The voices grew distant as the men went down the hill to the beach, where they had put their boat. Jack crept quietly through the low passage into the small cave with the tiny entrance. He put his ear down to the entrance and listened. The sound of voices floated up to him. He heard the sound of oars being put ready. He heard the sound of the boat being pushed on to the water. Then came the sound of splashing.

"They're going!" he called. "They really are!"

The others crowded round Jack. Then, when he thought it was safe, they all squeezed out of the tiny cave entrance and crept out on the hillside. Well hidden in the

135

tall bracken, they watched the boatful of men being rowed away—away—away! The splashing of the oars, and the men's voices, came clearly to the four children as they stood there.

Nora suddenly began to cry. The excitement had been so great, and she had been so brave, that now she felt as if she must cry and cry and cry. And then Peggy began—and even Mike and Jack felt their eyes getting wet! This was dreadful—but oh, it was such a glorious feeling to know they had not been discovered, and that their dear little island, their secret island, was their very own again.

A low and mournful noise came from the inside of the hill—it was poor old Daisy the cow, sad at being left alone in the cave.

The children couldn't help laughing now! "Do you remember how Daisy frightened those men!" chuckled Jack.

"She frightened me too," said Peggy. "Honestly, I nearly jumped out of my skin—if my dress hadn't been well buttoned up I believe I would have jumped *right* out of myself!"

That made the others laugh still more—and half-laughing, half-crying, they sat down on the hillside to wait till the boat was out of sight.

"I really thought they'd found us when that men got up to the part we had blocked up," said Jack.

"Yes—it was a jolly good thing we *did* block it up!" said Peggy. "We would most certainly have been found if we hadn't!"

"And it was a good thing Mike sank the boat," said Nora. "If they had found a boat here they would have gone on looking for us till they'd found us."

"I wonder what they meant when they said that such a surprise was waiting for us," said Mike. "It couldn't have been a nice surprise, I suppose?"

"Of course not!" said Peggy.

"They're almost out of sight," said Nora. "Do you think it's safe to get up and do a dance or something, Jack? I'm just longing to shout and sing and dance after being shut up in the cave for so long!"

"Yes, we're safe enough now," said Jack. "They won't come back. We can settle into the caves for the winter quite happily."

"Shall we light a fire on the beach and have a good hot meal?" said Peggy. "I think we could all do with one!"

"Right," said Jack, and they set to work. Nora sang and danced about as she helped to fetch things. She felt so happy to think that they were safe, and that their secret island was their very own once more.

Soon they were eating as if they had never had a meal in their lives before. Then a loud moo from the hillside reminded them that Daisy was still there. So, leaving the girls to clear up, Jack sped off with Mike to get out Daisy and the hens.

"You're a good old cow, Daisy," Jack said to her, rubbing her soft nose. "We hoped you wouldn't moo when those men were hunting for us—but you knew better, and you mooed at them—and sent them off!"

The days were much shorter now, and night came early. It did not seem long before the sun went and the stars shone out in the sky. The children fetched the lantern from the cave and, taking their book, they went to Willow House. It was Nora's turn to read, and they all lay and listened to her. It was pleasant in Willow House with the lantern shining down softly, and the smell of the heather and bracken rising up. It was nice to be together and to know that the great hunt was over and they were safe.

"I'm sleepy," said Jack, at last. "Let's have some chocolate and a last talk and go to bed. You know, we shall soon have to think seriously of going to live in the caves. It won't be nice weather much longer!"

"We'll decide everything tomorrow," said Mike sleepily, munching his chocolate.

They were soon asleep, for the day's excitement had quite tired them out. But how lovely it was to wake the next day and know that the hunt was over and that they were safe for the winter. How they sang and joked and teased one another as they went down to bathe!

"Oooh!" said Nora, as she slipped into the water. "It's getting jolly cold to bathe in the lake, Jack. Have we got to do this all the winter?"

"Of course not," said Jack. "We'll have to give it up soon—but it's nice whilst it's warm enough."

That week the weather became really horrid. Storms swept over the lake and the children thought it looked just like the sea, with its big waves curling over and breaking on the beach with a crash. The waves ran right up the beach and it was impossible to make a fire there. The children got soaked with rain, and they had to dry their clothes as best they could by a fire they lighted outside the big cave. This was a good place for a fire, because the wind usually blew from the other direction and the fire was protected by the hill itself.

"I think we'll have to give up Willow House now and go to live in the caves," said Jack one morning, after a very wild night. The wind had slashed at the trees all night long, the rain had poured down, and, to the children's dismay, a little rivulet of rain had actually come into Willow House from the back and had soaked the heather bed Peggy and Nora were lying on. The girls had had to get up in the middle of the night and go to the front room, where the boys slept. This was a squash, but the front room was dry.

The leaves were falling from the trees. Every tree and

bush had flamed out into yellow, crimson, pink, brown or orange. The island was a lovely sight to see when the sun came out for an hour or two, for then its rays lighted up all the brilliant leaves, and they shone like jewels. But now the leaves were falling.

Leaves were dropping down in Willow House from the branches that made the roof. It was funny to lie in bed at night and feel a leaf drop lightly on to your cheek. Willow House looked different now that there were so few green or yellow leaves growing on the roof and walls. It was bare and brown.

Nora caught a cold and began to sneeze. Jack said they must move to the caves at once, or they would all get cold—and if they were ill, what would happen? There was no doctor to make them well!

They dosed Nora with hot milk and wrapped her up in the two new blankets Jack had bought in the village one week when he had been marketing. They set her at the back of the outer cave, with a candle beside her, for it was dim in that corner. She soon got better, and was able to help the others when they made their plans for living in the cave.

"We'll make this outer cave our living-room and bedroom!" Jack said, "and the inner one shall be our storeroom. We'll always have a fire burning at the entrance, and that will warm us and cook our food. This is going to be rather fun! We shall be cave-people this winter!"

Days In The Cave

That week the children made all their plans for passing the winter in the cave. Already all their stores were safely placed in the inner cave. It was just a question of getting the outer cave comforable and home-like. Peggy was wonderful at this sort of thing.

"You two boys must make a few shelves to put round the cave," she said. "You can weave them out of stout twigs, and put them up somehow. We will keep our books and games there, and any odd things we want. You must somehow manage to hang the lantern from the middle of the roof. Then, in the corner over here we will have our beds of heather and bracken. You boys can bring that in, too. If it's wet we'll dry it by the fire. The bracken is getting old and dry now—it should make a fine bed."

Peggy swept up the floor of the cave with a brush made of heather twigs, and then she and Nora threw fine sand on it which they had brought from the beach. It looked very nice. The boys brought in the heather and bracken for the beds. Peggy arranged them comfortably, and then threw a blanket over each bed but one. There were only three blankets—two new ones and one old one—so it looked as if someone must go without.

"What's the fourth bed going to have for a blanket?" asked Jack.

And then Peggy brought out a great surprise! It was a fur rug, made of rabbit skins that she had carefully cleaned, dried, and sewn together! How the others stared!

"But how lovely, Peggy!" said Jack. "It's a most

beautiful fur rug, and will be as warm as toast. We'll take it in turns to have it on at night."

"Yes, that's what I thought," said Peggy, pleased to find the others admired her rabbit rug so much. "It was very hard to sew the skins together, but I did it at last. I thought it would be a nice surprise for when the cold weather came!"

Soon the cave began to look very homely indeed. The shelves were weighed down with the books and games. The lantern swung in the middle, and they all knocked their heads against it before they became used to it there! The beds lay neatly in the corners at the back, covered with blankets and the rabbit rug. In another corner stood the household things that Peggy was always using—the kettle, the saucepans, and so on.

And then Jack brought out a surprise—a nice little table he had made by himself! He had found the old plank the children had brought with them months ago when they first came to the island, and had managed, by means of a saw he had bought during his marketing, to make a good little table for Peggy!

It was a bit wobbly. The four legs were made of tree branches, the straightest Jack could find, but it was difficult to get them just right. He had sawn the plank into pieces, and nailed them together to make a square top to the table, and this was very good. Peggy was delighted!

"Now we can have meals on the table!" she cried. "Oh, that will be nice! And I can do my mending on the table, too—it will be much easier than crouching on the floor!"

"But what about chairs?" asked Nora. "You can't sit up to the table without chairs!"

"I'm making stools," said Jack—and so he was! He had found an old tree broken in two by the wind on the other side of the hill. With his saw he was sawing up the trunk, and each piece he sawed out was like a solid stool—just a piece of tree-trunk, but nice and smooth to sit on!

The days passed very happily as they made the cave into a home. It was fun to sit on their little stools beside Jack's table and eat their meals properly there. It was fun to watch the fire burning at the entrance of the cave, getting brighter and brighter as night came on. It was lovely to lie on a soft heathery bed at the back of the cave, covered by a warm blanket or rabbit rug, and watch the fire gradually die down to a few glowing embers.

It was very cosy in the cave when the wind howled round the hillside. The light from the lantern shone down, and sometimes Peggy had an extra candle beside her when she sewed. The boys scraped at a bit of wood, carving something, or played a game with Nora. Sometimes they read out loud. The fire burnt brightly and lighted up the cave brilliantly every now and again when extra big flames shot up. It was great fun.

There was always plenty to do. Daisy still had to be milked each morning and evening. She seemed quite happy living in the grassy field, and the boys had built her a sort of shelter where she went at night. There were the hens to feed and look after. They were in a yard near the cave now. They were not laying so many eggs, but the children had plenty of stores and did not worry about eggs.

There was the usual cooking, washing, and clearing-up to do. There was water to be got from the spring. There was firewood to hunt for and pile up. Peggy liked to find pine-cones because they burnt up beautifully and made such a nice smell.

November passed by. Sometimes there were lovely fine days when the children could sit out on the hillside and bask in the sun. Sometimes there were wind-swept days when the rain pelted down and the clouds raced across the sky, black and ragged. Then the lake was tossed into white-topped waves.

142

Mike and Jack had got the boat up again and mended it. They had pulled it up the beach as far as they could to be out of reach of the waves.

When December came, the children began to think of Christmas. It would be strange to have Christmas on the island!

"We'll have to decorate the cave with holly," said Jack. "There are two holly-trees on the island, and one has red berries on. But there is no mistletoe."

"Christmas will be funny with only just ourselves," said Peggy. "I don't know if I will like it. I like hearing carols sung, and seeing the shops all full of lovely things, and looking forward to Christmas stockings and crackers, and things like that."

"Before our Daddy and Mummy flew off in their aeroplane and got lost, we used to have Christmas with them," Nora said to Jack. "It was lovely then. I remember it all!"

"I wish Daddy and Mummy hadn't gone away and got lost for ever," said Mike. "I did love them—they were so jolly and happy."

Jack listened as the three children told him all they had done at Christmas time when their father and mother had been with them. He had always lived with his old grandfather, who had never bothered about Christmas. To Jack this all seemed wonderful. How Mike, and Nora, and Peggy must miss all the happy and lovely things they used to do when they had their father and mother with them!

The boy listened and made up his mind about something. He would take the boat and row off to the end of the lake just before Christmas. He still had some money —and with that he would buy crackers, a doll for Nora, a new work-box for Peggy, something for Mike, and some oranges and sweets! They should have a fine Christmas!

He said nothing to the others about it. He knew that they would be terribly afraid that he might be caught again. But he did not mean to go to the same village as before. He meant to walk to the one five miles away, where he would not be known, and buy what he wanted there. He was sure he would be safe, for he meant to be very careful indeed!

December crept on. The days were dull and dreary. Jack planned to go off in the boat one morning. He would tell the others he was just going for a row to get himself warm. He would not tell them about his great surprise for them!

A good day came when the pale wintry sun shone down, and the sky was a watery blue. Peggy was busy clearing up after breakfast. Mike meant to rebuild Daisy's shelter, which had been rather blown about by the wind. Nora was going to look for pine-cones.

"What are *you* going to do, Jack?" asked Peggy.

"Oh," said Jack, "I think I'll take the old boat out and go for a row to get myself warm. I haven't rowed for ages!"

"I'll come with you, Jack," said Nora.

But Jack didn't want anyone with him! "No, Nora," he said, "you go out and look for cones. I shall be gone a good while. Peggy, could you let me have some food to take with me?"

"Food!" said Peggy in amazement. "However long are you going for, Jack?"

"Oh, just a few hours," said Jack. "Some exercise will do me good. I'll take my fishing-line, too."

"Well, put on your overcoat, then," said Peggy; "you'll be cold out on the windy lake."

She put some rolls and a hard-boiled egg into a basket, together with a bottle of milk. Jack said goodbye and set off down the hillside. Nora came with him, half sulky at not being allowed to go in the boat.

"You might let me come, Jack," she said.

"You can't come today, Nora," said Jack. "You will know why when I come back!"

He pushed off and rowed out on to the lake, which was not very rough that day. He rowed hard, and Nora soon left the beach and went to seek for cones. She thought she would try and see where Jack was fishing, after a time, and went to the top of the hill—but, try as she would, she could see no sign of the boat. She thought that very strange.

Hours went by, and Jack did not come back. The others waited for him, wondering why he had gone off alone and why he had not come back.

"Do you think he's gone to the village again to get anything?" asked Peggy at last. "Nora says she couldn't see his boat anywhere on the lake when she looked—and if he was fishing anywhere near, we should easily see him!"

"Oh, dear!" said Mike, worried. "If he goes to that village he'll be caught again!"

But Jack hadn't been caught. Something else had happened—something very extraordinary!

Jack Has A Great Surprise

We must go back to Jack and find out what had been happening to him. He had been such a long time away from the island—far longer than he would have been if he had just gone shopping. What could have kept him?

Well, he had got safely in the boat to the far end of the lake, and had tied the boat up to a tree. Then he had slipped through the wood, and taken the road that led to the distant village, five miles away. It would take him nearly an hour and a half to get there, but what fun it would be to do a bit of shopping again!

The boy padded along the wintry road. It was muddy and cold, but he was as warm as toast. He jingled his money in his pocket and wondered if he could buy all he wanted to. He did badly want to get a doll for Nora, for he knew how much she would love it!

He carried the food Peggy had given him, and, when he got near the village, he sat up on a gate and ate it. Then off he went again. He did not think anyone would know him to be one of the runaways, for surely people had forgotten all about them by now! It was half a year since they had first run off to the island! But he was keeping a sharp look out in case he saw anyone looking at him too closely!

He went into the village. It was a big, straggling one, with a small High Street running down the middle. There were about six shops there. Jack went to look at them. He left the toy and sweet shop till last. He looked at the turkeys in the butcher's shop, some with red ribbons on.

He looked into the draper's shop and admired the gay streamers that floated all about it to decorate it for Christmas. It was fun to see shops again.

And then he came to the toy shop. It was lovely! Dolls stood in the window with their arms stretched out as if they were asking people to buy them. A railway train ran on lines. A little Father Christmas stood in the middle, carrying a sack. Boxes of chocolate, tins of toffee, and big bottles of brightly-coloured sweets were in the shop, too.

Jack stood gazing, wondering which doll to buy for Nora. He had already seen a nice little work-basket for Peggy, and had spied a book for Mike about boats. There was a box of red crackers at the back of the window, too, which he thought would do well for Nora. It would be such fun to pull them on Christmas Day in the cave, and wear paper hats there!

Jack went into the shop. It had two or three other people there, for the shop was a post office, too, and people were sending off Christmas parcels. The shop assistant was weighing them—and it was a long business. Jack waited patiently, looking round at all the toys.

The people in the shop were talking to one another. At first Jack did not listen—and then he heard something that made him prick up his ears.

This is what he heard:

"Yes, it's a great pity those children were never found," said one woman. "Their father and mother are quite ill with grief, I've heard."

"Poor things," said the second woman. "It's bad enough to come down in an aeroplane on a desert island, and not be found for two years—and then to come back safe to see your children—and learn that they've disappeared!"

Jack's eyes nearly dropped out of his head. What did this mean? Could it possibly—possibly—mean that Mike's father and mother had turned up again. Forgetting all about being careful, Jack caught hold of the arm of the first woman.

"Please" he said, "please tell me something. Were the three children you are talking about called Mike, Peggy and Nora—and is it *their* father and mother that have come back?"

The woman in the shop stared at the excited boy in astonishment. "Yes," said the first woman. "Those were the children's names. They disappeared in June with another boy, called Jack, and have never been found. And in August the missing father and mother were found far away on a Pacific Island, and brought back safely here. Their aeroplane had come down and smashed, and they had been living there until a ship picked them up."

"But their children had gone," said the shop assistant joining in, "and it almost broke their hearts, for they had been worrying about them for months and longing to see them."

"What do *you* know about all this?" suddenly said one of the women. "You're not one of the children, are you?"

"Never mind about that," said Jack impatiently. "Just tell me one thing—where are the father and mother?"

"They are not far away," said the shop assistant. "They are staying at a hotel in the next town, hoping that the children will still be heard of."

"What hotel?" said Jack eagerly.

"The Swan Hotel," said the shop assistant, and then the women stared in amazement as Jack tore out of the shop at top speed, his eyes shining, and a look of the greatest excitement on his brown face!

He ran to the bus-stop. He knew that buses went to the town, and he had only one thought in mind—to get to the Swan Hotel and tell Mike's father and mother that their children were safe! Never in his life had Jack been

148

so excited. To think that things would all come right like this, and he, Jack, was the one to tell the father and mother!

He jumped into the bus, and could not keep still. He leapt out of it when it rumbled into the town and ran off to the Swan Hotel. He rushed into the hall and caught hold of the hall-porter there.

"Where are Captain and Mrs. Arnold?" he cried. Mike had often told him that his father was a captain, and he knew the children's surname was Arnold—so he knew quite well whom to ask for.

"Here, here, not so fast, young man," said the porter, not quite liking the look of the boy in the old overcoat, and worn-out shoes. "What do you want the Captain for?"

"Oh, tell me, please, where are they?" begged Jack—at that moment a man's voice said:

"Who's this asking for me? What do you want, boy?"

Jack swung round. He saw a tall, brown-faced man looking down at him, and he liked him at once, because he was so like Mike to look at.

"Captain Arnold! I know where Mike and Peggy and Nora are!" he cried.

The Captain stared as if he had not heard aright. Then he took Jack's arm and pulled him upstairs into a room where a lady sat, writing a letter. Jack could see she was the children's mother, for she had a look of Peggy and Nora about her. She looked kind and strong and wise, and Jack wished very much that she was his mother, too.

"This boy says he knows where the children are, Mary," said the Captain.

What excitement there was then! Jack poured out his story and the two grown-ups listened without saying a word. When he had finished, the Captain shook hands with Jack, and his wife gave him a hug.

"You're a fine friend for our children to have!" said the

Captain, his face shining with excitement. "And you really mean to say that you have all been living together on that little island and nobody has found you?"

"Yes," said Jack, "and oh, sir, is it true that you and Mrs. Arnold have been living on an island, too, till a ship picked you up?"

"Quite true," said Captain Arnold, with a laugh. "Our plane came down and smashed—and there we were, lost on an island in the Pacific Ocean! Little did we know that our children were going to live alone on an island, too! This sort of thing must be in the family!"

"John, we must go at once to them," said Mrs. Arnold, who was almost crying with joy. "Quickly, this very minute. I can't wait!"

"We'd better get a proper boat," said Jack. "Our old boat is a leaky old thing now."

It wasn't long before a car was brought round to the door, and Jack, Captain and Mrs. Arnold were motoring to the lakeside. They hired a big boat from a fisherman there, and set off to the secret island. Jack wondered and wondered what the children would say!

Meanwhile the three children were getting more and more worried! It was past tea-time now, and getting dark. Where *could* Jack be?

"I can hear the splash of oars!" cried Peggy at last. They ran down to the beach, and saw the outline of the boat in the twilight coming near to the island. And then Mike saw that it was a bigger boat than their own—and there were three people in it, instead of one!

"That means Jack's been caught—and these people have been sent to get us!" he thought, and his heart sank. But then, to his amazement, he heard Jack's clear voice ringing out over the darkening water.

"Mike! Peggy! Nora! It's all right! I've brought a Christmas present for you!"

The three children stared. Whatever could Jack mean? But when the boat landed, and Captain and Mrs. Arnold sprang out, they soon knew!

"Mummy! Oh, Mummy! And Daddy!" shrieked the children, and flung themselves at their father and mother. You couldn't tell which were children and which were grown-ups, because they were all so mixed up. Only Jack was alone. He stood apart, looking at them—but not for long. Nora stretched out her hand and pulled him into the crowd of excited, happy people.

"You belong, too, Jack," she said.

Everyone seemed to be laughing and crying at the same time. But at last it was so dark that no one could see anyone else. Jack lighted the lantern that Mike had brought down to the beach, and led the way to the cave. He badly wanted Captain and Mrs. Arnold to see how lovely it was.

They all crowded inside. There was a bight fire crackling just outside, and the cave was warm and cosy. Jack hung the lantern up and placed two wooden stools for the children's parents. Peggy flew to heat some milk, and put out rolls of bread and some potted meat she had been saving up for Christmas. She did so want her mother to see how nicely she could do things, even though they all lived in a cave!

"What a lovely home!" said Mrs. Arnold, as she looked round and saw the shelves, the stools, the table, the beds, and everything. The cave was very neat and tidy, and looked so cosy and friendly. How they all talked! How they jumped up and down and laughed and told first this thing and then the other! Only one thing made Captain and Mrs. Arnold angry—and that was the tale of how unkind Aunt Harriet and Uncle Henry had been.

"They shall be punished," said Captain Arnold, and that was all he said about them.

Daisy chose to moo loudly that night, and Captain Arnold laughed till the tears came into his eyes when he heard about the night that poor Daisy had had to swim behind the boat to the island! And when he heard how she had mooed and frightened away the people who had come to look for them, he laughed still more!

"Someone will have to write a book about your adventures," he said. "I never in my life heard anything like them. *We* didn't have such thrilling adventures on *our* island! We just lived with the native people there till a boat picked us up! Very dull indeed!"

Jack disappeared at that moment, and when he came back he carried a great load of heather. He flung it down in a corner.

"You'll stay with us tonight, won't you, Captain?" he said. "We'd love to have you. Please do."

"Of course!" said Captain Arnold. And Mrs. Arnold nodded her dark head. "We will all be together in the cave," she said. "Then we shall share a bit of your secret island, children, and know what it is like."

So that night the children had visitors! They all fell asleep on their heather beds at last, happy, excited, and very tired. What fun to wake up tomorrow with their own father and mother beside them!

The End Of The Adventure

Mike awoke first in the morning. He sat up and remembered everything. There were his father and mother, fast asleep on their heathery bed in the corner of the cave! It was true then—he hadn't dreamt it all! They were alive and well, and had got their children again—everything was lovely.

Mike crept out to light the fire. He could not possibly go to sleep again. The day was just creeping in at the cave entrance. The sky was a very pale blue, and the sun was trying to break through a thin mist in the east. It was going to be fine!

When the fire was crackling merrily everyone woke up. Nora flung herself on her mother, for she could not believe she really had a mother again, and had to keep hugging her and touching her. Soon the cave was filled with talk and laughter.

Peggy and Nora got the breakfast. Mike showed his father the inner cave and their stores. Jack flew off to milk Daisy. The hens clucked outside, and Nora fetched in four brown eggs.

Fish from Jack's line, eggs, rolls, the rest of the potted meat, and a tin of peaches made a fine breakfast, washed down with hot tea. The fire died down and the sunshine came in at the cave entrance. Everyone went outside to see what sort of a day it was.

The lake sparkled blue below. The bare trees swung gently in the breeze. Nora told her mother all about the wild raspberries and strawberries and nuts, and Peggy chattered about the seeds they had planted, and the baskets they could make.

And then Captain Arnold said, "Well, I think it's about time we were going."

The children looked up at him. "Going! What do you mean, Daddy? Leave our island?"

"My dears," said Captain Arnold, "you can't live here always—besides, there is no need for you to, now. You are not runaways any more. You are our own children that we love, and we must have you with us."

"Yes," said Mrs. Arnold. "We must all go back to a proper home, and you must go to school, my dears. You have been very brave and very clever—and very happy, too—and now you can have a lovely home with us, and we will all be happy together."

"But what about Jack?" asked Nora, at once.

"Jack is ours, too," said Mrs. Arnold. "I am sure his grandfather will be glad for us to have him for always. He shall have me for his mother, and your father shall be his, too! We will all be one big family!"

Jack wanted to say such a lot but he couldn't say a single word. It was very strange. His face just went red with joy, and he held Nora's hand so tightly that he hurt her without meaning to. He was just about the happiest boy in the world at that moment.

"Mummy, I shall so hate leaving our dear, dear island," said Nora. "And Willow House, too—and our cosy cave and the bubbling spring—and everything."

"I think I might be able to buy the island for you," said Daddy. "Then, in the holidays you can always come here and run wild and live by yourselves if you want to. It shall be your very own."

"Oh, Daddy!" shouted the children, in delight. "We shan't mind going to school and being proper and living in a house if we've got the island to go back to in the holidays! Oh, what fun it will be!"

"But I think you must leave it now and come back home

for Christmas," said Mrs. Arnold. "We have our own old home to go back to—you remember it, don't you? Don't you think it would be nice to have Christmas there—and a Christmas pudding—and crackers—and stockings full of presents?"

"Yes, yes, yes!" shouted all the children.

"It's just what I longed for!" said Nora.

"I was going to buy you some red crackers yesterday, Nora," said Jack, "but I heard the great news before I had bought anything!"

"You shall all have red crackers!" said Captain Arnold, with a laugh. "Now, what about getting off in the boat?"

"Just give us time to say good-bye to everything," said Peggy. "Mummy, come down and see Willow House. We made it ourselves and it's so pretty in the summer, because you see, it's a *live* house, and grows leaves all the time!"

In an hour's time everyone was ready to leave. The hens were bundled once more into a sack and were most annoyed about it. Daisy was left, and Captain Arnold said he would send a fisherman over for her. It was too cold for her to swim behind the boat. Most of the children's stores were left, too. They would be able to use them when they next went to the island.

Peggy took the rabbit-rug she had made. That was too precious to leave. They brought the books too, because they had got fond of those. They had stored everything carefully in the inner cave, and thrown sacks over them in case of damp. They couldn't help feeling a bit sad to leave, although they knew they were going to their own happy home again.

At last everyone was in the boat. Captain Arnold pushed off and the sound of oars came to Daisy's ears as she stood pulling at the thin winter grass. She stood watching the boat as it bobbed away on the waves.

"Good-bye, dear secret island," said Nora.

"Good-bye, good-bye!" said the others. "We'll come back again! Good-bye, Daisy, good-bye, everything!"

"And now let's talk about all we're going to do at Christmas," said Mrs. Arnold, cheerfully, for she saw that the children were sad at leaving their beloved little island.

It was not long before the four children and their father and mother (for Jack counted them as his parents too, now) were settled happily in their own home. There was such a lot of excitement at first, for the children had to have new dresses, new suits, new underclothes, new socks, new shoes! Mrs. Arnold said that although Peggy had really done her best to keep them tidy, they were quite dropping to pieces!

So off they went shopping, and came back feeling as grand as kings and queens, all dressed up in their new things! Peggy looked fine in a blue coat and skirt with a little blue hat. Nora wore red, and the two boys had suits and overcoats of dark blue.

Jack felt queer in his. It was the first time in his life he had ever had anything new of his own to wear, for he had always gone about in somebody's old things before! He felt very grand indeed.

The children looked at one another and burst out laughing.

"How different we look now!" said Mike. "Think of our dirty old rags on the island! But it's good to be really properly dressed again—and the girls *do* look nice!"

It was strange at first to sleep in a proper bed again. The girls slept in a pretty room and had a little white bed each. The boys slept in the next room, and had two brown beds. At first they all wondered where they were when they awoke in the morning, but after a few days they got used to it.

Christmas drew near. They all went out to buy presents

for one another. It was most exciting. They went to London and marvelled at the great shops there. They watched all kinds of ships and boats sailing along in a big tank. They saw model trains tearing round and round a little countryside, going through tunnels, stopping at stations, just like a real train. It was all very exciting after living such a peaceful life on the island.

Christmas was lovely. They hung up their socks at the end of their beds—and in the morning what fun they had finding the things packed tightly in the long stockings! Tiny dolls in the girls', oranges, sweets, nuts, needle-books and balls—and in the boys' were all kinds of things, too. Bigger presents were at the foot of the bed, and *how* excited all the children were unpacking them!

"This is better than Christmas in the cave!" said Nora, unpacking a great big smiling doll with curly golden hair. "Oh, Jack! Did you really buy this for me? Oh, how lovely, lovely, lovely!"

Soon the bedrooms were full of dolls, books, trains, balls, aeroplanes and motor-cars! It was the loveliest Christmas morning the children had ever had—and certainly Jack had never in his life known one like it! He just simply couldn't believe his luck.

"You deserve it all, Jack," said Nora. "You were a good friend to us when we were unhappy—and now you can share with us when we are happy."

There was a Christmas-tree after tea, with more presents—and as for the crackers, you should have seen them! Red ones and yellow ones, blue ones and green ones! Soon everyone was wearing a paper hat, and how the children laughed when Captain Arnold pulled a cracker and got a tiny aeroplane out of it!

"Well, you can't fly away in *that*, Daddy," cried Peggy.

"You won't ever fly away again, Daddy, will you?" said Nora, suddenly frightened in case her father and mother

157

should fly off again and be lost, so that the four children would be alone once more.

"No, never again," said her father. "Mummy and I have made such a lot of money out of our flying now, that we can afford to stay at home and look after you. We shall never leave you again!"

It was four happy children who went to bed that night. The boys left the door open between their room and the girls', so that they might all talk to one another till they fell asleep. They could not get out of this habit, for they had always been able to talk to one another in bed on the island.

"It's been a lovely day," said Peggy sleepily. "But I do just wish something now."

"What?" asked Mike.

"I do just wish we could all be back in our cosy cave on our secret island for five minutes," said Peggy.

"So do I," said everyone, and they lay silent, thinking of the happy days and nights on the island.

"I shall never, never forget our island," said Nora. "It's the loveliest place in the world, I think. I hope it isn't feeling lonely without us! Good-night, secret island! Wait for us till we come again!"

"Good-night, secret island!" said the others. And then they slept, and dreamt of their island—of the summer days when they would go there once more, and live merrily and happily alone, in the hot sunshine—of winter days in the cosy cave—of cooking over a camp fire—and sleeping soundly on heathery beds. Dear secret island, only wait, and you shall have the children with you once again!

THE END

The Secret of
Killimooin

The Secret of Killimooin was first published in the UK
by Basil Blackwell Ltd in 1943

First published as a single volume by Armada in 1965

Copyright © Enid Blyton 1943

A Fine Surprise

Three excited boys stood on a station platform, waiting for a train to come in.

"The train's late," said Mike, impatiently. "Five minutes late already."

"I'm going to tell the girls the news," said Jack.

"*I'm* going to tell them!" said Prince Paul, his big dark eyes glowing. "It's *my* news, not yours."

"All right, all right," said Mike. "You tell Nora and Peggy then, but don't be too long about it or I shall simply have to burst in!"

The three boys were waiting for Nora and Peggy to come back from their boarding-school for the summer holidays. Mike, Jack and Prince Paul all went to the same boys' boarding-school, and they had broken up the day before. Mike was the twin brother of Nora, and Peggy was his other sister, a year older than Mike and Nora.

Jack was their adopted brother. He had no father or mother of his own, so Captain and Mrs Arnold, the children's father and mother, had taken him into their family, and treated him like another son. He went to boarding-school with Mike, and was very happy.

Prince Paul went to the same school too. He was a great friend of theirs, for a year or two back the children had rescued him when he was kidnapped. His father was the King of Baronia, and the little prince spent his term-time at an English boarding-school, and his holidays in his own distant land of Baronia. He was the youngest of the five.

"Here comes the train, hurrah!" yelled Mike, as he heard the sound of the train in the distance.

"The girls will be sure to be looking out of the window," said Jack.

The train came nearer and nearer, and the engine chuffed more and more loudly. It ran alongside the platform, slowed down and stopped. Doors swung open.

Prince Paul gave a yell. "There they are! Look! In the middle of the train!"

Sure enough, there were the laughing faces of Peggy and Nora, leaning out of the window. Then their door swung open and out leapt the two girls. Nora was dark and curly-haired like Mike. Peggy's golden hair shone in the sun. She had grown taller, but she was still the same old Peggy.

"Peggy! Nora! Welcome back!" yelled Mike. He hugged his twin-sister, and gave Peggy a squeeze too. All five children were delighted to be together again. They had had such adventures, they had shared so many difficulties, dangers and excitements. It was good to be together once more, and say, "Do you remember this, do you remember that?"

Prince Paul was always a little shy at first when he met the two girls. He held out his hand politely to shake hands, but Peggy gave a squeal and put her arms round him.

"Paul! Don't be such an idiot! Give me a hug!"

"Paul's got some news," said Mike, suddenly remembering. "Buck up and tell it, Paul."

"What is it?" asked Nora.

"I've got an invitation for you all," said the little prince. "Will you come to my land of Baronia with me for the holidays?"

There was a shriek of delight from the two girls.

"PAUL! Go to Baronia with you! Oh, I say!"

"Oh! What a marvellous surprise!"

Paul beamed. "Yes, it *is* a fine surprise, isn't it?" he said. "I thought you'd be pleased. Mike and Jack are thrilled too."

"It will be a real adventure to go to Baronia," said Mike. "A country hidden in the heart of mountains – with a few beautiful towns, hundreds of hidden villages, great forests – golly, it will be grand."

"Oh, Paul, how decent of your father to ask us!" said Nora, putting her arm through the little prince's. "How long will it take us to get there?"

"We shall fly in my aeroplane," said Paul. "Ranni and Pilescu, my two men, will fetch us tomorrow."

"This is just too good to be true!" said Nora, dancing round in joy. She bumped into a porter wheeling a barrow. "Oh – Sorry, I didn't see you. I say, Mike, we'd better get our luggage. Can you see a porter with an empty barrow?"

All the porters had been engaged, so the five children had to wait. They didn't mind. They didn't mind anything! It was so marvellous to be going off to Paul's country the next day.

"We thought we were going to the seaside with Daddy and Mummy," said Nora.

"So we were," said Jack. "But when Paul's father cabled yesterday, saying he was sending the aeroplane to fetch Paul, he said we were all to come too, if we were allowed to."

"And you know how Daddy and Mummy like us to travel and see all we can!" said Mike. "They were just as pleased about it as we were – though they were sorry not to have us for the holidays, of course."

"We are not to take many clothes," said Jack. "Paul says we can dress up in Baronian things – they are much more exciting than ours! I shall feel I'm wearing fancy dress all the time!"

The girls sighed with delight. They imagined themselves dressed in pretty, swinging skirts and bright bodices – lovely! They would be real Baronians.

"Look here, we really *must* get a porter and stop talking," said Nora. "The platform is almost empty. Hi, porter!"

A porter came up, wheeling an empty barrow. He lifted

the girls' two trunks on to it and wheeled them down to the barrier. He got a taxi for the children and they all crowded into it. They were to go to their parents' flat for the night.

It was a very happy family party that sat down to a big tea at the flat. Captain and Mrs Arnold smiled round at the five excited faces. To come home for holidays was thrilling enough – but to come home and be told they were all off to Baronia the next day was almost too exciting for words!

Usually the children poured out all the doings of the term – how well they had played tennis, how exciting cricket had been, how fine the new swimming-pool was, and how awful the exams were. But today not a word was said about the term that had just passed. No – it was all Baronia, Baronia, Baronia! Paul was delighted to see their excitement, for he was very proud of his country.

"Of course, it is not a very big country," he said, "but it is a beautiful one, and a very wild one. Ah, our grand mountains, our great forests, our beautiful villages! The stern rough men, the laughing women, the good food!"

"You sound like a poet, Paul," said Peggy. "Go on!"

"No," said the little prince, going red. "You will laugh at me. You English people are strange. You love your country but you hardly ever praise her. Now I could tell you of Baronia's beauties for an hour. And not only beauties. I could tell you of wild robbers . . ."

"Ooooh," said Peggy, thrilled.

"And of fierce animals in the mountains," said Paul.

"We'll hunt them!" Mike chimed in.

"And of hidden ways in the hills, deep forests where no foot has ever trodden, and . . ."

"Oh, let's go this very minute!" said Nora. "I can't wait! We might have adventures there – thrilling ones, like those we've had before."

The little prince shook his head. "No," he said. "We shall have no exciting adventures in Baronia. We shall live in my father's palace, and wherever we go there will be guards with us. You see, since that time I was kidnapped, I am never allowed to go about alone in Baronia."

The other children looked disappointed. "Well, it sounds grand to have a bodyguard, I must say, but it does cramp our style a bit," said Mike. "Are we allowed to climb trees and things like that?"

"Well, I have never been allowed to in my own country," said Paul. "But, you see, I am a prince there, and I have to behave always with much dignity. I behave differently here."

"I should just think you do!" said Mike, staring at him. "Who waded through the duck-pond to get his ball, and came out covered with mud?"

"And who tore his coat to rags squeezing through a hawthorn hedge, trying to get away from an angry cow?" asked Jack.

"I did," said Paul. "But then, here, I am like you. I learn to behave differently. When you go to Baronia you, too, will have different manners. You must kiss my mother's hand, for instance."

Mike and Jack looked at him in alarm. "I say! I'm not much good at that sort of thing!" said Jack.

"And you must learn to bow – like this," said the little prince, thoroughly enjoying himself. He bowed politely from his waist downwards, stood up and brought his heels together with a smart little click. The girls giggled.

"It will be fun to see Mike and Jack doing things like that," said Nora. "You'd better start practising now, Mike. Come on – bow to me. And, Jack, you kiss my hand!"

The boys scowled. "Don't be an idiot," said Mike, gruffly. "If I've got to do it, I will do it – but not to you or Peggy."

"I don't expect it will be as bad as Paul makes out," said his mother, smiling. "He is just pulling your leg. Look at him grinning!"

167

"You can behave how you like," said Paul, with a chuckle. "But don't be surprised at Baronian manners. They are much better than yours!"

"Have you all finished tea?" asked Captain Arnold. "I can't imagine that any of you could possibly eat any more, but I may be wrong."

"I'll just have one more piece of cake," said Mike. "We don't get chocolate cake like this at school!"

"You've had four pieces already," said his mother. "I am glad I don't have to feed you all the year round! There you are – eat it up."

There was very little packing to be done that evening – only night-clothes and tooth-brushes, flannels and things like that. All the children were looking forward to wearing the colourful Baronian clothes. They had seen photographs of the Baronian people, and had very much liked the children's clothes. They were all so thrilled that it was very difficult to settle down and do anything. They talked to Captain and Mrs Arnold, played a game or two and then went off to bed.

Not one of them could go to sleep. They lay in their different bedrooms, calling to one another until Mrs Arnold came up and spoke sternly.

"One more shout – and you don't go to Baronia!" After that there was silence, and the five children lay quietly in their beds, thinking of the exciting day tomorrow was going to be.

Off To Baronia

It was wonderful to wake up the next morning and remember everything. Jack sat up and gave a yell to wake the others. It was not long before everyone was dressed and down to breakfast. They were to go to the airport to meet Ranni and Pilescu, the big Baronians, at ten o'clock. All the things they were taking with them went into one small bag.

"Mummy, I'm sorry I won't see much of you these hols." said Peggy.

"Well, Daddy and I may fly over to Baronia to fetch you back," said her mother. "We could come a week or two before it's time for you to return to school, so we should see quite a bit of you!"

"Oh – that would be lovely!" said Nora and Peggy together, and the boys beamed in delight. "Will you come in the White Swallow?"

The White Swallow was the name given to Captain Arnold's famous aeroplane. In it he and Mrs Arnold had flown many thousands of miles, for they were both excellent pilots. They had had many adventures, and this was partly why they liked their children to go off on their own and have their own adventures too.

"It doesn't do to coddle children too much and shelter them," said Captain Arnold many a time to his wife. "We don't want children like that – we want boys and girls of spirit and courage, who can stand on their feet and are not afraid of what may happen to them. We want them to grow up adventurous and strong, of some real use in the world! So we must not say no when a chance comes along to help them to be plucky and independent!"

"If we can grow up like you and Mummy, we shall be all

right!" said Peggy. "You tried to fly all the way to Australia by yourselves in that tiny plane – and you've set up ever so many flying records. We ought to be adventurous children!"

"I think you are," said her mother, with a laugh. "You've certainly had some marvellous adventures already – more than most children have all their lives long!"

When the car drew up at the door to take the children to the airport, they all clattered down the steps at once. "It's a good thing it's a big car!" said Mike. "Seven of us is quite a crowd!"

Everyone got in. The car set off at a good speed, and soon came to the big airport. It swept in through the gates. Mike, who was looking out of the window, gave a loud shout.

"There's your aeroplane, Paul! I can see it. It's the smartest one on the air-field."

"And the loveliest," said Nora, looking in delight at the beautiful plane towards which they were racing. It was bright blue with silver edges, and it shone brilliantly in the sun. The car stopped a little way from it. Everyone got out. Paul gave a yell.

"There's Pilescu! And Ranni! Look, over there, behind the plane!"

The two big Baronians had heard the engine of the car and they had come to see if it was the children arriving. Pilescu gave a deep-throated shout.

"Paul! My little lord!"

Paul raced over the grass to Pilescu. The big red-bearded man bowed low and then lifted the boy up in his strong arms.

"Pilescu! How are you? It's grand to see you again," said Paul, in the Baronian language that always sounded so strange to the other children.

Pilescu was devoted to the little prince. He had held him in his arms when he was only a few minutes old, and had vowed to be his man as long as he lived. His arms pressed so tightly round the small boy that Paul gasped for breath.

"Pilescu! I can't breathe! Let me down," he squealed. Pilescue grinned and set him down. Paul turned to Ranni, who bowed low and then gave him a hug like a bear, almost as tight as Pilescu's.

"Ranni! Have you got any of the chocolate I like so much?" asked Paul. Ranni put his hand into his pocket and brought out a big packet of thick chocolate, wrapped in colourful paper. It had a Baronian name on it. Paul liked it better than any other chocolate, and had often shared it with Mike and Jack, when a parcel had arrived for him from Baronia.

Ranni and Pilescu welcomed the other children, beaming in delight to see them all, and Captain and Mrs Arnold too. They had all shared a strange adventure in Africa, hidden in a Secret Mountain, and it was pleasant to be together again.

"Look after all these rascals, Pilescu," said Mrs Arnold, as she said goodbye to the excited children. "You know what monkeys they can be!"

"Madam, they are safe with me and with Ranni," said Pilescu, his red beard flaming in the sun. He bowed from his waist, and took Mrs Arnold's small hand into his big one. He kissed it with much dignity. Mike felt perfectly certain he would never be able to kiss anyone's hand like that.

"Is the plane ready?" asked Captain Arnold, climbing into the cockpit to have a look round. "My word, she is a marvellous machine! I'll say this for Baronia – you have some mighty fine designers of aircraft! You beat us hollow, and we are pretty good at it, too."

All the children were now munching chocolate, talking to Ranni. The big bear-like man was happy to see them all again. Nora and Peggy hung on to him, remembering the thrilling, dangerous days when they had all been inside the Secret Mountain in Africa.

A mechanic came up and did a few last things to the

engine of the great aeroplane. In a minute or two the engines started up and a loud throbbing filled the air.

"Doesn't it sound lovely?" said Mike. "We're really going!"

"Get in, children," said Pilescu. "Say your goodbyes – then we must go."

The children hugged their parents, and Paul bowed, and kissed Mrs Arnold's hand. She laughed and gave him a squeeze. "Goodbye, little Paul. Mind you don't lead my four into trouble! Jack, look after everyone. Mike, take care of your sisters. Nora and Peggy, see that the boys don't get up to mischief!"

"Goodbye, Mummy! Goodbye, Daddy! Write to us. Come and fetch us when the hols are nearly over!"

"Goodbye, Captain Arnold! Goodbye, Mrs Arnold!"

The roar of the aeroplane drowned everything. Pilescu was at the controls. Ranni was beside him. The children were sitting behind in comfortable armchairs. The engine roared more loudly.

"R-r-r-r-r-r-r! R-r-r-r-r-r-r—!" The big machine taxied slowly over the runway – faster – faster – and then, light as a bird, it left the ground, skimmed over the hedges and the trees, and was up in the sky in two minutes.

"Off to Baronia!" said Mike, thrilled.

"Adventuring again," said Jack. "Isn't this fun?"

"The runway looks about one inch long!" said Nora, peering out of the window.

"In half an hour we shall be over the sea," said Paul. "Let's look out for it."

It was grand to be in the big aeroplane once more. All the children were used to flying, and loved the feeling of being high up in the sky. Sometimes clouds rolled below them, looking like vast snow-fields. The sun shone down on the whiteness, and the clouds below the plane became almost too dazzling to look at.

Suddenly there was a break in the clouds, and Mike gave a yell.

"The sea! Look – through the clouds. Hi, Ranni, Ranni, isn't that the sea already?"

Ranni turned and nodded. "We are going very fast," he shouted. "We want to be in Baronia by lunch time."

"I'm so happy," said Nora, her eyes shining. "I've always wanted to go to Baronia, Paul. And now we're really going."

"I am happy too," said Paul. "I like your country, and I like you, too. But I like Baronia better. Maybe you also will like Baronia better."

"Rubbish!" said Mike. "As if any country could be nicer than our own!"

"You will see," said the little prince. "Have some more chocolate?"

The children helped themselves from Paul's packet. "Well, I certainly think your chocolate is better than ours," said Mike, munching contentedly. "Look, there's the sea again. "Doesn't it look smooth and flat?"

It was fun watching for the sea to appear and reappear between the gaps in the clouds. Then the plane flew over land·again. The clouds cleared away, and the children could see the country below, spread out like an enormous, coloured map.

They flew over great towns, wreathed in misty smoke. They flew over stretches of green countryside, where farms and houses looked like toys. They watched the rivers, curling along like blue and silver snakes. They flew over tall mountains, and on some of them was snow.

"Funny to see that in the middle of summer," said Mike. "How's the time getting on? I say – twelve o'clock already! We shall be there in another hour or so."

The plane roared along steadily. Ranni took Pilescu's place after two hours had gone by. He sat and talked to the children for a while, gazing devotedly at the little prince. Mike thought he was like a big dog, worshipping his master! He thought Paul was very lucky to have such friends as Ranni and Pilescu.

A palace that almost seemed to have come straight from a fairy tale!

"Soon we shall see the palace," he said, looking down. "Now we are over the borders of Baronia, Paul! Look, there is the river Jollu! And there is the town of Kikibora."

Paul began to look excited. It was three months since he had been home, and he was longing to see his father and mother, and his little brothers and sisters.

Mike and Jack fell silent. They wondered if Paul's mother would be at the airfield to greet them. Would they have to kiss her hand? "I shall really feel an awful idiot," thought Mike, uncomfortably.

"There is the palace!" cried Paul, suddenly. The children saw a palace standing on a hillside – a palace that almost seemed to have come straight from a fairytale! It was a beautiful place, with shining towers and minarets, and below it was a blue lake in which the reflection of the palace shone.

"Oh! It's beautiful!" said Nora. "Oh, Paul – I feel rather grand. Fancy living in a palace! It may seem ordinary to you – but it's wonderful to me!"

The aeroplane circled round and flew lower. Beside the palace was a great runway, on which the royal planes landed. Ranni's plane swooped low like a bird, its great wheels skimmed the ground, the plane slowed down and came to a halt not far from a little crowd of people.

"Welcome to Baronia!" said Paul, his eyes shining. "Welcome to Baronia!"

The Palace In Baronia

Ranni and Pilescu helped the five children down from the plane. Paul ran straight to a very lovely lady smiling nearby. He bowed low, kissed her hand, and then flung himself on her, chattering quickly in Baronian. It was his mother, the queen. She laughed and cried at the same time, fondling the little prince's hair, and kissing his cheeks.

Paul's father was there, too, a handsome man, straight and tall, dressed in uniform. Paul saluted him smartly and then leapt into his arms. Then he turned to four smaller children standing nearby, his brothers and sisters. Paul kissed the hands of his little sisters and saluted his brothers. Then they kissed, all talking at once.

Soon it was the other children's turn to say how-do-you-do. They had already met Paul's father and liked him, but they had never seen the little prince's mother. Nora and Peggy thought she looked a real queen, lovely enough to be in a fairy tale. She wore the Baronian dress beautifully, and her full red and blue skirt swung gracefully as she walked.

She kissed Nora and Peggy and spoke to them in English. "Welcome, little girls!" she said. "I am so glad to see Paul's friends. You have been so good to him in England. I hope you will be very happy here."

Then it was the boys' turn to be welcomed. Both of them felt hot and bothered about kissing the Queen's hand, but after all, it was quite easy! Mike stepped forward first, and the Queen held out her hand to him. Mike found himself bending down and kissing it quite naturally! Jack followed, and then they saluted Paul's father.

"Come along to the palace now," said the Queen. "You

must be very hungry after your long journey. We have all Paul's favourite dishes – and I hope you will like them too."

The children were glad that Paul's mother could speak English. They had been trying to learn the Baronian language from Paul, but he was not a good teacher. He would go off into peals of laughter at the comical way they pronounced the difficult words of the Baronian language, and it was difficult to get any sense out of him when he was in one of his giggling fits.

The children stared in awe at the palace. They had never seen one like it before, outside of books. It was really magnificent, though not enormous. With the great mountain behind it, and the shining blue lake below, it looked like a dream palace. They walked through a garden full of strange and sweet-smelling flowers and came to a long flight of steps. They climbed these and entered the palace through a wide-open door at which stood six footmen in a line, dressed in the Baronian livery of blue and silver.

After them clattered the little-brothers and sisters of Paul, with their nurses. Peggy and Nora thought the small children were sweet. They were all very like Paul, and had big dark eyes.

"We shan't be bothered much with these babies," said Paul, in rather a lordly voice. "Of course, they wanted to welcome me. But they live in the nurseries. We shall have our own rooms, and Pilescu will wait on us."

This was rather a relief to hear. Although the children liked the look of Paul's father and mother very much, they had felt it might be rather embarrassing to live with a king and queen and have meals with them. It was good to hear that they were to be on their own.

Paul took them to their rooms. The girls had a wonderful bedroom overlooking the lake. It was all blue and silver. The ceiling was painted blue with silver stars shining there. The girls thought it was wonderful. The

177

bedspread was the same beautiful blue, embroidered with shining silver stars.

"I shall never dare to sleep in this bed," said Peggy, in an awed voice. "It's a four-poster bed – like you see in old pictures – and big enough to take six of us, not two! Oh, Nora – isn't this marvellous fun?"

The boys had two bedrooms between them – one big one for Mike and Jack, with separate beds. "About half a mile apart!" said Jack, with a laugh, when he saw the enormous bedroom with its two beds, one each end. Paul had a bedroom to himself, leading out of the other one, even bigger!

"However do you manage to put up with living in a dormitory with twelve other boys, when you have a bedroom like this at home?" said Mike to the little prince. "I say – what a wonderful view!"

Mike's room had two sets of windows. One set looked out over the blue lake and the other looked up the hillside on which the palace was built. It was a grand country.

"It's wild and rugged and rough and beautiful," said Paul. "Not like your country. Yours is quite tame. It is like a tame cat, sitting by the fire. Mine is like a wild tiger roaming the hills."

"He's gone all poetic again!" said Mike, with a laugh. But he knew what Paul meant, all the same. There was something very wild and exciting about Baronia. It looked so beautiful, smiling under the summer sun – but it might not be all it seemed to be on the surface. It was not "tamed" like their own country – it was still wild, and parts of it quite unknown.

The children washed in basins that seemed to be made of silver. They dried their hands on towels embroidered with the Baronian arms. Everything was perfect. It seemed almost a shame to dirty the towels or make the clear water in the basins dirty and soapy!

They went with Paul to have lunch. They were to have it with the King and Queen, although after that they would have meals in their own play-room, a big room near their bedrooms, which Paul had already shown them. The toys there had made them gasp. An electric railway ran down one side of the room, on which Paul's trains could run. A Meccano set, bigger than any the children had ever seen, was in another corner, with a beautiful bridge made from the pieces, left by Paul from the last holidays. Everything a boy could want was there! It would be great fun to explore that play-room!

The lunch was marvellous. The children did not know any of the dishes, but they all tasted equally delicious. If this was Baronian food they could eat plenty! Paul's mother talked to them in English, and Paul's father made one or two jokes. Paul chattered away to his parents, sometimes in Baronian and sometimes in English. He told them all about the things he did at school.

Jack nudged Mike. "You'd think Paul was head-boy to hear him talk!" he said, in a low tone. "We'll tease him about this afterwards!"

It was a happy meal. The children were very hungry, but by the time lunch was nearing an end they could not eat another scrap. Jack looked longingly at a kind of pink ice-cream with what looked like purple cherries in it. But no – he could not even manage another ice.

Ranni and Pilescu did not eat with the others. They stood quietly, one behind the King's chair and one behind Paul's. A line of soldiers, in the blue and silver uniform, stood at the end of the room. The four English children couldn't help feeling rather grand, eating their lunch with a king, a queen, and a prince, with soldiers on guard at the back. Baronia was going to be fun!

Paul took them all over the palace afterwards. It was a magnificent place, strongly built, with every room flooded with the summer sunshine. The nurseries were full of Paul's younger brothers and sisters. There was a baby in a carved cradle too, covered by a blue and silver rug. It opened big dark eyes when the two girls bent over it.

The nurseries were as lovely as the big play-room that belonged to Paul. The children stared in wonder at the amount of toys.

"It's like the biggest toy-shop I've ever seen!" said Jack. "And yet, when Paul's at school, the thing he likes best of all is that little old ship I once carved out of a bit of wood!"

Paul was pleased that the others liked his home. He did not boast or show off. It was natural to him to live in a palace and have everything he wanted. He was a warm-hearted, friendly little boy who loved to share everything with his friends. Before he had gone to England he had had no friends of his own – but now that he had Mike, Jack, Peggy and Nora, he was very happy. It was marvellous to him to have them with him in Baronia.

"We'll bathe in the lake, and we'll sail to the other side, and we'll go driving in the mountains," said Paul. "We'll have a perfectly gorgeous time. I only hope it won't get too hot. If it does, we'll have to go to the mountains where it's cooler."

The children were very tired by the time that first day came to an end. They seemed to have walked miles in and around the palace, exploring countless rooms, and looking out of countless turrets. They had gone all round the glorious gardens, and had been saluted by numbers of gardeners. Everyone seemed very pleased to see them.

They had tea and supper on the terrace outside the play-room. Big, colourful umbrellas sheltered the table from the sun. The blue lake shimmered below.

"I wish I hadn't eaten so much lunch," groaned Mike, as he looked at the exciting array of cakes and biscuits and sandwiches before him. "I simply don't know what to do. I know I shan't want any supper if I eat this tea – and if supper is anything like lunch, I shall just break my heart if I'm not hungry for it."

"Oh, you'll be hungry all right," said Paul. "Go on – have what you want."

Before supper the children went for a sail on the lake in

Prince Paul's own sailing boat. Ranni went with them. It was lovely and cool on the water. Jack looked at the girls' burnt faces.

"We shall be brown as berries in a day or two," he said. "We're all brown now — but we shall get another layer very quickly. My arms are burning! I shan't put them in water tonight! They will sting too much."

"You'll have to hold your arms above your head when you have your bath, then," said Mike. "You will look funny!"

The children were almost too tired to undress and bath themselves that night. Yawning widely they took off their clothes, cleaned their teeth and washed. A bath was sunk into the floor of each bedroom. Steps led down to it. It seemed funny to the children to go down into a bath, instead of just hopping over the side of one. But it was all fun.

The girls got into their big four-poster, giggling. It seemed so big to them after the narrow beds they had at school.

"I shall lose you in the night!" said Nora to Peggy.

The boys jumped into their beds, too. Paul left the door open between his bedroom and that of Mike's and Jack's, so that he might shout to them. But there was very little shouting that night. The children's eyes were heavy and they could not keep them open. The day had been almost too exciting.

"Now we're living in Baronia," whispered Peggy to herself. "We're in Baronia, in . . ." And then she was fast asleep, whilst outside the little waves at the edge of the lake lapped quietly all night long.

An Exciting Trip

The first week glided by, golden with sunshine. The children enjoyed themselves thoroughly, though Nora often complained of the heat. All of them now wore the Baronian dress, and fancied themselves very much in it.

The girls wore tight bodices of white and blue, with big silver buttons, and full skirts of red and blue. They wore no stockings, but curious little half-boots, laced up with red. The boys wore embroidered trousers, with cool shirts open at the neck, and a broad belt. They, too, wore the half-boots, and found them very comfortable.

At first they all felt as if they were in fancy dress, but they soon got used to it. "I shan't like going back to ordinary clothes," said Nora, looking at herself in the long mirror. "I do so love the way this skirt swings out round me. Look, Mike – there are yards of material in it."

Mike was fastening his belt round him. He stuck his scout knife into it. He looked at himself in the mirror, too. "I look a bit like a pirate or something," he said. "Golly, I wish the boys at school could see me now! Wouldn't they be green with envy!"

"They'd laugh at you," said Nora. "You wouldn't dare to wear those clothes in England. I hope the Queen will let me take mine back with me. I could wear them at a fancy-dress party. I bet I'd win the prize!"

That first week was glorious. The children were allowed to do anything they wanted to, providing that Ranni or Pilescu was with them. They rode little mountain ponies through the hills. They bathed at least five times a day in the warm waters of the lake. They sailed every evening. They went by car to the nearest big town, and rode in the buses there. They were quaint buses, fat and squat, painted blue and silver. Everything was different, every thing was strange.

"England must have seemed very queer to you at first, Paul," said Mike to the little prince, realizing for the first time how difficult the boy must have found living in a strange country.

Paul nodded. He was very happy to show his friends everything. Now, when he was back at school again in England, and wanted to talk about his home and his country, Jack and Mike would understand all he said, and would listen gladly.

Towards the end of the first week Pilescu made a suggestion. "Why do you not take your friends in the aeroplane, and show them how big your country is?" he asked Paul. "I will take you all."

"Oh *yes*, Pilescu – let's do that!" cried Mike. "Let's fly over the mountains and the forests, and see everything!"

"I will show you the Secret Forest," said Prince Paul, unexpectedly.

The others stared at him. "What's the Secret Forest?" asked Jack. "What's secret about it?"

"It's a queer place," said Paul. "Nobody has ever been there!"

"Well, how do you know it's there, then?" asked Mike.

"We've seen it from aeroplanes," said Paul. "We've flown over it."

"Why hasn't anyone ever been into this forest?" asked Peggy. "Someone *must* have, Paul. I don't believe there is anywhere in the whole world that people haven't explored now."

"I tell you no one has ever been in the Secret Forest," said Paul, obstinately. "And I'll tell you why. Look – get me that map over there, Mike."

Mike threw him over a rolled-up map. Paul unrolled it and spread it flat on a table. He found the place he wanted and pointed to it.

"This is a map of Baronia," he said. "You can see what

a rugged, mountainous country it is. Now look – do you see these mountains here?"

The children bent over to look. The mountains were coloured brown and had a queer name – Killimooin. Paul's brown finger pointed to them. "These mountains are a queer shape," said the little prince. "Killimooin mountains form an almost unbroken circle – and in the midst of them, in a big valley, is the Secret Forest."

His finger pointed to a tiny speck of green shown in the middle of Killimooin mountains. "There you are," he said. "That dot of green is supposed to be the Secret Forest. It is an enormous forest, really, simply enormous, and goodness knows what wild animals there are there."

"Yes, but Paul, *why* hasn't anyone been to see?" asked Mike, impatiently. "Why can't they just climb the mountains and go down the other side to explore the forest?"

"For a very good reason!" said Paul. "No one has ever found a way over Killimooin mountains!"

"Why? Are they so steep?" asked Nora, astonished.

"Terribly steep, and terribly dangerous," said Paul.

"Does anyone live on the mountain-sides?" asked Peggy.

"Only goatherds," said Paul. "But they don't climb very high because the mountains are so rocky and so steep. Maybe the goats get to the top – but the goatherds don't!"

"Well!" said Mike, fascinated by the idea of a secret forest that no one had ever explored. "This really is exciting, I must say. Do, do let's fly over it in your aeroplane, Paul. Wouldn't I just love to see what that forest is like!"

"You can't see much," said Paul, rolling up the map. "It just looks a thick mass of green that's all, from the plane. All right – we'll go tomorrow!"

This was thrilling. It would be grand to go flying again, and really exciting to roar over the Killimooin mountains and peer down at the Secret Forest. What animals lived there? What would it be like there? Had anyone ever trodden its dim green paths? Mike and Jack wished a hundred times they could explore that great hidden forest!

The next day all five children went to the runway beside the hangar where Paul's aeroplane was kept. They watched the mechanics run it out on to the grass. They greeted Ranni and Pilescu as the two men came along.

"Ranni! Do you know the way to fly to Killimooin mountains? We want to go there!"

"And when we get there, fly as low down as you can, so that we can get as near to the Secret Forest as possible," begged Nora.

Ranni and Pilescu smiled. They climbed up into the aeroplane. "We will go all round Baronia," said Pilescu, "and you will see, we shall fly over Killimooin country. It is wild, very wild. Not far from it is the little palace the King built last year, on a mountain-side where the winds blow cool. The summers have been very hot of late years in Baronia, and it is not healthy for children. Maybe you will all go there if the sun becomes much hotter!"

"I hope we do!" said Paul, his eyes shining. "I've never been there, Pilescu. We should have fun there, shouldn't we?"

"Not the same kind of fun as you have in the big palace," said Pilescu. "It is wild and rough around the little palace. It is more like a small castle. There are no proper roads. You can have no car, no aeroplane. Mountain ponies are all you would have to get about on."

"I'd like that," said Jack. He took his seat in the big plane, and watched the mechanics finishing their final checks on the plane. They moved out of the way. The engine started up with a roar. Nobody could hear a word.

Then off went the big plane, as smoothly as a car, taxiing over the grass. The children hardly knew when it rose in the air. But when they looked from the windows, they saw the earth far below them. The palace seemed no bigger than a doll's house.

"We're off!" said Jack, with a sigh. "Where is the map? You said you'd bring one, Paul, so that we could. see exactly where we are each minute."

It really was interesting to spread out the map, and try to find exactly where they were. "Here we are!" said Jack, pointing to a blue lake on the map. "See? There's the lake down below us now – we're right over it – and look, there's the river flowing into it, shown on the map. Golly, this is geography really come alive! I wish we could learn this sort of geography at school! I wouldn't mind having geography every morning of the week, if we could fly over the places we're learning about!"

The children read out the names of the towns they flew over. "Ortanu, Tarribon, Lookinon, Brutinlin – what funny names!"

"Look – there are mountains marked here. We ought to reach them soon."

"The plane is going up. We must be going over them. Yes – we are. Look down and see. Golly, that's a big one over there!"

"Aren't the valleys green? And look at that river. It's like a silvery snake."

"Are we coming near the Secret Forest? Are we near Killimooin? Blow, I've lost it again on the map. I had it a minute ago."

"Your hand's over it, silly! Move it, Jack – yes, there, look! Killimooin. We're coming to the mountains!"

Ranni yelled back to the children. "Look out for the Secret Forest! We are coming to the Killimooin range now. Paul, you know it. Look out now, and tell the others."

In the greatest excitement the five children pressed their faces against the windows of the big plane. It was rising over steep mountains. The children could see how wild and rugged they were. They could not see anyone on them at all, nor could they even see a house.

"Now you can see how the Killimooin mountains run all

round in a circle!" cried Paul. "See – they make a rough ring, with their rugged heads jagged against the sky! There is no valley between, no pass! No one can get over them into the Secret Forest that lies in the middle of their mighty ring!"

The children could easily see how the range of mountains ran round in a very rough circle. Shoulder to shoulder stood the rearing mountains, tall, steep and wild.

The aeroplane roared over the edge of the circle, and the children gazed down into the valley below.

"That's the Secret Forest!" shouted Paul. "See, there it is. Isn't it thick and dark? It fills the valley almost from end to end."

The Secret Forest lay below the roaring, throbbing plane. It was enormous. The tops of the great trees stood

The aeroplane roared over the edge of the circle

187

close together, and not a gap could be seen. The plane roared low down over the trees.

"It's mysterious!" said Nora, and she shivered. "It's really mysterious. It looks so quiet – and dark – and lonely. Just as if really and truly nobody ever has set foot there, and never will!"

Hot Weather!

The aeroplane rose high again to clear the other side of the mountain ring. The forest dwindled smaller and smaller. "Go back again over the forest, Ranni, please do!" begged Jack. "It's weird. So thick and silent and gloomy. It gives me a funny feeling!"

Ranni obligingly swung the big plane round and swooped down over the forest again. The trees seemed to rise up, and it almost looked as if the aeroplane was going to dive down into the thick green!

"Wouldn't it be awful if our plane came down in the forest, and we were lost there, and could never, never find our way out and over the Killimooin mountains?" said Nora.

"What a horrid thought!" said Peggy. "Don't say things like that! Ranni, let's get over the mountains quickly! I'm afraid we might get lost here!"

Ranni laughed. He swooped upwards again, just as Jack spotted something that made him flatten his nose against the window and stare hard.

"What is it?" asked Nora.

"I don't quite know," said Jack. "It couldn't be what I thought it was, of course."

"What did you think it was?" asked Paul, as they flew high over the other side of the mountain ring.

"I thought it was a spiral of smoke," said Jack. "It couldn't have been, of course – because where there is smoke, there is a fire, and where there is a fire, there are men! And there are no men down there in the Secret Forest!"

"*I* didn't see any smoke," said Mike.

"Nor did I," said Paul. "It must have been a wisp of low-lying cloud, Jack."

"Yes – it must have been," said Jack. "But it *did* look like smoke. You know how sometimes on a still day the smoke from a camp fire rises almost straight into the air and stays there for ages. Well, it was like that."

"I think the Secret Forest is very, very strange and mysterious," said Peggy. "And I never want to go there!"

"I would, if I got the chance!" said Mike. "Think of walking where nobody else had ever put their foot! I would feel a real explorer."

"This is Jonnalongay," called Ranni from the front. "It is one of our biggest towns, set all round a beautiful lake."

The children began to take an interest in the map again. It was such fun to see a place on the big map, and then to watch it coming into view below, as the aeroplane flew towards it. But soon after that they flew into thick cloud and could see nothing.

"Never mind," said Ranni. "We have turned back now, and are flying along the other border of Baronia. It is not so interesting here. The clouds will probably clear just about Tirriwutu, and you will see the railway lines there. Watch out for them."

Sure enough, the clouds cleared about Tirriwutu, and the children saw the gleaming silver lines, as Pilescu took the great plane down low over the flat countryside. It was fun to watch the lines spreading out here and there, going to different little villages, then joining all together again as they went towards the big towns.

"Oh – there's the big palace by the lake!" said Nora, half-disappointed. "We're home again. That was simply lovely, Paul."

"But the nicest part was Killimooin and the Secret Forest," said Jack. "I don't know why, but I just can't get that mysterious forest out of my head. Just suppose that *was* smoke I saw! It would mean that people live there – people no one knows about – people who can't get out and never could! What are they like, I wonder?"

"Don't be silly, Jack," said Mike. "It wasn't smoke, so there aren't people. Anyway, if people are living there now, they must have got over the mountains at some time or other, mustn't they? So they could get out again if they wanted to! Your smoke was just a bit of cloud. You know what funny bits of cloud we see when we're flying."

"Yes, I know," said Jack. "You're quite right, it couldn't have been real smoke. But I rather like to think it was, just for fun. It makes it all the more mysterious!"

The aeroplane flew down to the runway, and came to a stop. The mechanics came running up.

"You have had the best of it today!" one called to Ranni, in the Baronian language, which the children were now beginning to understand. "We have almost melted in the heat! This sun – it is like a blazing furnace!"

The heat from the parched ground came to meet the children as they stepped out of the plane. Everything shimmered and shook in the hot sun.

"Gracious!" said Nora. "I shall melt! Oh for an ice-cream!"

They walked to the palace and lay down on sunbeds on the terrace, under the big colourful umbrellas. Usually there was a little wind from the lake on the terrace – but today there was not a breath of air.

"Shall we bathe?" said Jack.

"No good," said Mike. "The water was too warm to be pleasant yesterday – and I bet it's really hot today. It gets like a hot bath after a day like this."

A big gong boomed through the palace. It was time for lunch – a late one for the children. Nora groaned.

"It's too hot to eat! I can't move. I don't believe I could even swallow an ice-cream!"

"Lunch is indoors for you today," announced Ranni, coming out on to the terrace. "It is cooler indoors. The electric fans are all going in the play-room. Come and eat."

None of the children could eat very much, although the dishes were just as delicious as ever. Ranni and Pilescu, who always served the children at meal-times, looked quite worried.

191

"You must eat, little Prince," Ranni said to Paul.

"It's too hot," said Paul. "Where's my mother? I'm going to ask her if I need wear any clothes except shorts. That's all they wear in England in the summer, when it's holiday-time and hot."

"But you are a prince!" said Ranni. "You cannot run about with hardly anything on."

Prince Paul went to find his mother. She was lying down in her beautiful bedroom, a scented handkerchief lying over her eyes.

"Mother! Are you ill?" asked Paul.

"No, little Paul – only tired with this heat," said his mother. "But listen, we will go to the mountains to the little castle your father built there last year. I fear that this heat will kill us all! Your father says he will send us tomorrow. How we shall get there with all the children and the nurses I cannot imagine! But go we must! I don't know what has happened this last few years in Baronia! The winters are so cold and the summers are so hot!"

Paul forgot that he had come to ask if he could take off his clothes. He stared at his mother, thrilled and excited. To go to the mountains to the new little castle! That would be fine. The children could explore the country on mountain ponies. They would have a great time. The winds blew cool on the mountain-side, and they would not feel as if they wanted to lie about and do nothing all day long. "Oh, mother! Shall we really go tomorrow?" said Paul. "I'll go and tell the others."

He sped off, forgetting how hot he was. He burst into the play-room, and the others looked at him in amazement.

"However can you possibly race about like that in this heat?" asked Jack. "You must be mad! I'm dripping wet just lying here and doing nothing. It's hotter than it was in Africa – and it was hot enough there!"

"We're going to the new little castle in the mountains tomorrow!" cried Paul. "There's news for you! It will be

cool there, and we can each have a pony and go riding up
and down the mountains. We can talk to the goatherds,
and have all kinds of fun!"

Jack sat up. "I say!" he said. "Did you hear Pilescu say
that your new little palace was near Killimooin? Golly,
what fun! We might be able to find out something about
the Secret Forest!"

"We shan't!" said Paul. "There's nothing to find out.
You can ask the goatherds there and see. Won't it be fun
to go and stay in the wild mountains? I *am* glad!"

All the children were pleased. It really was too hot to
enjoy anything in the big palace now. The idea of
scampering about the mountains on sturdy little ponies
was very delightful. Jack lay back on the couch and
wondered if it would be possible to find out anything
about the Secret Forest. He would ask every goatherd he
saw whether he could tell anything about that mysterious
forest, hidden deep in the heart of Killimooin.

"If anyone knows anything, the goatherds should
know," thought the boy. Then he spoke aloud. "Paul,
how do we go to the mountains where the little castle is?
Do we ride on ponies?"

"No – we drive most of the way," said Paul. "But as
there is no proper road within twenty miles, we shall have
to go on ponies for the rest of the way. I don't know how
the younger children will manage."

"This is a lovely holiday!" said Nora, dreamily. "Living
in a palace – flying about in aeroplanes – peering down at
the Secret Forest – and now going to live in a castle built in
the wild mountains, to which there is not even a proper
road. We *are* lucky!"

"It's getting hotter," said Mike, with a groan. "Even the
draught from the electric fan seems hot! I hope it will get a
bit cooler by the time the evening comes."

But it didn't. It seemed to get hotter than ever. Not one
of the five children could sleep, though the fans in their
big bedrooms went all night long. They flung off the

sheets. They turned their pillows to find a cool place. They got out of bed and stood by the open windows to find a breath of air.

By the time the morning came they were a heavy-eyed, cross batch of children, ready to quarrel and squabble over anything. Paul flew into a temper with Ranni, and the big man laughed.

"Ah, my little lord, this heat is bad for you all! Now do not lose your temper with me. That is foolish, for if you become hot-tempered, you will feel hotter than ever! Go and get ready. The cars will be here in half an hour."

The boys went to have cool baths. It was too hot to swim in the lake, which was just like a warm bath now. They came out of the cold water feeling better. Mike heard the noise of car engines, and went to the window. A perfect fleet of cars was outside, ready to take the whole family, with the exception of Paul's father. The five older children, the five younger ones, Paul's mother, three nurses, and Ranni and Pilescu were all going.

"Come on!" yelled Paul. "We're going. Nora, you'll be left behind. Hurry up!"

And into the cars climbed all the royal household, delighted to be going into the cool mountains at last.

Killimooin Castle

It took quite a time to pack in all the five younger children. One of the nurses had the baby in a big basket beside her. The other nursery children chattered and laughed. They looked pale with the heat, but they were happy at the thought of going to a new place.

Ranni and Pilescu travelled with the four English children and Prince Paul. There was plenty of room in the enormous blue and silver car. Nora was glad when at last they all set off, and a cool draught came in at the open windows. The little girl felt ill with the blazing summer heat of Baronia.

"The new castle is called Killimooin Castle," announced Paul. "I've never even seen it myself, because it was built when I was away. It's actually on one of the slopes of Killimooin. We can do a bit of exploring."

"You will not go by yourselves," said Ranni. "There may be robbers and wild men there."

"Oh, Ranni – we must go off by ourselves sometimes!" cried Jack. "We can't have you always hanging round us like a nursemaid."

"You will not go by yourselves," repeated Ranni, a little sternly, and Pilescu nodded in agreement.

"Killimooin is about two hundred miles away," said Paul. "We ought to get there in four or five hours – as near there as the roads go, anyway."

The great cars purred steadily along at a good speed. There were five of them, for servants had been taken as well. Behind followed a small van with a powerful engine. In the van were all the things necessary for the family in the way of clothes, prams and so on.

The countryside flew by. The children leaned out of the

windows to get the air. Ranni produced some of the famous Baronian chocolate, that tasted as much of honey and cream as of chocolate. The children munched it and watched the rivers, hills and valleys they passed. Sometimes the road wound around a mountain-side, and Nora turned her head away so that she would not see down into the valley, so many hundreds of feet below. She said it made her feel giddy.

"I don't know what we would do if we met another car on these curving roads that wind up and up the mountain-side," said Peggy.

"Oh, the roads have been cleared for us," said Paul. "We shan't meet any cars on the mountain roads, anyway, so you needn't worry."

They didn't. The cars roared along, stopping for nothing – nothing except lunch! At half-past twelve, when everyone was feeling very hungry, the signal was given to stop. They all got out to stretch their legs and have a run round. They were on a hillside, and below them ran a shining river, curving down the valley. It was a lovely place for a picnic.

As usual the food was delicious. Ranni and Pilescu unpacked hampers and the children spread a snow-white cloth on the grass and set out plates and dishes.

"Chicken sandwiches! Good!" said Mike.

"Ice-cream pudding! My favourite!" said Nora.

"About thirty different kinds of sandwiches!" said Jack. "I am glad I feel so terribly hungry."

It was a good meal, sitting out there on the hillside, where a little breeze blew.

"It's cooler already," said Nora, thankfully.

"It will be much cooler in Killimooin Castle," said Ranni. "It is built in a cunning place, where two winds meet round a gully! It is always cool there on the hottest day. You will soon get back your rosy cheeks."

Everyone climbed back into the cars when lunch was finished, and off they went again. "Only about an hour

196

*The little sturdy animals trotted away up the rough
mountain path*

more and the road ends for us," said Pilescu, looking at
his watch. "It goes on round the mountains, but leaves
Killimooin behind. I hope the ponies will be there, ready
for us."

"How is the baby going to ride a pony?" asked Nora.
"Won't she fall off?"

"Oh, no," said Pilescu. "You will see what happens to
the little ones."

After about an hour, all the cars slowed down and
stopped. The children looked out in excitement, for there
was quite a gathering in front of them. Men with ponies
stood there, saluting the cars. It was time to mount and
ride, instead of sitting in a car!

It took a long time to get everyone on to the sturdy,
shaggy little ponies. Nora soon saw how the little children

were taken! The bigger ponies had a big, comfortable basket strapped each side of them – and into these the younger children were put! Then with a man leading each pony, the small ones were quite safe, and could not possibly fall!

"I'm not going in a basket," said Nora, half afraid she might be told to. But all the other children could ride and were expected to do so. Each child sprang on to the pony brought beside him or her and held the reins. The ponies were stout and steady, very easy to ride, though Nora complained that hers bumped her.

"Ah no, Nora – it is you who are bumping the pony!" said Pilescu, with a laugh.

The little company set off. The nurses, who had all been country girls, thought nothing of taking their children on ponies to the castle. The smaller boys and girls chattered in high voices and laughed in delight at the excitement.

The men leading the ponies that carried baskets or panniers leapt on to ponies also, and all the little sturdy animals trotted away up the rough mountain path that led to the new castle. The people who had come to watch the royal family's arrival waved goodbye and shouted good wishes after them. Their cottages were here and there in the distance.

The little company turned a bend in the path, and then the children saw the towering mountains very clearly, steep and forbidding, but very grand. Up and up they had to go, climbing higher little by little towards the castle Paul's father had built the year before. No houses, no cottages were to be seen. It was very desolate indeed.

"Look at those goats!" said Peggy, pointing to a flock of goats leaping up the rocky slopes. "What a lot of them! Where's the goatherd?"

"Up there," said Paul. "Look – by that crooked tree."

The goatherd stared down at the company. He had the flaming red beard that most Baronians had, and he wore ragged trousers of goat-skin, and nothing else.

"He looks awfully wild and fierce," said Nora. "I don't think I want to talk to goatherds if they look like that!"

"Oh, they are quite harmless!" said Ranni, laughing at Nora's scared face. "They would be more frightened of you than you would be of them!"

It was fun at first to jog along on the ponies for the first few miles, but when the road grew steeper, and wound round and round, the children began to wish the long journey was over.

"There's one thing, it's lovely and cool," said Jack.

"It will be quite cold at nights," said Ranni. "You will have to sleep with thick covers over you."

"Well, that will be a change," said Jack, thinking of how he had thrown off everything the night before and had yet been far too hot. "I say – I say – is that Killimooin Castle?"

It was. It stood up there on the mountain-side, over-looking a steep gully, built of stones quarried from the mountain itself. It did not look new, and it did not look old. It looked exactly right, Nora thought. It was small, with rounded towers, and roughly hewn steps, cut out of the mountain rock, led up to it.

"I shall feel as if I'm living two or three hundred years ago, when I'm in that castle," said Peggy. "It's a proper little castle, not an old ruin, or a new make-believe one. I do like it. Killimooin Castle – it just suits it, doesn't it?"

"Exactly," said Jack. "It's about half-way up the mountain, isn't it? We're pretty high already."

So they were. Although the mountains still towered above them, the valley below looked a very long way down. The wind blew again and Nora shivered.

"Golly, I believe I shall be too cold now!" she said, with a laugh.

"Oh, no – it's only the sudden change from tremendous heat to the coolness of the mountains that you feel," said Ranni. "Are you tired? You will want a good rest before tea!"

"Oh, isn't it nearly tea-time?" said Mike, in disappointment. "I feel so hungry. Look – we're nearly at that fine flight of steps. I'm going to get off my pony."

The caretakers of the castle had been looking out for the royal arrivals. They stood at the top of the flight of steps, the big, iron-studded door open behind them. The children liked them at once.

"That is Tooku, with Yamen his wife," said Pilescu. "They are people from the mountains here. You will like to talk to them sometime, for they know many legends and stories of these old hills."

Tooku and Yamen greeted the children with cries of delight and joy. They were cheerful mountain-folk, not scared at the thought of princes and princesses arriving, but full of joy to see so many little children.

It seemed no time at all before the whole company were in their new quarters. These were not nearly so grand and luxurious as those the children had had in the big palace, but not one of them cared about that. The castle rooms were small, but with high ceilings. The walls were hung with old embroidered tapestries. There were no curtains at the narrow windows – but, oh, the view from those windows!

Mountains upon mountains could be seen, some wreathed in clouds, most of them with snow on the top. The trees on them looked like grass. The valley below seemed miles away.

"Killimooin Castle has quite a different feel about it," said Jack, with enjoyment. "The palace was big and modern and everything was up to date. Killimooin is grim and strong and wild, and I like it. There's no hot water running in the bedrooms. I haven't seen a bathroom yet – and our beds are more like rough couches with rugs and pillows than beds. I do like it."

It was great fun settling down in the castle. The children could go anywhere they liked, into the kitchens, the towers, the cellars. Tooku and Yamen welcomed them anywhere and any time.

It was deliciously cool at Killimooin after the tremendous

heat of the palace. The children slept well that first night, enjoying the coolness of the air that blew in at the narrow windows. It was good mountain air, clean and scented with pine.

Next morning Ranni spoke to the five children. "You have each a pony to ride, and you may ride when and where you will, if Pilescu or I are with you."

"Why can't we go alone?" said Paul, rather sulkily. "We shan't come to any harm."

"You might lose your way in the mountains," said Ranni. "It is an easy thing to do. You must promise never to wander off without one of us."

Nobody wanted to promise. It wasn't nearly so much fun to go about with a grown-up, as by themselves. But Ranni was firm.

"You must promise," he repeated. "No promise, no ponies. That is certain!"

"I suppose we must promise, then," said Jack. "All right – I promise not to go wandering off without a nursemaid!"

"I promise too," said Mike. The girls promised as well.

"And you, little lord?" said big Ranni, turning to the still-sulky boy.

"Well – I promise too," said Paul. "But there isn't any real danger, I'm sure!"

Paul was wrong. There *was* danger – but not the kind that anyone guessed.

Blind Beowald, The Goatherd

Two days later a great mist came over Killimooin and not even Ranni and Pilescu dared to ride out on their ponies, although they had said that they would take the children exploring round about.

"No one can see his way in such a mist," said Ranni, looking out of the window. "The clouds lie heavy over the valley below us. Up here the mist is so thick that we might easily leave the mountain path and go crashing down the mountain-side."

"It's so disappointing," sighed Paul. "What can we do instead?"

Yamen put her head in at the door as she passed. "You can come down to tea with Tooku and me," she invited. "We will have something nice for you, and you shall ask us all the things you want to know."

"Oh, good," said Jack. "We'll ask all about the Secret Forest. Maybe they know tales about that! That will be exciting."

Tea-time down in the big kitchen of the castle was great fun. An enormous fire glowed on the big hearth, and over it hung a black pot in which the soup for the evening meal was slowly simmering. A grand tea was spread on the wooden table, and the children enjoyed it. There were no thin sandwiches, no dainty buns and biscuits, no cream cakes – but, instead, there were hunks of new-made bread, baked by Yamen that morning, crisp rusks with golden butter, honey from the wild bees, and a queer, rich cake with a bitter-sweet taste that was delicious.

"Yamen, tell us all you know about the Secret Forest," begged Nora, as she buttered a rusk. "We have seen it when we flew over in an aeroplane. It was so big and so mysterious."

"The Secret Forest!" said Yamen. "Ah, no one knows anything of that. It is lost in the mountains, a hidden place unknown to man."

"Doesn't anyone live there at all?" asked Jack, remembering the spire of smoke he thought he had seen.

"How could they?" asked Tooku, in his deep, hoarse voice, from the end of the table. "There is no way over Killimooin mountains."

"Hasn't anyone *ever* found a way?" asked Jack.

Tooku shook his head. "No. There is no way. I have heard it said, however, that there is a steep way to the top, whence one can see this great forest – but there is no way down the other side – no, not even for a goat!"

The children listened in silence. It was disappointing to hear that there really was no way at all. Tooku ought to know, for he had lived among the mountains for years.

"Ranni won't let us go about alone," complained Paul. "It makes us feel so babyish, Tooku. Can't you tell him the mountains are safe?"

"They are not safe," said Tooku, slowly. "There are robbers. I have seen them from this very castle. Ah, when this place was built last year, the robbers must have hoped for travellers to come to and fro!"

"What robbers?" asked Jack. "Where do they live? Are there many of them?"

"Yes, there are many," said Tooku, nodding his shaggy head. "Sometimes they rob the poor people of the countryside, coming in the night, and taking their goats and their hens. Sometimes they rob the travellers on the far-off road.'

"Why aren't they caught and punished?" demanded the little prince indignantly. "I won't have robbers in my country!"

"No one knows where these robbers live," said Yamen. "Aie-aie – they are a terrible band of men. It is my belief that they have a stronghold far up the mountains."

"Perhaps they live in the Secret Forest!" said Jack.

"Oh, you and your Secret Forest!" said Nora. "Don't keep asking about it, Jack. You've been told ever so many times there's no way for people to get to it."

"Are there any wild animals about the mountains?" asked Mike.

"There are wolves," said Yamen. "We hear them howling in the cold wintertime, when they can find no food. Yes, they came even to this castle, for I saw them myself."

"How frightening!" said Nora, shivering. "Well, I'm jolly glad I promised Ranni I wouldn't go out without him or Pilescu! I don't want to be captured by robbers or caught by wolves."

"You don't want to believe all their stories," said Peggy, in a low voice.

Yamen heard her, and although she did not understand what the little girl said, she guessed.

"Ah!" she said, "you think these are but tales, little one? If you want to know more, go to the goatherd, Beowald, and he will tell you many more strange tales of the mountain-side!"

Beowald sounded rather exciting, the children thought. They asked where he could be found.

"Take the path that winds high above the castle," said Tooku. "When you come to a crooked pine, struck by lightning, take the goat-track that forks to the left. It is a rocky way, but your ponies will manage it well. Follow this track until you come to a spring gushing out beside a big rock. Shout for Beowald, and he will hear you, for his ears are like that of a mountain hare, and he can hear the growing of the grass in spring, and the flash of a shooting star in November!"

The next day was fine and clear. The children reminded Ranni of his promise and he grinned at them, his eyes shining in the brilliant sunlight.

"Yes, we will go," he said. "I will get the ponies. We will take our lunch with us and explore."

"We want to find Beowald the goatherd," said Paul. "Have you heard of him, Ranni?"

Ranni shook his head. He went to get the ponies, whilst Nora and Peggy ran off to ask Yamen to pack them up some lunch.

Soon they were all ready. Ranni made them take thick Baronian cloaks, lined with fur, for he said that if a mist suddenly came down they would feel very cold indeed.

They set off up the steep mountain-way that wound high above the castle. The ponies were sure-footed on the rocky path, though they sent hundreds of little pebbles clattering down the mountain-side as they went. They were nice little beasts, friendly and eager, and the children were already very fond of them.

Ranni led the way, Pilescu rode last of all. It was a merry little company that went up the steep mountain that sunny morning.

"We've got to look out for a crooked pine tree, struck by lightning," said Jack to Ranni, who was just in front of him. "Then we take the goat-track to the left."

"There's an eagle!" said Nora, suddenly, as she saw a great bird rising into the air, its wings spreading out against the sun. "Are eagles dangerous, Pilescu?"

"They will not attack us," said Ranni. "They like to swoop down on the little kids that belong to the goats and take them to feed their young ones, if they are nesting."

"I wonder if we shall see a wolf," said Peggy, hoping that they wouldn't. "I say, isn't it fun riding up and up like this! I do like it."

"There's the crooked pine tree!" shouted Paul. "Look – over there. We shall soon come up to it. Isn't it ugly? You don't often see a pine tree that is not tall and straight."

The crooked pine tree seemed to point to the left,

'There's an eagle!" said Nora, suddenly

where the path forked into two. To the left was a narrow
goat-track, and the ponies took that way, their steady
little hooves clattering along merrily.

It was lovely up there in the cool clear air, with the
valley far below, swimming in summer sunshine.
Sometimes a little wispy cloud floated below the children,
and once one floated right into them. But it was nothing
but a mist when the children found themselves in it!

"Clouds are only mists," said Nora. "They look so solid
when you see them sailing across the sky, especially those
mountainous, piled-up clouds that race across in March
and April – but they're nothing but mist!"

"What's that noise?" said Jack, his sharp ears hearing
something.

"Water bubbling somewhere," said Nora, stopping her
pony. "It must be the spring gushing out, that Tooku and

206

Yamen told us about. We must be getting near where Beowald should be."

"Look at the goats all about," said Peggy, and she pointed up the mountain-side. There were scores of goats there, some staring at the children in surprise, some leaping from rock to rock in a hair-raising manner.

"Goats have plenty of circus-tricks," said Mike, laughing as he watched a goat take a flying leap from a rocky ledge, and land with all four feet bunched together on a small rock not more than six inches square. "Off he goes again! I wonder they don't break their legs."

"They must be Beowald's goats," said Peggy. "Ranni, call Beowald."

But before Ranni could shout, another noise came to the children's ears. It was a strange, plaintive noise, like a peculiar melody with neither beginning nor end. It was odd, and the children listened, feeling a little uncomfortable.

"Whatever's that?" asked Peggy.

They rode on a little way and came to a big rock beside which gushed a clear spring, running from a rocky hole in the mountain-side. On the other side, in the shelter of the rock, lay a youth, dressed only in rough trousers of goat-skin. Round his neck, tied by a leather cord, was a kind of flute, and on this the goatherd was playing his strange, unending melodies.

He sat up when the children dismounted. The children saw that his strange dark eyes were blind. There was no light in them. They could see nothing. But it was a happy face they looked on, and the goatherd spoke to them in a deep, musical voice.

"You are come!" he said. "I heard you down the mountain two hours since. I have been waiting for you."

"How did you know we were coming to see you?" asked Paul in astonishment.

Beowald smiled. It was a strange smile, for although his mouth curved upwards, his eyes remained empty and dark.

"I knew," said Beowald. "I know all that goes on in my mountains. I know the eagles that soar above my head. I know the wolves that howl in the night. I know the small flowers that grow beneath my feet, and the big trees that give me shade. I know Killimooin as no one else does."

"Well, Beowald, do you know anything about the Secret Forest then?" asked Paul, eagerly. The other children could now understand what was said in the Baronian language, though they were not able to speak it very well as yet. They listened eagerly for Beowald's answer.

Beowald shook his head. "I could take you where you can see it," he said. "But there is no way to it. My feet have followed my goats everywhere in these mountains, even to the summits – but never have they leapt down the other side. Not even for goats is there any path."

The children were disappointed. "Are there robbers here?" asked Jack, trying to speak in Baronian. Beowald understood him.

"Sometimes I hear strange men at night," he said. "They creep down the mountain path, and they call to one another as the owls do. Then I am afraid and I hide in my cave, for these robbers are fierce and wild. They are like the wolves that roam in the winter, and they seek men to rob and slay."

"Where do the robbers live?" asked Paul, puzzled.

Beowald shook his head, gazing at the little prince with his dark blind eyes. "That is a thing I have never known," he said. "They are men without a home. Men without a dwelling-place. That is why I fear them. They cannot be human, these men, for all men have a dwelling-place."

"That's silly," said Jack, in English. "All men have to live somewhere, even robbers! Paul, ask Beowald if they could live somewhere in a mountain cave, as he does."

Paul asked the goatherd, but he shook his head. "I know every cave in the mountains," he said. "They are my caves, for only I set foot in them. I live up here all the summer, and only in the cold winter do I go down to the valley to be with my mother. In the good weather I am happy here, with my goats and my music."

"Play to us again," begged Peggy. The goatherd put his wooden flute to his lips and began to play a strange little tune. The goats around lifted their heads and listened. The little kids came quite near. A great old goat, with enormous curling horns, stepped proudly up to Beowald and put his face close to the goatherd's.

Beowald changed the tune. Now it was no longer like the spring that ran down the mountain-side, bubbling to itself. It was like the gusty wind that blew down the hills and swept up the valleys, that danced and capered and shouted over the pine trees and the graceful birches.

The children wanted to dance and caper too. The goats felt the change in the music and began to leap about madly. It was an odd sight to see. Jack looked at the blind youth's face. It was completely happy. Goats, mountains – and music. Beowald wanted nothing more in his quiet, lonely life!

A Day In The Mountains

"Can't we have lunch here with Beowald?" asked Paul, suddenly. "I feel very hungry, Ranni. It would be lovely to sit here in the wind and the sun and eat our food, listening to Beowald."

"I expect the goatherd would rather eat with you than play whilst you gobble up all the food!" said Ranni with a laugh. "Ask him if he will eat with you."

The goatherd smiled when he heard what Ranni said. He nodded his head, gave an order that scattered his goats, and sat quite still, gazing out over the valleys below as if he could see everything there.

"Where do you sleep at night?" asked paul. "Where is your cave?"

"Not far from here," answered Beowald. "But often I sleep in the daytime and walk at night."

"But how can you find your way then?" said Peggy, thinking of the darkness of the mountain-side and its dangerous ledges and precipices.

"It is always dark for me," said Beowald. "My ears see for me, and my feet see for me. I can wander in these mountains for hours and yet know exactly where I am. The pebbles beneath my feet, the rocks, the grass, the flowers, they all tell me where I am. The smell of the pine trees, the scent of the wild thyme that grows nearby, the feel of the wind, they tell me too. I can go more safely over this steep mountain with my blind eyes than you could go, seeing all there is to be seen!"

The children listened to the blind goatherd, as Ranni and Pilescu set out the lunch. There were sandwiches for everyone, and hard, sweet little biscuits to eat with cheese made from goats' milk. Beowald ate with them, his face happy and contented. This was a great day in his life!

"Beowald, take us up to where we can see the Secret Forest," begged Paul. "Is it very far?"

"It will be two hours before we get there," said the goatherd. He pointed with his hand, and it seemed to the children as if he must surely see, if he knew where to point. "The way lies up there. It is steep and dangerous. But your ponies will take you safely."

The children felt thrilled at the idea of seeing the Secret Forest from the summit of the mountain. They were very high up now, though the summit still seemed miles away. The air was cold and clear, and when the wind blew, the children wrapped their fur-lined cloaks around them. They could not imagine how Beowald could wear nothing but trousers.

When they had eaten all they could, they stood up. Ranni fetched the little ponies, who had been nibbling at the short grass growing where the mountain-side was least rocky. The children sprang into the saddles and the ponies jerked their heads joyfully. Now, they thought, they were going back home!

But they were mistaken. Beowald led the way up a steep, rocky track that even goats might find difficult to tread.

"I can't think how Beowald knows the way," called Peggy to Nora. "There isn't a sign of any path, so far as I can see."

"It's probably one that only the goats know," said Ranni. "See, that old goat with the great curling horns is before us. It almost looks as if he is leading the way!"

"Ah, my old one knows when I need him," said the goatherd, and he put his flute to his mouth. He played a few merry little notes and the big goat came leaping lightly down to him. "Stay by me, old one," said Beowald.

The goat understood. He trotted in front of Beowald, and waited for him when he leapt up on to a rock.

211

Beowald was as nimble as a goat himself, and it was amazing to the children to think that a blind youth should be so sure-footed. But then Beowald knew every inch of the mountain-side.

Up they went and up. Sometimes the way was so steep that the ponies almost fell as they scrambled along, and sent crowds of stones rumbling down the mountain-side. Ranni and Pilescu began to be doubtful about going farther. Ranni reined in his fat little pony.

"Beowald! Is the way much steeper?" he asked. "This is dangerous for the children."

"Ranni! It isn't!" cried Paul indignantly. "I won't go back without seeing over the top. I won't!"

"We shall soon be there," said Beowald, turning his dark eyes to Ranni. "I can smell the forest already!"

The children all sniffed the air eagerly, but they could smell nothing. They wished they had ears and nose like Beowald's. He could not see, but he could sense many things that they could not.

They came to a narrow ledge and one by one the ponies went round it, pressing their bodies close against the rocky side of the mountain, for a steep precipice, with a fall of many hundreds of feet, was the other side! Nora and Peggy would not look, but the boys did not mind. It was exciting to be so high.

The old goat rounded the ledge first, and Beowald followed. "We are here!" he called.

The ledge widened out round the bed – and the children saw that they were on the other side of Killimooin mountains! They were not right at the top of the mountain they were on, but had rounded a bend on the shoulder, and were now looking down on the thing they wanted so much to see – the Secret Forest!

"The Secret Forest!" cried Paul, and Jack echoed his words.

"The Secret Forest! How big it is! How thick and dark! How high we are above it!"

All eight of them stared down into the valley that lay hidden and lost between the big ring of mountains. Only Beowald could not see the miles upon miles of dark green forest below, but his eyes seemed to rest on the valley below, just as the others' did.

"Isn't it mysterious?" said Jack. "It seems so still and quiet here. Even the wind makes no sound. I wish I could see that spire of smoke I thought I saw when we flew down low over the forest in the aeroplane."

But there was no smoke to be seen, and no sound to be heard. The forest might have been dead for a thousand years, it was so still and lifeless.

"It's funny to stand here and look at the Secret Forest, and know you can't ever get to it," said Mike. He looked down from the ledge he was standing on. There was a sheer drop down to the valley below, or so it seemed to the boy. It was quite plain that not even a goat could leap down.

"Now you can see why it is impossible to cross these mountains," said Ranni. "There is no way down the other side at all. All of them are steep and dangerous like this one. No man would dare to try his luck down that precipice, not even with ropes!"

The girls did not like looking down such a strange, steep precipice. They had climbed mountains in Africa but none had been so steep as this one.

"I want to go back now," said Nora. "I'm feeling quite giddy."

"It is time we all went," said Ranni, looking at his watch. "We must hurry too, or we shall be very late."

"I can take you another way back," said Beowald. "It will be shorter for you to go to the castle. Follow me."

With his goats around him, the blind youth began to leap down the mountain-side. He was as sure-footed as the goats, and it was extraordinary to watch him. The ponies followed, slipping a little in the steep places. They were tired now, and were glad to be going home.

Down they all went and down. Nora gave a sudden shout that made the others jump. "I can see Killimooin Castle. Hurrah! Another hour and we'll be home!"

They rounded a bend and then suddenly saw a strange place built into the rocky mountain-side. They stopped and stared at it.

"What's that?" asked Paul. Ranni shook his head. He did not know and neither did Pilescu.

"It looks like some sort of temple," said Nora, who remembered seeing pictures of stone temples in her history book. But this one was unusual, because it seemed to be built into the rock. There was a great half-broken archway, with roughly-carved pillars each side.

"Beowald! Do you know what this place is?" asked Jack. The goatherd came back and stood beside Jack's pony.

"It is old, very old," he said. "It is a bad place. I think bad men once lived there, and were turned into stone for their wickedness. They are still there, for I have felt them with my hands."

"What in the world does he mean?" said Peggy, quite frightened. "Stone men! He's making it up!"

"Let's go and see," said Jack, who was very seldom afraid of anything.

"No, thank you!" said the girls at once. But the boys badly wanted to see inside the queer, ruined old place. Beowald would not go with them. He stayed with the two girls.

"Come on. Let's see what these wicked stone men are!" said Jack, with a grin. He dismounted from his pony, and passed through the great broken archway. It was dark inside the queer temple. "Have you got a torch, Mike?" called Jack. Mike usually had a torch, a knife, string, and everything anyone could possibly want, somewhere about his person. Mike felt about and produced a torch.

He flashed it on – and the boys jumped in fright. Even Ranni and Pilescu jumped. For there, at the back of the

214

He flashed it on – and the boys jumped in fright

temple-like cave, was a big stone man, seated on a low, flat rock!

"Oooh!" said Paul, and found Ranni's hand at once.

"It's an old statue!" said Jack, laughing at himself, and feeling ashamed of his sudden fright. "Look – there are more, very broken and old. Aren't they odd? However did they get here?"

"Long, long ago the Baronians believed in strange gods," said Ranni. "These are probably stone images of them. This must be an ancient temple, forgotten and lost, known only to Beowald."

"That sitting statue is the only one not broken," said Jack. "It's got a great crack down the middle of its body though – look. I guess one day it will fall in half. What a horrid face the stone man has got – sort of sneering."

"They are very rough statues," said Pilescu, running his

215

hand over them. "I have seen the same kind in other places in Baronia. Always they were in mountain-side temples like this."

"Let's go home!" called Nora, who was beginning to be very tired. "What sort of stone men have you found? Come and tell us."

"Only statues, cowardy custard," said Jack, coming out of the ruined temple. "You might just as well have seen them. Gee-up, there! Off we go!"

Off they went again, on the downward path towards Killimooin Castle, which could be seen very plainly now in the distance. In a short while Beowald said goodbye and disappeared into the bushes that grew just there. His goats followed him. The children could hear him playing on his flute, a strange melody that went on and on like a brook bubbling down a hill.

"I like Beowald," said Nora. "I'd like him for a friend. I wish he wasn't blind. I think it's marvellous the way he finds the path and never falls."

The ponies trotted on and on, and at last came to the path that led straight down and round to the castle steps. Ranni took them to stable them, and Pilescu took the five tired children up the steps and into the castle.

They ate an enormous late tea, and then yawned so long and loud that Pilescu ordered them to bed.

"What, without supper!" said Paul.

"Your tea must be your supper," said Pilescu. "You are all nearly asleep. This strong mountain air is enough to send a grown man to sleep. Go to bed now, and wake refreshed in the morning."

The children went up to bed. "I'm glad we managed to see the Secret Forest," said Jack. "And that funny temple with those old stone statues. I'd like to see them again."

He did – and had a surprise that was most unexpected!

Robbers!

A few days went by, days of wandering in the lower slopes of the mountain, looking for wild raspberries and watching the swift shy little animals that lived on the mountain. Yamen and Tooku told the children more tales, and nodded their heads when Jack told them of the ruined temple and the queer statues.

"Ah yes – it is very old. People do not go near it now because it is said that the statues come alive and walk at night."

The children screamed with laughter at this. They thought some of the old superstitions were very funny. It seemed as if Yamen really believed in fairies and brownies, for always when she made butter, she put down a saucer of yellow cream by the kitchen door.

"It is for the brownie who lives in my kitchen!" she would say.

"But, Yamen, your big black cat drinks the cream, not the brownie," Nora would say. But Yamen would shake her grey head and refuse to believe it.

Yamen used to go to buy what was needed at the village near the foot of the mountain each week. She had a donkey of her own, and Tooku had two of these sturdy little creatures. Tooku used sometimes to go with Yamen, and the third donkey would trot along behind them, with big baskets slung each side of his plump body, to bring back the many things Yamen bought for the household.

One day Yamen and Tooku started out with the third donkey behind them as usual. They set off down the track, and the children shouted goodbye.

"We shall be back in time to give you a good tea!" called Yamen. "You shall have new-baked rusks with honey."

But when tea-time came there was no Yamen, no Tooku. Ranni and Pilescu looked out of the great doorway of the castle, puzzled. The two should be in sight, at least. It was possible to see down the track for a good way.

"I hope they haven't had an accident," said Nora.

An hour went by, and another. The children had had their tea, and were wandering round the castle, throwing stones down a steep place, watching them bounce and jump.

"Look!" said Ranni, suddenly. Everyone looked down the track. One lone donkey was coming slowly along, with someone on his back, and another person stumbling beside him. Ranni ran to get a pony and was soon galloping along the track to find out what had happened.

The children waited anxiously. They were fond of Tooku and Yamen. As soon as the three climbed the steps of the castle, the children surrounded them.

"What's the matter, Yamen? Where are the other donkeys, Tooku? What have you done to your arm?"

"Aie, aie!" wept Yamen. "The robbers came and took our goods and our donkeys! Tooku tried to stop them but they broke his arm for him. Aie-aie, what bad luck we have had this day! All the goods gone, and the two fine little donkeys!"

"They took all three," said Tooku, "But this one, my own good creature, must have escaped, for we heard him trotting after us as we hastened back home on foot."

"What were the robbers like?" asked Jack.

"Strange enough," answered Yamen. "Small and wiry, with strips of wolf-skin round their middles. Each had a wolf's tail, dyed red, hanging behind him. Aie-aie, they were strange enough and fierce enough!"

"We heard tales in the town," said Tooku, to Ranni and Pilescu. "Many travellers have been robbed. These robbers take goods but not money. They come down from the mountains like goats, and they go back, no man knows where!"

"Have the villagers searched for their hiding-place?"

asked Ranni. "Have they hunted all about the mountain-sides?"

"Everywhere!" said Yamen. "Yes, not a place, not a cave has been forgotten. But nowhere is there a sign of the fierce robbers with their red wolves' tails!"

"Poor Yamen!" said Nora. The frightened woman was sitting in a chair, trembling. Pilescu bound up Tooku's arm. It was not broken, but badly gashed. The children felt very sorry.

Paul's mother soon heard of the disturbance and she was angry and upset. "To think that such things should happen in Baronia!" she cried. "I will send word to the king, and he shall send soldiers to search the mountain-side."

"The mountain-folk themselves have already done that," said Ranni. "If they have found nothing, the soldiers will find even less! It is a mystery where these men come from!"

"Perhaps they come from the Secret Forest!" said Jack. The others laughed at him.

"Idiot! Come from a place where nobody can go to!" said Mike.

"You children will not stir from this place without Ranni or Pilescu!" said Paul's mother.

"Madam, they have already promised not to," said Ranni. "Do not be anxious. They are safe with us. We have always our revolvers with us."

"I wish we hadn't come here now," said the Queen, looking really worried. "I wonder if we ought to go back. But I hear that it is hotter than ever in the big palace."

The children had no wish to return when they heard that. "We shall be quite safe here," said Paul. "The robbers will not dare to come anywhere near this castle, mother!"

"Silly child!" said his mother. "Now that they know we are here, and that travellers will go to and fro, they will be all the more on the watch. They will haunt the road from here to the high road, and from here to the next village. I must get some more servants from the big palace. We must only go about in small companies, not alone."

This was all very exciting. The boys talked about the robbers, and Mike felt three or four times an hour to see if his big scout-knife was safely in his broad belt. Paul thought of all the terrifying things he would do to the robbers if he caught them. Mike thought it would be marvellous to shut them all up in a cave somewhere. Jack pictured himself chasing the whole company down the mountain-side.

The girls were not so thrilled, and were not much impressed when the three boys promised to take care of them.

"What could you do against a company of robbers?" asked Nora.

"Well, this isn't the first time we've had adventures, and had to fight for safety," said Mike, grandly.

"No, it's true we've had some exciting times and very narrow escapes," said Peggy. "But I don't particularly want to be chased and caught by robbers, even if you boys rescue me in the end!"

"Perhaps it's the stone men in the cave that come alive and rob people!" said Paul, with a grin.

"I'd like to go and have a look at those statues again," said Jack. "Ranni, can we go tomorrow? It's only about an hour's ride."

"I don't want to go too far from the castle," said Ranni. "Well – we'll go as far as that old temple if you really want to. Though why you should want to see ancient statues, broken to pieces, when you've already seen them once is a puzzle to me!"

The children set off the next day to go to the old temple. They were on foot, as it really was not a great distance away, and Ranni said it would be good for them to walk. So up the mountain they trudged.

It was late afternoon when they started. They had their

220

tea with them. The sun shone down warmly and the children panted and puffed when they went up the hillside, so steep and stony.

"There's the old temple," said Jack, at last, pointing to the ruined archway, hewn out of the mountain rock. "It really is a funny place. It seems to be made out of a big cave, and the entrance is carved out of the mountain itself. Come on – let's go in and have another look. Nora, you come this time, and Peggy. You didn't come last time."

"All right," said Peggy. "We'll come."

They all went into the old temple, and switched on the torches they had brought. Once again they gazed on Beowald's "stone men," and smiled to think of his idea that the statues had once been wicked men, turned into stone.

The biggest statue of all, at the back of the cave, sat on his wide flat rock, gazing with blank eyes out of the entrance. He seemed to be in much better repair than the others, who had lost noses, hands and even heads in some cases. Jack flashed his torch around, and suddenly came to a stop as he wandered around.

"Look here!" he said.

The others came to him and looked down at the ground, where his torch made a round ring of bright light. In the light was the print of a small bare foot. Jack swung his torch here and there, and on the floor of the temple other footprints could be seen – all small and bare, the toes showing clearly.

"Someone comes here quite a lot!" said Jack.

"More than one person," said Mike, kneeling down and looking closely at a few prints with his torch. "These are not the prints of the same person's feet. Look at this print here – all the toes are straight – but this one has a crooked big toe-print. And that one is a little larger than the others."

"It couldn't be Beowald's prints, could it?" asked Nora, remembering the bare feet of the goatherd.

"No. His feet are much bigger than those shown in these prints," said Mike. "I remember thinking what big feet he had."

"Well – could it be the robbers' footprints?" cried Peggy, suddenly.

"It might be," said Jack. "But they are plainly not here – not living here, I mean! Anyway, they would be discovered easily enough if they did live here. Beowald would know."

Ranni called the children. "Come along. Tea is ready. We must hurry now, because it looks as if a mist is coming up."

The children hurried out of the dark temple into the bright sunshine. They sat down to have their tea, telling Ranni and Pilescu what they had seen. But the two big Baronians were not much impressed.

"The prints are probably made by the feet of the goatherds sent to search every nook and cranny of the mountain-side, to look for the robbers' hiding-place," said Ranni.

This was disappointing. The children had quite made up their minds that they must belong to the robbers! Mike pointed down the hillside.

"Look at the clouds down there below us," he said. "They seem to be creeping up towards us."

"They are," said Pilescu, beginning to gather up the tea things. "Come along. I don't want to get lost in a mountain mist!"

They all set off down the mountain-side. Jack suddenly spied some juicy wild raspberries, and slipped off the path to get them. Before he had eaten more than a dozen he found himself surrounded by a thick grey mist!

"Blow!" said Jack, making his way back to the path. "I can't even see the others now! Well, I know the path, that's one thing!"

He shouted, but could hear no answer. The others had gone round a bend, and could not hear him, though usually a shout in the mountains echoed round and round. But the thick mist muffled the sound, and Jack could hear no reply to his yell.

"I'll just go on and hope to catch the others up," thought the boy. He set off, but after a while he had no idea of the right direction at all. The mist became thicker and thicker and the boy felt cold. He pulled his fur-lined cloak round him, and wondered what to do.

Something familiar about the rocky face of the mountain caught his eye. "Well – look at that! I'm right back at the old temple!" said Jack, in astonishment. "I've doubled back on the path somehow, and reached the temple-cave again. Well, I can't do better than shelter inside till the mist clears. Maybe it won't be long. They come and go very quickly."

He went inside the cave where the old stone images were. He found a corner where he could sit, and he

Then one of the men went to the entrance of the cave

223

squatted down to wait. He yawned and shut his eyes. He hoped Ranni and Pilescu would not be very angry with him.

He dozed lightly, whilst the mist swirled round outside. He was awakened by the sound of voices, and sat up, expecting to see the other children coming into the temple to look for him. He half got up – and then sank back in the greatest astonishment.

The cave was full of strange, hoarse voices, speaking in the Baronian language, but using a broad country accent that Jack could not understand. It was dark there, and the boy could not see the people to whom the voices belonged. He dared not switch on his torch.

Then one of the men went to the entrance of the cave and looked out, calling back that the mist was still there, but was clearing rapidly. Jack looked at him in amazement. He was small and wiry, and wore no clothes at all except for a strip of skin round his middle. The boy crouched back in his corner, suddenly scared.

The mist thinned outsided the cave, and the man at the entrance was joined by others. They went out, and Jack saw that each man had a wolf's tail behind him, dyed red. They were the robbers!

There were many of them. Where had they come from? They had not been in the cave when the boy fell asleep, and if they had entered, he would have heard them. Where *had* they come from? There must be some secret entrance in the temple itself. But where could it be?

The Amazing Statue

The cave was now empty. Jack got up cautiously and crept to the entrance. The mist was almost gone. Not a sign of the strange men was to be seen.

"They must have gone off to rob someone again!" thought the boy. "I'll take a good look round the cave now I'm here and find out where those men came from. There *must* be some hidden entrance at the back. Possibly there's a big cave farther in, where they live. This is awfully exciting!"

But before he could put on his torch and look round he heard the sound of shouts outside.

"Jack! Jack! Where are you?"

It was Ranni's voice. Jack ran out of the old temple-cave. Ranni was some way down the mountain-path. The boy shouted loudly.

"Ranni! I'm here, quite safe! I got lost in the mist."

"Come along quickly, before the mist comes again!" ordered Ranni.

"But Ranni, wait! I've made a discovery!" yelled Jack.

"Come along at once," shouted Ranni, sternly. "Look at the mist coming up. It will be thicker this time. Come now, Jack."

There was nothing for it but to go to Ranni. Jack leapt down the path, and as soon as he reached the big Baronian, he began to tell him what he had seen. But Ranni, anxious about the returning mist, paid little heed to the boy's excited chatter, and hurried him along as fast as he could go. Jack had no breath left to talk after a while, and fell silent. He could see that Ranni was cross with him.

The others had reached the castle safely. Ranni hurried

Jack inside the door, just as the mist swirled up again, thick and grey.

"And now!" he said sternly, turning to Jack. "Will you kindly tell me why you left us all? I had to go back and find you, and I might have hunted the mountain-side for hours. I am not pleased with you, Jack."

"I'm sorry, Ranni," said Jack, humbly. "I just went to pick some raspberries, that's all. Ranni, I saw the robbers!"

"I do not want to talk to you," said Ranni. "You have displeased me." He went to his own room, leaving Jack behind.

Jack stared after the Baronian, rather hurt, and feeling decidedly small. He went to find the others.

"Jack! What happened to you?" cried Nora, rushing to him. "We lost you, and Ranni went back."

"I've some news," said Jack, and his eyes gleamed. "Strange news, too!"

"What?" cried everyone.

"I wandered about a bit, when the mist overtook me," said Jack, "and suddenly I found I was back at the old temple. So I went in out of the mist, and sat down to wait till it cleared. I dozed off for a bit – and suddenly I awoke and found the cave becoming full of voices! I heard more and more of them, and then a man went to the entrance of the cave and looked out – and it was one of the robbers!"

"Jack! Not really!" cried Peggy.

"Yes, really," said Jack. "When the mist cleared a bit, they all went out of the entrance, and I saw the wolves' tails they had, dyed red. They did look extraordinary."

"Did they come into the cave to shelter then?" asked Mike.

"No – that's the funny part," said Jack. "They didn't! I feel absolutely certain that they came into the cave by some secret way – perhaps at the back of the temple. I believe there must be a big cave further in, where they live."

"So those footprints we saw must be theirs, after all," said Paul. "Oh, Jack – this is awfully exciting, isn't it! What did Ranni say when you told him?"

"He wouldn't listen," said Jack. "He was angry with me."

"Well, he'll soon be all right again," said Paul, cheerfully. "Ranni's temper never lasts long. I know that."

Paul was right. Ranni forgot his anger in a very short time, and when he came into the children's room, he was his usual smiling self. The boys went to him at once.

"Ranni! We know where the robbers hide!"

"Ranni, do listen, please. Jack saw the robbers."

This time Ranni did listen, and what he heard made him call Pilescu at once. The two men were eager to hear every word that Jack had to tell.

"It looks as if we shall be able to round up the robbers quickly now," said Ranni. "Good! You must be right, Jack – there is probably a secret entrance somewhere in the cave, leading from a big cave farther in."

"We must make a search as quickly as possible," said Pilescu. "Ranni, the moon is full tonight. You and I will take our most powerful torches and will examine that temple from top to bottom tonight!"

"Oh, Pilescu, let me come too?" begged Jack.

"And me!" cried Mike and Paul together.

Pilescu shook his big head. "No – there may be danger. You must stay safely here in the castle."

Jack was angry. "Pilescu! It was *my* discovery! Don't be mean. You *must* take me with you. Please!"

"You will not come," said Pilescu, firmly. "We are responsible for your safety in Baronia, and you will not be allowed to run into any danger. Ranni and I will go tonight, and tomorrow you shall hear what we have found."

The two men went out of the room, talking together. Jack stared after them fiercely. The boy was almost in tears.

"It's too bad," he said. "It *was* my discovery! And they're going to leave me out of it. I didn't think Ranni and Pilescu would be so mean."

The boy was hurt and angry. The others tried to comfort him. Jack sat and brooded for a little while and then he suddenly made up his mind.

"I shall go, too!" he said to the others, in a low tone. "I shall follow them and see what they find. I won't miss this excitement."

"But you promised not to go out alone," said Mike, at once. All the children thought the world of their promises and never broke one.

"Well, I *shan't* be alone – I shall be with Ranni and Pilescu, and they won't know it!" grinned Jack, quite good-tempered again now that he had thought of a way to join in the adventure. For adventure it had become, there wasn't a doubt of that!

The others laughed. It was quite true. Jack would certainly not be alone!

So, that night, after they had gone to bed, Jack kept his ears pricked to listen to any sounds of Ranni and Pilescu leaving. The moon swam up into the sky and the mountain-side was as light as day. The boy suddenly heard the low voices of the two Baronians, and he knew they were going down the passage to make their way to the great front door.

He had not undressed, so he was ready to follow them. After them he went, as quietly as a cat. The others whispered to him:

"Good luck!"

"Don't let Ranni see you or you'll get a spanking!"

"Look after yourself, Jack!"

The big front door opened, and shut quietly. Jack waited for a moment, opened it, and crept after the two men. He had to be careful to keep well in the black shadows, for it was easy to see anyone in the moonlight.

Up the mountain track behind the castle went Ranni and Pilescu. They did not speak, and they made as little noise as they could. They kept a sharp look-out for any sign of the robbers, but there was none. Word had come to the castle that evening that a company of local people, returning from market, had been set upon and robbed that afternoon, and the two Baronians had no doubt that the robbers were the men that Jack had seen in the cave.

"If we can find the entrance to their lair, we can get soldiers up here, and pen the whole company in, and catch them one by one as they come out," said Ranni, in a low tone. Pilescu nodded. He heard a sound, and stopped.

"What is it?" whispered Ranni.

"Nothing," answered Pilescu, after a pause. "I thought I heard something."

He had! He had heard the fall of a stone dislodged by Jack, who was following them as closely as he dared! The boy stopped when Pilescu stopped, and did not move again until the two men went forward.

In about an hour's time they were at the old temple. The moon shone in at the ruined entrance. Ranni gave a startled exclamation as he went in, for the moon shone full on the face of the old stone image at the back. It seemed very lifelike!

"Now," said Ranni, flashing his torch round the cave. "You take a look that side and I'll take this. Examine every inch of the rock."

The moon suddenly went behind a big cloud and the world went dark. Jack took the chance of slipping into the cave without the two men seeing him. He thought he could hide behind the images, as the men worked round the cave. He stood behind one near the entrance and watched Ranni and Pilescu examining the rocky wall, trying to find some hidden entrance to another cave beyond.

"I can find nothing," said Pilescu, in a low voice.

Jack stood behind the statue and watched, hoping that one of the men would discover something. How he wished he could help too – but he was afraid of showing himself in case Ranni was angry again.

He stared at the big squatting statue at the back of the

cave. The moon had come out again and was shining full on the image. As Jack watched, a very strange thing began to happen!

The statue's face began to widen! It began to split in half! Jack stared in astonishment and horror. What could be happening? Was it coming alive? Were those old tales true, then?

Then he saw that the whole statue was splitting slowly and silently in half. The two halves were moving apart. It all happened so smoothly and silently that Ranni and Pilescu heard no sound at all, and had no warning.

Jack was so amazed that he could not say a word. The statue split completely in half, the two halves moving right apart – and then, from the floor of the flat rock beneath, a man's shaggy head appeared, full in the moonlight – the head of one of the robbers!

Jack gave a yell. "Ranni! Pilescu! Look out! The robbers are coming! Look at the statue!"

Ranni and Pilescu, amazed at Jack's voice, and at what he said, swung round quickly. They stared in the utmost amazement at the split statue, and saw the head and shoulders of the robber below. With a wild yell the robber leapt up into the temple, calling to his friends below:

"Come! Come! Here are enemies!"

In half a minute the cave was full of robbers. Ranni and Pilescu, taken completely by surprise, had their hands bound. They fought and struggled fiercely, but the robbers were too many for them.

Ranni remembered Jack's voice, and knew that the boy must be somewhere about. He must have followed them! Ranni called out in English:

"Don't show yourself, Jack. Go and give warning to the others."

Jack did not answer, of course. He crouched down behind a statue, watching the fight, knowing that it would be useless to join in, and hoping that the robbers would not see him.

Before his astonished eyes, the boy saw the wolf-tailed men force the two Baronians down through the hole beneath the great statue. Every robber followed. Then the statue, smoothly and silently as before, began to move. The two halves joined together closely, and the image was whole once more, its cracked face shining in the moonlight.

"No wonder there was such a crack down the middle of it!" thought the boy. "It wasn't a crack — it was a split, where the two halves joined! Golly, this is awful. I wonder if it's safe to go."

He waited for a while and then stole quietly out of the cave, looking behind him fearfully as he went. But no robber was there to follow him. The boy sped swiftly down the track in the moonlight, anxious to get to the others.

They were all awake. Jack got them into his room and told them hurriedly all that had happened. Paul was shocked, and anxious to hear about Ranni and Pilescu, whom he loved with all his heart.

"I am going to rescue them," he announced, getting into his clothes at once.

"Don't be an idiot, Paul," said Mike. "You can't go after robbers."

"Yes, I can," said Paul, fiercely, and his big dark eyes gleamed. "I am a Baronian prince, and I will not leave my men in danger. I go now to find them!"

When Paul got ideas of this sort into his head, there was no stopping him. Jack groaned. He turned to the girls.

"We'd better go with Paul and keep the idiot out of danger. You go and wake Tooku and Yamen and tell them what has happened. They will think of the best thing to do. Don't frighten Paul's mother, will you?"

Paul was already out of the front door, running down the steps in the moonlight. Ranni and Pilescu were in danger! Then he, their little prince must rescue them. Mike and Jack tore after him. A big adventure had begun!

The Beginning Of The Adventure

Mike and Jack soon caught up with Paul. The boy was struggling up the steep track as fast as he could go. He had no clear idea as to exactly what he was going to do. All he knew was that he meant to find Ránni and Pilescu and rescue them from the robbers.

"Paul! You're going the wrong way," panted Jack, as he came up to Paul. "You really are an idiot. You'd be lost in the mountains if we hadn't come after you. Look – you go this way, not the one you're taking."

Paul was glad to have the others with him. He pulled his fur-lined cloak around him, for he was cold. The others were wearing theirs too. They climbed steadily up the mountain-side, the moon showing them the way quite clearly. Mike hoped that clouds would not blow up, for it would be impossible to find their way in the dark. He thought of Beowald, the blind goatherd. He did not mind the dark. It made no difference to him at all!

Up they went and up, and an hour went by. Paul did not seem to be at all tired, though Jack's legs ached badly. But then he had already been to the temple-cave and back once before that night!

They came near the cave, and trod softly, keeping to the shadows, in case any of the robbers should be about. Suddenly a figure showed itself from behind a rock! Quick as lightening Jack pulled the other two down beside him in a big shadow, and the three of them crouched there, their hearts beating painfully. Was it a robber, left on guard? Had he seen them?

The moon went behind a small cloud and the mountain-side lay in darkness. Jack strained his eyes and ears to find out if the night-wanderer was anywhere near.

Then he heard the plaintive notes of the little flute that Beowald played! It must be the goatherd, wandering at night as he so often did.

"Beowald!" called Jack, softly. "Where are you?"

The moon sailed out from behind the cloud and the boys saw the goatherd seated on a nearby rock, his head turned towards them.

"I am here," he said. "I heard you. I knew you were friends. What are you doing up here at night?"

Jack came out from his hiding-place. He told Beowald in a few words all that had happened. The goatherd listened in amazement.

"Ah, so that is why I thought the stone men came to life at night!" he said. "It was robbers I heard coming forth from the temple, and not the stone men. There must be a deep cave below the floor of the temple. I will come with you to find it."

The goatherd led the way to the cave. The moon went in again behind a cloud, and the boys were glad to be with Beowald for the last piece of their climb. They could not have found their way otherwise. But darkness did not matter to the blind youth. He found his way as surely as if he were seeing the path in daylight!

They came near to the temple, treading very cautiously. Not a sound was to be heard. "We'd better creep into the cave whilst the moon is behind a cloud," whispered Jack. "Paul, ask Beowald if he thinks any robbers are about now. His ears are so sharp that surely he would know."

Paul whispered to Beowald in the Baronian language. The goatherd shook his head. "There is no one near," he said. "I have heard nothing at all, and my ears would tell me if a robber was in the cave. I should hear him breathing."

The boys crept silently into the dark cave. When they were in, the moon shone out and lighted up the strange stone face of the big statue at the back. It seemed to look sneeringly at the three boys.

233

Jack went up to the image, and ran his fingers down the crack that he had seen widen into a split when the statue divided into halves. He wondered how he could find out the working of the strange image. There must be some way of opening it, both from above and below. What was it? He must find it, or he would not be able to find the place where the robbers had taken Ranni and Pilescu.

But no matter how he felt and pushed and pulled, the crack remained a crack, and did not widen into a split. The other two boys tried as well, but they had no more success than Jack. They looked at one another in despair.

"Let my fingers try," said the voice of Beowald. "My eyes cannot see, but my fingers can. They can feel things that only the whiskers of a mouse could sense!"

This was perfectly true. The blind youth's fingers were so sensitive that they could tell him more than the eyes of others could tell them. The boys watched Beowald run his fingers down the crack in the middle of the statue. They watched him feel round the staring stone eyes. They followed his quivering fingers round the neck and head, touching, feeling, probing, almost like the feelers of an enquiring butterfly!

Suddenly Beowald's sensitive fingers found something and they stopped. The boys looked at him.

"What is it, Beowald?" whispered Prince Paul.

"The statue is not solid just here," answered the goatherd. "Everywhere else it is solid, made of stone – but just behind here, where its right ear is, it is hollow."

"Let me feel," said Jack eagerly, and pushed away the goatherd's fingers. He placed his own behind the right ear of the statue, but he could feel nothing at all. The stone felt just as solid to him there as anywhere else. The other boys felt as well, but to them, as to Jack, the stone was solid there. How could Beowald's fingers know whether stone was solid or hollow behind a certain spot? It seemed like magic.

Beowald put his fingers back again on the spot he had

234

found. He moved them about, pressed and probed. But nothing happened. Jack shone his torch on to the ear. He saw that it was cleaner than the rest of the head, as if it had been handled a good deal. It occurred to him that the ear itself might be the place containing a spring or lever that worked the statue so that it split in half.

The left ear was completely solid, Jack saw – but the right ear, on the contrary, had a hole in it, as have human ears! Beowald found the hole at the same time as Jack saw it, and placed his first finger inside it. The tip of his finger touched a rounded piece of metal set inside the ear. Beowald pushed against it – and a lever was set in motion that split the stone image silently into half!

Actually it was a very simple mechanism, but the boys did not know that. They stared open-mouthed as the statue split completely down the crack, and the two halves moved smoothly apart. Beowald knew what was happening, though he could not see it. He was afraid, and moved back quickly. He half-thought the statue was coming alive, when it moved!

"Look – there's a hole underneath the statue, in the middle of the low rock it sits on," said Jack, and he shone his torch down it. The hole was round in shape, and would take a man's body easily. A rope, made of strips of leather, hung down the hole from a staple at the top.

"That's the entrance to the robber's lair!" said Jack, in a low voice. "No doubt about that! I bet their cave is below this one, in the mountain itself."

"I'm going to see," said the little prince, who seemed that night to be more than a small boy. He was a prince, he was growing up to be a king, he was lord of Baronia, he was going to take command and give orders! Jack pulled him back as he was about to go down into the dark hole.

"Wait! We might all fall into a trap. Don't do anything silly. We shan't help Ranni and Pilescu by being foolish."

"I will go to rouse the local people and to bring help," said Beowald. "I would like to come with you, but I am no

235

good in a strange place. My feet, my ears and my hands only help me when I am on my mountain-side. In a strange place I am lost."

"We will go down the hole and find out what we can," said Jack. "You get the others and follow us as soon as you are able to. The girls will have told Tooku and Yamen by now, and maybe they will be on the way here with one or two of the servants. I expect Paul's mother will send for some soldiers, too."

Beowald did not understand all that Jack said, for the boy did not speak the Baronian language very well as yet. Paul quickly translated for him, and Beowald nodded his head.

"Do not fall into the hands of the robbers," he said. "Why do you not wait here until I come back?"

"I go to rescue my men," said Prince Paul haughtily. "Where they go, I follow."

"You must do as you wish," said the goatherd. Jack slid down into the hole, and took hold of the rope. He went down and down, whilst Mike shone his torch on to him. Beowald waited patiently, seeing nothing, but knowing by his ears all that was happening.

The hole went down for a long way. Jack swung on the rope, his arms getting tired. Then he found that there were rough ledges here and there on the sides of the hole, on which he could rest his feet now and again, to relieve his arms.

The hole came to an end at last. Jack felt his toes touching ground once more. He let go the rope and felt round with his hands. He could feel nothing. The hole must have come out into some kind of cave. The boy could hear no sound of any sort, and he thought it would be safe to switch on his torch.

He switched it on, and saw that, as he had imagined, he was in a cave, through the roof of which the hole showed, dark and round. "I wonder if this is the robbers' lair," thought the boy, flashing the torch around. But there was

He found rough ledges here and there

nothing at all in the rocky cave, whose rugged walls threw back the gleam of the torch.

Mike's feet appeared at the bottom of the hole and the boy jumped down beside Jack. Then came Paul. They all stood together, examining the cave.

"It doesn't look as if anyone lives here at all," said Mike. "There are no beds where you might expect the robbers to sleep, not a sign of any pot or pan. I don't believe this is their lair."

"Well, what is it, then?" demanded Jack. "I saw them go down here, didn't I? Goodness knows how Ranni and Pilescu were taken down, with their hands tied! Where can they be?"

"They're nowhere here at all," said Paul, flashing his torch into every corner. "It's odd. What can have become of them?"

It really was a puzzle. Jack began to go round the little cave, his footsteps echoing in a weird way. He flashed his torch up and down the walls, and suddenly came to a stop.

"Here's another way out!" he said. "Look! It's quite plain to see. I'm surprised we didn't see it before when we shone our torches round."

The boys looked. They saw that halfway up the opposite wall of the cave was a narrow opening. They jumped on to a ledge and peered through it. It was plain that it led out of the cave, and was a passage through the rock.

"Come on," said Jack. "This is the way the robbers must have gone. I'll go first!"

He was soon in the passage that led from the cave. He flashed his torch in front of him. The way was dark and rough, and the passage curved as it went, going downwards all the time. Where in the world did it lead to!

The River In The Mountain

As the boys crept down the rocky passage, they suddenly heard a curious noise in the distance. They stopped.

"What's that noise?" asked Jack. It was a kind of rumbling, gurgling sound, sometimes loud and sometimes soft. The boys listened.

"I don't know," said Mike, at last. "Come on. Maybe we shall find out."

On they went again, and very soon they discovered what the queer noise was. It was made by water! It was a waterfall in the mountain, a thing the children had not even thought of! They came out into a big cave, and at one end fell a great stream of water. The cave was damp and cold, and the boys shivered.

They went over to the curious waterfall. "I suppose the snow melts on the top of the mountain and the water finds its way down here," said Jack, thoughtfully. "It must run through a rocky passage, something like the one we have just been in, and then, when the passage ends, the water tumbles down with that rumbling noise. I'm quite wet with the spray!"

The water fell steadily from a hole in the roof of the cave, where, as Jack said, there must be a tunnel or passage down which the water ran before it fell into the cave.

"Where does the water go to, I wonder?" said Mike. "It rushes off into that tunnel, look – and becomes a kind of river going through the mountain. I think it's weird. I wonder if the robbers live in *this* cave – but there still seems to be no sign of them or their belongings. After all, if people live somewhere, even in a cave, they scatter a few belongings about!"

But there was nothing at all to be seen, and, as far as the boys could see, no way of getting out of the "waterfall cave," as they called it.

They wandered round, looking for some outlet – but the water seemed to have found the only outlet – the tunnel down which it rushed after falling on to the channelled floor of the cave.

The boys went back to the water and gazed at it. Jack saw that through hundreds of years the waterfall had worn itself a bed or channel on the floor of the cave, and that only the surface water overflowed on to the ground where the boys stood. The channel took the main water, and it rushed off down a tunnel, and then was lost to sight in the darkness.

"I suppose the robbers couldn't possibly have gone down that tunnel, could they?" said Paul suddenly. "There isn't a ledge or anything they could walk on, is there, going beside that heaving water?"

The boys tried to see through the spray that was flung up by the falling water. Jack gave a shout.

"Yes – there *is* a ledge, and I believe we could get on to it. For goodness' sake be careful not to fall into that churning water! We'd be carried away and drowned if so, it's going at such a pace!"

The boy bent down, ran through the flying spray, and leapt on to a wet ledge beside the water, just inside the tunnel into which it disappeared. He nearly slipped and fell, but managed to right himself.

He flashed his torch into the tunnel and saw the amazing sight of the heaving, rushing water tearing away down the dark vault of the mountain tunnel. It was very weird, and the noise inside the tunnel was frightening.

Paul and Mike were soon beside Jack. He shouted into their ears. "We'd better go along here and see if it leads anywhere. I think this is the way the robbers must have gone with Ranni and Pilescu. Keep as far from the water as you can and don't slip, whatever you do!"

The boys made their way with difficulty along the water-splashed tunnel. The water roared beside them in its hollowed-out channel. The noise was thunderous. Their feet were soon wet with the splashing of the strange river.

"The tunnel is widening out here," shouted back Jack, after about an hour. "Our ledge is becoming almost a platform!"

So it was. After another minute or two the boys found themselves standing on such a broad ledge that when they crouched against the back of it, the spray from the river no longer reached them.

They rested there for a while. Paul was terribly tired by now. Mike looked at his watch. It was four o'clock in the morning! The sun would be up outside the mountain – but here it was as dark as night.

"I feel so sleepy," said Paul, cuddling up against Mike. "I think we ought to have a good long rest."

Jack got up and looked around the broad platform for a more comfortable resting-place. He gave a shout that quickly brought the others to him.

"Look," said Jack, shining his torch on to a recess in the wall of the tunnel at the back of the platform. "This is where the robbers must sometimes rest before going on to wherever they live!"

In the recess, which was like a broad shelf of rock, lay some fur rugs. The boys cuddled into them, snuggled up to one another, closed their eyes and fell asleep at once. They were tired out with their night's travel.

They slept for some hours, and then Jack awoke with a start. He opened his eyes and remembered at once where he was – on the inside of the mountain! He sat up – and suddenly saw the platform outside the recess where the boys were, was lighted brightly. Voices came to him – and he saw a flaring torch held high. What could be happening now?

The other boys did not wake. They were too tired to

hear a sound! Jack leaned out of the rugs and tried to see who was holding the torch. He had a nasty shock – for it was held by one of the robbers! When Jack saw him turn round and his red wolf-tail swing out behind him, he knew without a doubt that the robbers were there within a few feet of him.

The boy tried to see what they were doing. They were at the edge of the river, at the end of the rocky platform. As Jack watched he saw two more men come up from the ledge that ran beside the river. It was plain that the broad platform they were on narrowed into the same sort of ledge that ran beside the upper part of the river. The men were coming up from lower down – and they were dragging something behind them, something that floated on the water. Jack could not see what it was, for the light from the torch flickered and shook, making shadows dance over everything.

The men called to one another hoarsely. They did something at the edge of the water, and then, without a glance toward the recess in which the boys were sleeping, they turned and made their way up the tunnel through which the boys had come, keeping along the ledge in single file. They were going up to the temple-cave, Jack was sure.

"Going to rob people again, I suppose!" thought the boy, excitedly. "They've taken Ranni and Pilescu somewhere further down, and tied them up, I expect – left them safe, as they thought. Golly, if only we could find out where they are, we could rescue them easily now that the robbers have left them for a while."

He looked at his watch. It showed ten minutes to nine! It was morning. Would Yamen and Tooku, Beowald and the villagers have arrived at the temple-cave yet, and meet the robbers on their way? Jack could not imagine what would happen. He woke the others and told them what he had seen.

"The thing to do now is to get along as quickly as we

242

can, and find out where Ranni and Pilescu are," he said.
"The robbers have gone in the opposite direction. Come on,
I saw where they came from. It's plain they follow the
river."

The boys shook off the warm rugs. Jack flashed his torch
round the comfortable recess to make sure they had left
nothing behind. The light fell on a tiny shelf at the back. In it
was something wrapped in a cloth. Jack unwrapped it in
curiosity. Inside was a big Baronian loaf, crusty and stale.

"We'd better soak it in water and eat some," said Jack,
pleased. "I'm hungry enough to enjoy bread and water,
even if you two aren't! I suppose the robbers leave bread
here to help themselves to when they rest in these rugs."

When they pulled off the crust of the big loaf they found
that the bread was not too hard to eat after all. They did not
even need to soak it in water. Paul, as usual, had a big
packet of the honey-flavoured Baronian chocolate with him,
and the three boys thoroughly enjoyed their strange meal
beside the rushing mountain river.

There was a flattish sort of cup on the little shelf where
they had found the bread; and the boys dipped this into the
clear river water and drank. It was as cold as ice, and tasted
delicious.

Jack bent down to fill the cup again and something caught
his eye, as he flashed his torch round. He stopped and gave
a surprised exclamation.

"Whatever's that? Look – that thing over there?"

The others looked. Tied by a leather thong to a jutting
rock was what looked like a hollowed-out raft. It was broad
and flat, with a hollow in the middle. The sides were
strengthened with strip upon strip of leather, bound tightly
over the edges.

"It's a raft-boat, or boat-raft, whatever you like to call it!"
said Mike, surprised. "I've never seen anything like it before. Isn't it odd? What's it for?"

"To go down the river, I imagine!" said Jack, joyfully.
"My word, we shall soon get along if we use that raft!"

"But how did the men get here on it?" said Paul, puzzled. "They couldn't float against the current, and it's very strong here."

"They probably crept up on the narrow rocky ledge that seems to run beside the river all the way," said Jack. "But behind them each time they come, they must drag a raft like this, which they use to get themselves back quickly. I say, this is getting awfully exciting! We can take the raft for ourselves, and that will mean that we leave the robbers I saw just now far behind us, for they will have to walk along the ledge as we did, instead of using their boat. Come on – let's try it!"

"I shouldn't be surprised if it takes us right to the place where Ranni and Pilescu are prisoners," said Paul. "Undo that leather thong, Mike, and let's get into the funny boat."

The boys untied the leather strip, and got into the

Down they went on the rushing mountain river

244

hollow centre of the solid raft. It was absolutely un-sinkable, made out of wood from a big tree, hollowed out carefully in the middle. The boys soon found out why the edges were bound so thickly and firmly with strips of leather!

They let the raft go free on the rushing stream. At once they floated into the dark tunnel from which Jack had seen the robbers come. The raft swung round and round as it went, and bumped hard against the rocky sides of the strange dark tunnel. The leather edges took off the worst jolts, but even so, the boys had to cling tightly to the raft to prevent themselves from being jerked overboard!

"This is the most exciting thing we've ever done!" shouted Jack, above the roar of the water. "Golly, aren't we going fast! I hope we don't come to a waterfall!"

Down they went on the rushing mountain river, down and down in the darkness. The raft rushed along as fast as a speed boat, and the three boys gasped for breath. Where did the river flow to?

In The Secret Forest

The raft rushed along, swinging and bobbing. Sometimes the water was smoother, and then the raft floated more slowly, but on the whole it rushed along at a terrific pace. Once the roof of the tunnel was so low that the boys had to crouch right down on the raft to prevent their heads being bumped hard against it.

"We're going down and down," said Jack. "The river must be running right through the mountain in a downward direction, and I suppose will come out at the other side."

"The other side! Do you mean where the Secret Forest is?" cried Mike.

Jack nodded his head and his eyes gleamed eagerly in the light of Mike's torch. "Yes! If the river *does* come out into the open, and I suppose it must at last, we shall be somewhere on the mountain-side overlooking the Secret Forest itself. So, you see, there *is* a way of getting there! And the robbers know it. I shouldn't be surprised if that really was smoke I saw that day we flew over it in the aeroplane."

The boys felt even more excited, if that was possible! They sat on the weird raft-boat and thought about their night's adventure. It was stranger than any they had ever had. This mountain river seemed never-ending. How long did it go and on and on?

After about two hours a startling thing happened. Jack saw a light, bright and golden, far ahead of them. "Look!" he said. "What's that?"

They floated rapidly nearer and nearer to the gleam, and soon they saw what it was. It was daylight, sunlight, bright and golden. They were soon coming out into the open air!

"We'll be able to get off the raft and stretch our legs a

bit!" said Jack, thankfully, for they were all beginning to feel very cramped indeed. But Jack was wrong. There was no getting off that raft yet!

It suddenly shot out into the open air, and the boys blinked their eyes, dazzled by the sudden bright sunshine. When they could see properly, they saw that they were indeed on the other side of the steep Killimooin mountains!

Below them, not very far away, was the Secret Forest! The mountain river, after having flowed for miles through the mountain tunnels, was now flowing down the slopes of the hill, taking the raft with it. It spread out into a wide river, and the raft sailed along in the middle, where the current was swift and strong. There appeared to be no dangerous waterfall to navigate! That was very fortunate, Jack thought.

"Do you suppose this river goes right down to the Secret Forest?" said Mike, trying to see where it flowed, far ahead of them. He caught glimpses of silver here and there, near the forest. It really did look as if the river flowed to it!

"I believe it does," said Jack, as the raft floated swiftly down the current. "We are getting nearer and nearer!"

After some time the river was very near to the great forest. The boys could see how wide and thick and dark it was. Now it no longer looked merely a great stretch of green; they could see the trees themselves, tall and close-set together. The river flowed on and on towards it.

The raft reached the outermost fringe of trees, and the river then disappeared into the forest. The boys were swept along on the raft, and as soon as they entered the forest, the sunshine disappeared, and a dim green light was all they had to see by.

"How dark and thick the trees are!" said Jack, awed. "The river must go right through this forest."

"I wonder where it goes to," said Mike. "Rivers all go to the sea. How can this one get out of this closed-in valley? You would think it would make a big lake – all this water flowing down the mountain-side like this, with nowhere to escape to!"

This was a puzzle, too. The boys thought about it as the raft swung along beneath the arching trees. Then, quite suddenly, they were in a big, wide pool, like a small lake, completely surrounded by trees. The river flowed through the pool, and out at the opposite side.

The raft swung to the side of the pool, and Jack gave a cry of surprise.

"This is where the robbers live! Look at those strange houses, or whatever you like to call them!"

The boys saw that round the lake-side were strange, bee-hive shaped houses, made of branches of trees and dried mud. From a hole at the top smoke appeared. Then Jack knew that he had been right when he thought he had seen a spiral of smoke from the aeroplane! The smoke from the bee-hive houses joined together as it rose into the air, and made a straight streak of blue smoke that hung almost motionless, for no wind came into that still valley.

No one was to be seen. If there was anyone in the huts, they must be sleeping, Jack thought! Their raft swung silently to the bank and the three boys leapt off at once. They crouched down in the bushes watching to see if anyone had noticed them. But nobody had. Not a soul appeared from the curious huts.

The boys were very hungry indeed, but they dared not go to ask for food. They whispered together, wondering what to do. Behind them was the deep, dark forest. In front was the great pool, out of which flowed the river, disappearing into the depths of the Secret Forest.

"Do you suppose all the robbers have gone up to the temple-cave?" whispered Mike. Jack shook his head. "No," he said. "I only saw five or six. Hundreds must live here. Sh! Look, there are some children!"

The boys saw four or five children coming from the forest, going towards the huts. They had nothing on at all, except for a strip of skin round their waists. They were dirty, and their bright hair was tangled and long. They wore bright bird-feathers behind their ears, and looked real little ruffians.

A woman appeared at the door of one hut, and the children shouted to her. Paul turned to the others.

"Did you understand what those children said? They said they had been to see the big men who were prisoners! So Ranni and Pilescu must be here somewhere. Shall we try going along that path where the children came from?"

"We should get completely lost in the Secret Forest," said Mike, feeling scared. "There are probably wolves here too. I almost wish we hadn't come. We should have waited and come with the others!"

"We will go down the forest path," said Paul, suddenly becoming the Prince of Baronia again. "Stay here if you do not wish to follow me. I, myself, will find Ranni and Pilescu!"

There was nothing for it but to follow Paul. He skirted the pool carefully and then found the narrow path down which the robber-children had come. It ran between the thickly-growing trees, and was evidently much used. Here and there the trees were curiously marked as if with an axe.

"Perhaps it's the way the robbers have of marking their way through the forest," said Paul.

"Yes – sort of signposts," answered Jack, who had thought the same thing. "Well, as long as I see those marks, I shan't feel lost!"

They went on down the narrow, twisting path. It curved round trees, wandered between the thick trunks, and seemed never-ending. Now and again the children saw the axe-marks on a tree-trunk again. The forest was very quiet and still. No wind moved the branches of the trees. No bird sang. It was very mysterious and silent.

Jack's sharp ears heard the sound of voices. "Someone's coming!" he said. "Shin up a tree, quick!"

The three chose trees that did not seem too difficult to climb quickly. They were up them in a trice. A squirrel-like animal bounded away in alarm from Jack. The boy peered down between the branches.

He saw three more children going along, fortunately towards the pool they had left. They shouted to one another, and seemed to be playing some sort of hopping game. They soon passed, and did not guess that there were three pairs of anxious eyes following their movements from the branches above them.

As soon as the robber-children were out of sight the boys jumped down and went on again. "I hope that they haven't hidden Ranni and Pilescu too far away!" said Jack, with a groan. "I'm getting tired again and awfully hungry!"

"So am I," said Mike. Paul said nothing. He meant to go on until he found his men. He did not seem to be tired, though he looked it. Jack thought he was a very plucky boy indeed, for he was younger and smaller than the other two, and yet managed to keep up with them very well.

Jack stopped again and motioned to the others to listen. They stood still, and heard voices once more. Up a tree they went at once, but this time the voices did not come any nearer. Paul suddenly went red with excitement. He leaned towards Jack, who was on the branch next to him.

"Jack! I think that is Pilescu's deep voice. Listen!"

They all listened, and through the forest came the deep tones of Pilescu's voice, without a doubt. In a trice the boys had shinned down the tree again and were running down the path towards the voices.

They came out into a small clearing. In the middle of this there was a hole, or what looked like a hole from where the boys stood. Across the top of the hole were laid heavy beams of wood, separated each from the other by a few inches, to allow air to penetrate into the hole.

It was from this hole or pit that the voices came. Mike took a quick look round the clearing to see if anyone was there. But it seemed to be completely empty. He ran across to the pit.

"Ranni! Pilescu?" he cried, and Paul tried to force apart the heavy logs of wood.

"Ranni! Are you there? Pilescu, are you hurt?" cried Paul, in a low voice.

There was an astonished silence, and then came Ranni's voice, mingled with Pilescu's.

"Paul! Little lord! What are you doing here? Paul, can it be you?"

"Yes – I'm here and Mike and Jack," said Paul. "We have come to rescue you."

"But how did you get here?" cried Ranni, in amazement. "Did you come through the mountain and down the river into the depths of the Secret Forest?"

"Yes," said Mike. "It has been a tremendous adventure, I can tell you."

"Are you all all right?" asked Pilescu.

"Yes, except that we're awfully hungry," said Jack, with a laugh.

"If you can move those logs, with our help, we will give you food," said Ranni. "We have some here in this pit. The robbers put bread and water here, and we have plenty. Goodness knows what they meant to do with us. I suppose they captured us because they knew we had found the secret of their coming and going, and did not want us to tell anyone."

The boys began to try and move the heavy logs. Ranni and Pilescu helped them. They shifted little by little, though it was as much as the whole five of them could do to move them even an inch! At last, however, there was enough space for Ranni and Pilescu to squeeze out of the pit, and haul themselves up on to the level ground.

They sat there panting. "Not a nice prison at all," said Ranni, jokingly, as he saw tears in Paul's eyes. The boy had been very anxious about his two friends, and now that he had Ranni's arm about him again, he was so relieved he felt almost like crying.

"Funny boy, isn't he!" whispered Mike to Jack. "So awfully brave, and yet he cries like a girl sometimes."

"We'd better hide quickly," said Ranni. "The robbers may come back at any moment and we don't want them to find us all here. They would have five prisoners then, instead of two! Let's push the logs back exactly as they were, Mike. It will puzzle the robbers to know how we escaped, when they see that the logs have apparently not been moved!"

Back To The Robber Camp

It was easy to shift the logs back into position for now Ranni and Pilescu were able to use the whole of their strength, instead of being hindered by being in a deep pit. They finished their task and then went to discuss their next move under some thick bushes at the edge of the clearing.

They had a good view of the path from there and could see anyone coming, though they themselves could not be seen. They sat down and talked earnestly. Jack told the two Baronians all that had happened, and they were amazed.

"Shall we try and get back home the way we came?" asked Mike. "Perhaps that would be best."

"I don't know about that," said Ranni. "Once the robbers discover that we are gone, they will be on the look-out for us, and probably men will be guarding the way back, ready to take us again."

"Well, what else is there to do?" asked Paul, impatiently.

"Let us think carefully, little lord," said Ranni. "Can there be any other way out of this Secret Forest, so well-hidden within the great Killimooin mountains?"

Everyone was silent. It was quite impossible to climb the surrounding mountains, even if they could make their way through the depths of the forest towards them.

Jack spoke at last. "Ranni, where do you suppose this river goes to? It must go somewhere. If it was penned up in this valley, it would make a simply enormous lake, and doesn't do that, or we should have seen it from the air, when we flew over."

Ranni sat and thought. "It must go somewhere, of

course," he said. "Maybe it finds its way underground, as it did in the mountain. You think perhaps it would be a good idea to follow the river, Jack, and see if we can float away on it, maybe through a tunnel in one of the mountains, to the other side."

"We could try," said Jack, doubtfully. "We could go back to the queer beehive-like houses tonight and see if our raft is still there. If it is, we could board it and go off on the river. The river won't take us backwards, that is certain, so we shall have to go forwards with it!"

"Well, we will try that," said Ranni, though he did not sound very hopeful. "Let us eat now, shall we? You must, as you said, be very hungry."

The Baronians had brought the bread with them from the pit. All five began to eat, thinking of the adventure that lay ahead. Pilescu looked at the three boys. He saw that they were worn out.

"We will find a good hiding-place and rest there," he said to Ranni. "We shall need to be fresh for tonight. Come, then. I will carry Paul. He is already half asleep!"

But before they could creep away, they heard the sound of voices, and saw three or four robber-women coming down the path, carrying pitchers of water and more bread! They had evidently come to bring food to the prisoners. Very silently the five vanished into the trees.

The women went to the pit and placed the food and water beside it. They had apparently been told to take it there and leave it, so that the men could hand it down to the prisoners when they came later, and could move the logs a little apart. It was beyond the women's strength to move them.

The women peered curiously between the logs, and were amazed when they could not see the prisoners. They chattered together excitedly and then peered down again. It was dark in the pit, but even so, they should have been able to catch sight of the two men. Had not the children been to see them that morning and come back with tales of their fierce shouts and cries, their fiery red hair and beards? Then why could not these things be seen and heard now?

The women became certain that the prisoners were not there. Yet how could they have escaped? The logs were still across the mouth of the pit, and no men could move those without help from outside! It was a mystery to them. Chattering loudly, they fled away back to the robber encampment to tell the news. They left the food and water beside the empty pit.

As soon as the women had gone, Ranni slipped out of his hiding-place and went to the pit. He took the bread and ran back to the others.

"This may be useful!" he said. He tied a leather thong around it, and hung it at his back. It was a flat, round loaf, easy to carry.

"Now we will find a good hiding-place," said the big Baronian. Pilescu picked up Paul in his arms and the two men strode away into the forest to find a safe hiding-place to rest until night came.

Presently they found one. A great rock jutted up between the thickly-growing trees, and underneath it was a well-hidden hole, draped by greenery. Once in the shelter of that rock, no one would see them.

"Do you know the way back to the clearing, Pilescu?" asked Paul, sleepily, as the big man arranged him comfortably on the ground, on the fur-lined cloaks that he and Ranni had taken off for the time being. They made good rugs for the three tired boys.

"I know it, little lord. Do not worry your head," said Pilescu. "Now sleep. You must be wide-awake tonight, for you may need all your wits about you!"

The boys soon slept. They had had so little sleep the night before, and were so exhausted with all their adventures, that it was impossible to keep awake. The men kept a watch. They had been very touched to know that the boys had followed them to rescue them. Now it was their turn to watch over the boys, and save them from the robbers!

The sun began to slide down towards the west. The day was going. Ranni dozed, and Pilescu kept watch. Then Pilescu dozed whilst Ranni kept eyes and ears open. He heard excited cries towards the evening, coming from the clearing, and guessed that the robbers had discovered their escape. Then all was silence again. The Secret Forest was the most silent place that Ranni had ever been in. He wondered if the wind ever blew down in that valley, and if birds ever sang. It made him .jump when a mouse-like creature scurried over his foot.

Twilight came creeping into the forest. It was always dim there, and difficult to see the sunshine. Twilight came there before the outer world had lost its daylight. Ranni looked at his watch. Half-past seven. The boys still slept. Let them sleep for another hour or two, and then they would creep through the darkness of the forest, back to the clearing where they had left the raft.

Jack awoke first. He stretched himself and opened his eyes, looking into complete darkness. He wondered where he was. Then he heard Ranni speaking in a low voice to Pilescu, and everything came back to him. He was in the Secret Forest, of course – hidden under that rock! He sat up at once.

"Ranni! Pilescu! What time is it? Is everything all right?"

"Yes," said Ranni. "Soon we will go to get the raft. We will wake the others now, and eat. Paul! Mike! It is time to wake!"

Soon all five of them were eating the hard bread. Ranni had some water in his flask, and everyone drank a little. Then they were ready to go.

By the light of his torch Ranni made his way back to the clearing where the pit was. He flashed his light around. There was no one there at all. The logs had been dragged away from the pit, when the robbers had come to see if what their women had said was true.

"We will take the path back," said Ranni. "It is over there. Take hands and go in single file. We must not lose hold of one another. I go first. You next, Paul. Then Mike and Jack, and Pilescu last. Now – are you ready?"

They found the path and went along it quietly in single file. The boys felt excited, but perfectly safe now that they had Ranni and Pilescu.

Ranni halted after a while. He flashed his torch here and there. He had gone from the path!

"We are not very far from it," he said. "I saw the axe-marks in a tree only a little way back. We must look for them."

It was anxious work looking for the axe-marks which would tell them they were once more on the right path. Mike felt very uncomfortable as he wondered what would happen if they really got lost in that enormous forest! He thought he saw two gleaming eyes looking at him from between the trees and he jumped.

"Is that a wolf?" he whispered to Jack. But it was only his imagination! There was no wolf, merely a couple of shining leaves caught in the light of Ranni's brilliant torch!

"Ah!" said Ranni, at last, in a glad voice. "Here is the path again. And look, there are axe-marks on that tree. Now we can go forward again. Keep a look-out, all of you, for the axe-marks that tell us we are on the right path."

Everyone watched anxiously for the marks after that. It was impossible to stray far from the path if they followed the marks. They were made at regular intervals, and the little company soon made steady progress.

"We must be near the encampment!" said Ranni at last, in a low voice. "Can you hear the lapping of water? I think we are nearing that big pool."

In another minute his torch shone on to the glittering waters of the pool. They had reached the cluster of huts. If only the robbers did not see or hear them!

A Way Of Escape?

Everything was quiet. There were only a few small night-sounds – the lapping of the water, the squeal of some small animal, the splash of a fish jumping. There was nothing else to be heard at all.

The five stood quite still beside the big pool, listening. A curious sound came on the air, and the boys clutched one another.

"It's all right," whispered Ranni, a laugh in his voice. It's only one of the robbers snoring in the nearest hut!"

So it was. The sound came again, and then died away. Ranni, who had switched off his torch, switched it on again. He wanted to find the raft that Paul had told him about. Luckily it was quite near him, about ten yards away, tied to a tree.

"Did you come down the mountain river on a raft like that?" whispered Paul to Ranni. The big man answered in a low voice.

"We came on a raft only as far as the outlet of the river, just where it leaves the mountain. The men steered the raft to the bank there, and we all jumped off. They tied up the raft and we walked the rest of the way to the Secret Forest. Apparently, whenever the robbers go up to the Temple Cave they walk along the ledge beside the mountain river, and drag a raft up with them, floating it on the rushing water. It must be hard work!"

"Oh! Then that's why there are no rafts to be seen on this pool," said Jack, who had been puzzling about this. "They only use them inside the mountain, to bring them down quickly."

"Sh!" said Pilescu, warningly. "We had better not talk any more. Hold your torch higher, Ranni, so that I can see to untie the raft."

It did not take long to free the raft. Ranni found a broken branch to use as a paddle. He did not want to be completely at the mercy of the river. With the branch to use, he could steer a little, and, if necessary, bring the raft to the bank.

"Get on the raft," whispered Ranni. They all got into the hollowed-out piece in the centre. it was a tight fit! Ranni pushed the raft into the centre of the big pool, where it was caught in the current that flowed through it. The raft swung along at once, very slowly but surely. Soon it was out of the pool and on the river, which ran through the Secret Forest for miles.

It was very weird and mysterious, swinging along on the swift river, through the heart of the dark forest. Sometimes branches of trees swept down low and bumped the heads of the travellers, scraping their faces. It was impossible to prevent them. Ranni tried shining his torch so that they might have warning of overhanging boughs but the river was swift, and the down-sweeping branches were on them before they knew.

The boys huddled against one another, stiff and uncomfortable. When a big branch nearly took Paul overboard and gave him a great bruise on his forehead, Ranni decided to moor the raft till the night was over. He did not expect the robbers to pursue them down the river, because they had no boats.

So he tied the raft to a tree, and the five of them nibbled bread and talked in low voices. Ranni fell off to sleep after a while, but the boys were wide-awake now. Pilescu kept watch. It seemed a long long time till dawn, but at last it came. The trees were so thick just there that the boys could see no sunlight, only a gradual lightening around them, as the tree trunks began to show, and the leaves to take on colour.

"We'll go on now," said Ranni. He untied the raft and on they went again, caught by the strong current. Now they could see when branches of trees would scrape over the raft, and Ranni steered to avoid them.

The river wound in and out, and suddenly took a great curve, almost doubling back on itself.

"I hope it doesn't flow back very far!" said Pilescu. "We don't want to land back near the robber camp!"

The river did wind back a good way, and at one part, although the little company did not know it, it was only about a mile from the robbers! It had a strange course in the Secret Forest. It flowed half-way through, doubled back, and finally flowed out of the trees about six miles from where it first flowed in. The travellers did not know this, though Ranni could tell, by the position of the sun, that they were now travelling almost in the opposite direction.

The trees suddenly thinned, and sunshine flooded down here and there, almost dazzling the two men and the three boys. The river flowed more rapidly, and the raft bobbed about.

"We are coming out of the Secret Forest!" said Jack, shading his eyes and looking forward. "The trees are getting thinner and thinner. Where does this river go. I wonder? I do wish it would take us right through the mountains somewhere and out at the other side. Then we could just walk round them till we come to Killimooin Castle."

"Not so easily done!" said Pilescu.

A shout made them turn their heads. To their horror, between the trees, they saw one of the robbers! He called out something, and then ran off to tell his comrades, his red wolf-tail swinging behind him.

Six or seven more came running with him after a few minutes, and they stood watching the raft as it swung along in the distance.

One robber yelled something after them. "What did he say?" asked Jack. Ranni looked a little solemn.

"He speaks a curious dialect," he said, "But I think I understood him to say, "Soon, soon, you will be in the middle of the earth!" I wonder what he meant."

Everyone thought about it. "Do you think it means that the river goes down underground?" asked Jack. "Well if it does, it's what we want, isn't it?"

"It depends on whether there is room for the raft or not," said Ranni. "We must keep a sharp look-out."

The river ran on. The boys saw the mountains of Killimooin around them. In front of them, slightly to the left, was the one they knew, on the other side of which Killimooin Castle was built. It looked very different from this side, but the summit was the same shape.

Suddenly they heard a terrific roaring sound ahead of them. Quick as thought Ranni plunged the tree-branch into the water and tried to steer the raft out of the current. But it was very swift and the raft kept on its course.

Jack saw that the big Baronian looked pale and anxious as he tried in vain to swing the raft from its steady course. "What's the matter?" he asked.

"Can you hear that noise?" said Ranni. "I think the river makes a fall somewhere ahead – maybe a big waterfall. We don't want to be caught in it. I can't get this raft out of the current.

Pilescu suddenly slipped overboard, and, taking the raft with one hand, tried to swim to the shore with it. But he could not move it from the swift current.

"Jump!" he cried to the others. "Jump, and swim. It is our only hope. We are getting near the fall."

Everyone jumped into the water. Paul was the weakest swimmer and big Ranni took him on his back. The raft went bobbing off by itself.

Pilescu helped Mike and Jack, but it was a stiff struggle to get to the bank of the swiftly-running river. They sat there, exhausted, hoping that no robber would come by, for they had no strength to resist anyone!

They recovered after a while. The hot sun dried their clothes, and steam began to rise from them.

"I wonder what happened to the raft," said Jack.

"We'll go and see!" said Ranni. "The noise is so

tremendous here that the waterfall, or whatever it is, can't be very far ahead. I think it must be where that fine mist hangs in the air over there, like smoke."

They walked on beside the river, over rough ground. The noise became louder and louder. Then they suddenly saw what happened to the mountain river!

They rounded a big rock and came to the place where fine spray flew. The great silver river rushed by them – and then disappeared completely!

No river flowed ahead. The whole of the water vanished somewhere in that little place. Ranni went forward cautiously. He called to the others:

"It's a good thing we got off the raft when we did! The river goes right down into the earth here!"

All the others joined Ranni. The spray soaked them as they stood there, trying to see where the volume of water went to.

It really was most extraordinary. There appeared to be a great cavern or chasm in the ground into which the river emptied itself with a terrific roar. The water fell into the enormous hole and completely disappeared.

"So that's what the robber meant when he shouted that we should soon be in the middle of the earth," said Jack. "That water must go deep down into enormous holes and crevices among the rocks. I suppose it goes right under the surrounding mountains and comes out somewhere else as a river again. How amazing!

"What a mercy we leapt off the raft!" said Mike, feeling scared at the thought of what might have happened if they and the raft together had plunged down into the heart of the earth. "Golly! This river has an exciting course! Through the mountain, down the slope, into the Secret Forest, out again, and down this chasm. Well – there's no way out for us here, that's certain."

The five travellers left the curious place, and went to sit by a sun-warmed rock to dry their spray-wet clothes once more.

Everyone jumped into the water

"The robbers must think we are all lost in the depths of the earth now," said Pilescu. "They will not be on the watch for us any more. That is something to the good, at any rate."

"What are we going to do?" asked Paul

"There is only one thing to do, my little lord," said Pilescu. "We must go back the way we came!"

"What! Up into the mountain, beside the river all the way, and back to the temple-cave?" cried Paul. "Oh, we shall never do that!"

"We must," said Ranni. "It is the only way out. I am going to climb a high tree so that I may see where the river flows out of the mountain."

He climbed up the biggest tree nearby, and shaded his eyes for a long time. Then he came down.

"I cannot see where the river comes forth from

Killimooin," he said. "It is too far away. But I can see where the water enters the Secret Forest – or I think I can. We must go the east, and walk until we come to the river. We cannot miss it, for it will lie right across our path!"

"Let us have something to eat first," said Paul. "Where is the bread? There is plenty left, isn't there?"

There was not plenty, but there was enough. They sat and ate hungrily. Then Ranni rose, and everyone got up too.

"Now to find the river again," said Ranni. "We will skirt the Secret Forest until we come to the rushing water. Then we will follow it upwards to the mountain!"

The Terrible Storm

Meanwhile, what had happened to the two girls? They had done as the boys had suggested, and had awakened Tooku and Yamen at once. The couple sat up in their bed, bewildered at the children's extraordinary story. Ranni and Pilescu captured by the robbers! The statue that split into two! All the boys gone! It seemed like an unbelievable nightmare to Yamen and Tooku.

"We can do nothing tonight," said Tooku, nursing his injured arm. "The servants would be of no use to hunt for the boys and the others. They would be too afraid. Tomorrow, early, we must send the servants to gather together the villagers of the mountain-side."

The girls did not want to wait so long, but there was nothing else to be done. They went back to bed, but not to sleep. They cuddled together on a small couch, covered with a warm fur rug, and talked together, worried about the boys. At last, just before dawn, they dozed off, and were awakened by Yamen.

Soon everyone in the castle knew what had happened the night before. The servants went about with scared faces. Paul's mother heard the girls' story again and again, tears in her eyes as she thought of how Paul had marched off to rescue his men.

"He is a true little Baronian!" she said. "How glad I am that Mike and Jack are with him! Oh, why didn't they wait until we could send soldiers or armed villagers to find Ranni and Pilescu?"

A band of people came climbing up on mountain ponies, fetched by servants of the castle and by the goatherd, Beowald. They had been amazed at the tale told to them, but all of them were determined to rescue their "little lord" as they called Paul.

Beowald was with them. He led them up the hill to the old temple-cave. The villagers shrank back in fear when they saw the queer stone images. The statue of the sitting man, at the back, was now whole again. The robbers that the boys had seen the night before had come up to the cave, found the statue in half, and, fearing that their secret had been discovered, had closed the two halves together once more and gone back into the cave below.

Peggy and Nora watched Blind Beowald put his finger into the right ear of the statue. The villagers cried out in wonder when they saw the stone man split in half, and divide slowly. Beowald pointed down to the hole that the statue hid so well.

"That is the way," he said.

The villagers went to the hole and looked down. They shivered. They did not want to go down at all. Thoughts of mysterious magic, of mountain-spirits, filled their heads.

But one bolder than the rest slid down the rope, calling to the others to follow. One by one they went down. The girls wanted to go too, but Tooku and Yamen forbade them sternly. "This is men's work," they said. "You would only get in the way." So the girls had to go back to the castle, where Paul's mother sat waiting for news, white and anxious.

Nora and Peggy tried to comfort her by telling her of the adventures they and the boys had had before, and how they had always won through in the end. The Queen smiled at them, and sighed.

"You are adventurous children!" she said. "Wherever you go, you have adventures. I shall be glad when this adventure is over!"

There was no news at all that day. The search party did not return. Beowald came down from the temple to say that although he had listened well by the hole, he had heard nothing. For the first time he was angry with his blindness, for he badly wanted to follow his friends into the mountain. But he did not dare to, because he would be completely lost in a place he did not know.

Towards tea-time the sky suddenly darkened. The girls went to the window. Yamen was with them, and she looked out too.

"A storm is coming," she said, pointing to the west. "A great storm. You must not be frightened, little ones. Sometimes, when the weather has been hot, the big clouds blow up, and the lighning tears the sky in two, whilst the thunder roars and echoes round."

"We are not afraid of storms, Yamen," said Nora. "It ought to be a wonderful sight, a storm in the Killimooin mountains!"

The sky grew so black that the girls could not see to read. Great clouds began to roll round the mountain itself, and soon the castle was completely swallowed up in the thick, swirling mists. Thunder rumbled in the distance. The little children in the nurseries of the castle began to cry.

"There's the lighning!" said Nora, as a vivid flash appeared, and everything was lighted up clearly for an instant. "Oh – what thunder! I've never heard anything like it!"

Killimooin seemed to be in the midst of the storm. Thunder cracked round the castle, and the lightning shivered the sky to pieces. It was as dark as night between the flashes.

"Although the two girls were not afraid of storms, they were awed by this one. The noise was so terrific and the lightning was so grand.

Then the rain came. Rain? It sounded more like a waterfall pouring down on the castle, lashing against the windows, forming itself into rivulets that rushed down the hillside at top speed. Never in their lives had the two girls seen or heard such rain. It almost drowned the thunder that still rolled around!

"Well, it's a mercy the boys are not out in this, but are somewhere in a cave," said Nora, trying to be cheerful.

But the boys were not in a cave! No, they were making their way towards the river where it entered the Secret Forest! They were almost there, and could see its shining waters. They were glad, because now they felt that they knew their way. They had only to follow the river's course backwards to the mountain, and climb up beside it as it flowed down through the heart of the hill!

Then the sky darkened, and the storm blew up. First, it was very still, and Ranni glanced uneasily at the sky. He knew the Baronian storms! They were as grand as the mountains themselves!

The storm broke, just as the little party reached the river and began to follow its swift course backwards to the mountain. Thunder cracked above their heads, and lightning split the darkened sky.

"We had better shelter," said Ranni, and looked about for somewhere to go. He did not want to stand under the trees in case they were struck by lightning. There were some thickly-growing bushes nearby with enormous flat leaves. The rain fell off the leaves as if they were umbrellas.

"We'll crawl under these bushes," said Ranni. "We can draw our cloaks over our heads. The rain will not soak through the fur lining."

But it did! It soaked through everything, and once again the company were wet! The boys hated the fierceness of this rainstorm. The drops pelted down, stinging them, slashing them, soaking through the bushes, their fur-lined cloaks, their clothes, and everything.

"What a storm!" said Paul. "It is the worst I ever remember in Baronia. I don't like it, Pilescu."

Pilescu pulled the small boy to him and covered him with his great arms. "You are safe with Pilescu," he said. "Not even the worst storm can harm you now!"

For two hours the rain poured down, never-ending. Jack was astonished to think that so much water could be held by clouds! It was as if someone up in the sky was emptying whole seas of water down on to the earth.

At last a break came in the clouds and a bit of brilliant blue sky showed through. The thunder died away. The lightning no longer flashed. The clouds thinned rapidly, and the rain stopped. The boys heaved sighs of relief. They were wet, cold and hungry. Ranni felt about in his big pockets and brought out some chocolate. It was very welcome.

"Now we must get on," he said. "If the sun comes out strongly, before it sets, we shall soon be dry again. We have a long climb ahead before we reach the place where the river gushes forth from the mountain. Shall I carry you for a while, little lord?"

"Certainly not," said Paul. "I can walk as well as Mike and Jack!"

But after three hours of hard walking the little prince was only too glad to be hoisted on to Pilescu's broad back! They made their way slowly on and up, the noise of the water always in their ears. They saw no sign of the robbers at all, though they kept a sharp look-out for them.

When evening began to fall they reached the place where the river flowed out of the mountain-side, rushing and roaring as if in pleasure to see the sun. They sat by the water and rested. They were all tired now.

"Well, we must begin our watery climb now," said Ranni, at last. "It will take us some hours to follow the river up to where it falls into the cave above. The way will be steep and often dangerous. Paul, I am going to tie you to me, for if you fall into the river, I cannot save you. You will be whirled away from me in an instant."

"Well, tie Mike and Jack to Pilescu, then," said Paul. "I don't want to be the only one."

In the end, all five were roped together, so that if one fell, the others might pull him up again to safety. Then the five of them entered the cavernous hole in Killimooin mountain, and prepared to climb up beside the rushing torrent.

There was a narrow ledge, as Ranni had guessed. It was

wet and slippery, and sometimes so narrow that it seemed impossible to walk on it. But by finding firm hand-holds in the rocky wall of the tunnel, the climbers managed to make their way steadily upwards.

Once Paul slipped and fell. He almost jerked Ranni off his feet, too. The boy half fell into the rushing water, but Ranni caught hold of the rope and tightened it quickly. The boy was pulled back to the ledge, and knelt there, gasping with fright.

"You are safe, little Paul. Do not be afraid," said Ranni, comfortingly, shouting above the rushing of the water.

"I'm not afraid!" yelled Paul, and got to his feet at once. He had had a bad scare, but he would not show it. Ranni felt proud of the little prince.

The toiled upwards, not saying a word, because it was soon too much effort to shout to make themselves heard above the noise of the river. It seemed as if they had been climbing up the narrow ledge for hours, with Ranni's torch showing the way at the front, and Pilescu's at the back, when the five saw something that startled them exceedingly.

The light from Ranni's torch fell on something swirling down the torrent! In surprise Ranni kept his torch pointed towards it – and the little company saw that it was a raft, on which were five or six of the small, wiry robbers, bobbing rapidly downwards to the Secret Forest!

The robbers saw them too, and uttered loud cries of amazement. In half a minute they were swept away down the river, out of sight, lost in the long black tunnel through which the water rushed downwards.

"They saw us!" yelled Jack. "Does it matter, do you think? Will they come after us?"

Ranni and Pilescu stopped to consider the matter. They thought it was possible that the robbers *would* turn back and pursue them. It would be easy to swing their raft against the side and leap out. They could drag their raft up behind them, as they apparently did each time they climbed up to the temple-cave.

"Ranni!" yelled Jack, again. "Do you think they'll come after us?"

"We think it is likely," replied Ranni. "We must push on quickly. Come, there is no time to be lost."

The five of them set off again. It was a hard and tiring journey. They were splashed continually by the river, which also overflowed time and again on to the ledge so that their legs were always wet. Sometimes the tunnel was very low, and once the company had to go down on hands and knees and crawl like that round a bend of the ledge, their heads touching the roof of the tunnel!

Ranni's torch gave out and Mike was glad he had one with him to lend to Ranni, for it was necessary to have two, one at the back of the line and one at the front.

"How much further have we to go?" groaned Paul. "How much further, Ranni?"

A Journey Up The Mountain River

It was a long, long climb. Ranni shone his torch on to his watch, and saw that it was nearly midnight! No wonder poor Paul was groaning, and wondering how much further they had to go. Even the two men were tired.

"Ranni, there's a sort of platform place somewhere," said Jack, remembering the broadening out of the ledge, where he and the others had slept in a recess at the back two nights before.

Ranni and Pilescu did not know about this. Jack shouted into their ears, telling them about it, and the two Baronians hoped that they would soon come to it. Then they would all have a rest. One or other could be on watch in case the robbers came!

Up they went again, stumbling over the rough, rocky ledge that ran beside the river. Once Mike slipped and fell headlong into the water. He pulled Jack right off his feet, and both boys disappeared. Paul gave a scream of fright.

But Pilescu stood steady, and gripped the rope. He pulled Jack and Mike firmly back to the side and helped the soaking boys out. The were shivering as much with fright as with cold! It was not at all a nice feeling to take a plunge unexpectedly into the icy mountain water. They were glad that Ranni had had the idea of roping everyone together. Jack hoped that neither of the big Baronians would fall into the river, for he was sure that if they did they would jerk the boys in after them! But Ranni and Pilescu were sure-footed, having been used to climbing hills and mountains all their lives, and neither of them slipped!

Paul was getting so tired that he could hardly stumble along. It was impossible for Ranni to carry him, for he needed both his hands, one to hold the torch, and the other to find hand-holds for himself. His heart ached for the tired boy stumbling along just behind him.

It was a long time before they came to the platform. Ranni did not even know he had come to it. He went along the ledge, feeling the wall, not noticing at first that he was getting further from the river. Mike gave a shout.

"I believe it's the platform! Oh good! This ledge is widening out tremendously!"

Ranni and Pilescu stopped and flashed their torches around. It *was* the platform, as the boys called it! Thank goodness for that.

"There's the recess where we slept, look!" shouted Mike. The men saw the hollowed-out recess in the wall at the back, lined with fur rugs. They saw something else, too. On the little shelf above was more bread, placed there by the robbers the company had seen swinging down on their raft two or three hours before!

"Now this is really good," said Ranni. He set Paul on his knee, took the bread, and broke it into pieces. Mike and Jack took some and began to eat hungrily. But Paul was too exhausted. He could eat nothing. His head fell forward on Ranni's broad chest, and he was asleep at once.

"You boys must rest on those rugs on that rocky couch there," said Ranni, speaking to Mike and Jack. "I will hold Paul in my arms to warm him. Pilescu will keep watch for the robbers in case they come back."

Mike and Jack flung themselves on to the strange resting-place at the back of the platform, and pulled the fur rugs over them. They were asleep in half a second. The two Baronians were sleepy too, but Pilescu was on guard and did not dare even to close his eyes.

Ranni fell asleep holding Paul. Only big Pilescu was awake. He felt his eyes closing. He had switched off his torch, for he did not want the robbers to see any light, if they came back. It was difficult to keep awake in the dark, when he was so tired!

His head nodded. He stood up at once. He knew it would be impossible not to sleep if he remained seated. He began to walk up and down the platform, like a lion in a cage. That kept him awake. He was not likely to fall asleep on his feet.

He paced steadily for two hours. Then he stiffened and listened. He could hear voices! They echoed up from the tunnel below. It must be the returning robbers!

"They have managed to get their raft to the side and land, and have turned back to come after us!" thought Pilescu. "What are we to do? They will be on us before we can escape. How I wish I had a gun with me!"

But the robbers had taken away all the weapons carried by the Baronians. Neither Ranni nor Pilescu had anything to defend themselves with, except their bare hands. Well, they could make good use of those!

The voices came nearer. Pilescu woke Ranni and whispered the news to him. Ranni put the sleeping Paul into the recess at the back, with the other boys. He did not wake.

"We will cover ourselves with our cloaks and sit with our backs to the wall, on either side of the recess," whispered Ranni. "It is just possible that the robbers may not see us, and may not guess that we are resting here. They would think that we were going ahead as fast as we could."

They could not hear any voices now. They guessed that the robbers were very near. They carried no torch but were coming along the ledge they knew so well, in complete darkness.

Ranni's sharp ears caught the sound of panting. A robber was on the platform! The two Baronians sat perfectly still, hoping that the three sleeping boys would make no sound. They had covered them completely with the rugs so that any snoring might not be heard. It was amazing that Ranni had been able to hear the robbers, because the river made almost as much noise there as anywhere else.

There came the sound of a loud voice and it was clear that all the robbers were now on the platform. Ranni and

Pilescu strained their ears for any signs that the wolf-tailed men were going to explore the wide ledge.

There appeared to be no more sounds at all. Neither Ranni nor Pilescu could hear panting or voices. They sat like statues, hardly breathing, trying to hear any unusual sound above the noise of the water.

They sat like that for ten minutes without hearing a sound. Then, very silently, Ranni rose to his feet. He felt for his torch, and pressed down the switch suddenly. The light flashed out over the platform. It was quite empty!

"They've gone," whispered Ranni. "I thought they must have, for I have heard nothing for the last ten minutes. They did not think of searching this platform. They have gone higher up, probably hoping to catch us in the cave where the great waterfall is."

"That's not so good," said Pilescu, switching off his torch. "If they wait for us there, they will catch us easily. Jack said that Beowald was going to fetch the villagers to hurry after us – it is possible that they might have got as far as the waterfall cave, and might help us. But we can depend on nothing!"

"We will let the boys rest a little longer," said Ranni. "There is no need to rush on, now that the robbers are in front of us, and not at the back! I will watch now, Pilescu, whilst you sleep."

Pilescu was thankful to be able to allow himself to close his eyes. He leaned his big head against the wall at the back, and fell into a deep sleep at once. Ranni was keeping guard, his eyes and ears on the look-out for anything unusual. It was a strange night for him, sitting quietly with his sleeping companions, hearing the racing of the mountain river, watching for wolf-tailed robbers to return!

But they did not return. There was no sound to make Ranni alert. The others slept peacefully, and the boys did not stir. Ranni glanced at his watch after a long time had passed. Six o'clock already! It was sunrise outside the mountain. The world would be flooded with light. Here it was as dark as midnight, and cold. Ranni was glad of his warm cloak.

Pilescu awoke a little while later. He spoke to Ranni.

"Have you heard anything, Ranni?"

"Nothing," said Ranni. "It is nearly seven o'clock, Pilescu. Shall we wake the boys and go on? There is no use in staying here. Even if the robbers are lying in wait for us above, we must push on!"

"Yes," said Pilescu, yawning. "I feel better now. I think I could tackle four or five of those ruffians at once. I will wake the boys."

He awoke them all. They did not want to open their eyes! But at last they did, and soon sat munching some of the bread they had found on the little shelf nearby the night before.

Ranni told them how the robbers had gone by in the night without discovering them.

"It's not very nice to think they're somewhere further up, waiting for us!" said Mike, feeling uncomfortable. "I suppose they'll be in one of the caves. "We'll have to look out!"

"We'll look out all right!" said Jack, who, like Pilescu, felt all the better for his night's sleep. "I'm not standing any nonsense from wolf-tailed robbers!"

They left the platform, and made their way to the ledge that ran beside the river, beyond the platform. As usual Ranni went first, having tied them all together firmly.

"It's not so very far up to the waterfall cave from here, as far as I remember," said Jack. "About two hours or so."

They began to stumble along the rocky ledge again, the water splashing over their feet. The boys were surprised to find that the ledge was now ankle-deep in water.

"It wasn't when we came down this way," said Mike. "Was it as deep as this when you and Pilescu were brought down by the robbers, Ranni?"

"No," said Ranni, puzzled. "It barely ran over the ledge. Look out – it's quite deep here – the river is overflowing its channel by about a foot. We shall be up to our knees!"

So they were. It was very puzzling and rather disturbing. Why was the river swelling like that?

In The Cave Of The Waterfall

The higher they went, the deeper the water became that overflowed the ledge. The river roared more loudly, too. Ranni puzzled over it and then suddenly realized the reason.

"It is the terrific rainstorm that has caused the river to swell!" he called back, his voice rising over the roar of the water. "The rain has soaked deep into the mountain, and has made its way to the river. You know what a rainstorm we had yesterday – it seemed as if whole seas of water had been emptied down on the earth. The river is swelling rapidly. I hope it doesn't swell much more, or we shall find it impossible to get along."

This was a very frightening thought. It would be dreadful to be trapped in the mountain tunnel, with the rushing river rising higher and higher. The three boys put their best feet forward and went as quickly as they could.

When nearly two hours had gone by, they began to hope they were nearing the waterfall cave. The river by now had risen above their knees and it was difficult to stagger along, because the water pulled against them the whole time. Ranni and Pilescu began to feel very anxious.

But, quite suddenly, they heard the sound of the waterfall that fell down into the big cave! It could only be the waterfall they heard, for the noise was so tremendous. "We are nearly there!" yelled Ranni.

"Look out for the robbers!" shouted back Jack.

They rounded the last bit of the ledge, and, by the light of Ranni's torch, saw that at last they were in the big cave, from which led the passage that would take them to the cave below the temple. They all felt very thankful indeed.

There was no sign of the robbers. The five of them went

cautiously into the cave and looked round. By the light of Ranni's torch the waterfall seemed to be much bigger than they had remembered. It fell from a great hole in the roof of the cave, and then ran down the channel to the tunnel, where it disappeared.

"It is greater now," said Ranni. "It must be much swollen by all the rain that fell yesterday. It already fills the hole through which it falls."

"What will happen if the hole can't take all the extra water?" asked Jack, curiously.

"I don't know," said Ranni. "Now, what shall we do next? Where are those robbers? Are they lying in wait for us somewhere? Are they up in the cave below the temple – or have they gone out on the mountain-side to rob again?"

"Well there's nothing for it but to go and see," said Pilescu. You boys stay down here, whilst Ranni and I go through the passage to the other cave."

"No – we'll go with you," said Paul, at once.

"That would be foolish," said Pilescu. "There is no need for all of us to put ourselves in danger. You will stay here until I or Ranni come back to tell you that it is safe for us all to go back down the mountain-side to the castle."

The boys watched the two big Baronians disappear into the narrow passage at the end of the cave opposite the great waterfall. It was difficult to stay behind and wait in patience. They sat in a corner and watched the tremendous fall of water at the other end of the cave.

"It's roaring as if it was angry!" said Jack. "I don't believe that hole is big enough now for all the volume of water to pour through. It will burst it bigger. I'm sure of it!"

"Well, the hole's made through the solid rock," said Mike. "It will have to burst the rock!"

Even as they spoke, a frightening thing happened. The water falling from the roof seemed suddenly to become bigger in volume and noise – and the boys saw a great mass of rock fall slowly from the roof! As Jack had said, the hole was no longer big enough to take the rush of water, and the force of its rush had burst away part of the solid, rocky roof!

Water at once flowed over the floor of the cave, almost to the feet of the astonished boys. They leapt up at once, staring at the water falling from the roof at the other end of the cave.

"I say! I hope the whole roof doesn't give way!" said Jack. "There must be a terrific rush of water to burst through the rock like that."

Nothing more happened, except that the extra volume of water made more noise and flooded the floor of the cave almost up to where the boys stood.

"Well, anyway, we're safe," said Mike. "We are just at the opening of the passage that leads upwards to the other cave. The water comes from the other direction. If it gets deep in here we'll have to go up the passage, that's all, away from it."

It got no deeper, however, so the boys waited patiently. Twenty minutes went by, and there was no sign of the return of Ranni or Pilescu. Mike began to feel worried.

"I wish they'd come back," he said. "I feel as if I can't stay here doing nothing much longer!"

"Whatever are Ranni and Pilescu doing?" said Jack, impatiently. "They must be right out on the mountain-side by now!"

"Let's go up the passage and find out," said Paul, at last. "I simply can't sit here any longer."

"All right," said Mike. "Come on. We can easily rush back if we hear Ranni and Pilescu coming."

They made their way up the narrow, curving passage, leaving behind them the noise of the great waterfall. But before they were half-way up, they heard the sound of someone else coming down!

"That must be Ranni and Pilescu coming back!" said

Mike, in a low voice. "Come on – we'll get back. We don't want to get into trouble for not waiting, as we were told."

They stumbled back down the rocky passage, and came out once more into the cave of the waterfall. It was still falling at the other end, with a mightier roar than ever.

"Here they come!" said Mike, as a light shone out of the passage. He flashed his own torch upwards to welcome Ranni and Pilescu.

And then he and the other two boys stared in horror. Certainly it was Ranni and Pilescu returning – but returning as prisoners! Once again they were captives, angry, but completely helpless! Six or seven robbers were behind them, kicking them and pushing them, holding sharp-pointed knives behind their backs to urge them on.

"Ranni! What's happened?" cried Paul, springing forward.

But before anything could be explained, the robbers, with cries of satisfaction, leapt at the three boys and forced their arms behind them. Mike tried his hardest to get out his scout-knife but it was impossible!

The robbers bound the boys' arms and legs together with thongs of supple leather. No matter how they struggled, they could not free themselves. They were placed on the floor of the cave, like trussed chickens. Ranni and Pilescu stood roaring like angry bulls, trying to free their own hands, which had been tightly tied behind them as before. The robbers tripped them defly to the ground and tied their legs together, too.

Small as they were, the Secret Forest robbers were very strong. Ranni and Pilescu were big giants of men, but the robbers swarmed over them like ants, and by their very smallness and deftness they overcame the two big men.

The robbers chattered together exultantly. Now they had all five prisoners to take back. But suddenly one of them pointed to the water that flowed over the floor of the cave.

They all looked at it in surprise. Clearly they had never

seen water flowing over the floor of the cave before. They looked at the water falling from the now bigger hole in the roof of the cave, at the other end. They saw what had happened, and ran fearfully to the ledge that ran beside the roaring river.

The water was now above their knees. They had left their raft behind them, below the platform-ledge. They gazed in panic at the water. They could not hear themselves speak, so near the waterfall, and ran back to where the five prisoners were, shouting to one another in terror.

The noise of the water grew louder. Everyone gazed fearfully at the hole through which it poured from the roof. And then more of the rocky roof gave way and fell to the floor of the cave with a crash. Water followed it at once, forcing its way out, pouring down into the cave with a noise like thunder.

The robbers gave a scream of terror. They knew that never would they be able to get back to the Secret Forest if they did not go at once, for now that more and more water was pouring down, the river in the mountain tunnel would rise so high that no one would be able to walk beside it on the rocky ledge.

They disappeared in the spray. Jack raised his head and saw them dimly in the distance, trying to force their way on to the ledge beside the river where it entered the tunnel. It was above their waists!

"They'll all be drowned," said Jack. "The water will sweep them off the ledge. It's getting deeper and deeper."

"Don't worry about the robbers!" said Ranni, sitting up with a jerk. "It's ourselves we must worry about! Look at the water – it's right up to us now!"

So it was. It lapped round them. The five captives managed to get themselves upright, though it was difficult, with both hands and feet tied. They struggled with their bonds, but the robbers were too clever at knots for them to be undone or broken.

"We'd better try to get up the passage," said Ranni,

trying to hop towards it with his tied-up legs. But he fell at once. He cracked his head against a rock, for he could not save himself with his hands. He lay quite still, and Paul looked at him in terror.

"He's just knocked out for a minute or two, that's all," said Pilescu, comfortingly. But really, the big Baronian was as frightened now as little Paul. They were all in a terrible plight. At any moment more of the roof might fall in and the cave would be completely flooded with water. They could not help themselves to escape because they were so tightly bound.

"Ranni! Open your eyes!" begged Paul. One of the robbers had left a torch shining on a ledge nearby, and its light shone on to Ranni's face as he lay with his eyes shut, half-leaning against the rocky wall. "Pilescu! How did you get caught like this?"

"We went up into the cave below the temple," said Pilescu. "We found the statue was divided into half, and we climbed up. We could not see a robber anywhere. We went to the mouth of the cave and looked out. We could see nothing at all, because there is a thick mist on the mountain-side this morning. We went back into the cave to return to you, when into the cave rushed all the robbers and flung themselves on us. They must have seen us standing at the entrance. They were waiting for us there! We could not see them in the mist.

"Oh, Pilescu – just as we had got to the end of our journey!" cried Prince Paul. "What are we going to do now? Is Ranni badly hurt? He hit his head so hard on the rock!"

Ranni opened his eyes at that moment and groaned. His head ached badly. He tried to sit upright, and then re-membered everything with a rush.

"More of the roof is falling!" cried Jack. He was right. With another tremendous roar a great mass of rock again fell down at the other end of the cave, and a still greater volume of water poured out. It was now all round their legs. The five captives struggled to get up on ledges out of the way of it.

"It is rising higher now," said Mike, watching the water swirling in the cave. The bright light of the torch glittered on the blackness of the icy-cold water. It looked very threatening.

"Pilescu, what *are* we going to do?" said Jack, desperately. "We shall all be drowned soon if we don't do something! Oh, why didn't someone come after us – some of the servants, or villagers. Beowald said he would fetch some!"

Beowald, of course, *had* fetched the villagers, and they had gone down as far as the cave of the waterfall. But they had not been able to guess that the way the boys had gone was along the narrow, rocky ledge beside the rushing river. They had left the cave and gone back to the mountain-side, telling Beowald that he must be mistaken. No one had gone down into those caves below! The robbers and their prisoners must be somewhere on the mountain-side!

They had searched the mountains well, hallooing and shouting for hours. When the thick mist had come up, they had had to leave their search, for, good mountaineers as they were, they could lose themselves in the mist as easily as any child.

Beowald alone had not stopped searching. The mist did not hinder him, for neither darkness nor mists made any difference to him. He wandered about all night long, looking for his friends, the big mountain goat keeping him company.

When the sun was high in the sky Beowald made his way back to the temple-cave. He listened outside. There was no sound. He went to the big stone image at the back. It was still split in half. Beowald stood thinking. Should he go down himself, and seek for the others? The villagers had already said there was nothing below but empty caves, with rushing water in one. Beowald would be lost in a strange place. But something made him decide to try.

The blind goatherd slipped down into the hole, hanging

deftly on to the rope. Down he went, and down, and came at last to the little cave below. He explored it carefully with his hands stretched out in front of him, going round the rocky, irregular walls.

He soon found the opening that led into the narrow, rocky passage. He went down it, feeling before him and beside him with his hands. Down and down went the passage, curving as it descended.

Beowald came out into the cave of the waterfall, and stood there, deafened by the roar. Water swirled over his feet. At first he was so deafened by the terrific noise that he heard nothing more.

And then, to his extreme astonishment, he heard his name called.

"Beowald! Beowald!"

"Look – it's Beowald! Beowald, help us, quickly!"

Beowald the goatherd stood at the entrance of the waterfall cave, his blind eyes seeing nothing, his ears hearing voices he could hardly believe in!

But even more astonished were the five captives! Beowald had appeared before them, like a wizard, just as they had given up all hope of being saved!

Beowald To The Rescue!

'Beowald! Quick! Set us free!" shouted Ranni. The water was already high, and more and more was flooding into the cave. It had increased a great deal in the last few minutes. Ranni was afraid that the whole roof might give way beneath the terrific weight of water – and then there would be no hope for the little company at all.

"What is it? Where are you? What is this water?" cried Beowald, lost in this strange new world of roaring and wetness.

"Beowald! Listen to me!" shouted Ranni, urgently. "Listen carefully. You are standing at the entrance to a cave, where I and the others are, all bound tightly, so that we cannot walk, or free ourselves. Water is pouring into our cave, and we shall be drowned if you do not hurry. Step down, Beowald, walk towards my voice. Do not be afraid."

"I will come," said the blind goatherd. He stepped further into the water, and then stopped, afraid. He was never afraid in his own mountain world. He knew every inch, every rock, every tree. But this was all new to him and strange to him, and it frightened him.

"Hurry, Beowald, hurry!" cried Ranni. "Come to me, quickly. Get our your knife. Cut my bonds."

Beowald stumbled through the water and felt about for Ranni. His hands brushed the big Baronians face. Ranni was half-lying, half-sitting. On his head was an enormous bump where he had struck it against a rock. Beowald's fingers felt the bump, and he wondered what had caused it. His hands ran down Ranni's body and he felt that the man had his arms tied behind his back.

He took out his knife and, with a careful stroke, cut the

leather thongs that bound Ranni's hands together. The big man stretched out his arms gladly, trying to get some strength back into them for they were stiff and swollen with being bound so tightly.

He snatched Beowald's knife from him and cut the thongs that bound his ankles together. He stood up, and at once over-balanced, for the thongs had cut into his legs, and for the moment he could not stand on them. He rose again, and went to Paul.

In a trice the small boy was free, and was trying to get to the entrance of the passage. "Quick, quick!" he cried. "Set the others free, Ranni. They will be drowned!"

As quickly as he could Ranni cut the thongs that bound the others, and set them free. They tried to stagger out of the water that now swirled above their knees. The cave was rapidly filling.

Ranni picked up the torch that was still lying on the rocky ledge, shining brightly into the cave. He held it so that everyone could see how to get into the narrow passage that led upwards to the other cave, away from the water. Beowald had already gone into the passage, anxious to get back to the mountain-side he knew. He felt so strange and so lost underground.

Ranni swung his torch round the cave of the waterfall for the last time – and then he saw that what he had feared might happen, was about to happen! The whole roof of the big cave was giving way! The pressure and weight of the water above it, trying to find its way out of the already enlarged hole, was too much for it. It had to give way. The rain that had fallen in torrents on the mountain-top, had to get away somewhere, and it had found the ordinary channels in the mountain too small for it. It was forcing and pressing everything in its way – and now the roof of the cave had to give in to its enormous pressure.

With a terrific roar the roof fell in, and after it poured the biggest volume of water that Ranni had ever seen. He gave a shout of terror and rushed up the narrow passage after the others. He was afraid that the water might flood even that passage, and trap them before they could get into the other cave!

"What's the matter, Ranni, what's the matter?" cried Paul, hearing the terrified shout.

"Hurry! Hurry! The roof has fallen in and the cave is nothing but swirling water!" panted Ranni. "It will find its way up this passage, before it can get its own level and drain away downwards. Hurry, Paul; hurry, Mike!"

The five in front of him, frightened by the fear in his voice, hurried on as swiftly as they could, stumbling over the rough, rocky way. Beowald was terrified. He was afraid of falling, afraid of the unknown, afraid of the roaring of the water behind him.

The water had found the narrow passage and was making its way up there too. Ranni felt sure he could hear it lapping behind him! He pushed the others on, shouting and yelling, and they, full of panic, went staggering through the dark and winding passage.

"Thank goodness the passage goes upwards all the way," thought Ranni, thankfully, as he came to a steep piece. "Now we are safe! The water cannot reach us here. We are too high. Never will anyone be able to get down into the cave of the waterfall again. There will always be water there now that the roof has fallen in."

They came out into the cave below the temple at last. All of them sank down on the floor, trembling in every limb. Surely there had never been such a narrow escape.

"If Beowald had not come when he did, we should all have been drowned by now," said Paul, in a choking voice. "Oh, Beowald – however was it you came down there just at that moment?"

Far away, down the passage, the muffled roar of the water could still be heard. Beowald's voice rose clearly above it:

"The search party went down to this cave and to the waterfall cave, but they could not find you. They are seeking for you still out on the mountain. I was anxious, and when I came into the temple-cave, I felt that I must come down by myself, though I was afraid. That is how I found you."

"We have had such adventures!" said Mike, beginning to feel quite a hero. "We've been to the Secret Forest, Beowald!"

"That is marvellous," said the blind goatherd. "Surely no man has even set foot there before!"

"Oh, yes!" said Paul. "The robbers live there, Beowald. They must have lived there for years and years. Ranni, will the robbers ever be able to come up the mountain river now, climbing along that ledge, to get to Killimooin this side?"

"Never," said Ranni. "We are well rid of them!"

Little by little the boys stopped trembling from their exertions, and their hearts beat less fast. They began to feel able to stand. Mike got up and found that he was quite all right again.

"I want to get back to the castle," he said. "I want to see the girls and tell them all that has happened to us. My word, won't they be jealous of our adventures!"

"I want something to eat," said Paul. "I'm terribly hungry. I shall ask Yamen to give me the very nicest, most delicious food she's got."

The thought of food made everyone eager to set out again. Ranni got up and pulled Paul to his feet. "Well, come along then," he said. "We shall soon be home now!"

One by one they hauled themselves up the rope that led to the temple-cave. Their feet found the rough places to help them, as they went up, and at last all six of them were standing in the big temple-cave.

It seemed dark there, darker than it should have been. Ranni looked towards the entrance.

"We can't go home!" he said in disappointment. "Look at that mist! It is like a thick fog. We could not see our hands in front of our faces if we went out in that. We should be completely lost in two minutes."

"Well, we must stay here till the mist clears," said Pilescu. "I am afraid it will not clear for some hours. When the mountain mists are as thick as this one, they last a long time."

"Oh, Pilescu! We *must* get back now we're so near home!" said Paul, almost in tears. "We must! I'm so hungry I can't stay here one more minute."

Jack looked at the blind goatherd, who was standing, quietly listening.

"Beowald can guide us back," said Jack. "You know your way by night, or in the thickest mist, don't you, Beowald?"

Beowald nodded. "It is all the same to me," he said. "If you wish, I will take you back to Killimooin Castle. My feet know the way! Is the mist very thick? I can feel that there is one, but I do not know how thick."

"It's the thickest one I've ever seen," said Pilescu, peering out. "I'm not at all sure I like to trust myself even to you, Beowald!"

"You are safe with me on the mountain-side," said the goatherd. He took out his little flute and played one of his queer tunes on it. An enormous horned head suddenly appeared at the entrance of the cave, and everyone jumped in fright.

"Ha, old one, you are there!" cried Beowald, as he heard the patter of the big goat's hooves. "Keep by me, old one, and together we will lead these friends of ours safely down our mountain-side!"

"Take hands," ordered Ranni. "Don't let go, whatever you do. If anything happens, and you have to let go, shout and keep on shouting so that we keep in touch with one another. We have had enough narrow escapes for one day!"

Everyone took hands. Beowald went out of the cave, playing his flute, his left hand firmly clasped in Ranni's big one. Behind Ranni came Paul, then Mike, then Jack, then Pilescu, all firmly holding hands.

"I feel as if we're going to play 'Ring-a-ring-of-roses'!" said Jack, with a laugh.

"Well, don't let's play the 'all-fall-down' part," said Mike at once. "It wouldn't be at all a good thing to do on a steep mountain-side like this."

They felt light-hearted at the idea of going home at last. With Beowald's music sounding plaintively through the mist, they stumbled along down the steep mountain-path. Two or three times one or other of the boys fell, and broke hands. They shouted at once, and the party stopped and joined together again.

It was slow work walking in the thick mist. They could barely see the person in front. Only Beowald walked steadily and surely. He could see with his feet!

"Don't go too fast, Beowald," said Ranni, as he felt the little prince dragging behind him. "Remember, we cannot see anything – not even our own feet."

"Neither can Beowald!" thought Mike. "How marvellous he is! Whatever should we have done without him?"

They stumbled downwards slowly for more than an hour and a half. Then Ranni gave a shout.

"We're almost there! I can hear the hens clucking at the back of the castle, and a dog barking. Bear up, Paul, we are nearly home!"

They came to the flight of steps, and stumbled up them, tired out. Beowald slipped away with the big goat. The others hardly saw him go. They were so excited at getting back in safety. Killimooin Castle at last! They hammered on the big iron-studded door impatiently.

The End Of The Adventure

The door flew open – and there stood Yamen with Nora and Peggy close behind her. With screams of excitement and delight the two girls flung themselves on the boys. Yamen beamed in joy. The lost ones were home again! They were dragged indoors, and Yamen ran up the big stone staircase, shouting at the top of her voice:

"Majesty! They're back! The little prince is safe! He is safe!"

The whole household gathered to hear the story of the returned wanderers. Servants peered round the door. The smaller children, clinging to the hands of their nurses, gazed open-eyed at the untidy, dirty boys and the two big Baronians. Tooku, his arm still bound up, came running up from the kitchen. What an excitement there was!

"We've been to the Secret Forest!" announced Paul, grandly. He had forgotten his tiredness and his hunger. He was the Prince of Baronia, back from rescuing his men.

"The Secret Forest!" repeated Yamen, with awe in her voice, and all the servants sighed and nodded to one another. Truly their prince was a prince!

"No, Paul, no – you cannot have been there!" said his mother. She glanced at Ranni and Pilescu, who nodded, smiling.

"It's true, mother," said Paul. "We found that Ranni and Pilescu had been captured by the robbers, and taken down below the temple-cave. There's a mountain river flowing underground there, and it's the only way there is to the Secret Forest!"

Bit by bit the whole story came out. Everyone listened, entranced.

When Paul came to the part where the roof had fallen in and they had almost been drowned, his mother caught him up into her arms, and wept tears over him. Paul was very indignant.

"Mother! Let me go! I'm not a baby, to be cried over!"

"No – you're a hero, little lord!" said Yamen, admiringly. "I go to get you a meal fit for the greatest little prince that Baronia has ever had!"

She turned and went down to her kitchen, planning a really royal meal. Ah, that little Paul – what a prince he was! Yamen marvelled at him, and at the two English boys, as she quickly rolled out pastry on her kitchen table. She would give them such a meal. Never would they forget it!

"Where is Beowald?" asked the Queen, when she had listened again and again to the thrilling tale of how Beowald had appeared just in time to free them before the cave filled with water. "I must thank Beowald and reward him."

"Didn't he come in with us?" said Jack. But no, Beowald was not there. He was far away on his mountain-side, playing to his goats, hidden by the mist.

"Mother, I want Beowald to come and live with me," said Paul. "I like him, and he plays the flute beautifully. That shall be his reward, mother."

"If he wants to, he shall," promised the Queen, though she did not think that the blind goatherd would want such a reward. "Now, you must get yourselves clean, and then a good meal will be ready. Oh, how thankful I am that you are all back in safety!"

Half an hour later the whole party looked quite different. They were clean again, and had on spotless clothes. How tired they looked, thought the girls. But perhaps they were only hungry!

Yamen had prepared a marvellous meal. The smell of cooking came up from the big kitchen, and the five travellers could hardly wait for the first dish to appear – a thick, delicious soup, almost a meal in itself!

The boys had never eaten so much before. Ranni and

Pilescu put away enormous quantities, too. Paul had to stop first. He put down his spoon with a sigh, leaving some of his pudding on his plate.

"I can't eat any more," he said, and his eyelids began to close. Pilescu gathered him up in his arms to carry him to bed. Paul struggled feebly, half asleep.

"Put me down, Pilescu! I don't want to be carried! How could you treat me like a weakling?"

"You are no weakling, little lord!" said Pilescu. "Did you not rescue me and Ranni by your own strength and wisdom? You are a lion!"

Paul liked hearing all this. "Oh, well, Mike and Jack are lions too," he said, and gave an enormous yawn. He was asleep before he reached his bedroom, and Pilescu undressed him and laid him on the bed, fast asleep!

The girls hung on to Mike and Jack, asking questions and making them tell their story time and again.

"We were so worried about you!" said Nora. "When the villagers came and said they couldn't find any of you, it was dreadful. And oh, that terrible storm! We hoped and hoped you were not caught in it."

"Well, we were," said Jack, remembering. "And it was all because of that storm, and the torrents of rain that came with it, that the waterfall in the cave became so tremendous and swelled up the river that ran from it. I wonder if the robbers got down safely! My word, if they got down to where they left their raft, and got on to it, they'd go down that river at about sixty miles an hour!"

"Now Mike and Jack, you must go to bed, too," said big Ranni, coming up. "Paul is fast asleep. You have had a very hard time, and you need rest, too. Come."

The children themselves could hardly believe that all their adventures really had happened, when they awoke next day. The boys lay and blinked at the ceiling. They felt stiff, but happy. They had rescued Rannie and Pilescu. They had found the robbers. They had been in the Secret Forest. They couldn't help feeling very pleased with themselves.

"Mother, I'm going up on the mountain-side to find Beowald," said Paul at breakfast time. "I'm going to tell him he must leave his goats and come to live with me. When we go back to the palace he must come too. I shall never forget all he did for us."

"Take Ranni and Pilescu with you," said his mother. "I'm afraid of those robbers still."

"You needn't be," said Paul. "You will never see them again! Ranni! Will you come with me, and find Beowald?"

Ranni nodded. He and Pilescu looked none the worse for their adventure, except that Ranni had a great bump on his head.

The mist had entirely gone. The mountains shone clear all around, their summits sharp against the sky. The five children, with Ranni and Pilescu, mounted their ponies, and turned their shaggy heads up the mountain-side.

They came to the temple-cave after about an hour. Beowald was not anywhere there. Ranni lifted his great voice and shouted down the mountain-side:

"BEOWALD! BEOWALD!"

They heard an answering cry, musical and clear, coming from a distance. They sat down to wait for the blind goatherd. Paul was already planning a uniform for him. He would show Beowald what princely gratitude was!

Soon the children heard the playing of the little flute Beowald always carried with him. Then, rounding a curve nearby came a flock of capering goats. At the head of them marched the old goat with his big curling horns.

"Here he comes!" said the little prince, and he ran to meet the goatherd. Beowald came to sit down with the company, asking them how they felt after their adventure.

"Oh, Beowald – it was a thrilling time," said Paul. "I don't know what would have happened to us if it hadn't been for you. I want to reward you, Beowald. We are all grateful to you – but I, most of all."

"Do not speak to me of rewards, little lord," said the goatherd, and he played a little tune on his flute.

"Beowald, I want you tó come and live with me," said Paul. "You shall come back to the big palace, and I will give you a uniform. You shall no longer herd goats on the mountain-side! You shall be my man and my friend!"

Beowald looked towards the little prince with his dark, empty eyes. He shook his head and smiled.

"Would you make me unhappy, little prince? I would break my heart in a strange place, under a roof. The mountains are my home. They know me and I know them. They know the feel of my feet, and I know the song of their winds and streams. And my goats would miss me, especially this old one."

The big horned goat had been standing by Beowald all the time, listening as if he understood every word. He stamped with his forefoot, and came close to the goatherd, as if to say, "Master, I agree with you! You belong here! Do not go away!"

"I did so want to reward you," said Paul disappointed.

"You *can* reward me, little lord," said Beowald, smiling. "Come to see me sometimes, and let me play my tunes to you. That will be enough reward for me. And I will make you a flute of your own, so that you too may learn the mountain songs and take them back to the big palace with you."

"Oh, I'd like that," said Paul, picturing himself at once playing a flute, and making all the boys at school stare at him in admiration. "You must teach me all the tunes you know, Beowald!"

"Let's go into the cave and have a look round," said Jack. They all went in, but Ranni and Pilescu forbade the children to slip down the hole to the cave below.

"No," he said. "No more adventures whilst we are here! We have had enough to last us for a lifetime – or, at any rate, for two months!"

"Now the Secret Forest will never again be visited by

anyone!" said Mike. "The only way to it is gone. The water will always keep people from travelling through the mountain to get to it."

"And the robber-people will never be able to leave the Secret Forest!" said Jack. "How strange! They will have to live there, year after year, a people lost and forgotten."

This was a strange thought. "But perhaps it is a good punishment for robbers," said Nora, thoughtfully. "It will be like keeping them in a great prison, which they can never escape from to rob other people!"

"We shall never see the Secret Forest again," said Mike, sadly. "It is such an exciting place!"

But he was wrong. They did see it again, for when, towards the end of a lovely holiday, their mother and father flew over in the White Swallow to fetch the children. Ranni took the whole company, Captain and Mrs Arnold as well, in the blue and silver aeroplane, right over the Killimooin mountains, and over the Secret Forest!

"There it is, Daddy!" cried Mike. "Look! You can see where the river flows out of the mountain. Go down lower, Ranni. Look, there's where it goes into the Secret Forest – and where it comes out again, after doubling back on itself. Oh, and there's where it disappears into a chasm, falling right down into the heart of the earth!"

The aeroplane was now so low that it almost seemed as if it was skimming the tops of the trees! The robbers heard the great noise, and some of them ran out from the forest in wonder.

"There's one of the robbers – and another – and another!" shouted Paul. "Goodbye, robber-people! You'll have to live in the Secret Forest for ever and ever and ever."

The aeroplane swept upwards and left the Secret Forest behind. Over Killimooin it went, and the children heaved a sigh.

"It's been the loveliest holiday we've ever had!" said Nora. "I wonder what adventures we'll have *next* time?"

"You've had quite enough," said Ranni.

But they are sure to have plenty more. They are that kind of children!

The Secret of
Moon Castle

The Secret of Moon Castle was first published in the UK
by Basil Blackwell Ltd in 1953

First published as a single volume by Armada in 1965

Copyright reserved Enid Blyton 1953

Home From School

Two girls were standing at their front gate one sunny afternoon in July.

"The car ought to be here by now," said Nora. "I hope it hasn't had a puncture or anything. I'm longing to see Mike – and Jack too, of course."

"So am I," said Peggy, her sister. "I wonder if Paul will be with them? Is he going to spend his holidays with us – or go back to Baronia? I wonder."

Paul was the little Prince of Baronia, a great friend of Nora, Peggy, Mike and Jack. He went to the same school as the boys, and had had plenty of adventures with them.

"I expect he'll spend a few days with us first," said Nora, swinging on the gate. "He usually does, doesn't he? Then he'll have to go back to Baronia to see his parents – and all his many brothers and sisters!"

"It's a silly idea, our school breaking up two whole days before the boys'," said Peggy. "We go back earlier too – that's even more of a nuisance!"

"Here's a car – and it's bringing the boys!" said Nora, suddenly. "They've come in Paul's car – the big blue and silver one. I wonder if Ranni is driving it?"

Ranni was Paul's man, who had vowed to look after Paul from the moment when he was put into his arms on the day he was born. He was devoted to the little Prince, and had shared many adventures with him. And now here he was, driving the great Baronian blue and silver car, bringing the three boys home in state!

The girls swung the big gates open as the car came near. They yelled as the car swept in. "Mike! Jack! Paul! Hurrah! Welcome back!"

The car stopped with a squeal of brakes, and Ranni, who was at the wheel, smiled at them through his fiery red beard. Three heads were poked out of the nearest window.

"Hallo, girls! Jump in. We thought you'd be looking for us!" called Mike. The door was swung open, and the girls squeezed in at the back with the three boys making room for them.

Nora gave Mike a hug. He was her twin, and the two were very fond of each other. Except that Nora was smaller than Mike, they were very much alike, with black, curly hair and bright, merry eyes. Golden-haired Peggy was a year older, but Mike was as tall as she was.

"Hallo!" said Jack, giving each of the girls a friendly punch. "What do you mean by breaking up sooner than we did!"

Jack was not their brother. He had no parents, and the Arnolds had adopted him as a big brother for Mike, Nora and Peggy. He thought the world of them all, and grinned around happily, his blue eyes shining in his brown face.

Prince Paul never punched the girls in the friendly way that the other boys did. Baronian manners did not allow that! He bowed politely to each of the girls, smiling happily – but they hadn't the beautiful manners of Baronia, and fell on him like a couple of puppies.

"Is he still ticklish? Yes, he is! Paul, are you going to stay with us for the holidays – or just for a few days – or what?"

"Stop tickling me," said Paul, trying to push them off. "Hey, Ranni, Ranni! Stop the car and turn them out!"

The car swept up to the front door, and Ranni leapt out, grinning. He went to the back to get the school trunks piled there on top of one another.

The door flew open and Mrs Arnold stood there smiling. "Welcome back, boys!" she said. Mike ran to hug his mother. "We're home!" he shouted. "Good old home!"

Jack kissed Mrs Arnold, and then Paul followed his usual custom, bent over her hand with a deep bow, and kissed it

304

politely. The others used to laugh at Paul's grand manners, but they had got so used to them by now that they didn't really notice them.

"Come along in," said Mrs Arnold. "We'd better get out of Ranni's way. He's bringing the trunks in. Ranni, how *can* you manage two trunks at once!"

Ranni grinned. He was big, and enormously strong. Two trunks were nothing to him! He went up the stairs with them easily.

"Mother! What a lovely smell!" said Mike, sniffing. "Buttered toast – and hot scones!"

"Quite right," said his mother. "You've probably forgotten that you asked me to have them for tea as soon as you got home these holidays – though why you took it into your head to ask for such things on a hot July day I don't know."

Jack put his head in at the dining-room door. Tea was already laid there. "My word!" he said. "Home-made éclairs too – and the biggest chocolate sponge sandwich I ever saw! When do we have tea?"

"As soon as you've washed your hands," said Mrs Arnold. "I'll get the toast and scones brought in now, so don't be long."

They weren't long. All five of them tore upstairs, laughing and shouting, glad to be together again. Prince Paul was pleased too – he loved this English family, with its friendliness and generosity.

When they came down, someone else was with Mrs Arnold. The three boys smiled at the small, grey-eyed woman sitting beside Mrs Arnold.

"Dimmy!" they said, and went to shake hands. Paul, as usual, bowed from his waist, and then unexpectedly gave the little woman a hug.

Dimmy's real name was Miss Dimity, and she often came to help Mrs Arnold, especially when the children were home. They all liked her, and teased her – and although she looked so gentle and timid, she could be very firm indeed, as they had found out many a time.

"Good old Dimmy!" said Mike, and looked as if he was going to try to lift her up. She pushed him off.

"No, no, Mike – I know you're almost as big as I am now – but I'm really not going to be tossed about like a bag of potatoes! Sit down before the toast gets cold."

For a little while there was silence as the five children helped themselves from the full plates on the table. Paul gave a loud sigh.

"Now this is what I call *real* food – almost as good as Baronia. Mrs Arnold, I have been half-starved all the term!"

"Don't you believe it!" said Jack. "You should just see the whopping great parcels he gets from Baronia every week!"

"I can guess what they are like,' said Mrs Arnold. "Paul's mother often sends me one too – full of the most delicious things. I had a letter from the Queen, your mother, this morning, Paul. She sends you her love and is looking forward to seeing you."

"Oh – is Paul going to Baronia very soon?" asked Nora, in a disappointed voice. "Peggy and I haven't seen him for a whole term. Can't he stay with us for a bit?"

"Well, I have rather a surprise for you," said her mother, smiling round. "Paul's father and mother have an idea that they would like to come over here for a month or two, and get to know us all better. They want to bring two of Paul's brothers, as well, so that they may know a little of England before they come over here to school."

"Oh *Mother*! How super!" cried Peggy. "But there won't be room here for the King and Queen and servants – they're sure to bring servants, aren't they, Paul? They never travel anywhere without heaps of guards and menservants and maids. Surely they're not coming *here*?"

"No, dear – of course not," said her mother. "Don't be

silly! There's hardly room for you five to spread yourselves in the holidays. No – Paul's father wants us to look out for a really big place, where he can bring his wife, two boys, and about twenty servants."

"Gosh!" said Mike. "He'll want a castle!"

"That's just what he suggests," said Mrs Arnold, handing a plate of very buttery scones round.

"I say! Does he really?" said Nora. "Paul, did you know about this?"

Paul shook his dark head. His mouth was too full to speak! His eyes shone, and he tried to swallow down his mouthful too quickly, and began to choke.

There was a lot of banging on the back at this, and Paul went purple in the face.

"Do leave him alone," said Mrs Arnold. "You're making him much worse. Drink some tea, Paul."

"A castle! I say – what fun to ring up the estate agents, and say, 'Please will you send me particulars of a dozen or so castles'," said Mike.

"Mother, do they know what castle they're going to yet?" asked Nora. "Is it anywhere near here? Can we go and see it?"

"Idiot! You know there's no castle near here," said Mike.

"Let Mother answer my questions," said Nora. "Mother, what castle are they going to?"

"My dear child, I told you I only got the letter this morning," said her mother. "Paul's mother has only just thought of the idea. She has asked me to find out what I can, and perhaps go and see over any suitable place – not that I would know in the least whether a castle would be suitable to live in or not!"

"Well, I suppose they only want to rent one, not buy one," said Mike. "You'd better take Paul with you, Mother, and let him poke round a few old castles. He'll know what his mother will fancy! Anyone want this last scone? If so, say the word."

Nobody did, so Mike took it. Everyone began to talk

excitedly about the news Mrs Arnold had just given. Paul, recovered from his choking fit, talked more loudly than anyone. He was really thrilled.

"You will all be able to come and stay with me," he announced. "We will share this castle together. You shall know my two brothers. You shall . . ."

"Your mother may not want us," said Mike.

"She certainly won't want you for very long," said Mrs Arnold, with a smile. "A noisy crowd like you! Actually, she says in her letter that she hopes we will *all* go and stay for a little while, so it should be great fun."

"If only we can find a really *good* castle!" said Nora.

"What do you mean – a *good* castle?" said Mike. "You don't suppose we're going to look for half-ruined ones, do you? Mother, have you heard of any yet?"

"Mike – I only got the letter *today*," said his mother. "Now, finish your tea for goodness sake. We'll have any amount of castles to see by next week."

"Castle-hunting – I shall like that!" said Jack. "I wonder which we'll choose – a really exciting one, I hope!"

Choosing A Castle

The next few days were very exciting in more ways than one. For one thing it was great fun to be at home again – no lessons – no bells clanging – no prep in the evenings. For another thing it was most exciting to read through the particulars of various castles that could be rented.

There were not very many. Mrs Arnold looked through the papers that came, and quickly decided which offers were no good. Big mansions were offered as well, and it really seemed to Mrs Arnold that it might almost be better to take one of those for Paul's family. The castles seemed in such remote places, or had been empty for some time, with just a caretaker in.

"Oh *no*, Mother – do let's have a castle," said Mike. "A big house wouldn't be nearly such fun."

"I'm not thinking about how much fun I can provide for you children," said his mother. "I'm thinking about the difficulties Paul's mother will have, in a big, bare castle, with very old-fashioned ways of lighting and heating."

"But Baronia isn't modern, either," said Mike. "Paul's own castle hasn't got a lot of things that a big hotel in England would have, for instance. Mother, do find a castle. It sounds so much more exciting than a big house."

"Look through these," said his mother. "Take the papers with you, and pore over them with the others. They are all ones I think are no good. You will see what I mean when you read through the particulars."

Mike carried away the papers, feeling rather thrilled. What fun to try to choose a castle. He called the other four, and they took the papers out into the garden.

"Here you are – have one or two each," said Mike. "We'll all read through them, and see what we think. Mother's turned all these down."

They read solemnly through the particulars. "Castle and fifty thousand acres," said Jack. "Whew! Do people rent fifty thousand acres as well? Oh – *this* castle's no good. It's only got twelve rooms furnished – goodness knows how many your parents will want, Paul. It must be maddening to be a King and Queen and have to have such enormous places to live in."

"I like our castle in Baronia," said Paul. "But I would rather be an ordinary boy and live the life you do, Jack."

"I don't wonder Mother turned these down," said Mike, putting down his papers. "They're no good at all. Either the owners want to live in one wing of the castle too – or they want Paul's people to rent it for a whole year – or the place

309

isn't furnished. It's a lot more difficult than I thought it would be, to get a castle for a month or two!"

"There's one here," said Peggy, suddenly. "It sounds rather thrilling. I don't quite know why Mother turned it down. Listen."

The others turned to her. They were all lying on the grass, the papers spread around them. Peggy told them about the particulars she held in her hand.

"It's called Moon Castle," she said. "That's a lovely name, isn't it? Moon Castle! And it's big, but not too big – just about right for Paul's family. It's got caretakers in, so it should be in fairly good order. It can be had immediately, because the owners don't live in it. It's high on a hill with 'wonderful panoramic views over a countryside of moorland, wood and waterways'."

"It sounds good," said Mike, sitting up. "Go on – anything else?"

"It's very old," said Peggy. "It says here, 'a castle full of myth and legend', whatever that means. And it says, 'What stories its old walls could tell – tales of violence and mystery, hate and greed'. Goodness, it's just as well that old walls don't suddenly begin to talk, if that's the kind of thing they say!"

"It really does sound rather good," said Nora. "Why did Mother turn it down, I wonder?"

"There she is!" said Mike, as his mother came out into the garden, with a basket and a pair of scissors for picking flowers. "Mother! Hey, Mother! Why did you turn down Moon Castle? It sounds super."

"Moon Castle? Well, really because it sounds so very cut off from everywhere," said Mrs Arnold. "It isn't near any town – and the only village anywhere near is an old ruined one which has the queer name of Moon. I suppose that's how the castle got its name."

"But would it matter, being cut off from everywhere?" asked Peggy.

"It's called Moon Castle."

"Yes, I think so," said her mother. "For a big household such as Paul's mother would bring, you would need good shops at least *fairly* near – but the nearest shops are about twenty miles away, it seems to me. It sounded such a lonely, desolate place – it really gave me the creeps!"

"Oh *Mother*! But that's the sort of castle we'd all love," said Nora. "And Paul's mother would bring plenty of cars –wouldn't she, Paul? So that shopping would be easy."

"Well – not *plenty*," said Paul, laughing. "But enough."

"Another drawback is that there wouldn't be any people to make friends with," said Mrs Arnold. "No neighbours, for instance. What the poor, wretched caretakers do with themselves I really cannot imagine!"

"They probably get in a month's stores at once!" said Jack. He turned to the others, "I say, do you remember when we ran away to the Secret Island – where there were no shops – no neighbours except the rabbits and the birds – and everything was lonely and desolate? But what a wonderful time we had!"

"Yes. We did," agreed the others. Mike turned to his mother. "Mother, do let's see what this Moon Castle is really like. Can't we just go and *see* it? Paul, what do *you* think? Would your mother mind its being so far from everywhere – and having 'old walls that could tell tales of mystery and violence' and all the rest of it?"

Paul laughed. "No. Mother wouldn't mind a bit. I expect the walls of our own castle at home are far older than the walls of Moon Castle – and could tell just as fiercesome tales. Mrs Arnold, is the castle too far away for us to go and have a look at it?"

Mike glanced down at the papers in Peggy's hands. "It's nearest station is Bolingblow," he said. "I've never heard of it! Bolingblow – where is it?"

"It's about one hundred miles away," said his mother. She took the papers from Peggy and looked at them again. "Of course, I don't know how much of the castle is furnished

– it says 'partly furnished' – that might mean only two or three rooms. And we don't even know whether the furnishings are in good repair or not – they might be mouldering away!"

"Well, Mother, let's go and *see*,' said Mike, half-impatiently. "It will save such a lot of writing to and fro if we go and have a look. I must say I like the sound of it. It sounds sort of – sort of mysterious – and lost – it belongs to the past and not to nowadays. It . . ."

"Mike's going all romantic," said Nora, with a laugh. "Mike, you'll expect King Arthur's knights to go riding out of the castle, won't you?"

"Don't be an ass," said Mike. "Mother, can't we just go and *look*? Can't you telephone and say we're coming?"

"There's no telephone," said his mother. "That is another reason why I turned it down. The Queen of Baronia will not expect a castle without a telephone!"

"Oh," said Mike, thinking that his mother was quite right there. Then Miss Dimity unexpectedly put in a word. She had come up to listen to the conversation.

"I must say that *I* thought Moon Castle would have done very well for Paul's family," she said. "Except for being twenty miles away from shops, and no telephone, it sounded ideal to me. After all, Paul's mother will have powerful cars to send for any goods she wants – or to take messages. It might be worth seeing. We've got to hurry up and find one, because the family want to come almost immediately!"

"Let's go today," said Mike. "Nothing like doing things at once. Mother, ask Ranni to bring the car round. Let's go today!"

"Yes, do let's," said Paul. "I know what my parents are like! They will change their minds about a castle and a holiday here, if they don't get news of one very soon!"

"Oh dear – you do *rush* me so!" said Mrs Arnold, laughing. "Well – I suppose we'd better make up our minds and go and see this place at once. Paul, find Ranni and tell him. We will be ready in a quarter of an hour. We won't take a picnic lunch – though I should like to – but it would take too long to get ready. Mike, find the right maps, will you – we must look out the best way to go."

After that there was an enormous amount of rushing about, shouting and excitement. It was a very hot day, so the girls put on clean, cool cotton frocks. The boys put on coloured cotton shirts and shorts, except for Jack who considered himself too big and wore grey trousers.

Dimmy was not going. Even without her it would be a tremendous squash in the big blue and silver car belonging to Prince Paul. She waved them off.

"See you some time tonight," she said. "I hope you won't give the caretakers too big a shock, arriving so suddenly out of the blue! I shall be longing to hear all about the castle when you come back."

They went off excitedly. Paul and Mike were in front with Ranni. Mrs Arnold and the girls and Jack were behind. Mike had the map in front, and was poring over it, ready to tell Ranni the roads to take.

They were soon out in the country, speeding along between hedges, with fields of yellowing corn each side. The poppies gleamed in it here and there, and blue chicory flowers shone by the wayside.

"This way now," said Mike, as they came to a corner. "Then east for a good bit till we come to a bridge. Then to the town of Sarchester – then north towards Bolingblow. After that there are only minor roads shown on the map. I hope they will be good enough for a magnificent car like this!"

"Where do we have lunch?" asked Peggy.

"I *thought* somebody would ask that in a minute or two," said Mrs Arnold. "We'll have it at one o'clock, if we are near or in a town."

"We should be at Bolingblow by then," said Mike,

reckoning up quickly. "This car goes at such a speed, it simply *eats* up the miles."

"We should perhaps ask a few questions at Bolingblow about the castle," said Mrs Arnold.

"Yes, we could," said Peggy, and broke into a funny little song that made the others laugh.

> *"O Castle of the Moon,*
> *We're coming to you soon,*
> *This very afternoon,*
> *O Castle of the Moon!"*

The others picked up the words, and the car rushed on with everyone singing the silly little song:

> *"We're coming soon,*
> *O Castle of the Moon!"*

Moon Castle

Ranni drove the car into the town of Bolingblow at just after one o'clock. It was a pretty town with wide streets, and a market-place in the centre.

Mrs Arnold approved of it. "There are good shops here," she said. "And this hotel that Ranni has brought us to looks very nice. Old and picturesque and spotlessly clean."

They were all very hungry, and delighted to find a very good lunch being served. "Iced melon – good!" said Mike. "What's to follow? Cold chicken and ham and salad. Couldn't be better. All I shall want after that is an ice- cream or two."

The little waitress smiled at the hungry children, and took

315

their orders quickly. Soon they were all tucking in, too busy to talk.

When the bill was being paid Mrs Arnold asked the waitress one or two questions.

"Is the road to Moon Castle good, do you know? And about how long will it take us to get there in a car?"

"Moon Castle!" said the waitress, in surprise. "You can't go there. It's not open to the public, you know. No one is allowed to see over it."

"I hear it may be rented this summer," said Mrs Arnold. "I want to go and see it."

"Rented!" said the waitress. "Well, I would never have thought anyone would want to take an old, desolate place like that. It's such a way to the nearest town. Good gracious, nobody's lived there for years and years."

"Oh dear – then I don't expect it's in very good condition," said Mrs Arnold, feeling that her journey would probably be wasted. "There are caretakers, I believe."

"I don't know," said the waitress. "I did hear that once a month somebody comes over in a car to take back goods – food and oil and so on – so I suppose caretakers *are* there. My word! I wouldn't live in that lonely old place for anything. I've heard that queer things go on there – very queer."

"Ooooh! What? asked Nora at once.

"I don't know," said the little waitress. "All I know is that some brainy fellow went there once to ask to see some old books in the big library there – and he was frightened out of his wits! Said the books leapt out of the shelves at him, or something."

Everyone laughed. "That's good!" said Mike. "I'd love to live in a castle where books leapt out of bookshelves. I'd say, 'Hey there – is there a good mystery story waiting for me? Well, jump out, please, and I'll catch you!'"

The waitress didn't like being laughed at. She tossed her head. "Oh well – it's a queer old place that nobody knows much about nowadays. I wouldn't go near it if you paid me."

The children went off to find the car, smiling at the waitress's indignant face. They got into the car and Ranni looked round inquiringly at Mrs Arnold.

"The Castle, madam?" he asked. She nodded, and Mike looked at the map.

"Not such good roads now," he said. "Turn right at the end of the town, Ranni."

"I must say that I don't like what I hear about Moon Castle," said Mrs Arnold, as they drove off. "If nobody has lived there for so long – except the caretakers – the place must be in a very poor condition."

"Yes – it doesn't sound too good," said Mike. "How queer people are – owning a castle and never bothering about it at all! Gosh – what a road this is!"

Ranni had to slow down because the road became very bad just there, and continued bad all the rest of the way. It was full of ruts, and was uneven and in places very stony. The car went carefully.

"We should come to a fork in the road here," said Mike. "Yes, look – there it is. We take the left-hand fork, Ranni."

"That is a good thing," said Ranni. "We could not have taken the other fork! There is hardly any road to be seen!"

It was quite true. The right-hand fork was not really a road – just a fifth-rate cart-track, unused now, and overgrown. Peggy pointed to something in the distance, about half a mile up the track.

"Look," she said. "Houses of some sort. Mother, do you suppose that's all that is left of the ruined village of Moon. Why is it ruined, do you suppose?"

"Peggy, dear, how *should* I know?" said her mother. "The people probably found it too lonely and just left it."

"I can see a few of the roofs," said Peggy. "They look all tumble-down. It might be fun to go and explore a ruined village."

317

"Well, everyone to his taste," said her mother. "I can think of a lot of better things to do than wander through smelly old villages with not a soul there!"

"Why should it be smelly?" Peggy wanted to know, but just then the car wheels went into such a series of ruts that Mrs Arnold was half-afraid the springs would be broken. But Ranni assured her that they were very, very strong.

"Baronian cars are built for country like this," he said. "All bumps and jumps and humps. The springs cannot break, Madam Arnold. Soon we should see the castle. There is a hill over yonder. It must be there."

They all looked eagerly at the hill coming into view. It was very steep indeed, covered with trees on the slope. Jack gave a sudden exclamation.

"There's the castle – there, right at the top – well, almost at the top! It backs into the hill for protection from the

"There's the castle – there, right at the top!"

318

wind, I suppose. Look at that one great tower! It soars up higher than the hill. Just one tower. How queer!"

"Still, it *looks* like a castle, even if it's only got one tower," said Nora. "I think it's grand. It's got all sorts of turrets and bits and pieces sticking up round it. What a wonderful view it must have over the countryside. All the same – it *would* be lonely to live there always!"

"It certainly looks grand enough for your father and mother, Paul," said Jack. "I mean – it's a *proper* castle – strong and big and *commanding*-looking, if you know what I mean."

Paul did. He was rather taken with it, from the outside. It was such typical English countryside around too – and how his mother would love the little town of Bolingblow, the market-place, the corn-fields, and the countryfolk themselves.

"Well, commanding-looking or not, I can't believe that the inside will be worth seeing as far as furnishing is concerned," said Mrs Arnold. "I expect it has been allowed to fall to pieces! However, we shall soon see. We are nearly there now."

They were going up the steep hill now. Ranni had put the car into bottom gear, and it growled up slowly, the hill-road just as bad as the road they had left. The road wound to right and left in order to make the climbing of the hill easier.

The castle seemed even bigger and more overpowering as they came nearer. "It's watching us!" said Nora, suddenly. "It's saying: 'What is this horrible noisy thing coming to disturb my dreaming?' I'm sure it's watching us."

"Don't be silly," said Peggy, uneasily. "You do say such stupid things, Nora. My word – what a grand place it is! Towering up into the sky – its one great tower soaring up high. I like it! It belongs to the days of the old knights and their ladies, not to our days."

They came to a great gateway. The gates were shut. Jack

jumped out to open them. Ranni was afraid they might be locked, but they were not. Jack managed to open them, though they creaked and groaned as if they hated to be touched.

The car went through, and up a weed-covered drive that swept round to a great entrance. A flight of wide steps went up to a great door studded with iron nails.

"Well – here we are," said Mrs Arnold, in the sort of voice that meant she wished they weren't! She got out of the car, helped politely by Prince Paul. Ranni leapt up the steps to ring or knock – or whatever one did at a castle like this.

There was a great chain hanging down, with a wrought-iron handle on the end. "Is that the bell?" said Mike, doubtfully. "There's no knocker. Mother, look – there are cobwebs all over the door – even down the opening-crack. It looks as if the door hasn't been opened for years!"

"It does," said Mrs Arnold, beginning to wonder what they would find inside the castle – if they ever got there!

"Shall I pull this chain-thing and hope a bell rings?" said Mike. "Right – well, here goes!"

He gave the chain a big heave. Nothing happened. No sound came, no jingle, no clanging. Mike pulled again. Still nothing happened.

Then Ranni pulled it – and he gave it such a tug that the chain came off and dropped round his shoulders! He threw it down in disgust.

"So old that the rust has eaten into the chain!" he said. "I will hammer on the door."

He hammered with his great fists, and then shouted so that the echoes suddenly swept round them and made them jump.

Nobody came. The door remained fast shut. "Well," said Mrs Arnold, "this is most disappointing. I suppose we must just give it up."

"Oh *no*, Mother! We can't just tamely go back home

after actually getting to the front door!" said Mike, quite shocked. "Let's walk round a bit and see if we can see another door – a back door perhaps. Or don't castles have back doors? Has *your* castle got a back door, Paul?"

"Plenty," said Paul, grinning. "Look – we will go this way. There seems a kind of path."

They followed Paul, Mrs Arnold not at all liking the idea of trying to find another way in. She had quite given up the idea of taking the castle for Paul's parents, but she knew what an outcry the children would make if she insisted on their going back to the car at once.

The overgrown way led round the walls of the castle. They came to a small door set in the wall, but that had no bell, knocker or handle. They went on again and suddenly saw a little clearing, set within a small wall of its own.

"Look," said Peggy, and stopped. "Washing hanging out on a line! There *must* be somebody here, then! Yes, see – there's a fairly big door set in the wall there, that leads into that yard – or drying-ground, whatever it is – where the washing is. This must be the kitchen quarters. If we yell, somebody might hear us now."

Mike obligingly yelled, and made them all jump, for he had a most stentorian voice when he liked.

"HEY! IS ANYONE ABOUT?" he yelled.

Nobody answered. A few hens scuttled across the yard and disappeared under some bushes. A tabby cat streaked across and disappeared, too.

"HEY!" began Mike again, and stopped. Somebody had come cautiously out of the big door nearby – the one that led into the yard.

It was a little plump woman with grey hair. She was followed by two others, remarkably like her in face, but both tall and thin. All three stared at the visitors in surprise.

"What do you want?" said the plump woman, in a frightened voice. "Who are you? Why have you come here? No one's allowed here, you know."

321

Inside The Castle

Mrs Arnold stepped forward, with the estate agent's letter in her hand. "We have come to see over the castle," she said. "Is it convenient to do so now? We couldn't telephone you, of course, because the castle is not on the phone."

"But – but no one is allowed to see over the castle," said the little woman, and her two tall companions nodded their heads vigorously in agreement.

"We are not sightseers," said Mrs Arnold. "We got the particulars of the castle from the agents, who said that the castle could be viewed at any time, if we took with us this letter. It came with the particulars. It is possible that it might suit a friend of mine, who wants to rent a big place for a month or two."

"Well – my son isn't in," said the woman, looking very taken aback. "He told me nobody was to come in. He said nobody would ever want this place. Nobody has ever come to see it, to buy it, or rent it before. Nobody. I really don't know if I can let you in."

"But we have come all this way to see it!" protested Mrs Arnold. "This is ridiculous! I'm afraid you will get into serious trouble with the owners if you refuse to allow people to see over their castle with a view to renting it. You could be making them lose a great deal of money. Can't you see that? Your son has nothing to do with it!"

"Well, he said we weren't to let anyone in," said the woman, and she turned to her tall companions, not knowing what to do. They held a hurried conference in whispers. The children and Mrs Arnold waited impatiently. How unhelpful these women were!

The little plump woman turned round at last. "Well – I

don't know what my son will say," she said again, "but I suppose I must let you in! I and my two sisters are the caretakers."

"Yes – I'm afraid you *must* let us in and also take us round," said Mrs Arnold, firmly. "What does your son do here? Is he a caretaker too?"

"Oh no. My son is very, very clever," said the little woman, proudly. "He is a scientist. I can't tell you the number of exams he has passed."

"Why does he bury himself here then?" said Mrs Arnold, thinking that this mysterious son must be a spoilt and lazy fellow, living in luxury in the castle, waited on by the three women!

"He has work to do," said the little woman, speaking proudly again. "Important work that needs quiet and peace. I don't know *what* he'll say if people come to live in the castle."

"It really doesn't matter in the least what he says about it," said Mrs Arnold, getting annoyed. "The castle doesn't belong to him. If he makes this kind of trouble every time anyone comes to view it, he will certainly lose you your job! Now please don't say any more about your son, but just take us round at once."

"Yes, madam," said the little woman, looking scared. The other two remained quite silent, but followed behind the party, looking grim.

"What is your name?" asked Mrs Arnold, as they went down a passage.

"I'm Mrs Brimming, and my sisters are Miss Edie Lots and Miss Hannah Lots," said the little woman. "Er – would the person who wants the castle need the whole place?"

"Certainly," said Mrs Arnold. "Except your own quarters, of course. Why?"

Mrs Brimming said nothing in answer to that, but flashed a quick look at her two long-faced sisters. The children, finding Mrs Brimming too slow in her showing-round, went on in front, down the corridor, eager to see the castle.

They came out into a great hall, hung with magnificent brocade curtains. Suits of armour stood all round, gleaming brightly. Paul slapped one and it gave out a hollow noise. "I'd like to wear one of these!" he said. "I'd like to pull the vizor down over my face and peer through it."

"You'd be too small to wear a suit of armour," said Jack. "I could get into one nicely though!"

Mrs Arnold caught a look of alarm on Mrs Brimming's face. "It's all right!" she said, with a laugh. "They won't really walk about in these suits of armour! What a lovely hall this is!"

"Yes," said the woman, and led them to a big door. She swung it open. Inside was a really beautiful room, with graceful furniture upholstered in a royal blue, dimmed with the years. A carpet stretched the whole length of the room, its colours dimmed too, in a lovely soft pattern of blues, reds and creams. The children's feet sank into it as they trod over it.

"My mother would like this," said Paul, at once. "Oh, look at that clock!"

A great clock hung on the wall. It had been made in the shape of a church with a spire. As the children looked at it, a bell inside the church began to toll the hour. It was three o'clock.

"Look! There's an angel coming out of that door in the clock – at the bottom there!" cried Peggy. "A little angel with wings and a trumpet!"

The angel stood there with his trumpet, and then went slowly back again, and the door shut.

"I've never seen a clock like *that* before!" said Nora, in delight.

"There are many curious things here," said Mrs Brimming. "Lord Moon – the one who lived at the beginning of last century, collected many strange marvels from all over the world. There is a musical-box that plays a hundred different tunes, and—"

324

It gave out a hollow noise.

"Oh! Where is it?" cried Peggy, in delight.

But Mrs Arnold, glancing at her watch, saw that there was only time to look over the castle itself, certainly not to listen to musical-boxes playing a hundred tunes!

"You'll have time to set the musical-box going if we come here," she said. "We must hurry up. Will you show us all the rooms there are, except, of course, your own quarters, Mrs Brimming? My friend, who is the Queen of Baronia, will bring her own servants, and they will, of course, want the use of the kitchen."

"I see," said Mrs Brimming, looking as if she was about to remark that she really didn't know what her son would say to that! "Well, the kitchens are big enough. We use only a corner of them. I'll take you to the other rooms and then upstairs."

All the rooms were beautiful. Upstairs the bedrooms were just the same – magnificently furnished, with wonderful pictures, strange but beautiful ornaments, un- usual and most extravagant curtains. Some of them made Peggy think of "cloth of gold", they shone and shimmered so.

Nothing was mouldering, ragged, cobwebby or dirty. Everything was beautifully kept, and Mrs Arnold could not see a speck of dust anywhere. Queer as these three caretakers were, they had certainly tended the castle with the most loving and thorough care.

Upstairs there was a great room whose walls were lined with books from floor to ceiling. The children gazed in amazement. Except in the big public libraries they had never in their lives seen so many books together!

"How wonderful!" said Mike, staring. "I say – what a room for a rainy day! We could never, never get to the end of all these books!"

"They're old," said Jack. "I bet they wouldn't be very interesting. What a waste – to have thousands and thousands of books – and not a soul to read them!"

"My son reads them," said Mrs Brimming, proudly. Nobody said anything. Everybody was tired of Mrs Brimming's son!

On the third storey were great attics – rooms in which were stored enormous chests, old furniture and curious junk of all kinds.

"I don't think my friend would want the attics," said Mrs Arnold, who had been counting up the rooms as they went through them. "The first and second storeys would be enough. How beautifully the whole place is kept! Do you and your sisters keep it like this – does no one else help you?"

"No one," said Mrs Brimming, proudly, and the Misses Edie and Hannah Lots shook their heads too. They led the way downstairs again, to one of the rooms there. "We have been here by ourselves for years. We love this old castle. Our family has always been here, doing some kind of work – yes, our great-great-great-grandmother was here, when the present Lord's great-great-great-grandfather was lord. That's his picture over there."

The children looked at a great portrait that hung over the fireplace of the room they were in. It showed a grim-faced man with a lock of black hair falling over his forehead, his eyes looking quite fiercely at them.

"He doesn't seem to like us much," said Peggy. "I wish he wouldn't look quite so fierce. I shan't be in *this* room much, if we come here – I should never feel comfortable with great-great-great Lord Moon glaring at me!"

The others laughed. Then Mike suddenly thought of something. "We haven't been up the tower – the one, tall tower! We *must* see that!"

There was silence. Mrs Brimming looked at her sisters, and they looked back. Nobody said anything.

"Well – what about the tower?" said Mike again, surprised at the silence. "Can't we see it? I bet your mother will like the tower, Paul! She'll sit up at the top and gaze out

"He doesn't seem to like us much," said Peggy.

over the countryside. What a view there must be from the
top. Let's go and explore it."

"Well, I'll just stay here and discuss a few things with the
caretakers," said Mrs Arnold, who did not particularly
want to climb hundreds of stone steps up to the top of the
tall tower. "You can wander round. I suppose the tower is
in good order too, Mrs Brimming?"

"Yes, madam," said Mrs Brimming, after a little pause.
"There's nothing to see there, though. Nothing. I am sure
your friend will not want to use the tower – so many steps
up, you know – and only small, stone-walled rooms and
tiny windows – no use at all."

"It's locked," said one of the Miss Lots, unexpectedly.
"Fast–locked."

"Where's the key then?" said Mike at once. He wasn't
going to miss going to the top of the tower!

There was another pause. "It's lost," said the other Miss Lots.

"Lost for years," added the first one. "But there's nothing there to see."

"There's a view, surely!" said Mike, puzzled. He didn't believe all this about locked doors and lost keys. Why didn't the caretakers want them to see the tower? Had they neglected it?

"Well, you must find the key before my friend comes," said Mrs Arnold. "She will certainly like to see the view from the top of the tower. Now – I must just ask a few questions about such things as food and so on. You go off for twenty minutes, children, but keep out of mischief, please!"

"Of course!" said Peggy, indignantly. "Come on, Mike." She dropped her voice to a whisper. "Let's go and find the tower!"

An Unpleasant Fellow

They went out of the room, followed by the eyes of all three caretakers. They shut the door behind them. They were in the great hall, and the suits of armour gleamed all around. Peggy gave a little shiver.

"Now I feel as if these suits of armour are watching me!" she said. "Those two Miss Lots give me the creeps. What a peculiar family."

"The son sounds the most peculiar of the lot," said Mike. "I don't feel as if I'm going to like him somehow. But I say – what a castle! Paul, do you like it?"

"Yes, I do, very much," said the little Prince, his eyes shining. "And my mother will love it. So will my two brothers. There will be plenty of room here for all of us, you too! We shall have a grand time!"

"Now – where would the entrance to the tower be?" wondered Jack. "It's on the east side of the castle. So it must be in this direction – down this passage. Come on."

They all followed Jack. He took them down a dark passage hung with what seemed like tapestry, though it was difficult to tell in the dark.

"I wish I'd got a torch," said Mike. "We'd better bring our torches and plenty of batteries, because there only seem to be a few lights in this place, and I bet they don't switch them all on each night!"

They came to the end of the passage, and found themselves in a small square room, whose walls were lined with old chests. Mike lifted up a lid and looked inside. A strong smell of mothballs at once floated out. Nora sneezed.

"Rugs, I think – or curtains or something," said Mike, letting the lid shut with a bang. "I must say those three old caretakers really *do* take care of everything! Now – what about this tower?"

"There doesn't seem to be any entrance to it from here," said Jack, looking all round. He went to a hanging of tapestry that fell from the ceiling of the room to the floor, covering a space left between the many chests. He lifted up the tapestry and gave an exclamation.

"Here's the door to the tower – at least, I should think it leads to the tower."

The others crowded over to look. It was a tall, narrow door, black with age, and looked very strong. There was a handle made of a black iron ring, and an enormous keyhole.

Mike turned the handle to and fro. He could hear a latch clicking, but however hard he pushed at the door it would not open.

"Locked," he said, in disappointment. "And no key. Do you suppose it really *is* lost, Jack?"

"No," said Jack. "I'm sure they didn't want us to use the tower. I bet their awful son uses it – locks himself away from the three old ladies!"

"To do his wonderful scientific work, I suppose," said Mike, with a grin. "Or to laze the days away without anyone knowing. I wonder what he's like. He won't like having to keep in his place when your mother comes, Paul. He'll have to clear out of the tower, if he does use it – we'll have the view to ourselves then!"

Jack took hold of the iron handle and gave the door another shake, a very violent one. Just as he was doing this, footsteps sounded in the long corridor that led to the little square room where they stood.

The children swung round to see who was coming. Jack still had his hand on the iron ring of the tower door.

A man came into the room. He stopped short at once when he saw the children, and gazed at them, astounded. He was short, burly and very dark. His eyes seemed almost black, and his big nose and thin-lipped mouth made him very ugly.

He shouted loudly. "What are you doing here? How dare you? Clear out at once, the lot of you! Take your hand off that iron ring, boy. The door's locked, and you've no business to be snooping round my castle."

The children gasped. *His* castle! Whatever did he mean?

"It's Lord Moon's castle," said Jack, who was the only one who felt able to answer the angry man. "Are you Lord Moon?"

"It doesn't matter who I am!" said the man, taken aback at Jack's words. "I've told you to clear out. How did you get in? Nobody is allowed here, nobody!"

"My mother, the Queen of Baronia, is going to rent this castle from Lord Moon," said Prince Paul, suddenly finding his tongue, and speaking in the imperious way that often made the children laugh. But they didn't laugh now. They were glad of Paul's sudden imperiousness!

331

The man stared at Paul as if he couldn't believe his ears. His shaggy eyebrows came down low over his eyes so that they seemed to be only slits.

"What fairy-tale is this?" he demanded, suddenly. "The Queen of Baronia! I never heard of her! You clear out, I say – and if you ever come round here again I'll take the lot of you up to the top of the tower and throw you out!"

Jack tried again. "But it's true!" he cried. "We're all coming to stay here and we want to look at the tower rooms so that our friend can describe them to his mother. She will be sure to want to know what they are like. You seem to be able to get into the tower, so will you please unlock it for us?"

The man exploded into fury. He stuttered something, raised his hands and came towards them, looking so fierce that they backed away. The girls fled down the corridor. The boys stood their ground a moment, and then they too took to their heels! The man was strong and could have knocked all three of them down easily. He raced after them.

The five children ran down the passage, into the hall, and then flung open the door of the room where they had left Mrs Arnold and the three sister caretakers.

"Good gracious!" began Mrs Arnold, annoyed at this sudden entry, "I must say—"

After the children came the man, muttering fiercely. He stopped in surprise in the doorway. Then he marched in and addressed his mother.

"What's all this? I caught these children snooping round the castle. Who's this woman too?"

"Guy, calm yourself," said Mrs Brimming, in a shaky voice. "This is someone with a letter from the estate agents. She – she thinks her friend, the Queen of Baronia, would like to rent Moon Castle. She has come to see it – these children belong to her. And this small boy is the son of the Queen of Baronia – Prince Paul. It's – it's quite all right. They have every right to be here."

"Didn't I tell you nobody was allowed in?" said her son,

fiercely. "What's all this about renting? I don't believe a word of it."

Mrs Arnold began to feel alarmed. What an extraordinary man! She beckoned to Mike. "Go and fetch Ranni," she said. Mike sped off into the hall and went to the great front door. They had left Ranni and the car outside the flight of steps that led up to it from the drive. How Mike hoped he would be there, waiting!

The front door was well and truly bolted, and had two great keys in the locks. Mike dragged back the bolts, and turned the keys with difficulty. The door came open with a terrible groan, as if it resented being awakened from its long, long sleep.

Ranni was down in the drive, standing patiently beside the car. He saw Mike at once, and sprang up the steps, quick to note the urgency in the boy's face.

"Mother wants you," said Mike, and ran back down the hall to the room where he had left everyone. Big Ranni followed, his boots making a great noise on the stone floor.

Guy, the son of the scared Mrs Brimming, was now examining the letter, which he had almost snatched out of Mrs Arnold's hand when she had offered it to him to prove the truth of her words. His face was as black as thunder.

"Why didn't you write to make an appointment?" he demanded. "No one is allowed in without an appointment! And I must tell you that no one has rented this castle for years – not for years! I cannot—"

"You sent for me, madam?" interrupted Ranni's deep voice. Guy looked up at once, and was astounded to see the enormous Baronian standing beside Mrs Arnold.

"Yes, Ranni," said Mrs Arnold. "I have been over this castle, and I think your master, the King of Baronia, will find it to his liking. This man here – the son of one of the caretakers – does not appear to like our coming. Do you think your master will allow him to stay here when he brings his own servants?"

Ranni knew perfectly well what Mrs Arnold wanted him to say. He looked at Guy with much dislike. Then he bowed to Mrs Arnold and spoke loudly.

"Madam, you know my master's wishes. His Majesty will certainly not allow anyone here except the caretakers. I will get His Majesty's orders and convey them to this man. He will certainly have no right to be here or to object to anything."

The children looked at Guy triumphantly. Good old Ranni! Mrs Brimming gave a little cry. "But he's only my son. He always lives here. He didn't mean to be rude. It's only that . . ."

"I don't think we need to talk about it any more," said Mrs Arnold. "Your son will have to leave the castle while my friends are renting it. He appears to think the castle belongs to him!"

Guy had gone purple in the face. He took a step forward and opened his mouth – but nobody knew what he wanted to say because Ranni also took a step forward. That was enough! One glance at the big Ranni, with his flaming red beard and steady eyes, made Guy change his mind quickly. He muttered something under his breath, swung round and went out of the room.

"I think we'll go now," said Mrs Arnold, picking up the letter that Guy had flung down on a table. "I will tell the estate agents to contact Lord Moon and arrange everything quickly. My friends would like to come in ten days' time, as I told you – earlier if possible, if it can be arranged. I shall tell them how beautifully kept the castle is – and you may be sure that the Queen's servants will keep everything just as well."

"Madam – please don't tell Lord Moon that my son – that my son – behaved rudely," begged Mrs Brimming, looking suddenly tearful. "He – well, he helps to look after the castle too, you see – and he didn't know anyone was coming to see it – or rent it."

"That doesn't excuse his behaviour," said Mrs Arnold. "But I assure you I shall make no trouble for him or for you, if he makes none either. But he must certainly leave the castle while my friend's family is here. We expect *you* to remain here, of course – but not your son or any other relations or friends. We shall make that clear to Lord Moon."

Mrs Arnold said good day and walked to the front door, followed by the children and Ranni. The caretakers did not follow them. They remained behind, gloomy and upset.

But from an upstairs window two angry eyes watched the great blue and silver car set off down the drive. Nobody saw them but Ranni – and he said nothing!

Plans

When the five children got back home again, they found Captain Arnold there. He had been away on business, and was very glad to see them. He swung Peggy and Nora up in his arms, one after the other.

The boys clustered round him, glad to see him. "Where in the world have you been?" he demanded. "I came home expecting to find a loving wife and five excited children to greet me – and nobody was here except Dimmy!"

"I did my best to give him a good welcome," Dimmy said to Mrs Arnold. "But don't fret – he's only been in ten minutes! He hasn't had to wait long."

It was eight o'clock, and everyone was very hungry. "We'll tell you our news when we've washed and are sitting down to supper," said Mrs Arnold. "We've really had a most exciting day!"

So they told Captain Arnold all about how they had been

to visit Moon Castle – its magnificence, its grandeur, its loneliness – how beautifully it was kept by the three caretaker-sisters, and all about the angry son.

"Ha! He's been frightening people away, I expect!" said Captain Arnold. "Likes to think he's King of the Castle – probably brings his own friends there and impresses them very much. If I were Lord Moon I'd make a few enquiries as to why the castle hasn't been let before – and I'd find out how many friends of that son have been staying at the castle – living there for months, I expect! He sounds a bad lot."

"He soon came to his senses when Ranni appeared, though," said Mike, with a grin. "He hardly said a word after that."

"It's a most lovely place," said Mrs Arnold. "I shall ring up the agents first thing tomorrow, and tell them to get in touch with Paul's father. The place is quite ready to go into immediately. I could order all the food and other goods that will be needed. I made enquiries about what shops to go to when I was in Bolingblow."

"Do you think we'll be there next week?" said Paul, hopefully.

"I don't see why not," said Mrs Arnold. "I imagine your people will all fly over, Paul. If only we have a good summer! It's such lovely country round about the castle – real English countryside, Your mother will love it."

"Shall we go and stay with you as soon as your family come?" asked Nora, eagerly, turning to Paul.

"No, no," said her mother, answering for Paul. "Of course not. Only Paul will go to join them at first. We must give them time to settle in a little! But we will certainly join them later."

"Paul will be able to go up the tower before we do," said Peggy, enviously. "Paul, write and tell us about everything, won't you – the tower – and if the key is produced – and if that horrid man Mr Brimming has gone, and . . ."

"Of course he'll be gone," said her mother. "I certainly

will not have him hanging round the place. He seemed to me to be a little mad. The caretakers will have to keep out of the way too, and not interfere with the Queen's servants at all. I think they will be quite sensible – especially if that man isn't around. He seemed to have them under his thumb."

"I'll explore everything and take you everywhere when you come," promised Paul.

Dimmy was very interested to hear about it all. She was not going to the castle when the others did, but Paul said that she really must come just for the day. He was very fond of Dimmy. He turned to Captain Arnold, a thought suddenly striking him.

"Sir – will you be able to come too? Are you on leave for a time?"

"I hope so," said Captain Arnold, helping himself to a large plateful of trifle. "It's not certain, though. I might be off on a very interesting job."

"What job?" asked everyone, but he shook his head. "I shan't tell you till I know," he said. "I hope it will be after we come back from Moon Castle."

Nora yawned hugely, patting her hand over her mouth. "Oh dear – sorry, everyone, but I do feel so sleepy. I even feel too sleepy to have another helping of trifle, which is an awful pity!"

"It isn't," said Paul. "It means I can have it instead!"

Mike and Paul scrabbled for the last helping and made a mess on the table. "I knew that would happen," said Dimmy. "Never mind! It's nice to see every single dish finished up – so much easier to wash! Now there's Peggy yawning and Paul too."

"Get to bed, everyone," said Mrs Arnold. "I'd like a little peace with my husband! I haven't seen him for a very long time!"

The five children went up to bed, everyone yawning now. Mike wanted to talk about Moon Castle, but as both

337

Jack and Paul were sound asleep as soon as their heads were on the pillow, he had to lie and think instead.

Moon Castle! Fancy there being a castle like that – so very, very old – so beautifully kept – with such strange things in it. He remembered the church-shaped clock and the angel appearing at the church door. And he must remember to look for the musical-box that played a hundred tunes – and could he *possibly* try on a suit of armour? And – and . . .

But Mike was now as fast asleep as the others. Mrs Arnold sat downstairs and talked quietly with her much-travelled husband. He was one of the finest pilots in the world. How many times had he flown round the world? He had lost count! Mrs Arnold, too, was a fine pilot, and had gone on many record flights with her husband. She knew almost as much about aeroplanes as he did.

"This new job you spoke of?" she said. "Is it important? Can you tell me?"

"Yes, I'll tell you," said her husband. "It is to fly a new plane – a queer one, but a beauty! It's a wonderplane. It can rise straight up in the air at a great speed, for one thing, and it gains height in a most remarkable manner."

"Amazing!" said Mrs Arnold. "Will you be on a test flight with it, then? When will it be ready? Do you know?"

"I don't," said her husband. "Yes, it's a test flight, all right. I shall put it through a few hair-raising tests, you may be sure! The speed it goes! I've got to wear special clothes, and some queer apparatus over my head because of the enormous speed – faster than sound again, you know!"

"I want to come and see you take off," said Mrs Arnold. "I always bring you luck, don't I? The only time I couldn't come and watch, you had an accident. I must come and see you this very special, important time, my dear!"

"Yes – you must," said Captain Arnold, knocking out his pipe. "I only hope it doesn't come at a time when you want to go to Moon Castle with the Queen and her family. You'd enjoy that so much!"

"Well, if the times clash, I shall come with *you*, dear – and the children can go off to the castle with Dimmy," said his wife. "I *must* come with you and bring you luck when you fly this new plane."

They went off to bed, and soon everyone in the house was sleeping. How many dreamt about Moon Castle? Certainly all the five children did.

It was their first thought in the morning too. They pestered Mrs Arnold after breakfast to telephone the agents at once. She protested. "I *must* telephone Paul's mother first! It takes a little time to get a clear line to telephone Baronia."

But at last all the telephoning was done. The Queen approved heartily. She spoke to Paul too, and the boy was excited to hear his mother's voice coming so clearly over so many miles.

"Dear Paul!" said his mother, in the Baronian language. "I shall see you soon. And your brothers are so excited to be coming to England – such a wonderful country! Mrs Arnold will arrange everything as quickly as possible."

The agents were pleased to hear that Lord Moon's castle had been let. "It's the first time for years," they told Mrs Arnold. "We've had such difficulty in letting it. We've sent a few people there to see it – but they came back with queer stories – either they couldn't get in – or things were made difficult for them. I don't really know what happened. We do hope the Queen of Baronia will like her stay there. I am glad, too, to hear that the place is in such beautiful order. Perhaps we shall have better luck with it now."

Mrs Arnold thought that Mr Guy Brimming must have been the one who had made things difficult! She did not say so, but determined that she would make things very hard for that unpleasant fellow if he did not take himself off and remain away!

"Well, we don't even need to get into touch with Lord Moon," she told the children. "Apparently if the agents are

"I have arranged to take the castle for your mother, Paul."

satisfied, they are the judges as to whether the new tenants may go in, and when. So I arranged to take the castle for your mother, Paul, this day week!"

"Oh *good*!" said Paul, delighted. "Only seven days to wait! Well, I suppose Mother will let those three old ladies know what she wants in the way of food and so on – or are you going to do all that Mrs Arnold?"

"Oh, I shall do that," said Mrs Arnold. "What a shock for the three old things when loads of goods arrive day after day! They will hardly know where to put them!"

"Does it cost a lot to rent a castle?" said Mike, thinking that he might like to rent one himself some day.

"Good gracious, yes!" said his mother. "Why, are you thinking of renting one, dear? Just save up a few thousand pounds then!"

"Goodness!" said Mike, abandoning his ideas of castles at once. "Mother, you will be able to come too, won't you? I did hear you say something to Dimmy this morning that you might not be able to."

"Well – there's a chance that your father might like to have me with him when he goes to his new job," said his mother. "But I shall join you afterwards – and Dimmy can go with you, if it happens at an awkward time. But Daddy will soon know, and I'll tell you immediately! I promise!"

Captain Arnold came home that night with the news they wanted. "It's all right!" he said. "I'm to go next week – and as the job will probably only take a week, your mother and I will be home in time to join Paul and his people at Moon Castle in a fortnight's time – probably on the very day we have been asked!"

"Oh good!" said Mike. "Paul will have to go next week, of course, when his family come over – and then we can all go together the week after, when they are settled in."

"Better enjoy this week here while you're all

together," said Dimmy. "You'll be all alone with me next week!"

"Can't we go and watch the new tests too, Daddy?" asked Peggy. "Why can't we?"

"Oh, they're very hush-hush!" said her father. "No sightseers allowed. Cheer up – all our plans are going well these holidays! Nothing will go wrong, I'm sure!"

But he wasn't right about that – something *did* go wrong before the week was up!

Things Go A Little Wrong

The first inkling that things were going wrong came in three days' time, when Mrs Arnold got a letter from Paul's mother, the Queen.

"Any news from my mother?" asked Paul, eagerly. "What a long letter, Mrs Arnold!"

"Yes – it is," said Mrs Arnold. "Oh dear – one of your brothers is ill, Paul dear. It's Boris, who was coming to Moon Castle with your mother in a few days' time!"

"Oh," said Paul, dolefully. "What's the matter with him? He's not *very* ill, is he?"

"No. But they are afraid it is measles," said Mrs Arnold. "Oh, what a pity! Your other brother hasn't had measles, she says – so he will be in quarantine, if Boris has it, as they've been together, of course."

"Oh, Mrs Arnold – it won't mean that my mother can't come, will it?" said Paul, full of dismay. "What about Moon Castle? What about—"

"Well, we won't begin to worry till we know for certain Boris *has* got measles," said Mrs Arnold. "Your mother says it may not be. Perhaps she will come and bring some of the other children, and leave Boris and his brother behind, if they have measles. Don't worry about it."

But Paul did worry, of course. Their lovely, lovely plans! Bother Boris! He was always getting things. Now perhaps they wouldn't be able to go to Moon Castle – and it was going to be such an adventure!

Mike and the others were very disappointed too, because if the trip to England was cancelled they wouldn't have the fun of going to Moon Castle either!

"The only person who will be pleased about this is that horrid man Mr Brimming," said Mike, gloomily. "He'll rejoice like anything!"

Two more days passed. "Any news from my mother?" Paul asked at every post-time. "Mrs Arnold, we're supposed to have the castle the day after tomorrow, aren't we? What will happen if Mother decides not to come? Do you just tell the caretakers, or what?"

"Now don't keep worrying your head about it," said Mrs Arnold. "Your mother is going to telephone today after lunch. We shall know then."

"R-r-r-r-r-ing!" went the telephone bell after lunch, and the children rushed into the hall. Mrs Arnold pushed them firmly away. She took up the receiver. A voice came to her ear.

"A personal call from Baronia, please, for Mrs Arnold."

"I am Mrs Arnold," was the answer, and then came a lot of clicking noises and far-off voices.

The children stood round breathlessly, trying to hear what was said to Mrs Arnold. She listened carefully, nodding, and saying "Yes. Yes, I see. Yes, a very good idea. Yes. Yes. No, of course not. Yes, I agree."

The children, who could make nothing at all of all this, went nearly mad with impatience. Paul stood as close to Mrs Arnold as he could, hoping to catch a word or two from his mother's long talk. But he couldn't.

At last Mrs Arnold said good-bye, and put back the

receiver with a click. Paul gave a wail. "Why didn't you let me speak to her? Why didn't you?"

"Because it was a personal call, and because that wasn't your mother!" said Mrs Arnold, laughing at the little Prince's fierce expression. "Now listen and I'll tell you what was being said. It's not so bad as we feared."

"Why? Tell us – quick, Mother!" said Mike.

"That was your mother's secretary," said Mrs Arnold to Paul. "Boris *has* got measles – and Gregor, your brother, developed it two days ago. But it's only very slight indeed, and they'll be up and about in no time."

"What's going to happen then? Is Mother going to leave them and come over here?" demanded Paul.

"No. She doesn't want to leave them. But she is sure she will be able to come in about ten days' time, and bring them too," said Mrs Arnold. "So what she proposes is this – as she has rented the castle from the day after tomorrow, she thinks it would be a good idea for us all to go there and settle in till they come!"

"Oh how super!" cried Peggy and Nora together. Then Nora looked solemn. "But Mother," she said, "what about you and Daddy? You're going off with Daddy soon, aren't you, to those new tests? Shall you let him go alone after all, and come with us?"

"Well, dear, I think I *must* go with Daddy," said her mother. "I do bring him luck, you know. But Dimmy will go with you – won't you, Dimmy? And you'll have Ranni as well. And it will only be for a short time – a week or so. It will be nice for your mother to find you well settled in, Paul, and Dimmy able to show the servants the rooms, and where everything is to go."

"Yes. I'd be pleased to do that," said Dimmy, who had been listening to everything with interest. "I've not seen this wonderful castle – and now I shall! But when will the servants come? I don't feel that I can manage hordes of Baronian servants, all speaking a language I don't know! Not even with Ranni's help!"

344

"The servants will not come until the day before the Queen arrives," said Mrs Arnold. "The children can easily look after themselves, with your help. There will be any amount of food arriving, because I can't very well cancel that. I'll give you the lists, and you will know what is there. Well – what do you say, children?"

"Lovely! Super! Smashing!" said everyone at once. Peggy gave her mother a hug. "I wish you were coming too, though," she said. "Still – you'll come and join us when the Queen arrives, won't you? The plane tests will be over by then."

"I'll do my very best," said her mother. "Now – we'll have to get busy! There are your clothes to see to – the agents to ring up – and I must write a letter to the three caretakers to tell them that our plans are altered, and only you children are coming for the time being."

"I'll see to their clothes," said Dimmy. "They won't want to take a great deal this warm weather. Now, you children, if you want to take any special books or games you'd better look them out and let me have them to pack. And please, Mike, don't imagine that means you can take your whole railway set or anything like that!"

"How many books can we each take?" said Jack. Then he remembered the big library at the castle. "Wait, though – we'll have all those books to read we saw in the bookcases that covered the walls in the library at Moon Castle. We shan't mind a rainy day one bit!"

"Well, *I'm* taking a few books of my own," said Mike. "Those old books in the library might be too dull to read. I'm taking my favourite adventure books."

"We really ought to have a book written about *our* adventures," said Nora, going upstairs with Peggy. "They would make most exciting books."

"And everyone would wish they knew us and could share our adventures!" said Paul. "I bet most children would like to visit our Secret Island – the one we escaped to the first time I knew you – do you remember?"

"Come along, chatterboxes," said Miss Dimmy, pushing the children up the stairs. "Let me look at the clothes in your chests of drawers, and see exactly how much washing and ironing and mending I've got to do. You'll have to help, Peggy and Nora, if there's too much."

"Oh we will," they promised, feeling so happy at the thought of going off to Moon Castle that even the thought of mending clothes didn't depress them.

Captain Arnold was told the news when he got home that night. "Well, it's a mercy the boys have only got a slight attack of measles," he said. "It would have been maddening to cancel the visit to Moon Castle altogether. Anyway, the children will be all right with Dimmy."

Those two days were very full. Mrs Arnold rushed here and there, looking for this and that. Dimmy washed and ironed and mended without stopping. The boys began packing books and games at the bottom of the two big cases. Peggy and Nora began singing the silly little Moon song again!

> *"O Castle of the Moon,*
> *We'll see you very soon!"*

Mike added to it, after a great deal of thought:

> *"And many a happy hour*
> *We'll spend up in the tower!"*

"I wonder if that man will have gone," said Jack, suddenly. He called to Mrs Arnold. "I say, Mrs Arnold! Did you write to the caretakers? You haven't heard from them, I suppose?"

"There hasn't been time to hear from them," said Mrs Arnold. "Yes, I wrote, of course. I wrote to Mrs Brimming. Why?"

"I was just wondering about that man called Guy," said Jack. "I was hoping he would have gone."

"Oh yes, of course he will have gone," said Mrs Arnold. "I

told the agents that unless he went we would not rent the castle. You needn't worry about him. You won't see much of the old ladies either. I don't suppose – unless they do any dusting or cleaning till the Queen's servants arrive."

"Who's doing the cooking?" asked Peggy. "Dimmy? Will those three old women let her use the kitchen stove?"

"I don't know," said Mrs Arnold. "When I wrote I said they could choose what they would prefer to do – cook for you and be paid for it – or allow Dimmy to cook in the kitchen. I've no doubt they would rather do the cooking and earn a little extra money. I hope so, because it will be easier for Dimmy."

"I wish tomorrow would hurry up and come," said Nora, appearing with an armful of ironed clothes.

"Can't you think of anything else to say?" said Mike. "I've heard you say that about twelve times already. What's the time? Nearly tea-time. Well, this time tomorrow we'll be in the castle of the Moon!"

At last everything was packed and ready. The suitcases were shut. Dimmy went round to make sure that everything necessary had been packed and nothing left out. Mrs Arnold and her husband were also leaving on the day following. The children had not been told their address, as the tests were not to be made known – in fact even Captain Arnold was not sure exactly where he was to go the next day.

"I vote we all go to bed early," he said at supper-time. "I want to be absolutely fresh tomorrow – and you look tired out already, my dear," he said, turning to his wife. "So does Dimmy."

"*We're* not tired," said Mike. "But we'll go to bed early and make tomorrow come all the quicker! What time is Ranni coming for us in the car?"

"About half-past ten," said his mother. You can have your lunch at that hotel in Bolingblow again, if you like. And I suppose I need hardly warn you to take great care of

At last everything was packed and ready.

all that beautiful furniture at the castle during your stay – and . . ."

"Mother, we'll behave like Princes and Princesses!" said Mike, laughing. "Come on, everyone – let's go to bed. Hurrah for tomorrow – and the Castle of the Moon!"

The Castle Again

Everyone was in a great rush the next morning. The house was to be left empty for the time being. Mrs Hunt, the woman who cooked and helped in the house, was to go home, and to come in daily only to dust and open the windows. She would come and feed the hens too.

Captain Arnold had his bag ready, and Mrs Arnold had packed a small one for herself. Mike wanted to open one of the suitcases, and put in two books he suddenly longed to take at the last moment.

"You can't open them," said Dimmy. "You've done that twice already and messed everything up inside. Now I've locked the case and I've got the key safe!"

"Blow!" said Mike, and went to see if he could open Paul's school trunk, which he was taking with him. But Dimmy had artfully locked that too.

Ranni came round with the shining car at exactly half-past ten. He grinned at the excited children. "So we go back to the castle!" he said. "The poor car – she will bump herself to death!"

"Baronian cars don't mind bumps," said Paul. "You said so yourself! Anyway, I rather like them. Goodbye, Captain Arnold, and the very best of luck with your new tests."

"Thank you," said Captain Arnold. "If you hear something that sounds like a big sneeze, and it's gone almost before it's come, it'll be me in the new plane!"

Everyone laughed. Nora hugged her father. "Be careful, Daddy, won't you?" she said. "And good luck!"

Soon all the good-byes had been said and the car set off, with Captain and Mrs Arnold waving from the doorstep. They were off!

It was rather a squash in the big car again, but nobody minded except Dimmy, who said that Nora was the most fidgety person to sit next to that she had ever known in her life. But when Peggy took Nora's place Miss Dimmy changed her mind, and said that she thought Peggy was worse than Nora. Certainly none of the five children stopped talking or leaning out of windows, or stretching across one another for the whole journey.

They had lunch at Bolingblow again, and the same little waitress served them.

"We went to the castle," said Peggy. "It's WONDERFUL!"

"And we're going again now – to stay!" said Nora.

The waitress laughed. She didn't believe Nora. "No one stays there," she said. "So don't you try to pull my leg. It's got a bad name, Moon Castle has."

"Why has it?" asked Mike at once.

"Well – people say Things Happen there," said the waitress, mysteriously. "I told you before about the fellow who went to see some old books in the library there!"

"Oh yes – and they jumped out of the shelves at him!" said Peggy, with a giggle. "We do hope that will happen when *we're* there! But do please believe us – we really *are* going there to stay."

The waitress stared at them, still finding this difficult to believe. "I did hear say that any amount of goods have been ordered and sent to the castle," she said. "Any amount – food and stuff. Would that be for you?"

"Well, partly," said Peggy. "Do you know any more tales about the castle?"

"Noises!" said the waitress, lowering her voice as if she was half-afraid to speak. "Noises! I did hear there were very strange noises."

"What sort?" asked Mike, in great interest.

"I don't know. Nobody knows," said the girl. "Just noises. Don't you go to that castle. You go home while there's time!"

She went off with their plates. Peggy laughed. "This is very thrilling. Isn't it queer how all old places have strange stories about them? I wouldn't be a bit surprised if that man Guy put out these tales, just to keep the castle to himself and prevent people going there. I bet there aren't any Noises or Things that Happen!"

"I agree with you," said Mike. "It's just tales. Well – we'll soon find out. Personally I'd like something to happen."

"Not Noises," said Nora. "I don't like noises – queer noises, I mean – when you don't know what makes them."

"Like the wicker chair in our bedroom," said Peggy. "At night it suddenly gives a creak *exactly* as if somebody had sat down in it. But when I put my light on there's nobody there."

"Of course there isn't," said Dimmy. "It's merely the wickerwork relaxing after having to bear your big lump of a weight, Peggy!"

They were now on to ice-creams. They were so nice that Miss Dimmy ordered a second round. Nora patted her arm affectionately.

"I do like some of your habits, Dimmy," she said. "Like ordering another lot of ice-creams – and looking the other way when one of us orders a third lot."

"There'll be *no* third lot," said Dimmy. "I'm calling for the bill!"

The children grinned. They didn't really want a third ice-cream, but it was always fun to pull Dimmy's leg. The waitress came up with the bill.

"I've been talking to my friend over there about Moon Castle," she said in a low voice. "She's the niece of the grocer who sent up some of the goods. And she says the driver of the van was so scared when he got to the castle that he just dumped all the things in the drive, shouted 'Here they are!' jumped back into the van, and went down the hill as if a hundred dogs were after him."

"But why was he so scared?" said Nora, puzzled. "There's absolutely nothing frightening about the front door! The driver must be crazy!"

"I tell you, it's a scary place," said the waitress, who seemed quite determined to make the most of what little she knew. "Well – you come in here and see me when you've been there a day or two. I guess you'll have some queer tales to tell!"

The children laughed. "There are only three harmless old caretakers up there now," said Mike. "They would be more scared than anyone else if Things Happened, like you said."

"Ah – caretakers! Three of them – *that's* queer!" said the waitress.

"Why? Do they fly about on broomsticks at night?" asked Jack with a grin.

The waitress was cross. She piled the plates together loudly and walked off.

"Come on," said Mike. "Off to the castle of the Moon, we'll be there very soon – no, I've got it wrong. Anyway, come on, everyone!"

They went back to the car. Ranni was already in the driving-seat, waiting patiently. It was somehow rather comforting to see him there, big and burly and confident, after hearing the waitress's tales. They all got into the car, feeling very well-fed indeed. Now for the castle!

Ranni drove off. They followed the same road as before, bumpy and full of ruts. Ranni drove carefully. Nora and Peggy looked out for the fork that led to the ruined village.

"I meant to have asked the waitress if she knew anything about that," said Nora, regretfully. "But I forgot. I'm sure she would have had a wonderful story about it."

"Look – there's the fork to it," said Peggy. "I vote we go and explore it one day. It's only about a mile from here. I'd like to explore a ruined village."

They passed the fork and the children once more caught a glimpse of tumble-down roofs and a desolate group of houses huddled together.

And then they were on the steep road to the castle. They wound to and fro on the slope, their engine sounding loudly as they went. Not even the powerful Baronian car could go up in top gear!

The entrance gates were again shut and Mike hopped out to open them. Up the drive they went and swept round to the front door. That too was shut.

"Well – here we are," said Mike, looking up at the towering castle. "It seems awfully big when we're as near as this. Now, what happens? Do we ring the bell again? On no – you broke the chain, Ranni! I hope we don't have to go all round the back, like we did before."

"The chain is mended," said Ranni, and the children, looking towards the door, saw that he was right. "We can get in at the front this time!"

Jack leapt up the wide flight of steps and took hold of the iron handle at the end of the chain. He pulled it downwards.

This time a bell rang! A loud jangle sounded somewhere back in the castle, a cracked, harsh noise, as if the bell was big, but broken.

Ranni heaved the cases and Paul's trunk up the steps. Everyone stood patiently waiting for the door to open. Jack got impatient and rang the bell again. Then he jumped. The door was opening slowly and quietly in front of him.

But no one was there! The children stood there, expecting one of the old caretakers to appear. But no one came. Was someone behind the door?

The door was opening slowly and quietly in front of him.

Jack ran in to see. No – the hall was empty. "How queer!" said Dimmy. "Somebody *must* have opened the door in answer to the bell – but why should they disappear at once?"

"One of the Queer Things that Happen!" said Mike, with a chuckle. "Oh well – I expect one of the sisters did open it, but got so scared of Ranni and his red beard that she fled at once. It's so dark in the hall that we wouldn't notice anyone scuttling away. Shall I give you a hand, Ranni?"

Ranni wanted no help. "You go and find someone and ask if everything is ready for us," he said, standing inside the hall. Jack looked at Dimmy.

"Shall I go and get Mrs Brimming?" he asked. Dimmy nodded, and Jack sped off, trying to remember the way to the back quarters.

He came back almost immediately with Miss Edie Lots who was looking rather scared. "I've found one of them," said Jack, pleased. "She says she didn't hear the bell, and doesn't believe anyone opened the door."

"Rubbish," said Dimmy. "Miss Lots, is everything ready for us to come in? You got Mrs Arnold's letter, I expect – and the one from the agent, telling of our change in plans."

"Oh yes. Yes," said Miss Edie, sounding rather breathless. "We heard that only the children were coming and a Miss Dimity. Yes. Everything is ready. You will choose what bedrooms you want yourself. And the packages have come – dozens of them! They are all in the kitchen. Yes."

"Thank you," said Dimmy. "We'll get straight in now, then – and I'll come and examine everything in the kitchen later on. Now, children – come upstairs and show me the bedrooms. What a truly magnificent place this is!"

Up the stairs they went in excitement, talking nineteen to the dozen. What fun they were going to have!

Settling Into The Castle

Ranni followed the children upstairs with the luggage. Dimmy thought she had better follow quickly too, before the children took unsuitable bedrooms for themselves! She marvelled as she went up the broad flight of stairs – what a wonderful place this was!

"What carpets! What hangings! What magnificent pictures!" she thought, leaning over the broad banister and looking down into the great hall. The front door was still open and sunlight flooded through it, gleaming on the suits of armour, standing on their pedestals.

"Not a speck of dust anywhere!" marvelled Dimmy. "Those caretakers may be strange but they do know how to take care of things!"

Ranni had put the luggage down on the great landing, and now passed Dimmy to fetch the rest of it. He stopped beside her.

"I would like a small room not far from my little master, the Prince," he said, politely. "Or one opening out of his, if that is possible."

"Very well, Ranni. I will see to that," said Dimmy, thinking for the hundredth time how devoted Ranni was to Paul. Servant – friend – guardian; Ranni was everything!

She hurried towards the sound of chattering and laughter. Where were those children?

They were in an enormous bedroom that looked out over the countryside for miles. Nora swung round to Dimmy, her eyes shining.

"Dimmy! Can Peggy and I have this room? It's wonderful! Look at the view!"

"I shouldn't think you can for one moment," said

Dimmy, amazed at the size of the room. "This must be one of the biggest rooms. Paul's mother should have it!"

"Oh no, Dimmy – there are much bigger rooms than this!" protested Nora. "Come and see!"

Feeling quite dazed, Dimmy followed Nora into room after room, all beautifully furnished, all beautifully kept. The views were marvellous.

Finally they came to a suite of smaller rooms, leading out of one another, but each with its own door to the landing. There were three of these, two of them double rooms and one single room.

"Now these would do beautifully for you five children," said Dimmy, at once. "No, don't argue, Nora – the room you wanted was far too big. Let me tell you this – you will probably have to keep it spotlessly clean and tidy yourself, if the caretakers are not going to take on the job – and you'd do much better to have these small rooms, which will be very easy to keep tidy."

"Oh," said Nora, disappointed. "Well – I suppose you're right, Dimmy. And it *would* be nice to have three rooms all together like this." She went to the door and shouted.

"Peggy! Mike! Come here – there are three rooms all together here!"

They all came running. Jack approved at once. "Yes – Mike and I could have this middle one – and you two girls the one to the left of us – and Paul the one to the right – the single room. Couldn't be better!"

He went to the window and looked out. "I never in my life saw such views!" he said. "Never! I say – is that a bit of the ruined village we can see? I'm sure I can see roof-tops and a chimney or two!"

They all crowded together at the window. "Yes!" said Mike. "It must be. Look – you can just make out a bit of the road there, too – the fork to the village comes about there. I say, we *must* go and explore it sometime."

Dimmy had wandered off. She wanted to find a room for

357

herself, and one for Ranni too. She found a small room for Ranni a little way down the corridor, but alas, it looked on to the hill at the back of the castle, and was rather dark, because the walls were so near the hillside itself. The hill rose up behind the castle like a cliff.

Only the tall tower rose high above the hilltop. Dimmy thought what a wonderful view there must be from that! She looked for a room for herself, hoping to find one with a view.

She found a tiny little room at the end of the corridor. It had no bed in it, but seemed more like a little sitting-room. She decided to move a bed into it from another room, and use the little room for herself – it had such a wonderful view that she felt she would rather have it than a bigger one without a view.

She went back to the children. They had called Ranni and he had brought their luggage in. Dimmy smiled at the big, bearded fellow. "I've found a room for you, Ranni," she said. "Quite nearby. But it hasn't a view."

However Ranni, brought up in a country of high mountains and sweeping valleys, had no wish for a view. He had had plenty of those in Baronia! He was very pleased with his little room, because it was so near Paul.

"There aren't any basins with running water," said Nora, looking at the great old-fashioned washstands. "Do we have to use these enormous jugs? I shall hardly be able to lift mine!"

"Use the bathrooms," said Mike. "I counted seven on this floor already! There's one just opposite our rooms. It's got a shower and everything."

"Dimmy, isn't this fun?" said Nora. "Have you got a room for yourself – a nice one? Oh Dimmy, won't it be lovely living in a castle like this? It will take me ages to find my way around properly."

Dimmy felt rather the same – but it was amazing how quickly they learnt where all the rooms were, and the quickest way here, there and everywhere! There were two main staircases, and two or three smaller ones.

"We can have a marvellous time chasing one another and playing hide-and-seek," said Mike. "All these staircases to get away on! You know, Paul, it's a very good idea to let us come here on our own, before your people come – we shan't have such fun when they're here, really, because all the rooms will be occupied, and people won't like us rushing everywhere."

"No, they won't," said Paul, thinking of the different way he would have to behave when his family came, with all their servants. "Let's make the most of it this week!"

Dimmy went down to see the three caretakers. She rang a bell from what she imagined to be the drawing-room, but nobody came. So she found her way to the enormous kitchens.

There were two fireplaces in the biggest kitchen, one with a fire, the other empty. Great cooking stoves lined the walls. Six or seven sinks showed up here and there. Dimmy paused at the door. Goodness – what a place!

Sitting at an open window at the far end were the three sisters. Dimmy had already seen the one called Edie Lots. She walked over to them.

They stood up as she came, looking nervous.

"Please sit down," said Dimmy, thinking what a queer trio they were. "I will sit with you too, and find out what is the best way to manage till Her Majesty, the Queen of Baronia, comes next week."

They all sat down. None of the three said a word. Dimmy talked pleasantly, and got Mrs Brimming to open her mouth at last.

She arranged that the three should look after the children, herself and Ranni, and should continue to clean the castle and keep it tidy until the Baronian servants came.

"Everything will go to rack and ruin then, I suppose!"

said Mrs Brimming, dolefully. "My son said it would. Those foreign servants!"

"That's not a fair thing to say," said Dimmy. "You will find that the Baronians will take a pride in the place and keep it beautifully. In any case, that is hardly your business. You may be sure that the Queen will see that nothing goes wrong. Now do please cheer up – after all, Lord Moon must try to make a little money out of a beautiful castle like this, empty for years!"

"My son says that Lord Moon wouldn't let it to foreigners if he knew about it," said Mrs Brimming. "He says it's only the agents that have let it, without consulting Lord Moon. He says—"

Dimmy began to feel as annoyed as Mrs Arnold had felt over this interfering son! "I'm afraid it is no business of your son's," she said. Then she remembered that one of the conditions Mrs Arnold had made was that the interfering fellow – what was his name – yes, Guy – should go away.

"I suppose your son is no longer here, now that the castle has been let?" she said.

"Of course he's not here," said Miss Edie Lots, in a loud voice. She glared at Dimmy, and seemed about to say a lot more – but Mrs Brimming nudged her sharply and she stopped.

Dimmy left them soon after that. "I suppose they all adore this Guy," she thought, as she went to find the children and help them to unpack. "Well, it's a good thing he's gone. He certainly wasn't in the kitchens. Now – which is the way to our rooms? Good gracious – it's a mile walk to find them, really it is!"

The children had begun their unpacking. They wouldn't let Dimmy help. "No, Dimmy – you've got your own unpacking to do," said Nora. "You always forget that we have to unpack our own things at school! We can do it all right now, honestly we can!"

"When do we have tea – and where?" called Mike. "I'm hungry already."

"I've arranged it for half-past four," said Dimmy. "And we're using the smallest room downstairs, off the right-hand side of the hall – the room where there are some queer old musical instruments on the walls."

"Oh yes – I know it," said Peggy. "It's a queer-shaped room – what do you call it – L-shaped."

"Yes – it's just like a letter L," said Jack. "With the bottom part of the L having windows all down the side. I vote we put a table there, and have our meals looking out of the window. We can see for miles then!"

They unpacked everything and arranged their things in the great drawers, leaving half of them empty, of course, because their clothes took up very little room!

"The drawers of these great chests are so enormous that I could almost get into one!" said Paul, coming into the boys' room, which was between his and the girls'. "Are you nearly ready? I had much more to unpack than you and I've finished first."

"Well, *we'd* have finished sooner if we'd just thrown everything higgledy-piggledy into drawers, like you have." said Mike. "Get off those jerseys, Paul. There's plenty of carpet to stand on without treading on my clothes!"

"Don't be so fussy," said Paul. "What time's tea? I could do with some."

But, like the others, he had to wait till half-past four. What should they do after that? Mike had an idea at once.

"The tower! We'll see if it's unlocked now. It jolly well ought to be!"

Queer Happenings

Mrs Brimming brought up a really delicious tea. The children approved of it so heartily, and said so in such loud voices, that Mrs Brimming actually smiled!

"Thank you, Brimmy," said Nora, unexpectedly. Dimmy looked at her sharply, and the others stared at Mrs Brimming, expecting her to object at once.

But to their surprise she didn't seem to mind at all. In fact, she actually smiled again. "Fancy your calling me that!" she said. "I haven't been called that since I was nurse to Lord Moon's youngest, years ago! They all called me Brimmy in those days!"

She then scurried out of the room like a frightened hen, evidently as surprised as the children that she had made such a long speech!

"What cheek to call her Brimmy when you've only seen her twice!" said Mike to Nora. "But you just hit her on a tender spot – didn't she, Dimmy?"

"Brimmy and Dimmy," said Nora, with a giggle. "I could make a nice rhyme up about Brimmy and Dimmy."

"Well, I'd rather you didn't," said Dimmy, pouring out tea. "I'm used to your silly ideas, but Mrs Brimming isn't. I'm quite sure she wouldn't like to hear you all singing a ridiculous song about her."

"All right," said Nora. "Anyway, there aren't any decent rhymes to Brimmy or Dimmy. I say – what a smashing chocolate cake. Nice and big too. Big enough for us all to have a second slice."

"You really mustn't finish that enormous cake today," said Dimmy. "I'm sure Mrs Brimming meant it to last us a whole week."

"Well, Brimy will have a whole lot of different ideas about us before the week is up," said Mike. "Where did these biscuits come from? They're not home-made."

"I looked at some of the piles of goods that have arrived," said Dimmy. "I told Mrs Brimming she could open what she thought would do for us – but she had already made this lovely chocolate cake."

"Well, I'm beginning to think she's not a bad sort, after all," said Jack. "What do you think, Paul?"

Paul thought that anyone who could make a chocolate cake as good as the one he was eating must be a good sort. Dimmy laughed. She listened to the friendly chatter of the five children, poured them out more cups of tea, cut slices of cake and sponge sandwich, and decided that they really were a nice set of children.

"What are you going to do after tea?" she asked.

"We're going to see the tower," said Mike promptly. "It ought to be unlocked now. Like to come, Dimmy?"

"I don't think so," said Dimmy. "I want to go and see that the beds are all made, and if they are aired properly. Mrs Brimming didn't know which rooms we were going to choose and I saw that she had piles of sheets airing by the fire – probably for us. I shall see to all that, and I'm sure she will help me. You go and explore the tower if you like."

"Right – we'll leave Brimmy and Dimmy to gossip together over sheets and pillow-cases," said Mike, getting up. "Everybody finished? Oh, sorry, Dimmy – I didn't see that your cup wasn't empty." He sat down again.

"Don't wait for me, please," said Dimmy. "I always enjoy a quiet cup after you've all gone! Go along now, and do whatever you want to do!"

"Dimmy's jolly glad to finish her tea in peace," said Nora, tickling the back of Dimmy's neck affectionately as she passed her chair. "She's been busy looking after us the whole of the meal. If you want any help with the beds, call us, Dimmy, and we'll come."

They trooped out of the room. Dimmy sat back peacefully, and poured out another cup of tea. They had had their meal in the curious L-shaped room as they had planned, and the table had been set in front of the windows, in the short bottom part of the L. Dimmy gazed out of the window at the view.

The room was silent. Dimmy couldn't even hear the voices of the children in the distance – she heard only the sound of her spoon stirring her tea slowly.

TWANG!

Dimmy jumped. The sound came so suddenly, and so very unexpectedly that for a minute she couldn't imagine what it was!

TWANG! There it was again. What could it be? Dimmy suddenly remembered the old musical instruments hung on the wall in the other part of the room – in the long part of the L. She smiled.

"Silly children!" she thought. "One of them has crept back to play a joke on me and make me jump. Mike, I expect! He's crept in and twanged one of the strings of some instrument. Silly boy."

She stirred her tea again, listening for a giggle.

TWANG! TWANG!

"I can hear you!" called out Dimmy, cheerily. "Twang all you like – I don't mind!"

DONG!

"Run away and play," called Dimmy. "Silly children!"

DONG!

Dimmy wondered what instrument made the "dong" noise. It was a queer sound – but then the musical instruments on the wall beyond were very queer-looking – old, foreign and most unusual. Perhaps the "dong" noise was made by that thing that looked like a drum but had stout strings stretched across it. Anyway, she wasn't going to bother to get up and see.

DONG!

"That's enough," said Dimmy. "You ought to know when a joke is played out."

She listened for a giggle, or the scuffle of feet creeping away, but she heard nothing. She began to drink her tea. No more of the twanging, donging noises came, and Dimmy was certain that whichever of the children had played the trick on her had crept away.

She went to see about the beds, and was soon in a deep discussion with Mrs Brimming about sheets and pillowcases. She felt sure that the children were now busily exploring the tower.

But they weren't! They were all very angry indeed, because the tower door was still locked!

They had gone down the tapestry-covered corridor, and into the square-shaped room lined with great oak chests. Mike went straight to the tapestry that hung over the tower door to cover it.

He pulled it to one side, expecting to see the door.

He gaped in amazement, and turned startled eyes to the other four behind him. "It's gone!" he said. "There's no door here!"

The five looked hurriedly round the room. They could see no door at all – in fact, the whole wall was lined with chests. But about three feet from the tapestry hanging was a very tall chest, taller than the others.

"I bet it's behind that chest!" Jack said, and stepped over to it. "I *thought* that tapestry was hanging in a different place when I saw it just now. Give me a hand, Mike – we'll pull this chest away."

They tugged at it. It was astonishingly heavy, and needed all five of them to move it. Nobody thought of taking out the contents of the drawers to make the chest easier to handle!

Behind the chest, just as Jack had thought, was the tower door – tall, narrow – and locked!

"That's that awful man again!" said Jack, fiercely,

365

"It's gone! There's no door here!"

366

pulling at the ring handle. "What does he think he's doing? Fancy thinking he'd hide the door by putting a chest in front of it, and hanging the tapestry somewhere else. He must be mad. What's the point, anyhow?"

"The point is that he doesn't want anyone to go into the tower – because he's got some secret there," said Mike. The others nodded in agreement. Nora shook the handle, and then bent down and peered though the keyhole.

"I can see stone steps beyond the door," she said. "Oh how could that horrible man do such a thing! Whatever will your mother say, Paul, when she finds that this kind of thing is being done?"

"Perhaps by the time your mother's family comes, the door will be unlocked," said Jack slowly. "Maybe Mr Brimming hasn't had time to clear out of the tower – and thinks that he can stop us going in by tricks like this."

"Yes. I expect that's it," said Paul. "I bet he's made himself a kind of home in this tower – thinks of it as his own – and resents us coming. I bet he's got all his furniture in there still!"

"Well, if we suddenly find the key in the lock, and the tower is empty, we'll know we were right," said Jack. "He'll probably move out one dark night."

"It's *maddening*," said Peggy, shaking the handle in her turn, as if she thought that a little temper would make the door open. She put her mouth to the keyhole.

"Hey!" she shouted. "We know you're up there! Come down and unlock this door!"

Jack pulled her away. "Don't be so *silly*, Peggy," he said. "You wouldn't like it a bit if he came tearing down those stairs and flung the door open and glared at you out of his horrid eyes!"

Peggy looked at the door, rather alarmed. "No sound of footsteps!" she said, with a laugh. "He wouldn't hear my shouting, anyway. It wouldn't carry through that thick door and up those stone steps."

Mike was looking in the big chest they had hauled away from the door. "I'd like to know what makes it so jolly heavy," he said. "We *almost* couldn't drag it away. Look – rugs – cloth of some kind – and what's this in the bottom drawer of the chest, wrapped up in blue curtains?"

They all leaned over him as he knelt down, feeling in the big bottom drawer, He tugged at the cloth that wrapped up some great, heavy objects which could hardly be moved.

Nobody could move them an inch, and everyone grew very curious about what the heavy things could be. Jack took hold of a corner of one of the cloths and pulled hard until the heavy bundle unrolled.

"Rocks! Stones big enough to be called small rocks! My word, what a time he must have had, bringing them here to weight this chest down. I wonder the drawer didn't break – but these chests are very old and solid."

"No wonder we could hardly move the thing," said Paul. What are we going to do?"

"Leave the chest moved out of place so that Mr Guy Brimming can see we've discovered his little joke – a jolly silly one," said Jack. "He probably didn't reckon there'd be five of us to move it. Well! *Somehow* we've got to get into this tower – and it's certainly not going to be easy!"

Twang-Dong Again!

The five children left the chest where it was, pulled right away from the tower door. Guy Brimming would certainly know they had gone to explore the tower, found the door hidden, and discovered it behind the chest! Would he do anything further? They would wait and see.

They decided to go back to the L-shaped room and tell

Dimmy. She wasn't there, so they went to find her in the bedrooms upstairs, remembering that she was going to see to the beds. She was there, as they thought, just finishing Paul's room. She was alone.

"Oh Dimmy – have you done the beds all by yourself?" said Nora. "I'm sorry! I thought you'd be sure to call Peggy and me if you didn't have help."

"It's all right, dear – Mrs Brimming and one of the Lots came up to help me," said Dimmy. "I don't know which one – they're so alike, those two Lots. They've only just gone."

"We couldn't get into the tower, Dimmy," said Peggy, solemnly.

"The door was still locked," said Mike.

"And *some*body had tried to hide it by pulling a chest in front," said Paul. "What do you think of that?"

Dimmy laughed at their very solemn faces. "Well – I don't *really* think very much of it," she said. "I expect there are things in the tower that need to be cleaned, or perhaps cleared out. Maybe it's been used for storing all kinds of things in – and I've no doubt the tower will be unlocked and ready for anyone to use by the time Paul's family arrive next week."

"I think you're wrong, Dimmy," said Jack. "I think there's something *mysterious* about it. I'm sure it's something to do with that fellow Guy."

"You think a lot of foolish things," said Dimmy. "I'll mention it to Mrs Brimming – and you'll see, she'll have a quite ordinary explanation for it. Maybe the key is lost, as they said before."

"Well – but why was the door *hidden* this time?" persisted Jack. "And why was the chest that hid it weighted down with rocks so that it was almost impossible to move?"

"Rocks! Nonsense!" said Dimmy. "You're joking. And, by the way, talking of jokes – TWANG! DONG!"

She made a loud twanging sound with her mouth and

then a loud dong. The children stared at her in wonder. She laughed.

"Yes – you can look as inncent as you please!" she said. "But *I* know those innocent faces of yours! Aha! It was funny, wasn't it – TWANG! DONG!"

The children looked rather alarmed at this Twang-Dong speech. They stared at Dimmy, and then looked at one another.

"What exactly do you mean, Dimmy?" asked Nora at last. "Honestly, we can't imagine what you're getting at."

Dimmy looked rather annoyed. "Well, as you very well know, one of you – or maybe two or three of you, I don't know – crept back to the tea-room and twanged and donged one or two of the musical instruments on the wall," she said. "So don't deny it. It was a good joke, I agree, and the first time I jumped like anything. But don't pretend to be innocent now!"

"Not one of us went back to play a trick," said Jack, astonished. He looked round at the others. "We didn't, did we? We went straight to the tower door, and we've been there ever since. We don't know a thing about this twanging and donging."

Dimmy found it difficult to believe him. "Well, well – perhaps the instruments play a little tune by themselves," she said. "Anyway – I'd be glad to know which one of you it was, when you've made up your minds that the joke is now ended."

The five children left Dimmy and went down to the sitting-room, where they had had tea. They were very puzzled. "What on earth did Dimmy mean?" said Mike. "TWANG! DONG! I really thought she had gone suddenly dippy when she made those noises! We certainly don't know anything about them."

"Perhaps old musical instruments are like wicker chairs," said Peggy. "Perhaps their strings relax or something and make a noise."

"I never heard of such a thing before," said Mike. "Let's have a good look at them."

They stood beside the walls and looked at all the queer instruments – some were like big guitars, some like banjos, and there were tom-toms and tambourines – any amount of instruments were there, many of which the children had never seen before.

Jack touched a string, and it twanged softly. Soon they were all touching the various strings and knocking on the drums and tom-toms, so that a weird noise filled the room.

They got tired of it after a time. "I really think Dimmy must have fallen asleep or something, when we left her," said Jack. "Instruments just *don't* play themselves. Come on – let's have a game. Who says Racing Demon?"

Everyone did, and they took the cards from the cupboard where they had put their various games.

Dimmy came in, in the middle of the first game. "What a nice peaceful sight!" she said. "I'll get some mending to do, so don't ask me to play. I don't like those top-speed games!"

She got some sewing, and came to sit beside them at the window. The children were playing on the table where they had had tea. Dimmy glanced out of the window, marvelling at the wonderful view she could see for miles on miles. The sky was very blue, the distance was blue too. The sun was going down, and there was a golden light over everything.

Jack began to deal again. "Wait a moment before you begin another game," said Dimmy. "Look out there – did you ever see anything so lovely?"

They all gazed out of the window, and Nora began to make up a few lines of poetry in her mind. It was a very peaceful moment.

TWANG!

Everyone jumped violently and Dimmy dropped the pair of scissors she was holding.

371

"There!" said Dimmy. *"That's the noise I heard before!"*

"There!" said Dimmy, in a whisper. "That's the noise I heard before. Wasn't it one of you, then?"

"No – we told you it wasn't," said Nora. "And anyway, we're all here now. Not one of us has moved to the other part of the room, where the guitars and things are."

Nothing more happened. Jack got up and went round the bend of the L-shaped room into the long part where the walls held so many instruments. Nobody was there. The door was open and he shut it.

"Nobody there," he said, and sat down. "Maybe somebody crept in and twanged a guitar. I wonder who the joker is!"

He began to deal once more.

TWANG!

Everyone jumped again, it was so loud. Jack and Mike raced round the bend of the room. The door was still shut!

"But someone might have crept in, twanged, and gone out quickly," said Jack. "Look – there's a key in the door. We'll turn it and lock the door – then the joker will be completely done!"

He turned the key. Dimmy looked rather startled. She had quite thought that one of the children had played the joke on her after tea – but now she saw that they had told the truth. Somebody else was doing the twanging!

DONG!

Jack slapped his cards down. "This is silly!" he said. "I locked the door!"

Mike disappeared into the other part of the room. "It's still locked!" he called. "Well and truly locked. Can't be opened at all."

He took a look at the instruments on the wall, wondering which one had twanged. He looked for a quivering string, but could see none. He went back to the others, as puzzled as they were.

DONG!

"Blow it," said Jack. "*Who's* doing it?"

"I don't think anyone is," said Dimmy, picking up her scissors, which she had dropped again. "I think it's just one or two of the instruments doing it on their own – perhaps it's this hot weather – making them expand or something."

"Well, there doesn't seem anything else to think," said Peggy, "except—"

"Except what?" asked Jack, as Peggy stopped.

"Well – except that we heard that Queer Things Happen here," said Peggy. "Don't you remember what the waitress said at that hotel? 'Strange Noises – Queer Happenings.'"

"Don't!" said Nora. "I didn't believe it. And I don't want to believe it now."

"And do you remember she said that books jumped out of the bookshelves?" said Peggy. "Oh dear – I hope things don't begin to jump about."

"Now listen to me," said Dimmy, in a suddenly brisk voice, "this kind of talk is foolish and ridiculous. I don't want to hear any more of it. Fancy believing the silly tales of a waitress! Books jumping! Too silly for words!"

"Well – but we *did* hear a Queer Noise," said Peggy.

"I dare say we did – but we've decided that it's the hot weather making the strings of some instrument or other expand, and go twang and dong," said Dimmy.

DONG!

"Yes, just like that," said Dimmy firmly, as the curious dong noise came from round the bend of the room. "Nobody is there. The door is locked – and if the instruments like to sigh and make a noise because it's hot, what does it matter?"

TWANG!

"Well, I expect you're right, Dimmy," said Nora. "If it's only noises like that I don't mind a bit. Let's go on with the game!"

Jack began once more to deal, and they gathered up their cards, listening all the time for another twang or dong.

But none came! They began to forget about it and played with a lot of noise. Dimmy watched them, glad that they were no longer puzzled. But she was very puzzled indeed.

Was she right in thinking that the noises had been natural ones? Yes, of course she must be right. She looked out of the window at the view. The sun was sinking low.

Bang-bang!

Everyone jumped so much that half the cards slid off the table. Dimmy leapt to her feet. *Now* what was it?

A voice came from the other side of the door – a plaintive, puzzled voice.

"Please, Miss Dimity, we're bringing your supper, and the door's locked."

"Gosh – that was only Brimmy knocking at the door!" said Jack, in great relief. He ran to open it. Brimmy was there with a large tray, and behind her were the two solemn sisters, also with trays.

Nobody explained the locked door. It suddenly began to seem rather silly. At the sight of a very nice supper all six completely forgot both Twang and Dong, and willing hands took the trays and set the table!

"Aha!" said Jack. "A meal fit for a King – and certainly fit for a Prince! Dimmy – are we ready? One, two, three, begin!"

An Interesting Discovery

It was fun to go to bed that night in the little suite of three rooms. The doors between were left open so that shouting could go on between the three boys and the two girls.

Nobody felt sleepy at all. When they were all in pyjamas, the girls and Paul went to sit on the beds in the middle room to talk to Mike and Jack. It wasn't long before a pillow-fight began, of course. With shrieks and thuds the fight raged round the room, and a chair went over with a bang.

"We'll have Dimmy in if we make too much row," panted Mike. "Oh you beast, Paul – you've taken my pillow. Give it back!"

Thud! Biff! Giggles and shrieks, bare feet pattering all over the bedroom, and someone pinned in a corner! And then Nora gave an agonized yell.

"Paul! Ass! Your pillow's gone out of the window!"

There was a pause in the battle at once. Paul looked rather abashed as Mike rounded on him. "Idiot, Paul! What did you do that for?"

"It sort of flew out of my hand," explained Paul, and went to the window. He leaned out so far that Jack caught him by his pyjama trousers, afraid that he might pitch out and join the pillow. "I can see it," he said. "It's down on the grass below. I'll get it."

He ran to the door of his room and opened it. Dimmy was just coming up the corridor! She saw him and called out.

"Paul! You ought to be in bed long ago. What are you doing?"

"Just looking out," said Paul. "Are you coming to bed now, Dimmy?"

"Yes, I am – and I shall come along just before I get into bed and make sure you are all asleep," said Dimmy, firmly. "So if you have any ideas of playing catch or hide-and-seek round the castle corridors, just put them out of your head! I suppose you've been pillow-fighting or something – you look so hot and tousled."

"We've had a bit of a fight," said Paul, grinning. "Good night, Dimmy." He shut the door and went back to the others, who had leapt into their beds as soon as they had heard Dimmy's voice.

"It was Dimmy," said Paul, poking his head into the boys' room. "She's just going to bed – but she's coming along last thing to see if we're alseep. Blow! What shall I do about the pillow? I don't like to go down and hunt for it now in case she comes along."

"Wait till she's been along and I'll go with you," said Mike. "It's getting dark now – we'll take our torches and slip out when it's safe. Get into bed now, for goodness' sake. Ranni will be along next!"

Mike was right. Ranni came along in about five minutes' time and quietly opened Paul's door to make sure he was in bed and asleep. There was no sound as Ranni switched on the light and saw a curled-up heap in Paul's bed. He went out quietly and shut the door. Paul heaved a sigh of relief.

When Dimmy came at last both the girls were fast asleep – and so was Paul! Dimmy had a word with Mike and Jack, said good night, and went out.

Mike sat up in bed. "Paul!" he called in a low voice. "Are you ready?"

No answer! Paul was far away, lost in delightful dreams of towers and castles and ruined villages. Mike scrambled out of bed and went to wake him – but Jack called him back.

"Let him be! He'll probably make some noise and wake up Ranni. We two will go. Got your torch?"

Without bothering to put on their dressing-gowns the two boys crept out of the room in slippers, each with his torch. The night was so warm that they felt hot even in pyjamas! It was dark now, too, and they crept along the dim corridors, flashing their torches when they came to the stretches of darkness between the lights which glowed dimly along the corridors at intervals.

"Better go out of the front door," whispered Mike. "We might bump into Brimmy or one of the Lots if we go towards the kitchen, and we're not sure yet where any other door is."

"Do you remember how the front door opened with-

They unbolted the great door.

out anyone there to open it, when we came today?" whispered Jack. "I'd forgotten it till now."

"Must have been one of the Lots, I expect," said Mike. "It would be just like them to scurry away as soon as they opened the door! Here we are – isn't it enormous?"

They unbolted the great door, hoping that no one would hear them. They turned the big key, and then twisted the handle. The door opened very quietly indeed, swinging back easily on its hinges.

The two boys went down the big flight of steps outside. "Round to the right," said Jack, in a low voice. "We'll keep close to the walls, and then we are bound to come to where the pillow fell."

The walls of the castle were not built in a straight line, but bulged out into odd shapes, sometimes rounded, sometimes square, as if the builder had planned queer-shaped rooms, or had planned towers that he had not completed.

"The pillow ought to be somewhere about here," whispered Jack, and shone his torch down on to the grass. Then he looked upwards to try to make out if they were under their bedroom windows.

He caught Mike's arm suddenly, and whispered in his ear. "Mike! The tower's over there, look – do you see what I see?"

Mike looked up – and saw the enormously high tower against the dark night sky, where stars shone, giving out a faint light. He gave a sudden exclamation.

"The windows! They're lighted! Somebody's in the tower!"

The two boys gazed up at the great tower. "Three of the narrow windows are lighted," whispered Jack. "Three! Somebody's very busy in there tonight!"

"Perhaps that man Guy is clearing out, as we thought," said Mike. "Clearing out his belongings, I mean."

"I wonder if it *is* that fellow," said Jack, gazing up, and wishing he could see into one of the windows just for a minute or two.

"Let's stay and watch for a bit – whoever is there might come to the window," said Mike. So they sat down on the thick grass and watched the lighted windows of the tower. Once they saw someone passing across a window, but couldn't make out if it was Guy or not.

They grew tired of watching, at last. "Let's get the pillow and go," said Jack, getting up. Then he had an idea and caught hold of Mike's arm. "Wait! What about sneaking along to that little square room where the tower door is, and seeing if the door's unlocked? We know someone is in the tower now."

"Yes! Smashing idea," said Mike, thrilled. "We might creep up the steps, even – and see what's going on. Come on – we'll go now."

They made their way back to the front door. It was still open, for which Jack was very thankful. He couldn't help thinking that a door which could apparently open by itself might also shut by itself! However, there it was, half-open just as they had left it.

They went in, shut, locked and bolted the door again, went past the silent suits of armour and then set off to the little square room. Down the tapestried passage they went, and into the square room.

It was in darkness, and neither boy could find a light switch. They turned on their torches, and at once weird shadows leapt round the walls. The boys flashed their torches to the place where the door should be. The chest was still out of its place, where they had left it. The tall, narrow door showed up plainly, set deeply in the wall.

Mike tiptoed to it and took hold of the handle. He turned it carefully. Then he groaned.

"No good!" he said. "It's still locked. Blow! No adventure tonight."

"We were silly to hope it would be open," said Jack. "That fellow wouldn't take any chances of being discovered in the tower, I'm sure. He'd be furious if he thought we had been out and had seen the lighted windows!"

"Well – it's no good waiting about here," said Mike. "Blow that fellow! I'd like to go and explore that tower more than anything else in the world! Why is he so secretive? Has he got something up there he doesn't want anyone to see? Why does he lock himself up?"

"I suppose because he knows he ought to have left the castle by now," said Jack. "I say – let's put something against the bottom of the door, so that when he opens it he pushes the obstacle away."

"What's the point of that?" asked Mike.

"Just to let him know we're about!" grinned Jack. "He'll know we're suspicious, he'll know we think there's someone up the tower, and that we'll be watching to see if the obstacle we put here is moved. He can certainly put it back again if he goes *out* of the door – but when he goes back he won't be able to – and we'll find it out of its place, and know that he's gone back up the tower again."

"All right – we'll get a rug out of one of the chests," said Mike. They got one, folded it lengthways, and shoved it firmly against the bottom of the door.

"Perhaps the door opens inwards *into* the tower," said Jack, "and not outwards, into this room. If it does, the rug won't prove anything. He could open the door, see the rug, and step over it without moving it."

"No. The door opens into this room," said Mike, and pointed to a curving line on the stone floor. "See where part of the bottom edge has scraped the stone each time it has been opened."

"Yes, you're right," said Jack, tucking the rug even more firmly against the door. He yawned widely. "Gosh, I'm sleepy now. Let's go to bed. Got the pillow?"

"Yes," said Mike, picking up the pillow from the floor. "Well, Paul's pillow certainly gave us the chance of making sure the tower is occupied!"

They went back to their rooms, keeping a sharp lookout for Ranni, who got up several times a night, as a rule, to see that his little master was safe! They didn't want to run into him.

The girls and Paul were still asleep. Mike put Paul's pillow at the end of his bed, and then he and Jack climbed thankfully between their sheets, and snuggled down.

"Good night," said Jack. "We'll ask Brimmy about the tower tomorrow, and see what she says!"

There was no answer. Mike was asleep already!

381

Jack Hears A Good Many Things

Next morning the two boys told the others about the lighted windows in the tower that they had seen the night before. The girls laughed when they heard about the rug that the boys had put in front of the door. "We'll go to the square room immediately after breakfast," they decided, "and see if it's still there."

But the rug had disappeared! The door was still shut and locked. Mike stared round the room. "Guy must have come out of the tower, seen the rug, and put it away somewhere. He just didn't bother to put it back. He doesn't care whether we suspect anything or not."

Jack was opening the many chests and peering inside. "Here it is!" he called at last. "Just chucked in here, still folded lengthways."

"Well – he knows we're on his track," said Nora, thrilled.

"I wish we were," said Jack. "As long as he slips in and out without anyone seeing him and challenging him, and as long as he keeps the tower locked up, we can't possibly do anything about it."

"We can ask Brimmy," said Nora. "She's doing some dusting and sweeping in the rooms downstairs. I saw her as we came here. Let's go and ask her."

They went to find Brimmy. She was on her knees, sweeping vigorously, her face very red.

"Excuse me, Brimmy," began Mike, "that tower door is still locked. Where's the key please?"

Brimmy looked up nervously, pushing some stray hairs away from her face. "The key?" she said. "Well now, perhaps it's still lost."

"It isn't," said Jack. "Somebody's been in and out of the tower door, so we know there must be a key."

"I daresay it's been found then," said Brimmy, beginning to sweep vigorously again. "There's – er – there's things in that tower that must be cleared out before the Queen comes."

"What things?" said Jack, determined to find out *some*thing. "Do they belong to Lord Moon? Are they very precious? Is that why they are locked up?"

"Maybe," said Brimmy, sounding annoyed as well as nervous. "There's things I don't want to talk about, so please don't ask so many questions. You're only renting the castle, not buying it! Everything will be unlocked, cleaned and ready for the Queen when she comes next week. You don't need the tower, and it's not safe for children."

"Why?" asked Nora.

"Oh, these questions!" said Brimmy, pushing more hair out of her eyes and looking really harassed. "Will you please leave me to my work, or I'll complain to Miss Dimity? I'm sure she wouldn't let you go up the tower, anyway, and risk falling out of those high windows. They're really dangerous."

At that moment Ranni appeared at the door. "Miss Dimity is going to take the car into Bolingblow for some things she needs," he said. "Would you like to come too?"

"Yes!" said everyone, and went out of the room, much to Mrs Brimming's relief.

"Listen – I'm not coming," said Jack, as soon as they were out of hearing. "You go, all of you – and I'll hide around somewhere. I've an idea that Brimmy will go and warn that Guy fellow, as soon as she thinks we're all safely out of the way. I might be able to find out something."

"Right," said Mike. "Well – we'll think of you snooping around while we're having big ice-creams!"

Jack hid in his room while the others went off. When they were safely gone he went cautiously into the long corridor outside his room. No one was about. He decided to go downstairs by one of the back staircases. He might hear Brimmy telling the two Miss Lots something.

The staircase led to what seemed to be staff bedrooms on the ground floor. Not a sound was to be heard. Jack passed the open doors of the bedrooms and went down an uncarpeted passage, glad that he had on rubber shoes.

He rounded a corner and came to an entrance to one of the kitchens. And then he heard voices! He stood at the half-open door, trying to make out if they were the women's voices.

Yes – they were certainly women's voices, worried and anxious. And then came a man's voice, raised as if in anger.

"Well, I can't! It won't be finished for some days. I can't help it. You'll have to make what excuses you can. It's your own fault for disobeying orders and letting people see over the place. But that tower will be locked, I tell you – so make what excuses you like about it. You don't know what you've done, letting these people into the castle just now!"

Then Jack heard angry footsteps on the stone kitchen floor, footsteps that sounded as bad-tempered and determined as the voice! The boy slid quietly behind a cupboard.

A man went by to the back stairs down which Jack had come. Jack peered out at him. Was it Guy? Yes, it was, he was sure of it. Jack debated with himself – should he follow him and see if he went back to the tower – he might even be able to see where the key was kept! No – it would be safely in his pocket, anyway. That was no good.

Jack decided that on the whole it might be foolish to follow the angry man. He stayed where he was for a

Was it Guy? Yes, it was, he was sure of it.

minute or two and then came out from his hiding-place. He went into the big kitchen. Brimmy was at the far end, weeping, and the two Miss Lots were standing by gloomily. Brimmy gave a little cry when she saw Jack.

"I thought you'd gone out! Surely you aren't all back yet!"

"I didn't go," said Jack. "What's the matter, Mrs Brimming? Why are you crying?"

"Oh – just one of my headaches, that's all," said Brimmy, dabbing her eyes. "Do you want something to do? Why don't you go and listen to the musical-box with a hundred tunes? Or go and look round the library?"

Jack saw that she wanted to get rid of him. Perhaps she was afraid he would ask her some awkward questions. He changed the subject.

"Do you know anything about that old ruined village?" he asked. "We thought we'd go and explore it one day. Why did everyone leave it?"

There was dead silence. Jack looked at the three women in surprise. They looked as if they didn't know what in the world to say!

"What's up?" said Jack. "Anything mysterious about the village?"

"No. No, of course not," said Miss Edie Lots in a suddenly loud voice. "There used to be mines there, you know – tin mines, I believe. And then something happened and they were given up, and the people drifted away to Bolingblow. That's why it's tumble-down, all in ruins. It's a horrid, lonely place – a place that no one in their senses would go near – especially at night!"

"I see," said Jack. "It sounds *most* interesting! We'll really have to go and explore it."

"Those old mines are dangerous," said Brimmy, joining in suddenly, her voice rather shaky. "If you fell down a shaft, that would be the end of you."

"We shouldn't be so silly," said Jack, wondering why

the three women seemed so worried. What was going on here? What was that man Guy doing? If only he could get into the tower!

"Well – I'll go and find the musical-box," said Jack, thinking that it would be fun to get it out and have it ready for the others when they came back. "Where is it?"

"I'll show you," said Miss Edie Lots, in her harsh, loud voice. She led the way, and soon Jack found himself in the hall, and then going down one of the corridors that led to the rooms near their own sitting-room.

"I say," he said, as he followed Miss Lots. "I say – a funny thing happened yesterday. You know those old musical instruments hanging on the wall in the room we've taken for our sitting-room, don't you? Well – they suddenly go TWANG! or DONG! – just like that! Queer, isn't it? Have you ever heard them?"

Miss Edie clutched at him, and Jack was surprised to see that she looked terrified. "You've heard them?" she said, in a loud whisper. "No! No! Oh, what dreadful thing is going to happen?"

"I've no idea," said Jack, politely. "What's up *now*? Why should anything dreadful happen because a bit of twanging and donging goes on?"

"It's the old legend," said Miss Edie, looking over her shoulder as if she expected a Twang or a Dong at any moment. "When those instruments make noises, something awful always happens!"

"What do you mean?" said Jack, with great interest. "Do you expect the castle to fall down or something – or the tower to blow up?"

"There's a legend – written in one of the old books in the library – that none but the Moon family may live here in peace," said Miss Edie. "They say that the spirit of the old castle gets angry and restless when others come, and queer things happen."

"I don't believe it," said Jack. "Beliefs like that belong to centuries ago, not to these days! You can't frighten *me* like that, Miss Lots!"

"I'm not trying to frighten you," said Miss Edie, forgetting to whisper in her annoyance with this unbelieving boy. "I've lived here all my life – I know that what I'm saying is true. I've seen dreadful things happen to those who have come here and defied the old legend. I could tell you many tales – people who have—"

"Save them up till the others come back, and then you can tell all of us," said Jack. "We'd absolutely love to hear those crazy old tales. They're such fun."

Miss Edie glared at him. She simply could not make out this smiling boy who disbelieved all she said. Most people were scared. She lowered her voice.

"The spirit of the old castle is restless again," she said, sounding really mysterious. "I can feel it! No wonder those noises came again. Now other things will happen. They always do"

"How smashing!" said Jack, sounding delighted. "What kind of things? My word, the others will be thrilled to hear all this!"

Miss Edie had now had enough of Jack. "I am not going to tell you things just for you to laugh at," she said, looking most unpleasant. "You can wait and see what happens – but be sure that my words will come true! Those noises always come first – a warning, no doubt."

"No doubt at all," agreed Jack, cheerfully. "Awfully kind of the old spirit of the castle to warn us in such an exciting way. Well – where's this musical-box? I'd like to set it going, if the spirit of the castle has no objection!"

All Very Peculiar

Miss Edie led him into a room that seemed very dark because it faced towards the hillside behind the castle, and not to the valley below.

"Do you want the light on?" she said, sounding cross. "The switch is over there."

"No thanks," said Jack. "Oh, is that the musical-box? My word, how enormous – and what a beauty!"

He went over to a long wooden box. It was about five feet long and a foot and half wide, and stood on a pedestal. Both box and pedestal were of walnut, and were beautifully carved. Little dancing figures ran all round the box and the pedestal too, carved by a clever and loving hand.

"How do you work it?" asked Jack, lifting up the lid, and peering inside at shining brass rollers set with myriads of tiny teeth.

There was no answer, and Jack looked round. Miss Edie had gone without a word! Jack grinned. Did she really think she could frighten him with those silly old tales? He wished the others could have been there to listen to everything.

"Now how does this box work?" he thought, bending over it. "Ah – here are the instructions on the lid. It has to be wound up. I wonder who made it. It must be very, very old!"

He wound it up carefully, and pushed back the lever that set it going. The roller went smoothly and slowly round, and the musical box began to play a merry old tune.

Its sweet, melodious music filled the room and Jack

listened, quite entranced. There was something unearthly and fairylike about the tinkling tunes that followed one after another, all different. The boy recognized some of them, but others he had never heard.

A sound disturbed him. He looked round the dim room into which no sunshine ever came. He saw that it was the same room that had the portrait of a long-ago Lord Moon over the mantlepiece. The face stared down at him, dark and forbidding, the black lock falling over the forehead. The eyes seemed to be looking straight at Jack, angrily and fiercely.

"Sorry if I'm disturbing you, Lord Moon," said Jack, politely to the portrait, as another tune began to play. "Please don't look so fierce!"

The same sound came again to Jack's ears through the tinkling of the music. It seemed as if it came from somewhere by the mantlepiece. Was it a hiss?

Jack walked over to the great fireplace. He listened. Then he looked up at the big portrait above his head. Lord Moon stared down as if he could say a great many things to this stupid boy who was disturbing his peace.

And then a curious thing happened. Lord Moon's eyes seemed to become alive! They glowed angrily, and seemed to flash with anger. Then came the hiss again!

Jack backed away. He was not a timid boy, and had plenty of courage – but this was very unexpected, and very eerie too, in that dim room, with the musical-box playing its tinkling music all the time.

He backed into a stool and fell over. When he got up and looked at the portrait again, the eyes no longer glowed, though Lord Moon still looked as unpleasant as ever.

Jack stared up, surprised to find his heart beating fast. Had he imagined those eyes? Was it some sudden trick of the light? The hissing noise had stopped now too. Jack frowned and walked back to the musical-box. He suddenly looked back over his shoulder at the portrait. Were those eyes looking at him, alive again and angry?

They were looking at him, certainly, but there was no glint in them now. "Imagination!" said Jack to himself. "Well, if that's the sort of effect this castle is going to have on me, I'd better be careful! I could have sworn those eyes came alive for a moment!"

The musical-box ran down with a slowing up of the music. Jack began to wind it up again. Then he heard a voice calling loudly.

"Jack! *Jack*! Where are you?"

He jumped violently – but then laughed at himself. It was only Mike's voice – they were back from Bolingblow already!

He ran out of the room and went to find the others. "Here he is!" cried Nora's voice, and she ran to meet him. "Jack, you ought to have come with us! We had meringues and ices both together. We brought you a meringue back. Here it is."

She gave it to him. He went into the L-shaped sitting-room where the others were. Dimmy was there too, and they were helping her to sort out the shopping she had bought.

"What have *you* been doing. Jack?" asked Dimmy. "You should have come with us!"

"I've been playing that musical-box with a hundred tunes," said Jack. "In the room where that portrait of a long-ago Lord Moon is – with the horrid eyes!"

Something in his voice made Mike look up. "Anything interesting?" said Mike. Jack nodded his head towards Dimmy, and Mike understood at once that Jack had something interesting to say, but not till they were alone. Fortunately Dimmy departed from the room with an armful of shopping in a short time, and left the children alone together.

"Jack! You've got something to tell us!" said Mike.

"What is it? Did you hear anything? Did something happen?"

"Yes – I heard plenty – and something *did* happen," said Jack. "Listen!"

He told the others what he had overheard Guy say to his mother and aunts. He told them what Miss Edie had said about the old legend of the spirit of the castle. Everyone laughed.

"Fancy trying to make us believe that the Twang and Dong came because the castle was angry we were here!" said Mike. "How idiotic!"

TWANG!

There was a startled silence. The sound echoed through the air and then was gone.

"H'm! That was timed very well," said Jack, noting that Nora and Paul looked scared. "Now then, spirit of the castle – what about a Dong?"

"Don't, Jack!" said Nora, anxiously.

No Dong came. "The spirit of the castle's gone a bit deaf," said Jack, cheerfully. "It didn't hear my request."

TWANG! Everyone jumped again. Jack ran round the bend of the room and examined every stringed instrument there. Not one had a vibrating string to show that someone had twanged it, or that it had somehow done it of its own accord.

Jack went back. He had suddenly remembered the gleaming eyes of the portrait. He glanced at Nora and Paul again. They both looked a bit scared, so Jack decided not to say anything in front of them about the portrait. He would tell Mike – and perhaps Peggy – when they were alone with him.

"Where's the musical-box?" said Nora. "Let's go and hear it."

But it was too late to do that because at that moment the two Miss Lots appeared with the midday meal. Dimmy appeared too.

"Oh thank you," she said. "Just put the trays down, and we'll set the table as usual. What a lovely meal!"

Meringues and ices did not seem to have spoilt anyone's appetite. The children looked joyfully at the trays left on the sideboard, lifting the lids that covered the various dishes.

"Cold ham. Tongue! Tomatoes – heaps of them, look. Hard-boiled eggs in salad. Potatoes in their jackets. And an enormous trifle with cherries on the top."

"Stop fiddling about with the lids," said Dimmy. "Come along, you two girls – set the table, please. Mike and Paul, you carry everything over carefully when the cloth is on."

They were soon sitting down and tucking in. It always amazed Dimmy to see how much the five could eat. It looked as if not a single crumb or fragment would be left.

"If anyone wants a biscuit or fruit, they are both on the sideboard," said Dimmy at the end of the meal.

Only Mike could manage any, and he went to take a plum. Just as he was taking it, one of the now familiar noises came from somewhere behind him.

DONG!

"There's the Dong you asked for," called Mike to Jack, glancing round quickly at each of the instruments on the wall. He took his plum back with him to the others. Nobody said anything about the noise, not even Dimmy, and a loud chatter arose as usual.

CRASH! That *did* make them all jump!

"Whatever was that?" said Dimmy. "It sounded round the bend of the room again, where the instruments are."

They all went to look. A big blue jar lay in fragments on the floor. "Look at that!" said Dimmy, vexed. "It's fallen from that shelf. But how could it have happened? What a pity!"

"It's a good thing you were here with us, Dimmy," said Mike. "You might have thought one of us had broken it! We'll have to tell Mrs Brimming. I wonder what made the jar jump off like that – it must have been too near the edge."

393

Jack remembered all that Miss Edie Lots had told him, and he couldn't help feeling a bit uncomfortable. They went back into the windowed corner, where they had meals. The girls began to clear the table, and stack the dirty plates and dishes on the trays for the caretakers to take down when they came.

Miss Edie Lots appeared in a short while, followed by Mrs Brimming. They stared in dismay at the broken jar; the fragments still lay on the carpet because there was no brush to sweep them up.

"I can't imagine how it happened," said Dimmy, "but we heard a crash, and when we came into this part of the room we saw this broken jar. It must have been too near the edge of the shelf it was on, and have fallen down."

"It was *well* back on its shelf," said Miss Edie. "I dusted this room myself this morning."

"Well, I'm sorry – but none of us had anything to do with it," said Dimmy. "I can't think how it could have happened."

"It's the beginning!" said Edie Lots, in a peculiar voice that made everyone look at her in surprise.

"The beginning of *what*?" asked Dimmy.

"All kinds of things," said Edie. "You'd best be gone before worse happens. The old legend is coming true again. You ask *him* what I said!" She nodded her head towards Jack. "I tell you, it's the beginning – you shouldn't have come to this castle. Bad things will happen!"

"Please don't be so silly," said Dimmy, coldly. "I cannot imagine what you are talking about. Take the trays and go!"

394

The Ruined Village

Mrs Brimming looked upset, and Edie Lots pursed up her lips and looked angry and most unpleasant. Dimmy turned to the children.

"I'm going upstairs for a rest. It really is so very hot this afternoon. What are you going to do ? Go for a walk?"

"Well – we might go and explore that old ruined village," said Mike. "We passed the fork to it again this morning and we felt we really must go and see it soon."

Edie Lots stared round at him and opened her mouth as if to say something. Dimmy saw her, and was determined that she shouldn't be allowed to talk again – such nonsense as she talked too! So she began to speak herself, and went on firmly until the trays had disappeared out of the room, carried by Brimmy and Edie!

Edie had no chance to say whatever it was she had meant to say – though Jack could have guessed! She would have tried to put them off going to the mines.

"I'm going upstairs now," said Dimmy. "Don't start off for your walk for half an hour or so – not *immediately* after your enormous lunch. Have a read."

"Let's go and play that musical-box, Jack," said Nora. "I do so love those tinkly musical-boxes. Does it really play a hundred tunes?"

"Well, I counted only thirty-three, and then you called me," said Jack. "All right – we'll go and count a few more. It's a lovely box – the finest I've ever heard."

They went along to the dim room with the portrait. Jack glanced up at it, half-afraid he might see those eyes gleaming again. But they were just as usual, staring down fiercely and broodingly. The children went over to the musical-box.

Jack started it. The silvery tune tinkled out, and all the children listened in delight. Just as it ended, Dimmy came quickly into the room.

"Have any of you been into my room? Surely you couldn't have played such a silly joke on me?"

All five stared at her in surprise. "What joke?" asked Jack, at last. "You *know* we haven't been upstairs since lunch-time, Dimmy."

"Well – it's very strange then," said Dimmy, frowning.

"What's happened?" asked Jack.

"The whole room is changed round," said Dimmy. "The bed is in a different place. My clothes are put into different drawers. The photos I brought with me are lying flat on their faces – and one of the vases on the chest has fallen down and smashed."

"Just like that other one did!" exclaimed Mike. "But Dimmy – who in the world could have done such a silly thing to your room? *Your* room, too! Honestly, not one of us would do such a thing."

"No, I don't think you would," said Dimmy. "Well, it must have been done in spite, perhaps – I really don't know! I can't think that one of the caretakers could have done it, grown women as they are – it's such a silly, spiteful thing. But I suppose one of them *might* have done it, just because we've arrived here and are making more work for them."

Dimmy went out of the room. The children looked at one another. "Poor old Dimmy," said Peggy. "I don't know how anyone could possibly feel spiteful towards *her* – she's so kind."

"I bet it's Guy," said Paul. "Or the spirit of the castle, whoever he may be! But he's a nasty fellow if he likes to smash Lord Moon's vases!"

The musical-box was still tinkling on. "Has anyone counted the tunes?" said Jack. "I forgot to."

"Yes, I have," said Peggy. "We've got to forty-one now. Oh listen – here's Cherry Ripe! We had it at school last term. It's a very old tune."

They were all listening to Cherry Ripe when Jack heard a noise by the mantlepiece. A distant hiss, just as he had heard before. He looked across uneasily.

Mike had heard it too, and Paul, but the girls were too engrossed in the musical-box. Paul suddenly gave a loud cry that made them all jump violently.

"Shut up, Paul," said Nora, crossly. "You nearly made me jump out of my skin!"

Paul was staring at the portrait. Mike and Jack were doing the same.

"Its eyes!" gulped Paul. "They came alive! They looked at me."

Nora and Peggy looked at the portrait too. "Don't be so silly," said Peggy. "You're imagining things! The eyes are horrid – but they're only *painted* ones that seem to look at you. Don't be such an ass, Paul."

CRASH!

A picture fell suddenly off the wall behind them, and made them all jump again. Jack stared at it. Then he went over and looked at the picture cord it had hung on. He at once saw that the broken ends were frayed.

"It's all right!" he said cheerfully to the others. "Nothing to do with the glowering Lord Moon – just frayed-out picture cord."

"Well, I don't like it," said Paul, who looked quite pale. "I *did* see those eyes gleaming just as if they were alive. Didn't *you*, Mike? You were looking too."

Jack frowned quickly at Mike. He didn't want him to say anything in front of the girls, who had neither of them seen the eyes glowing as if they were alive.

So Mike said nothing in answer to Paul, but suggested that it was time they went for their walk. "This room is getting on my nerves," he said. "I can't bear that fellow,

Lord Moon, glowering at us, and pictures falling down. Stop the musical-box, Jack, we'll go out."

"We got to forty-three tunes," said Peggy. "Listen – what's that hissing noise?"

Everyone had heard the hiss that time, for the musical-box was now silent. Jack gave the girls no chance of finding out what usually followed the hiss, and he hustled them out of the room. "It's nothing. Let's go, or we shan't have time to get to that old village."

The girls went out obediently. Jack glanced back into the room. Yes – those eyes were gleaming again, as if they were alive. Was it a trick? What a peculiar one, if so!

They made their way to the front door and went out into the sunshine, which seemed quite dazzling after the dim room where they had played the old musical-box. Ranni was outside, doing something to the car.

"Oh Ranni! What a bit of luck you're here with the car!" said Paul. He turned to Jack eagerly. "He could take us to the fork of the road in the car, Jack – it would save a lot of time. Then we need only walk up the fork to the old village. It's so frightfully hot this afternoon."

"Good idea," agreed Jack and they all got in. Ranni was quite willing to take them. He was bored with so little to do. The car swept off down the drive and out of the gates. It wasn't long before they were down the hill and at the fork of the road.

"I'll wait here," said Ranni. "I can do a little polishing till you come back."

The five of them set off up the rough road. It had never been much more than a village lane at any time, but now it was so overgrown that in places it was like a field. Only the hedges each side showed the children that they were in an old lane.

It took them a quarter of an hour to reach the village. What a desolate sight!

Every house was empty, the windows were broken, the

Every house was empty.

roofs had gaps in them where tiles had fallen off. A few houses had once been thatched, and there were great holes in the straw roofs.

"This must have been the main street," said Jack, stopping. "Is that a little church? What a shame to let it fall to bits like that."

"How silent and still it is!" said Nora. "Poor old village – no one to walk down the streets, or bang a door or call out cheerily."

"What's that over there?" said Mike, pointing. "A lot of tumble-down sheds and shacks – and that looks like some kind of old machinery."

"It's the mines, of course," said Jack. "Don't you remember – we heard there were mines here once, before the people all drifted away from the village. I suppose they were worked out. They were tin mines."

Nobody knew anything about tin mines. They walked over to the shacks, and looked at the old, rusted machinery. Jack came to a shaft driven deep into the earth. He looked down it.

"Come and see – here's where the miners went down," he said. "And there's another entrance over here – a bigger one."

"Let's go down!" said Mike.

This was just what Jack wanted to do, but Peggy and Nora looked doubtful. "Do *you* want to come, Paul – or would you like to stay and look after the girls?"

"They can look after themselves, can't they?" said Paul, indignantly. "Or go back to Ranni. But don't they *want* to come down?"

"Not particularly," said Nora. "It looks so dark and horrid down there. How do you get down?"

"There's an iron ladder," said Mike, peering down. "Gosh, it's pretty rusty, though. I wonder if it's safe?"

"This one's better!" called Jack, who was looking at the bigger shaft not far off. "This is much more recent, I should think. We'll try this one. I'll go down first."

He climbed down over the edge of the shaft. The others peered after him, excited. Tin mines! What did one find in tin mines? Nora had a vague picture of sheets of tin neatly stacked everywhere, which was very silly, of course. Mike thought of rocks with streaks of tin in them!

Jack called out to them when he was halfway down. "This ladder's fine. Come on, Mike and Paul!"

The other two boys followed him. The ladder seemed strong and in good order, surprisingly so, considering how long the village must have been deserted. Jack was now at the very bottom and was waiting for the other two.

They jumped down beside him, one by one. A hollow, most peculiar voice came down the shaft. "Are you all right, boys?"

"It's Peggy," said Jack. "How queer her voice sounds, echoing down that shaft!" He shouted up loudly. "Yes. We're at the bottom. There are tunnels everywhere. We'll have a quick look and come back again!"

"Don't get lost!" came Peggy's voice again, hollow and full of echoes.

The boys had their torches with them. Jack had switched his on as soon as he got to the bottom of the shaft. He flashed it round.

There were tunnels, as he had said, radiating out from the shaft. They seemed quite ordinary tunnels. Nothing glinted in the walls, no metal shone anywhere. Jack shone his torch into each one.

"Which shall we take?" he said. "This is going to be quite an adventure!"

Down In The Mines

The three boys decided to take a fairly wide tunnel, and they went down it. The roof was low, and Jack, the tallest, had to walk with his head bent. They came to a cave-like room after a time, out of which two tunnels led.

"Look," said Jack, picking up a bent knife. "This must have belonged to one of the old workers – and that broken mug too."

They shone their torches round. The roof of the cave was shored up by big timbers, but one had given way and that side of the cave had collapsed.

"I hope these timbers will hold up the roof till we get back!" said Mike, shining his torch on them. "They must be very old now. Look – there's some funny old machine they must have used – all rusty and falling to bits."

They took the right-hand tunnel and went on. "We could spend a long time exploring these old mines," said Jack. "There seem to be heaps of tunnels. Hallo, what's this?"

They had come up to what looked like a rough wall, blocking the tunnel. They shone their torches on it. "It's not a wall," said Mike. "It's a fall from the roof. Blow! We can't go any farther this way."

Jack kicked at the heap of rubble, and it fell all round him. Another lot then fell from the roof, and rubble and stones rolled round the boys' feet.

"There's a hole in the middle of all this stuff," said Jack. "I'll shine my torch through and see if there's anything to be seen."

He was just about to do so when Mike gave an exclamation. "Jack! Don't shine your torch through. There's a light the other side of this rubble wall! Look – you can see it shining through the hole. What can it be?"

Jack stared in surprise. Yes – through the hole that had appeared in the fallen rubble came a dim light. He set his eye to the hole in excitement.

He saw a strange sight. Beyond the fall of rubble was a spacious cave, and from it led another tunnel. Jack could see the opening to it, dark and shadowy.

On the floor of the cave burned a fire. It burned slowly and clearly, sending up vivid green flames from its deep-red heart. What it was burning Jack could not see – nothing so far as he could make out!

The fire made a noise, almost as if squibs or small fireworks were going off in it all the time. After every little explosion a purple tinge came into the green flames, and they sent off circles of greenish-purple that floated away like smoke-rings.

Jack gazed and gazed, filled with amazement. What was all this? What was this strange fire, and why was it burning here, in the old mines? Did anyone know of it?

"Let *me* see," said Mike, impatiently, and pushed Jack aside. He put his eye to the hole in his turn, and gave a loud cry of wonder.

"Gosh! Whatever is it? A fire – a green fire, burning all by itself!"

Paul elbowed him away in excitement. "My turn to see!" he said, and then fell silent in amazement as he gazed through the hole at the leaping flames, and heard the crick-crick-crack of the constant explosions.

Jack pulled him away after a minute or two. "My turn again," he said, and gazed earnestly through the hole. The others, leaning close against him, felt him suddenly stiffen and catch his breath.

"What is it? What is it?" whispered Mike and Paul, and tried to pull Jack away so that they too might see – but Jack resisted them, and went on looking.

Then he started back suddenly, just as the others heard a deep roaring noise from behind the rubble. A curious tingling came into their arms and legs, and they began to rub them quickly.

"What did you see? Tell us!" said Mike, rubbing his legs which felt as if they had pins and needles from the top to the bottom.

"I saw a figure," said Jack, rubbing his legs too. "Gosh, why have I suddenly got pins and needles? I saw a very strange figure, with a hood right over his face so that I couldn't see it. He wore very loose things, and very big gloves, so I couldn't see his skin at all. He poured something on the fire, and it made that sudden roaring noise, and its flames changed to brilliant purple. I simply couldn't look at them!"

Mike went to peep again. But, how bitterly disappointing – the fire had disappeared! Not a flame was to be seen, although the curious roaring noise still went on. Then in the tunnel beyond, lighted by a strange glow, he saw two figures – not one, as Jack had seen, but two.

They came forward slowly with what looked like a small broom. One of them swept gently over the place where the fire had been, and a little heap of stuff appeared, gleaming and glowing in its own light. What colour was it?

Mike didn't know! He wasn't sure that he had ever seen a colour quite like that before. Was it green – purple – blue? No, none of these.

The men swept the little heap into a curious narrow shovel made of some glittering metal that seemed to make the heap of glowing dust disappear as soon as it touched it. Then one of them put a bag or sack over the shovel, and the two of them disappeared down the tunnel.

Mike told the others all this. They sat back in their own tunnel, amazed and rather alarmed. What had they seen? What was happening in these old ruined mines?

"I wish I could get rid of these pins and needles in my

He poured something on the fire!

arms and legs," said Jack, rubbing vigorously again. "As soon as I stop rubbing, the feeling gets worse."

"Same here," said Mike. "Jack – what do you make of all this?"

"Nothing," said Jack. "I'm absolutely stumped. These are only old tin mines – *tin*, mark you – quite ordinary stuff. And yet we find this queer affair going on – a strange and most peculiar fire of green flames, that cricks and crack – and roars – and sends off rings of curious colour. Then for no reason at all that we can see, it dies down – and what's left is collected by a couple of men in the strangest clothes I ever saw!"

"Do you suppose that fellow Guy has anything to do with this?" asked Paul, after a pause.

"He might have," said Jack. "But how do the men get into that cave? Not through the way *we* came, or they would have removed this wall of rubble. I wish we could find the right way in. Then we could perhaps hide and watch everything properly. Yes, and see who the men are, and where they take the shovelful of stuff to."

"Well – I don't feel inclined to wander through all these mazy tunnels and get lost for ever," said Mike. "Couldn't we get a map of the old mines? If so, we might trace out a way to the cave we've just been looking at."

"Yes. That's a good idea," said Jack. "We'll do that – and I bet I know where we could get a map from, too! In that old library! This land probably belongs to Lord Moon, and we're sure to be able to find a book – or books – about the castle and all this property, in the castle library. I've no doubt that he made a lot of money out of the tin dug from here – or some of the Lord Moons did. I expect the mines had fallen into ruin long before the present one inherited the castle."

Mike glanced at his watch to see what the time was. "Surely it's more than half-past three?" he said, astonished. "Oh – it's stopped."

To their surprise the watches of the others had stopped too. "Better get back," said Jack. "The girls will be worried. I suppose that queer fire stopped our watches – and gave us these pins and needles too!"

They each took one more look through the hole, and then, as they could see absolutely nothing at all now, except for a faint glow from the floor of the next cave, they made their way back to the foot of the shaft they had entered by.

Nora and Peggy were leaning over the top, feeling anxious. They heard Nora shouting as they came to the bottom of the shaft.

"Mike! *Jack*!"

"Coming!" yelled the three boys, and then they heard Ranni's deep voice booming down.

"It gets late. Hurry, please."

They climbed up, and were very glad indeed to find themselves in the sunshine once more. But how their pins and needles tickled and pricked when the sun fell on their arms and legs! The three boys rubbed and scratched at top speed, much to the amazement of the girls.

"You have been too long, and such a pit is dangerous," said Ranni, severely, to Paul. "I was just coming to fetch you, little Prince. I have left the car waiting at the fork."

"Our watches stopped," said Paul. He turned to the girls. "Have your watches stopped too, by any chance?" he asked.

"No," said Nora, glancing at hers and then at Peggy's. "What did you see down there? Anything thrilling?"

"Gosh, yes," said Jack. "We'll tell you when we get back to the car."

The girls listened in the greatest astonishment when the boys related their adventure. Ranni, at the wheel, heard every word, and he was horrified.

He stopped the car and turned himself round to face the children at the back. "You will not come here again," he said, sternly. "If this tale is true, this place is not for you. I will not have my little master mixed up in such dangers."

407

"They're not dangers," said Jack. "We weren't in any danger, Ranni, really we weren't!"

Ranni thought differently. "Something goes on here," he said. "Something secret. It is not for children to meddle with it. Jack – you must promise me never to go down those shafts again, nor to take Paul with you."

"Oh Ranni!" said Jack, protestingly. "I can't promise that, Ranni. I mean – we really must discover what all this means."

"You will promise me," said Ranni, unmoved. "If you do not, I will tell Miss Dimity, and she shall take you back home."

"You're jolly mean, Ranni," said Jack. But he knew Ranni of old. There was nothing for it but to promise!

"All right – we won't go down the beastly shafts again," he said, sulkily.

"Nor will you come to the village," persisted Ranni who was taking no chances.

"All right," said Jack again. "Anyone would think we were six years old and wanted looking after. Go on – let's get back."

Ranni drove off, satisfied. Jack made a few plans, which he outlined to the others. "Even though we've had to promise Ranni we won't go to the village, there's no reason why we shouldn't find out a bit more about the mines from old maps. We'll go to the castle library after tea!"

"And have books jumping on us from the shelves!" said Nora, with a giggle. "Like that waitress said!"

"Well, it will all add to the fun," said Jack. "I say – don't let's say anything about what we saw in that mine, when we get back to Dimmy. She *might* whisk us back home – there's no knowing what she'll do if she thinks there's something we can't cope with."

"Oh, my pins and needles!" groaned Mike. "How long will they last? Honestly, mine are worse than ever!"

"Here we are!" said Nora, as the car swept in at the gates. "You're lucky, you boys, even though you've got pins and needles – you've had a fine adventure, and we haven't!"

Pins And Needles – And Jumping Books!

Dimmy was wondering what had happened to them all, because they were so late back to tea. She sat at the tea-table, occasionally looking out of the window to see if the children were coming.

She was most relieved when she saw them walking into the room. "Ah – here you are," she said. "Have you had a good afternoon?"

"Yes. We went to the old village – where the tin mines are," said Mike. "Ranni took us in the car. Sorry we're late. We did quite a bit of exploring. It's a queer old place, that village."

"Yes," said Nora, who really *had* explored it with Peggy, while the boys had been down the mine. "The tumble-down houses are all covered with ramblers and blackberry sprays, and tall-growing weeds, Dimmy. It's a sad sort of place, really – not a soul there. Only birds, and one or two rabbits we saw scampering around."

"Go and wash," said Dimmy, "and then come back quickly. Mrs Brimming has managed to provide another good meal for you!"

They were soon sitting down at the table, washed and brushed. The boys had bathed their arms and legs in cold water to try to get rid of the pins and needles that still attacked them. The water helped them at first, but as soon as they sat at the table, the pins and needles came back again so fiercely that the three boys wriggled and rubbed themselves in pain.

"What *is* the matter?" said Dimmy. "Have you been stung by something?"

"No," said Mike.

"It's just pins and needles," said Jack. "It came on us suddenly in the village. But it won't stop!"

When Brimmy came to take the tea-tray, Dimmy spoke to her about the boys' pins and needles.

"Do you think they've been stung by something?" she said, anxiously. "I can't make it out. Look at them – they can't keep still for a minute. They're wriggling and squirming all the time."

"They've been near the mines!" said Brimmy, at once. "Been down into them too, I wouldn't be surprised! You can do only one thing, Miss Dimity. Put them to bed, and I'll give you some lotion I have so that you can soak bandages for their arms and legs. That will soon put them right."

"But what *is* this pins and needles?" said Dimmy. "Why should it come on them like this?"

"It's the illness that drove the people away from that old village," said Brimmy. "It came all of a sudden, they say. The men were working the mines as usual – and for some reason a great fire came. When it died down, the men went to work down in the mines again – but when they came up they all had this pins and needles."

"Good gracious!" said Dimmy. "Is it dangerous?"

"Oh no, Miss," said Brimmy. "These boys will soon get rid of it if they lie quiet with this lotion on their limbs. But when it first came to the village it soon attacked every man, woman and child in the place, and only when they got away from the place did the attacks stop."

"What caused these attacks then?" said Dimmy, most interested.

"I don't rightly know," said Brimmy. "They do say that the great fire had something to do with it – it set loose radiations or something down in the mine, and these seeped up into the air above, and gave the village people this pins and needles in their limbs – a kind of tickling and prickling that drove them nearly crazy!"

"And so they left the village, did they?" asked Jack.

"Yes. The place got a bad name," said Brimmy. "No one would work the mines, and so there was no money to be earned. In three years' time there wasn't a soul there – and it's been going to rack and ruin ever since. My, that's over a hundred years ago now! I remember my grandmother telling me how it all happened in her grandad's time. I did warn these children not to go there, Miss Dimity – but they're headstrong, aren't they?"

Dimmy wasn't going to say anything against the five children! "Perhaps you'll get that lotion you kindly said you'd let us have," she suggested. "Nora, go with Mrs Brimming and bring it back."

Dimmy thought that the three boys would be sure to make a fuss at having to go to bed at once, but they did not. "Pins and needles can be most terribly tiring when it doesn't stop at all!" complained Mike, rubbing his arms hard. "It's quite funny when you have it for a little while – but not when you've got to put up with it for hours!"

"You're right," said Jack, feelingly. "It's like hiccups – quite comical for a few minutes, but alarming after half an hour!"

They went to their rooms to undress. Dimmy said she would bring the lotion as soon as she had it. The boys opened their doors – and then stared.

Their rooms were completely changed round, just as Dimmy's had been! The beds were by the window, the clothes had been taken out of drawers and arranged on the tops of the chests, the vase of flowers was on the floor, and their shoes were on the window-sill.

"This is crazy!" said Jack, staring round. A shout from Paul told him that his room was the same. They went into the girls' room – and that was changed round too.

"Mad!" said Mike. "Who's doing it? And why?"

"If it's the spirit of the castle, he's been pretty busy!" said Paul.

411

"Stuff!" said Jack. "This is no spirit – this is someone spiteful. But what's the point?"

"All part of the Queer Happenings that the waitress foretold, I suppose," said Mike, taking his shoes from the window-sill. "Look here – let's change the rooms round quickly and put everything tidy. Don't let Dimmy see what's happened. If she gets the wind up we'll all be taken back home – and I'm *jolly well going* to find out a bit more myself."

"Hear, hear!" said the other two.

"Mike, go and put the girls' room right, I'll do ours, and Paul can do his," said Jack. "Buck up! Dimmy will be here in a trice."

They hurried as much as their pins and needles would let them! They had got their rooms right, and were just beginning to undress when Dimmy came in with a big bottle of green lotion and some strips of old sheet for bandages. She looked reproachfully at them.

"Oh! I did think you'd all be in bed! I suppose you've been monkeying about, as usual. I don't think you're as bad as you make out."

"We *are*," said Mike. "Look at my leg – I've scratched it almost raw already! Come on, do me first, Dimmy. I'm in bed now."

Dimmy put the bandages soaked with the green lotion on his legs and arms, wrapping them round loosely. Mike lay back in great relief. "That's super! Oh, how heavenly! That lotion feels as cold as ice. I can hardly feel the pins and needles now."

"Mrs Brimming says you'll be as right as rain in the morning," said Dimmy. "I must say it's very extraordinary – the whole tale of the village is queer. In fact, I think quite a lot of things are extraordinary here. I've half a mind to take you all back home."

Mike sat up, shocked. "Oh *no*, Dimmy! Don't be such a spoil-sport! It's grand here. There – you've made my pins and needles come back again by saying such a worrying thing."

"Rubbish!" said Dimmy, and began to bandage Jack. "Lie down, Mike, I'll leave the lotion near you, so that when the bandages dry off, you can soak them again. Do you want any books?"

"The girls will get us some from the library," said Mike, making up his mind to get Nora and Peggy to bring up some books about the castle and the mines too, if they could find them. "Ask Nora and Peggy to come up, will you, Dimmy?"

The girls came up and said yes, of course they would go down to the great library and try to find some books for the boys. So down they went. They bumped into Edie Lots as they came to the library door. She had a duster in her hand, and they imagined she must have been dusting the books.

She stood with her back against the library door as they came up, her face unsmiling.

"Oh – er – do you mind moving, we want to go into the library," said Peggy, seeing that Edie was standing there for them to pass her.

Edie stood aside and even opened the door for them. "What kind of books do you want?" she said. "There are no books for children here."

"Well – we thought we'd like to read up about the old castle – and the old village," said Nora. "Goodness – what thousands of books there are! We'll never be able to find what we want here. It would be like looking for a needle in a haystack!"

"I'll help you," said Edie obligingly. "I've dusted these books so often I almost know their titles by heart. You sit down there now, for a minute. I'll get the little ladder from the cupboard outside, so that I can climb up to the shelf where the books are that you want."

She disappeared. The girls did not sit down, they began to wander round, reading out the titles of the books at

413

High up on a shelf a book was tilting itself over.

random. Nora suddenly gave a cry, and Peggy turned round quickly. Nora had her hand to her head.

"Peggy! You threw a book at me!" said Nora crossly. "It hit me on the head."

"I didn't throw one," said Peggy in astonishment. They bent down to pick up the book – and immediately another crashed down beside them, hitting Peggy's foot. She swung round, alarmed. Where were the books coming from? Then she clutched Nora's arm, and pointed. High on a shelf a book was tilting itself over – then it seemed to spring from its place, and landed about two feet away from the children.

"This is just what the waitress said happened to the man who came here to see some of the old books," said Peggy in a whisper. "Look out – here's another!"

Sure enough, yet another book tilted itself backwards, and then with a spring was off the shelf and on the floor in a heap, lying wide open. It was near Nora and she glanced down fearfully at it.

On the open pages she saw a map. She picked up the book at once. A map! Would it show the mines?

She looked at the title. It was difficult to read because the lettering was old and dim. "*A History of Moon Castle and its Lands*," she read. "Gosh, this is just the book we want, Peggy!"

Miss Edie came in, carrying a small library ladder. She stopped when she saw the books on the floor. "Now don't you treat the books like that!" she said angrily. "I won't have it!"

"They jumped off the shelves themselves," said Nora, not expecting to be believed. But Edie did believe her! She threw the ladder down and ran off at top speed, looking scared out of her life! Was she pretending, or was she really scared? She certainly looked terrified!

"Let's take this book to the boys and go and tell them about the jumping ones!" said Nora. "Whatever will they say!"

Some Exciting Map-Reading

The boys were feeling very much more comfortable. As long as they kept their bandages soaked with the green lotion they had no more pins and needles – but if they got out of bed and walked about, then back came the prickling at once!

They were very pleased to see the girls. Ranni had been in, and had put Paul's bed into the middle room with Mike and Jack, so all three were now together.

"Ha! You've brought a book!" said Mike, and reached out to get it. "A history of the castle – and its lands! Good work! This is just what we wanted. How clever of you to find it so quickly."

"We didn't find it," said Nora. "We didn't even look for it. It leapt straight off a shelf and fell at our feet!"

"Don't be an ass," said Mike, opening the book. "That's only the waitress's tale!"

"It's her tale, certainly – but it's ours too," said Peggy. "Do listen, Mike. It *really* happened!"

Now the girls had the whole attention of all three boys, of course! They listened as the two girls told their strange little story. Then, in their turn, they told Peggy and Nora how they had found all three rooms changed round, with everything in a different place.

"I can't make out what's happening," said Mike. "It looks as if we're being driven away from here – but I'm not going! I'm sticking it out till Paul's family comes. If things are still odd then, well, your father can go into the matter, Paul. But I feel somehow, from what Jack overheard this morning, that it's the next few days that are important to somebody – Guy, perhaps – or the two men we saw down in the mines. We just don't know."

They began to discuss everything again – the Twang-Dong noises – the way the rooms had been upset – the books flying off the shelves – the hissing noise in the room where the musical-box was, and then Mike mentioned the gleaming eyes of the portrait, forgetting that the girls hadn't seen them. They listened, finding this difficult to believe.

"It must have been some effect of light," said Peggy.

"It wasn't," said Paul. "That room's so dark."

"Well, I give it up," said Peggy. "In fact, I give everything up. I just don't understand a thing. If the castle really had a spirit of its own I'd understand what's happened, because it might not like us, and might want us to go – but I can't believe in spirits of that kind!"

"Nor can I," said Jack, and the others said the same, except Paul. Paul had been brought up in far-off Baronia, a wild land of mountains and forests, where legends were believed in, and strange things actually happened. But here – well, here it was just impossible. And yet – what *was* happening then?

Mike was looking through the book. The pages, solid with small print, were not easy to read, so Mike was looking for maps.

He found a section of them, unexpectedly clearly drawn. Some of them opened out into big sheets, like motoring maps. Mike opened one and spread it out over his bed. Paul left his bed and clambered on to Mike's to see. Soon all the children were poring over bits of the big map.

"It's the castle," said Mike. "Here's a plan of the downstairs floor. Let's find our L-shaped sitting-room."

They found it at last – then they found the library – the room with the musical-box – the one with the clock like a church. They found the different staircases. What a maze of rooms this castle possessed!

They examined the next plan, which showed the first floor, where their own rooms were. "Here's our suite of rooms," said Mike, pointing. "One – two – three – all connected. And there's Ranni's room – and this must be Dimmy's. Look – what's this extra door shown here – opening into Paul's room? *Is* there a door there – look, it would be in the wall on the right-hand side of your bed, Paul. Did you notice a door there? I didn't."

"I'll go and see," said Paul, and leapt off the bed. He took a few steps and then hobbled back again. "Oooh, my pins and needles!" he said. "As soon as I take a step or two they come back worse than ever. Peggy, you go and look. I'm sure there isn't a door. I'd have noticed it, I know."

Peggy and Nora went off to Paul's room at once and looked at the right-hand wall. No – there was no door there. The room was panelled all round, but, except for the door that led out to the corridor and the one that led into the middle room of the suite, there was no other door to be seen.

"No door," they reported when they came back. "Either it's a mistake on the map, or else there was once a door and it's been removed and the wall panelled over."

"Where did the extra door once lead to?" asked Jack with interest. "Let me see now – if it had been in the right-hand wall of Paul's room, it would have led into that blue bathroom next to it, wouldn't it? Well, I suppose there wouldn't have been a bathroom there in the old days – so I daresay when the bathroom was built, the old door was done away with."

"You mean, the door just led into the room that was there *before* the bathroom?" said Peggy. "Let's have another look. It's marked with a T. I wonder why."

"Let me fold this map up," said Mike impatiently. "Take your hand off, Peggy. I'll shake out the next map."

He shook it out, and there was an excited exclamation at once. "It's the tower! A map of the old tower!"

So it was. The children pored over it with great interest. The tower was shown in a diagram, as if it were cut in half from top to bottom, and the children could quite clearly see how it was built, and could imagine what it was like inside.

"There's the door at the bottom – the one that's locked," said Mike, pointing. "Then the stone stairway is shown – quite big, really – then the room on the first floor, look – how strange, it's quite round. I wonder how big it looks in reality? It looks fairly small here. Then up goes the staircase again, from just outside the room – it gets wider above and then narrows again to the second-storey room."

"I rather imagined the tower was like that inside," said Paul. "It's a bit like one we have in a castle in Baronia. Look – up go the stairs to the third–floor room, and up again to the roof. What a view there would be from there!"

"These square marks in each room must be the fireplaces," said Mike, pointing. "And this line must be the chimney, connecting all the fireplaces, and leading the smoke somewhere out at the top."

Nora put her finger on a small door-shaped drawing shown in the fireplace on the second floor.

"What's that?" she said. "It can't be the door that shuts off the staircase outside the room, because that's shown here, look. And yet it *looks* like a door. What's that mark on it?"

"It looks like a letter T," said Jack.

That rang a bell in Peggy's mind at once. "T! Well, that secret door in Paul's room – the one we couldn't find – was marked with T too, when it was shown on the other map," she said. "T – T for Tower perhaps."

"Why should a door leading off Paul's room be marked with T for Tower?" said Mike scornfully.

"Well – it might have been a door that at one time *led* to the tower," said Peggy, sticking up for herself. "I mean – there might have been a passage from this suite to the tower at some time – the tower isn't so very far from this suite of rooms!"

Mike looked at her, thinking hard. "You know – she

might be right," he said to the others. "Wait now – let's see the other maps."

There were no other big maps, except one for the attics, which was not very interesting. But there was a curious little map, marked ALL COMMUNICATIONS, which puzzled the children for some time.

"'All communications' – that *might* mean such things as stairways, passages, corridors and so on, connecting one part of the castle to the other," said Mike. "This is rather a muddled map if it means those though. I can't make out any of the staircases, for instance."

"Communications might mean *secret* ways," said Paul suddenly. "All old castles have secret ways and secret doors. Ours has in Baronia. They were once used for all kinds of things – hiding-places – escape routes – ways to get in by when the castle was surrounded by enemies. I expect Moon Castle has got its own secret communications too!"

"You're probably right," said Mike, looking suddenly excited. He pored over the map again, and then traced a curving line with his finger. "This line is marked with T at this end – and T at the other," he said. "It might be showing the two doors and the connecting passage between Paul's room and the tower. I *say*! Wouldn't it be super if we could find a secret way into the tower?"

There was a hush of excitement, and then Paul pounded on the bed. "We must find it! We must! We could creep in on Guy then, and see what he is doing. We *must* find it!"

"Well – look at this," said Jack, pointing to the map again. "It looks as if the passage from that secret door in Paul's room leads inside the walls somewhere, and then comes out to another door – or perhaps an opening of some kind – *inside the chimney* of one of the tower rooms. What does everybody think?"

Everybody was only too anxious to think that Jack was right!

"I know how we can tell if we're right," said Mike. "We

420

could measure the width inside of Paul's room, and the width of the bathroom, and see what they come to, together – and then we could measure the walls of both, *outside*, in the corridor – and if that measurement is bigger than our first one, we'll know it includes a secret passage in between the two rooms!"

"Gosh – what a super idea!" said Peggy. "I'll get a tape-measure out of my work-basket this very minute!"

She soon found one, and she and Nora measured Paul's room from wall to wall – exactly fourteen feet. Nora popped her head into Mike's room. "Fourteen feet exactly," she said. "Now we're going to measure the bathroom."

They measured it carefully, and came back to report. "Eight feet," said Nora. "Eight and fourteen make twenty-two. Now we'll measure the walls *outside* the rooms, in the corridor, and see what we make the length there."

Carefully they measured the walls that stretched along the corridor, outside Paul's room and then the bathroom. They counted in excitement – and then raced back into Mike's room.

"The measurements are different! The inner walls measure twenty-two feet – but the outer ones measure twenty-four! What do you think of *that*?"

Mike looked excited. "Two feet missing! Just the width for a secret passage. Good work, girls. There *is* a passage that starts somewhere in Paul's room, goes between his room and the bathroom – and then curves away behind walls to the tower!"

"Shall we go and find the secret door now?" said Paul excitedly, and leapt out of bed again. But he was soon back groaning. The boys had forgotten to soak their bandages when they had got dry, and now their pins and needles were coming back badly. Poor Paul had started his up again at once by jumping out of bed.

"We'll have to leave the secret door for tonight," said Mike dolefully. "No, Peggy – you're not going to look for secret doors without us, so don't think it. It'll be something to do tomorrow. My word – we'll have some fun!"

In The Middle Of The Night

All the five children felt really excited that night when bedtime came. Nobody could sleep. As for Paul, he tossed and turned, wondering where in the world the secret door could be in his room – if there still was one!

"But there must be!" he thought. "Because we know there is a space in the walls between this room and the bathroom next door."

He had, of course, not been able to stop himself from tapping his wall, and banging it here and there to see if there *was* a door in the panelling! It certainly sounded hollow – there was no doubt about that!

He had to get into bed before he had really examined the right-hand wall properly, because his pins and needles came back again with a rush. Mike heard the tapping and called from the next room.

"Paul! No probing about for that secret door now! You just wait till everybody can hunt for it!"

"Right!" said Paul, safely in bed, stretching his tingling legs out straight and rubbing his arms. Ranni had moved his bed back into his room again, though Paul had wanted to stay in Mike and Jack's room for the night.

"I shall come in two or three times, little master, to see that you are all right," said big Ranni, who had been most concerned about Paul's legs. "Do not be frightened if you see me standing by you."

"I wish you wouldn't fuss so, Ranni," said Paul. But it was of no use to say that. Paul had been put into Ranni's care, and the big Baronian was by his side as much as possible.

Everyone went to sleep at last, the girls first, because they had no pins and needles to bother them. Paul tossed and turned for some time and then he too went to sleep.

He woke very suddenly, some hours later, and sat up wondering what had awakened him. In his dreams he thought he had heard a loud click.

He saw a figure over by the window, and lay down again. "Bother you, Ranni," he murmured. "You woke me up!" He lay watching Ranni, and then his eyes began to close. He wondered if Ranni would come and fuss him about his bandages, and decided to pretend to be asleep.

He heard no further sound for a minute or two and then opened his eyes again. He could not see anyone now – perhaps Ranni had gone. Good!

Another loud click made him open sleepy eyes again – that must be Ranni going out of the room. He thought he saw a shadow moving high up on the wall, and tried to wake himself up enough to see more clearly. No – he couldn't – he was too sleepy. Clicks and shadows and Ranni all merged into a muddled dream.

He didn't hear low voices in the next room. It was Mike and Jack talking. They too had awakened suddenly, though they didn't know why. Mike thought he heard a sound in the room, and strained his eyes to see where it came from. The room appeared to be very dark indeed – not the slightest light came from the window, and Mike couldn't see even one star in the sky.

Jack spoke in a low voice. "You awake, Mike? How are your pins and needles?"

"Not too good," said Mike. "I'm awfully sleepy and I don't want to get out of bed – but I simply *must* get that lotion and soak my bandages again."

He saw a dark figure over by the window.

"Yes, I must too," said Jack. "Blow these pins and needles. It's most peculiar to get them like this, just because we went down those mines."

There was a creaking of the two beds as the boys sat up. Mike felt for the torch he always had by his bedside. He couldn't find it.

"Put *your* torch on," he said to Jack. "I can't find mine."

"Right," said Jack, and fumbled about for it. But he couldn't find his either! "Where on earth did I put it?" he grumbled. "Oh for a bedside lamp to put on! Living in a castle is great, but I do miss some things we have at home. *Where's* my torch?"

"It's most awfully dark tonight!" said Mike. "Surprising, really, because when we went to sleep it was such a starry night – no moon, but millions of stars. It must have clouded up."

Jack got out of bed, determined to find his torch. "I may have left it on the window-sill," he said. "Ooooh – my pins and needles!"

He went towards the window and fumbled for the window-sill. He couldn't find it! Something thick and soft and heavy hung over it.

"I say!" said Jack suddenly, "who's pulled the curtains over our windows? No wonder we couldn't see a thing! These great heavy curtains are pulled across, making the room as black as pitch and frightfully stuffy. No wonder I was so hot in bed!"

"Well, *I* didn't pull them!" said Mike. "You know I hate sleeping with a shut window or pulled curtains. I suppose Dimmy came in and did that."

"But whatever for?" said Jack. "She's just the one that's all against it! Well, I'm going to pull them back again and get a bit of air. I bet it's a beautiful starry night."

There was a soft rattle of curtain rings as the heavy curtains were pulled across the window. Jack leaned out, taking deep breaths of the warm night-air. The sky was full of stars.

"That's better," said Mike, getting out of bed. "I can breathe now. Why, the room's quite light, there are so many stars!"

He leaned out of the window with Jack. It was really a beautiful night. The boys soon felt, however, that they must get some more lotion on their bandages – the pins and needles were beginning to prickle unbearably! They turned to find the bottle.

"We can see by the starlight, really," said Jack. "But I do wish I could find my torch. I *know* I put it by my bed!"

They got the sponge, soaked it with the lotion, and dabbed the sponge over their bandages. "That's better already," said Jack.

They went to the window for one last look out at the lovely night. Both boys at once saw something that made them stare and draw in their breath quickly.

"Look! What is it!" said Jack, startled.

"A light – a sort of glow – shimmering over the ruined village!" said Mike, amazed. "What colour is it? It's the same colour as that little heap of stuff we saw that the men swept up after the roaring fire!"

"Yes," said Jack, his eyes on the soft, shimmering haze that hung over the rooftops of the village far below. "My word – this is really very peculiar, Mike. What *is* going on here – and down in those mines? I'm sure it's something that man Guy is mixed up in."

"Some experiment, perhaps," said Mike. "If so, that's the reason why he doesn't like people renting the castle or even coming to look over it. And now that he knows the Baronians are coming here in a few days, he's got to finish up whatever this experiment is, and clear out. No wonder he's angry!"

The strangely coloured haze began to fade, though it still shimmered beautifully. The boys watched till it completely disappeared. "What a sight!" said Mike, going back to bed. "I bet he would be annoyed if he thought we'd seen that!

It's a thing he can't hide – something that would make people enquire into it if they saw it – and then his little experiments, or whatever they are, would be found out!"

"Gosh – of course – he *didn't* want us to see it!" said Jack. "That's why the curtains were drawn across the window, so that if we woke we shouldn't see a thing! That's why our torches are gone, so that if we woke we couldn't put them on and discover the curtains blocking out the light!"

"Well, of all the cheek!" said Mike, sitting up indignantly in bed. "Coming in here – drawing our curtains – hiding our torches! I say – do you suppose he did the same in the girls' room – and Paul's?"

"I bet he did," said Jack. "I'm going to look." He soon reported that Mike was right. The curtains had been carefully pulled across in each room! "I've dragged them back again," said Jack. "I expect you heard me. What's he done with our precious torches? If he's taken them away with him I *shall* be wild!"

"Well – we've seen what he didn't mean us to see," said Mike, pleased. "We're one up on him! I say – he must be quite scared of us, mustn't he – trying to stop us discovering what he's up to!"

"He knows we're snooping round," said Jack, getting into bed and lying down. "He must have found that rug we put against the tower door to see if he came in and out – he saw we'd moved the chest there, when he put it to hide the tower door."

"Fancy him daring to come along here in the middle of the night, and take our torches and draw our curtains," said Mike. "He would have to pass Ranni's door – and Ranni sleeps like a dog, with one ear always open."

"He may have come through that secret door – the one we haven't found yet," said Jack, sitting up straight again. "Down the secret passage, straight from the tower! He wouldn't need to pass anyone's door then – or bump into anybody. I bet that's what he did!"

"Gosh! I shall never get to sleep tonight now," said Mike. "What a place this is! Twang-dongs, breaking vases, jumping books, gleaming eyes, secret doors, peculiar mines – well, we've had a good many adventures, Jack – but this beats the lot!"

"And we're only just in the middle of it so far," said Jack. "Come on – we really must go to sleep, Mike. We *must* find that secret door in Paul's room tomorrow. It will be very, very well-hidden, I'm sure – but we'll find it!"

They settled themselves down to sleep. Their pins and needles had subsided again. They lay and looked through the uncurtained window into the starry sky, puzzling out this and that, feeling little surges of excitement now and again.

They went to sleep at last, and woke late in the morning. The girls were already up and about. Peggy heard Jack speaking to Mike and went in. "Hallo, sleepy-heads!" she said. "We're just going down to breakfast. How are your legs?"

"Well – they feel absolutely all right," said Jack, getting out of bed and trying them. "Not a twinge! Not a pin, not a needle! Good!"

"Then you don't want to stay in bed for the day or anything?" said Nora, pleased.

"Good gracious, no!" said Mike, leaping out too. "We're quite all right. I say – anyone lost their torches?"

"Yes," said Peggy and Nora together. "Ours have both gone. We thought you'd borrowed them."

Paul poked his head in at the door. "Are your legs all right?" he asked. "Mine are. Did I hear someone ask about torches? Mine's gone too!"

"Blow!" said Mike. "Not one of us has got a torch then. All right, girls, don't look so puzzled. Jack and I have got a bit of news for you – something that happened in the night, while you were snoring your heads off!

We're in the very middle of an adventure – the strangest one we've ever had. Just wait till Jack and I are dressed, and we'll tell you all about it – and we'll have to Make Plans. Aha, Plans! We're going to be very, very busy today!"

Where Is The Secret Door?

Dimmy was pleased to find that the boys' legs and arms were better. She told Brimmy so when she and Edie Lots came to collect the breakfast trays.

"That lotion is very good," she said. "I've never heard of anyone keeping a lotion for pins and needles before! How did you hear of it? Do you suffer from pins and needles yourself?"

"No. But my son does," said Brimmy; and Mike nudged Jack at once. "I bet he does," he said, in a low voice, and Jack grinned. "I bet he gets it every time he goes down those mines!"

"It's a pity it's raining," went on Brimmy. "It'll keep the children in."

"We've got plenty to do," said Jack at once, and winked at the others. They laughed. They knew what Jack's wink meant – they were going to hunt for that secret door in Paul's room. The girls and Paul had now heard of all the happenings of the night before, and were feeling very thrilled.

"Where are you going to play?" Dimmy asked the children after breakfast. "You can be in here, if you like, now the breakfast is cleared."

"Well – we rather thought we'd just go up to our suite of rooms and look for something we've lost," said Jack. "So you can sew here in peace, Dimmy. Anyway, we've got a game or two up there, so there's no need to disturb you with our shouts and yells!"

"You don't disturb me," said Dimmy. "But if you want to go up to your rooms, you can. But wait till they are dusted and cleaned. And by the way, you must put that book back into the library that you borrowed last night."

"Oh yes – I'll fetch it now," said Jack. "You four go and wait for me in the library." He sped off, and the others went to the library.

"I hope some books do a bit of jumping," said Nora. She looked up at the shelves. "Books – we're here!"

But, most disappointingly, nothing happened. The books that had fallen out the day before had been picked up and put away in their places. Only one gap showed in the shelves, and that was where the *History of Moon Castle* had leapt from!

Jack came in with the big book. He shut the door and looked round the room. "Any circus performances yet?" he said. The girls shook their heads.

"No. Most boring," said Nora. "The books are behaving just like books!"

There came a knock at the door. "Come in!" said Jack. The door opened and Edie Lots looked in. "I thought I heard you," she said. "Will you please not throw the books about as you did yesterday. Some are very valuable."

"We didn't throw them, you know we didn't," said Nora. "We told you what happened and you rushed off looking scared!"

Edie said nothing to that. She noticed the big book in Jack's hand. "Oh, you've come to put that back," she said. "I'll fetch the ladder for you – it belongs to that high shelf there."

She went off and in a minute or two came back with the ladder. She set it up against the shelves, and then went out again.

"She's a misery," said Mike. "I don't like her. I don't like any of them much. Well – does anyone want to have a squint at this book again before I put it back?"

"Let's not talk too loud," said Peggy, suddenly. "I have a feeling that Edie may be listening at the door. I'd like to have one more look at the book – where that secret passage to the tower is." She dropped her voice at the last words, so that no eavesdropper could hear her.

They all pored over the maps once again. "It's a pity it doesn't show the mines too," said Jack. "I'd like a book about those mines."

CRASH! They all jumped. A book lay near them, half-open, on its face. "Welcome, dear book!" said Jack. "Are you by any chance a book about the mines?"

He picked it up – but it wasn't. It was called *Rolland, the Duke of Barlingford. A History of his Horses.*

"Sorry, Duke Rolland," said Jack, "but your horses don't really interest me. Nice of you to throw yourself at my head, though!"

"Jack – look," whispered Mike, and Jack turned quickly. He saw that Mike and the others were staring at a picture over the mantelpiece. It was swinging slowly to and fro! It was a dark picture, of mountains and hills, of no interest at all – except that it was swinging to and fro like a pendulum!

Jack walked up to it and took hold of it. It stopped swinging immediately.

"I don't like it," said Nora. "It's worse than jumping books!"

THUD! CRASH!

The children swung round. Two more books lay on the ground – and then Jack caught sight of another one tilting up on the shelf. Over it went and down it came!

He took the ladder, put it below the shelf where the book had fallen from, and climbed up. He could see nothing that could cause the books to jump out.

"All the books have come from the same side of the

431

room, and from the same shelf-level," said Paul. "That's queer, isn't it?" Oh my goodness, there goes the picture again!"

Sure enough it had begun to swing, though more slowly than before. Jack stood on the ladder and watched it. What was the point of all these silly happenings? "Pass the books back to me," he said to Mike. "I'll put them in their places."

He put the last one in its place, and climbed down again, expecting more to fall out immediately.

"Let's get out of here," said Nora. "I really don't like all these happenings."

"Come on then – we'll go upstairs. Our rooms will be done by now, I expect," said Mike. So they left the library and went up to their suite of rooms. Mrs Brimming was just coming out of them with a duster and a brush and pan.

"I've finished them," she said. "Now I'm going to do Miss Dimity's."

The five children went into the rooms. Jack locked the outer doors of all three rooms. "If we're going to hunt for a secret door, we don't want anyone bursting in just as we've found it!" he said.

They all felt excited. They went into Paul's room and looked at the right-hand wall. It was panelled from floor to ceiling. At first sight it seemed impossible that there should be a door at all.

"I wonder you didn't hear the fellow coming through the secret door into your room last night," said Jack to Paul.

"Well – I did hear a click once or twice," said Paul. "But I thought it was Ranni coming into my room and going out again. He stood over there by the window – I saw his outline."

Jack thought for a moment. "Well, perhaps that *was* Ranni, Paul. The man who came in by the secret door

432

drew all our curtains across the window, as you know – so you wouldn't have been able to see his outline there, if the curtains were drawn. The man must have come after Ranni had been."

"Or else Paul saw him by the window just *before* he drew the curtains," said Nora. Jack nodded.

"Yes – that might be," he said. "Now come on – let's find this door. And mind – we don't give up till we've got it."

They each went to a portion of the right-hand wall, and began to search the panelling carefully. They pushed this panel and that. They pressed, they tapped. They leaned against the panels, they tried to shove them sideways.

"Well – we're not very successful," said Jack, at last. "I've examined my portion of the wall as high as six feet – but as far as I can see it's all ordinary panelling – no secrets anywhere. Let's change over places and try our hands at each other's bits of wall."

So they changed places, and began all over again. What a probing and tapping and pressing there was! The smallest knot of wood was examined, the tiniest crack!

In the middle of it all somebody tried the handle of the boys' door, and then tapped sharply on it. The five children, intent on their search, jumped in fright.

But it was only Dimmy, bringing up biscuits and plums for their elevenses. She was cross because the door was locked. Peggy flew to open it.

"What do you want to lock this door for?" demanded Dimmy.

"To keep out Brimmy and the Lots," said Jack, truthfully. "They're always snooping about. Oh thanks, Dimmy. You're a brick – chocolate biscuits and plums – I could do with those."

Dimmy went, and the children took a rest from their labours and ate all the biscuits and the plums, sitting on Mike's bed. They were very disappointed.

"We've been over an hour looking for that wretched

door," said Jack. "We *know* it must be there! It's pretty certain our night-visitor came through it from the tower passage. Why can't we find it then?"

"We'll try again," said Mike. He hated giving up anything. "Come on. I bet we'll find it this time."

But they did not. They had to give it up at last. "There's not a single inch we haven't examined," said Jack, with a groan. "It's beaten us. I really don't feel that I can possibly look panelling in the face again – I'm fed up with it!"

Everyone was. "Let's go out," said Nora. "It's stopped raining, and the sun's out. I hope to goodness nobody comes along while we're out and changes our rooms round again. That's such a silly trick."

"We'll lock the doors," said Jack, "and take the keys with us."

So when they left their rooms they locked each of the three corridor doors, though they left the ones connecting them wide open. Off they went into the sunshine, and wandered all round the enormous castle, exploring it thoroughly from the outside.

"It's almost lunch-time," said Nora, at last. "We must go in. Gosh, I'm filthy! Let's go straight up and wash, as soon as we get in. Dimmy will have a fit if she sees us like this."

They went up the stairs and came to their rooms. Jack took the keys out of his pocket. He unlocked the girls' room door and they all went in.

"Everything's all right," said Jack, pleased. "No change-round this time. Whoever the joker is, he or she couldn't get in today, because the doors were all locked. Good!"

"Look – my torch is back!" said Nora suddenly, pointing to the table beside her bed. "So is Peggy's."

"So's mine!" said Mike, running into the middle room, "and Jack's. But – the doors were all locked, weren't they?"

"They were," said Jack. "So – whoever brought back the torches came through the secret door – the one we couldn't

434

find. There's no other way in. It *is* there! It *is*! And he came through it. Oh, why can't we find it? Paul – can't you think of *anything* that might help? You're the one that heard the clicks, and saw a man. Think hard – tell us everything you heard or saw."

"I have," said Paul, frowning hard, trying to remember the least detail. "I just remember a last click, that I thought was Ranni going out of the room – and a sort of shadow high up on the wall – and—"

"A shadow! High up on the wall! That's it, that's it!" cried Jack, his eyes shining. "This entrance must be high up, of course – higher than we looked – that shadow must have been the secret visitor going back through the door – but a door that is set high up in the wall! We'll find it now – we will!"

A Strange Night Journey

The children could not stop then and there to look for the door, because it was past their lunch-time already. Dimmy would be coming to look for them, not at all pleased. In excitement they flew to the bathroom, washed their hands, and then rushed back to brush their hair.

Downstairs they went, to find Dimmy just about to set out to fetch them, looking most annoyed. Peggy caught her round the waist and gave her a sudden hug, which stopped Dimmy's scolding at once. She couldn't help laughing, as Peggy nearly swung her over.

"Don't be so violent," she said. "And please set the table quickly. The meal has been here for ten minutes."

All the children longed to discuss the secret door, and longed even more to set to work and find it, but, of course.

they did not want to discuss it in front of Dimmy. They would have to answer so many, many questions if they did. It was their secret, and they hugged it to themselves all lunch-time.

"I've told Ranni to be here with the car at two o'clock," said Dimmy, dropping a sudden bombshell. "Mrs Brimming has told me of a glorious bathing-pool about six miles from here, and, as it's so very hot today, I thought you would all enjoy a really good bathe. We're taking our tea with us, and our supper too!"

To her great surprise nobody seemed at all pleased. She did not know their tremendous impatience to get back to hunting for the secret door, now that they thought they knew where it was! She looked round, surprised at the lack of excitement.

"Don't you *want* to go?" she said. "What funny children you are! I thought you'd love it. I suppose you had made other plans. Well, never mind, your plans can wait till tomorrow. I've ordered the picnic tea and supper now. Fetch your bathing-things quickly after lunch, because I don't want to keep Ranni waiting."

Jack saw that Dimmy was disappointed because they didn't seem pleased. He was kind-hearted enough to pretend that he was thrilled, and he kicked the others under the table to make them follow his lead.

They played up valiantly, and soon Dimmy was thinking that she had been mistaken – the children really did want to go! Actually, when they went to fetch their bathing-things, they began to feel excited about the unexpected treat. A bathe would be heavenly this hot weather – and a picnic tea *and* supper would be heavenly too!

"The secret door won't run away," Jack said. "It will still be there, waiting for us this evening. We'll find it all right, now we are sure it's higher up in the panelling than we searched. I never thought of that. Let's enjoy ourselves, and look forward to a good hunt this evening!"

So they went off happily, and had a really wonderful time, bathing in a pool as blue as forget-me-nots, lying to dry themselves in the hot sun, and then bathing again and again. The picnic was better than they had hoped – and as for the supper, even Dimmy was amazed to see what Mrs Brimming had provided. They all enjoyed themselves thoroughly.

They were very tired when they got back. They had done so much swimming that their arms and legs ached all over! "You must go straight to bed," said Dimmy, seeing them yawn one after another. "You've had a lovely day – so have I – and we're all burnt a deeper brown than ever!"

They said good night to Dimmy and went upstairs. Their enthusiasm for the secret door was not quite so high as it had been. In fact, only Jack and Mike seemed able to hunt for it!

"We'll get into bed," said Peggy. "Nora and I can hardly stand. Do you mind looking for the door by yourselves, you and Mike, Jack? I'm sure Paul won't want to stand on chairs with you and tap the walls above his head! He can hardly keep awake."

"You get into bed, and Paul too – and Mike and I will tell you as soon as we've spotted the door," said Jack. "Good thing we've got our torches back. We can see what we're doing now."

The girls got into bed – and so did Paul, although he felt he really ought to go and help the two boys. He lay and watched them put chairs against the wall, and then, quite suddenly, fell fast asleep.

"Blow," said Jack, looking at him. "I meant to have asked him if there was a chair standing close to the wall when he woke up this morning; because it seems to me that whoever climbed back through the high-up door would certainly have to have a chair to stand on!"

"Yes, you're right," said Mike. "I remember seeing one, Jack – just about here, it was! Let's stand on one here and see if there's anything queer high up on the panelling above."

They put one of Paul's chairs in the place Mike pointed out, and Jack stood on it. He felt round the panelling there, and was lucky, almost at once!

"I've got something!" he said, in a low, excited voice. "A knob! I'm pressing it – gosh, this whole big panel is moving!"

Mike shone his torch up from below, his heart beating in excitement. Yes – a big panel had moved with a loud click to one side, and a dark gap showed in the wall. They had found the secret door! What a well-hidden one! Who would think of looking high up in the panelling for an entrance?

"Mike! See if the girls are awake," said Jack. "We'll tell them. Don't wake Paul. He's absolutely sound asleep. We'd have to yell the place down to wake him."

Mike went into the girls' room with his torch and came back immediately. "Sound asleep too," he reported. "I shook Nora, but she didn't even stir! We'd better go exploring alone, Jack. Anyway, it's probably better there should be only two of us!"

"Right," said Jack. "I think we'd better get a couple of our suitcases to put on this chair, to stand on. I don't see how we can climb into this hole unless we get a bit nearer to it!"

Mike fetched two suitcases and put them on the chair. It was easy to clamber into the hole then! Jack went first, making quite a noise, but Paul didn't even move!

"There are steps this other side," said Jack, feeling with his foot. "That's good! Pass me my torch, Mike. I've left it down there."

Mike passed it to him and Jack shone it into the passage. "Yes – it's a proper passage," he said. "About eighteen inches wide. I'll go down the steps. You get through and follow."

Mike clambered through the queer high-up door, and

Jack went first.

followed Jack down the steps into the passage. The steps
were more like a ladder clamped to the wall, but were quite
easy to get down.

Now the two boys stood one behind the other in the
passage. They both felt exultant. They had found the way!
Now where would this lead to? To a chimney of the tower?
And if so, what would they find there? A way out into a
room? And who would be in the room?

They began to make their way along the passage. It was

hot and stuffy. It ran straight for a little way and then bent sharply to the right. "I think we're walking behind the walls of some of the rooms on this floor," said Jack. "Hallo, we go downwards here – there's a slope."

They went downwards, and then very sharply upwards. The passage wound in and out, just as had been shown on the plan. And then, quite abruptly it stopped!

It came to an end against a stone wall. Up the wall some iron staples were set, evidently meant for climbing. "We go up here," said Jack, in a low voice, flashing his torch upwards.

They went up a little distance and then Jack stopped. "Can't go any farther up," he said. "There's a stone roof. But there's a grille or something here; just at the side of the iron staples. It's got a kind of handle. I'll pull it back. I hope it doesn't make a noise!"

He pulled it slowly back. It made not the slightest sound, and Jack guessed that it was well oiled. No doubt this was the way that the night-visitor used whenever he wanted to visit the three-room suite, or any other of the rooms on that floor, for any purpose!

Jack looked through the opening left by the sliding grille. He could see nothing but utter blackness. Was he looking into the chimney-piece of the room in the tower, which had been marked with a T door on the map? He must be! He listened. He could not hear a sound nor see a light.

"I'm climbing through the opening," he whispered to Mike, below him. "I think it's safe. Stay there till you hear a low whistle, then come up."

Jack climbed through the opening and felt about for some way to get down. His feet found some stone ledges, and he stepped down cautiously, not daring to put his torch on yet. He put out his hands and touched cold stone in front of him, at the back of him and at the sides! He decided to flick his torch on and off quickly.

When he did so he saw at once that he was standing

upright in a big chimney, his feet in the empty stone fireplace. He had only to bend down, walk forward, and he would be out in one of the tower rooms!

He bent down. There was pitch darkness in the room, but in a short time Jack made out a small strip of starry sky! He knew he was looking at one of the narrow tower windows, with the stars shining through it.

He gave a low whistle, and heard the sounds of Mike climbing up, then scrambling through the grille and down the stone ledges. Soon the two boys stood together in the dark room. Jack switched on his torch. The room was a sitting room – very comfortably furnished indeed. Nobody was there.

"What a lot of armchairs!" whispered Jack. "Guy believes in making himself comfortable. What do we do now?"

"Find the stone tower-stairway and go up it," whispered back Mike. "There are more rooms above. We know that from the map. Come on. The stairway will be outside that door over there."

They went carefully to the door and opened it. Outside was a dim light, evidently for lighting up the stairway. Jack fumbled round the curved stone wall until he found a switch, and turned off the light. "We shan't run so much risk of being spotted if we go up in the dark," he whispered. "Be careful, now. We don't know what we might come up against!"

They went silently up the stone steps in their rubber shoes. The stairway appeared to wind round and round the inside of the tower walls. They came to a door, which was a little ajar. The room beyond was in darkness.

Jack listened but could hear nothing. He pushed the door open, and looked in. He was sure nobody was there. He flashed on his torch quickly, and stared in astonishment.

"A bedroom!" he whispered to Mike. "But look at the beds – heaps of them! Whoever lives up here? Goodness, it

He flashed on his torch.

isn't only that Guy fellow – it's a whole lot of people. What *can* they be doing in this tower?"

"There's another room above this," whispered Mike, whose heart was thumping like a piston. "Perhaps something will be going on there."

They left the bedroom and went up the stone stairs again. Before they came to the next door, they heard loud voices!

They stopped at once, and pressed close together, hardly breathing. Some kind of quarrel was going on in that top room of the tower.

There were angry shouts in a foreign language. Then came the sound of something being flung over – a table perhaps?

"Who are they?" whispered Jack. "There sounds to be quite a lot. I vote we creep up and listen! Come on!"

A Truly Adventurous Time

The two boys crept up the few remaining stone steps and came to another door which, like the rest, was a little ajar. There was a small platform outside this door, and from it a narrower stairway led upwards.

Jack put his mouth to Mike's ear. "We'll scoot up these steps if anyone comes rushing out. They're not likely to think there's anyone up there at this time of night. I expect it only leads to the roof of the tower."

Mike nodded. He set his eye to the crack of the door, and so did Jack. The crack was wide and gave the boys a very good view of the whole room. They were astonished to see so many men.

Half of them were in the curious garb that the boys had seen being worn by the figures in the mine. Their heads

443

were hidden in a hood which had eye-holes covered by some stiff, transparent material. Jack thought it was probably to protect their eyes from the heat.

The other half were in ordinary clothes, but wore overalls over them. Jack gave Mike a nudge as he recognized Guy in overalls. There was no mistaking that ugly face with its fierce eyes!

It was plain that everyone was angry with Guy. They shouted at him in strange tongues. They shook their fists and threatened him. He stood there, glowering.

"You told us we were safe here, and could do our work in secret. You told us no one ever came to this castle, or to the mines. And now, before our work is finished, you say we have to clear out of this tower!"

Someone yelled something in a foreign language and Guy scowled.

"I've told you it's no fault of mine," he said. "We've been here, unseen, for nearly two years now – thanks to the help my mother and aunts have given me – ever since I first discovered the priceless metal in that old mine. I put you on to it, didn't I? I've helped you with my knowledge. But I tell you, if we stay here in this tower now, everything will be discovered. The place has been let – and the tower has got to be opened."

More yells. Then a quiet-looking man spoke up. "What you suggest, then, is that you take the stuff that is ready, and hide it away. And we leave this tower and go to live down in the mines, working there till the castle is empty of its tenants, and we can come back again and live in the tower while we finish our work?"

"Yes. And that's the only sensible thing to do," said Guy. "You know that. Lord Moon owns the castle – and the mines and everything in them, valuable or not. He thinks they are only tin mines – we know better. Because of that strange fire years ago, which drove the miners away and gave them that curious tingling disease, a new metal was formed. We've called it 'Stellastepheny', and it's going to be one of the most powerful and valuable in the world . . ."

More shouts, and someone pounded on a table.

"And you want us to let you go off and sell it, while we go down and live in the mines!" shouted one of the men in the hoods. "We don't trust you, Guy Brimming. We never did. You're not straight."

Guy looked round at them bitterly. "Not straight? And which of *you* is straight? Not one! Well, either you trust me, and we save something out of this – or you don't trust me, and all our work will be lost forever."

There was a heated discussion in all kinds of languages. Then the quiet-spoken man gave the verdict.

"All right. We *have* to trust you. Let's finish the last lot of stuff, and you can take it with the other. Then we'll take the secret way to the mines and stay there, at work, till we hear from you that things are safe. We've plenty of food down there."

"You're wise," said Guy, his face surly and unpleasant. "Get cracking, then. I want to go tonight. I'd hoped to scare the fools who want the castle – but they won't be scared. I daren't stay any longer."

"Right," said the quiet man. "We'll finish off this last lot of stuff, and you can take it and go. Then tomorrow we'll heave all the beds down into the cellars underneath the tower, so that no one suspects anything when they see the room. The other furniture won't matter. Then we'll clear up here. But tonight we must go to the mines. We all saw that light over the ruined village after we'd left last night. There will be many things to do there at once."

There was a good deal of muttering, but it was plain that everyone was now agreed. Jack and Mike watched the next proceedings in the greatest wonder.

One of the men put what looked like a glass cylinder in the middle of the floor. He clamped it down, and attached some glass tubes to it. Then the men in the loose robes and hoods brought up two or three narrow shovels covered in bags of some kind.

"Stand back," they said to the men in overalls. "Cover your faces."

Everyone stood back. Some of the men turned round to face the wall, and crouched down. Jack and Mike felt rather frightened, but they could not stop watching.

The hooded men uncovered their narrow shovels quickly and emptied the curious, shining, misty stuff on them into the wide opening at the top of the glass cylinder. Another man poured some colourless liquid into the tubes as the shimmering material slid into the cylinder.

And then the whole room seemed to disappear! A shimmering radiance came instead, that blotted out every single thing – a radiance that was of the same strange, unknown colour that the boys had seen hanging over the ruined village the night before.

Mike and Jack gazed through the crack, fascinated and entranced. What was this? They could see nothing at all in the room but this unearthly light. Men, chairs, floor, walls – everything was gone.

Jack's eyes began to hurt him. So did Mike's. They put their hands over them and stumbled away from the door and a little way up the stone steps. They sat down, unable to see for some time. No wonder the men had been told to cover their eyes!

"If that radiant stuff makes 'Stellastepheny' or whatever they called it, it's really wonderful," whispered Jack, at last. "I've never in my life seen anything like it."

"Listen – somebody's coming to the door," said Mike, clutching Jack's arm. "It must be Guy, with the stuff he wants to get away with tonight."

Somebody stumbled out of the open door and down the stone steps. The boys saw vaguely that he carried a metal box under his arm. Was the precious "Stellastepheny" in that? It must be.

"Let's follow and see if he goes out of the tower door at the bottom," whispered Jack. So they followed, and when they came to the bedroom, they saw that a light was there. Guy must have gone into that room. Perhaps he was getting a few of his clothes?

And then Jack did something so quickly that Mike could not at first make out what he was doing. He ran down the two steps to the door, shut it firmly, and turned a key that stuck out from the lock! There was a startled cry from inside, and an angry voice shouted:

"Who's that? What are you doing?" Then footsteps could be heard running over to the door. The man inside pulled at it violently, shouting again when he found it locked.

"Oh Jack! You've caught him! You've got him prisoner!" said Mike, in amazed delight. "He can't get out of that room. He can't even be heard in the room above."

"It won't matter if he is," said Jack. "I'm taking the key!" He took the key and put it into his pocket!

"What do we do now?" whispered Mike, his voice shaking with excitement.

"Shall we follow the men to the mine?" said Jack.

"No. Let's lock them into the top room, like you've locked Guy into this one," said Mike, almost choking over his brilliant idea.

"Come on, then!" said Jack, quite beside himself with all these sudden thrills. They raced up the stairs and came to the top room again. They peered cautiously through the crack.

The men were there, evidently getting ready to go, for all of them now had on the loose, hooded clothes. Jack saw that he must lock them in at once or they would be coming out. He banged the door, and felt for the key.

There wasn't one! Angry shouts came from inside, and Jack caught Mike's arm. "We must hide! There's no key!"

He pulled Mike up the steps that ascended to the roof, just as the door was wrenched open, and a man came out, looking very weird in his hooded garb.

"Who's that?" shouted the man. "Who's monkeying about with the door? Is it you, Guy?"

A murmur came from behind him, and he was pushed forward. "Of course it's Guy. Who else could it be? What's he doing, staying on here still? Come on, let's go down after him and see what he's up to."

Then the whole crowd of men poured down the stairs, never dreaming that two scared boys were on the stone steps just a little way above them!

They made a great noise, clattering down the stairs – such a noise that when Guy shouted to them as they passed the locked bedroom door, not one of them heard him. The boys, following down cautiously afterwards, heard him clearly, and grinned.

The men clattered right down to the foot of the tower, and then stopped. "He's not here. He's gone through the tower, after all," said one of them. "It must have been the wind that banged that top door shut! My, we must be scary to act like this!"

Another man produced a big key and fitted it into the tower door. He unlocked it and went out into the little square room beyond. The others followed.

One man gave a sudden exclamation. "I've forgotten to get my notes out of the sitting-room. I'll go and get them and catch you up. Give me the key and I'll lock the tower door behind me when I've got my notes."

He was given the key. Jack and Mike fled back up the steps, as silently as they could. If that man was coming to get something from the room above they would be caught if they did not get out of the way!

The man came up the stairs, slowly and heavily. He had not heard the boys. They shot past the door of the sitting-room and stood on the steps above, shaking with excitement. The man went into the room and switched on a torch. They heard him opening a drawer.

"Come on – we'll go down," said Jack, in a sudden

whisper. "It's our chance to get out of the tower before he locks it – and watch where he goes. There must be a secret way to the mines, as we thought!"

They ran silently down the steps to the very bottom, went out of the tall, narrow tower door, and crouched at the side of a chest, waiting.

Soon they heard footsteps and the man came down again. He pushed through the doorway, lighting his way with a torch, shut the door and locked it carefully. The boys watched breathlessly. What was he going to do?

He went to the side of the little square room, fumbled behind a chest and pulled at something there. In the very middle of the floor a big stone slid quietly downwards, as silently as if it had been oiled. The boys stared at the gap in the floor lit by the light of the man's torch. They were really amazed. Why, they had trodden over that stone a dozen times!

The man went over to the hole, sat down on the edge of it and let himself down carefully into the gap. He disappeared. After a few seconds the boys came out from their hiding-place and switched on a torch. Just as they flashed it they saw the stone rising slowly and silently back into place!

"Look at that!" said Jack. "I'm not sure we aren't in some peculiar kind of dream, Mike! What are we going to do now?"

"Follow that man!" said Mike promptly. Jack shook his head. "Too dangerous," he said. "I'd like to – but we might get lost underground trying to find where the man has gone. He's got too good a start. I know what we'll do!"

"What?" said Mike.

"Help me pull a heavy chest right over the stone that goes up and down!" said Jack. "Then none of the men will be able to get out. They'll be caught! If they lower the stone it won't provide a way out – because the chest will be on top! We'll have got them properly!"

So the two boys hauled one of the biggest chests right

over the stone trap door, and then stared at one another in delight.

"We've got Guy locked up in the bedroom of the tower –and we've blocked the way out for the others – unless they like to find their way through that wall of rubble we found in the mines, and come up the shaft. But I bet they won't do that!" Mike rubbed his hands in glee.

"*Now* what do we do?" said Jack. "Go to bed? Everyone is a prisoner, so we might as well! We'll tell Dimmy and Ranni in the morning – what a surprise for them, and the others, too! Come on."

"I hope we shan't wake up and find it's all a dream," said Mike. "Honestly, it's been one of the most adventurous nights we've ever had!"

An Exciting Finish

Next morning Mike and Jack were still sound asleep when the others were fully awake. It was Paul who woke them.

He came running into the boys' room. "I say, what happened last night? You found the secret entrance and never woke me! It's still open in my room. *I say*!"

The girls joined him, thrilled to hear his news. Mike and Jack woke up with a jump. Jack immediately remembered the happenings of the night before, and gave Mike an excited punch.

"I say, Mike, I wonder how all our prisoners are!"

Mike grinned, remembering everything in a rush. Goodness! What a night! Then Paul and the girls began to clamour to know all about the secret door, and if the boys had gone into the passage, and *what had happened*?

They could hardly believe their ears when the boys told

them. They listened, their eyes nearly falling out of their heads. All those men! Living in the tower too! and Guy finding out about that precious stuff, whatever it was – and getting men to work the mines for it, keeping it a dead secret.

"And he's locked up in the tower bedroom, you say!" cried Nora, with a squeal. "How *did* you think of such a thing! And all those men imprisoned underground! Quick – let's find Dimmy and Ranni!"

Dimmy was surprised to find five such excited children descending on her, as she sat waiting for them to come to breakfast. "Dimmy, Dimmy! Listen to what Jack and Mike have found out!" shouted Nora.

"I'm fetching Ranni," said Paul. "He ought to hear all this too," and he sped off, coming back with the big Baronian, who looked very puzzled at this sudden call.

Breakfast was forgotten as the children poured out their tale. Dimmy listened, almost speechless with astonishment. Ranni listened too, nodding his great head from time to time, and finally bursting into a great guffaw of laughter as he heard how Guy had been locked up in the tower bedroom.

He laughed still more when he heard how the two boys had put a heavy chest over the entrance to the underground passage to the mines. Then he looked grave.

"I should not laugh," he said apologetically to Dimmy, who looked very serious, and felt it. "There has been danger here for us – great danger. I can see that. Many things are clear to me now which puzzled me before."

"And to me too," said Dimmy soberly. "Well – the children seem to have managed everything very well without our help – but I think we should get the police in now, Ranni."

"Yes," said Ranni. "This is a serious busniess. Lord Moon must be told. He must fly back from America, or wherever he is."

"I had better ring for Mrs Brimming and the Lots," said Dimmy. "I am sure they knew all about this."

They did, of course. They were three frightened women as they stood before Dimmy and Ranni, and answered their stern questions.

Mrs Brimming wept bitterly and would not stop. Her two tall sisters were frightened, but Edie Lots was defiant as well.

"Don't blame my sister, Mrs Brimming," she said. "She never wanted her son to do this. But I urged him on. He's clever! He should be one of the greatest scientists in the world. He should—"

"He won't be," said Dimmy. "He has done wrong. The mines are not his, and he had no right to bring all those men here and put them into the tower like that. What will Lord Moon say when he knows all this?"

Mrs Brimming sobbed more loudly. The children felt sorry for her. Edie Lots spoke loudly.

"Lord Moon never comes here. He has no use for his castle or for the mines. Why shouldn't my nephew use them?"

"It is foolish to talk like that," said Dimmy. "Don't you realize that all of you will get into serious trouble over this?"

"I suppose all those queer happenings were caused by you three?" said Jack. "The jumping books – and Twang-Dong noises and so on. You wanted to scare us away, didn't you?"

"Yes," said Edie Lots, still defiant. "But I was the only one who worked them. My sisters wouldn't. My nephew Guy invented them – I tell you, he's a genius – and he showed me how to work them. The front door opening by itself – that's done by a wire. And the jumping books – there's a little passage behind the library bookcases, and Guy made some small holes in the back of one of the shelves; so that when I went into the passage behind I could poke my finger into a book, and send it leaping off the shelf."

"Very simple!" said Jack. "We didn't look for small holes at the back of the shelf! What about the Twang-Dong noises? How did the instruments on the wall make *them*?"

"They didn't," said Edie Lots, sounding quite proud. "There's a mechanical device up the chimney. When it goes off, it makes those two noises at intervals."

"Gosh! So that's why we could never spot who did it – even when the door was locked!" said Mike. "Oh – and what about those gleaming eyes in Lord Moon's portrait?"

"The canvas eyes have been scraped very thin, and then painted again, and a hole made in each," said Edie Lots. "And there is a light behind each eye that can be turned on from outside the room. I waited ouside when you were inside, and kept turning the light on and off. And the hissing noise was made by a bellows worked at the same time. My nephew thought of all those things."

"And did you change the rooms round – and break the vases?" asked Dimmy, entering suddenly into this extraordinary conversation.

"I did everything," said Edie, proudly. "I made the picture swing too. Guy arranged that." Her tall sister hung her head, and Mrs Brimming still sobbed, heart-broken. But Edie was proud and glad. She had helped her beloved nephew, and that was all she cared about!

"Oh well – it's rather disappointing – everything has got quite a reasonable explanation!" said Peggy. "But goodness me, some people would have been very scared!"

"Some people were," said Edie, and the children thought of the man who had gone to the library to look at the old books. How pleased the sisters must have been when he spread the tale of Queer Happenings about!

Nobody seemed to want any breakfast at all! Dimmy dismissed the three caretakers, and began to pour out the tea. Ranni sat down to join them, his arm round Paul. He seemed to think that Paul had escaped great dangers and must now be guarded every minute!

They talked soberly for some time. "I think you should take the car and go and inform the police, Ranni," said Dimmy. "I don't see that this will make any difference to Her Majesty the Queen of Baronia coming here, as arranged – but we must get this business settled up before she comes."

"Yes. Guy will have to come out of the tower bedroom, for instance!" said Nora.

Ranni got up to go. The children made a very poor breakfast, they were so excited and so eager to talk. They watched for Ranni to come with the police, and were thrilled when they heard the car hooting below to tell them he was back.

Things happened very quickly after that. Ranni had told the police most of the strange story. Two men were dispatched to get the angry Guy from the tower bedroom. They forced the tower door easily enough, and went up the stone stairs, having been presented with the bedroom key by Jack. Soon a very dishevelled Guy was being hustled into a police car, angry, astonished and bewildered.

His weeping mother and two aunts were not allowed to speak to him. Nothing was being done about them for the time being. Lord Moon would decide everything when he returned the next day, called back from America. He was flying over, most astonished at what the police had told him on the telephone.

As for the underground miners, they were soon rounded up by a most formidable posse of police. Jack and Mike got permission to go down the secret passage to the mines, behind the police, provided they stayed close to Ranni. Much to Paul's anger Ranni would not allow him to come.

The heavy chest was moved away from the stone trap door. Mike went to the side of the room and fumbled behind the same chest he had seen the man go to. He found an iron lever sticking a little way out of the wall. He pulled it – and lo and behold, the stone in the middle of the floor slid downwards, and exposed the opening to the secret passage!

Down they all went. The underground passage was not a pleasant one, for most of the way it was narrow, low-roofed and dripping wet. It led down the hill, meandering about. Ranni thought it must have been the bed of an underground stream, which had more or less dried up and left its bed as a tunnel.

They came into the mines at last, and at once the passage became dry and the roof rose high. The boys soon found themselves in a little tunnel near the place where they had seen the wonderful, roaring fire. It was just opposite the wall of rubble from behind which they had watched such a strange sight.

The men were all gathered together in the main cave, puzzled and anxious. They had been back to the trap door entrance, and had moved the stone trap door, to get out and back into the tower. But, of course, they had found the way blocked by the heavy chest, and had not dared to try to move it. In fact, they had no idea what it was! They had closed the stone trap door again and retreated into the mines.

When they saw the uniforms of the police, a murmur went up from the miners, who looked very strange in their queer hooded garments. Ranni was quite startled to see them!

The men had been expecting something like this ever since they had found the trap door blocked. They felt sure that Guy was at the bottom of it, and were ready to give away everything, to get even with him! It was not until they had told the police every single bit of information they knew that they were told that Guy was a prisoner too – and had been locked up all night in the tower bedroom!

"If only the men had known, they could have escaped

that way," said Jack, pointing to the wall of rubble on the opposite side of the cave. "They could have knocked down the rubble and escaped up a shaft. We knew that – but they didn't!"

"The things you kids know just don't bear thinking about," said a tall policeman, with a grin. "Keep behind your red-bearded friend, now – we don't need your help in front."

The prisoners were all taken away in police cars. Ranni and Dimmy sighed with relief. Goodness gracious – to think of all the secrets that had been going on in Moon Castle!

"I think we'll take the car and go into Bolingblow for lunch," said Dimmy, heaving an enormous sigh. "I'm sure Mrs Brimming and her sisters won't be able to provide anything like a lunch today!"

"Yes, let's go," said Nora, at once. "We can tell that waitress she was quite right. There *were* Queer Happenings and Noises in Moon Castle. Do let's."

"You're not to say a single word to her," said Dimmy. "It's nothing to do with her. We don't want the news all over the town, exaggerated and garbled – we'd never hear the last of it!"

"Dimmy – come and see the tower," begged Jack.

"No, thank you," said Dimmy, firmly. "I don't feel strong enough today to tackle that awful tower – though I *would* like to see the view from the top."

"My mother is still coming, isn't she?" said Paul anxiously. "You haven't put her off, have you, Dimmy?"

"On the contrary," said Dimmy. "I had a letter from her this morning – which, in all the excitement, I forgot to mention – and as your brothers are quite well again, they're all coming tomorrow! What do you think of that?"

"Smashing!" said Mike, at once. "It was going to be dull, now this adventure is over, waiting and waiting for them to come. Now we'll have hardly any waiting at all. Couldn't be better!"

"In fact, we've cleared up all the mysteries at exactly the right moment," said Jack. "Aren't we clever, Dimmy?"

Dimmy wouldn't say they were. She laughed and ruffled Jack's hair

TWANG!

"Oh, my goodness – don't say that awful Twang-Dong is still going!" cried Dimmy. "I can't bear it!"

DONG!

The children roared with laughter. Jack went round the bend of the L-shaped room and looked up the chimney, shining his torch there.

He put up his hand and pulled down a curious little contrivance of metal, springs and tiny hammers.

"There you are," he said, putting it on the table. "The Twang-Dong itself. One of the mysterious secrets of Moon Castle!"

"Hurrah for Moon Castle!" said Nora. "And hurrah for all its secrets, Twang-Dongs and everything!"

The Twang-Dong made a curious noise. Its mechanism seemed to be running down. It slowly raised one of its little hammers and struck the metal beneath.

DONG!

"It's finished," said Jack. "Finished – like this adventure. Well, it was GRAND FUN while it lasted!"

Enid Blyton
Five Find-Outers
Mystery Stories
in Armada

Have you read all the adventures in the "Mystery" series by Enid Blyton? Here are some of them:

The Rockingdown Mystery
Roger, Diana, Snubby and Barney hear strange noises in the cellar while staying at Rockingdown Hall. Barney goes to investigate and makes a startling discovery...

The Rilloby Fair Mystery
Valuable papers have disappeared – the Green Hands Gang has struck again! Which of Barney's workmates at the circus is responsible? The four friends turn detectives – and have to tackle a dangerous criminal.

The Ring o' Bells Mystery
Eerie things happen at deserted Ring o' Bells Hall – bells start to ring, strange noises are heard in a secret passage, and there are some very unfriendly strangers about. Something very mysterious is going on, and the friends mean to find out what.

The Rockingdown Mystery	£2.99
The Rilloby Fair Mystery	£2.99
The Ring o' Bells Mystery	£2.99

Have you read all the adventures in the "Mystery" series by Enid Blyton? Here are some of them:

The Rubadub Mystery

Who is the enemy agent at the top-secret submarine harbour? Roger, Diana, Snubby and Barney are determined to find out – and find themselves involved in a most exciting mystery.

The Rat-A-Tat Mystery

When the big knocker on the ancient door of Rat-A-Tat House bangs by itself in the middle of the night, it heralds a series of very peculiar happenings – and provides another action-packed adventures for Roger, Diana, Snubby and Barney.

The Ragamuffin Mystery

"This is going to be the most exciting holiday we've ever had," said Roger – and little does he know how true his words will prove when he and his three friends go to Merlin's Cove and discover the bideout of a gang of thieves.

The Rubadub Mystery	**£2.75**
The Rat-A-Tat Mystery	**£2.99**
The Ragamuffin Mystery	**£2.75**

The Chalet School Series
Elinor M. Brent-Dyer

Elinor M. Brent-Dyer has written many books about life at the famous alpine school. Follow the thrilling adventures of Joey, Mary-Lou and all the other well-loved characters in these delightful stories, available only in Armada.

1	The School at the Chalet	£2.99
2	Jo of the Chalet School	£2.99
3	The Princess of the Chalet School	£2.99
4	Head Girl of the Chalet School	£2.99
5	Rivals of the Chalet School	£2.99
6	Eustacia Goes to the Chalet School	£2.99
7	The Chalet School and Jo	£2.99
8	The Chalet Girls in Camp	£2.99
9	Exploits of the Chalet Girls	£2.99
10	The Chalet School and the Lintons	£2.99
11	A Rebel at the Chalet School	£2.99
12	The New House at the Chalet School	£2.99
13	Jo Returns to the Chalet School	£2.99
15	A United Chalet School	£2.99
16	The Chalet School in Exile	£2.99
17	The Chalet School at War	£2.99
55	Jane and the Chalet School	£2.50
56	Redheads at the Chalet School	£2.99
58	Summer Term at the Chalet School	£3.50
59	Two Sams at the Chalet School	£2.99

Chalet School Three-in-One (containing *The Chalet School in Exile*, *The Chalet School at War*, and *The Highland Twins at the Chalet School*) £4.99

Enid Blyton
School Stories
in Armada

Malory Towers Series

FIrst Term at Malory Towers	£2.99
Second Form at Malory Towers	£2.99
Third Year at Malory Towers	£2.99
Upper Fourth at Malory Towers	£2.99
In the Fifth at Malory Towers	£2.99
Last Term at Malory Towers	£2.99

St Clare's Series

The Twins at St Clare's	£2.99
The O'Sullivan Twins	£2.99
Summer Term at St Clare's	£2.99
Second Form at St Clare's	£2.99
Claudine at St Clare's	£2.99
Fifth Formers at St Clare's	£2.99

Other titles by
Enid Blyton
in Armada

Order Form

To order direct from the publishers, just make a list of the titles you want and fill in the form below:

Name ....

Address ....

....

....

....

Send to: Dept 6, HarperCollins Publishers Ltd, Westerhill Road, Bishopbriggs, Glasgow G64 2QT.

Please enclose a cheque or postal order to the value of the cover price, plus:

UK & BFPO: Add £1.00 for the first book, and 25p per copy for each additional book ordered.

Overseas and Eire: Add £2.95 service charge. Books will be sent by surface mail but quotes for airmail despatch will be given on request.

A 24-hour telephone ordering service is available to Visa and Access card holders: 041-772 2281